Freeman's
The Future
of New Writing

Previous Issues

Freeman's
The Future
of New Writing

Est. 2015

Edited by

John Freeman

Grove Press
New York

Associate Editor: Allison Malecha
Managing Editor: Julia Berner-Tobin
Copy Editor: Kirsten Giebutowski

Published simultaneously in Canada
Printed in the United States of America

FIRST EDITION

ISBN 978-0-8021-2729-7
eISBN 978-0-8021-8883-0

First Grove Atlantic paperback edition: October 2017

Library of Congress Cataloging-in-Publication data is available for this title.

Grove Press
an imprint of Grove Atlantic
154 West 14th Street
New York, NY 10011

Published in collaboration with the MFA in Creative Writing at The New School

THE NEW SCHOOL
CREATIVE WRITING

Distributed by Publishers Group West
groveatlantic.com

17 18 19 20   10 9 8 7 6 5 4 3 2 1

Contents

CONTENTS

Introduction

JOHN FREEMAN

The first book I received as a gift was *The Little Prince*. My grandmother mailed me a copy for my sixth birthday, the illustrated edition with dreamy watercolors painted by the author, Antoine de Saint-Exupéry. I was not a reader back then. I rode a yellow banana bike and imagined it was a chopper. I played whiffle ball and soccer and yearned for little else than to be a starting pitcher for the Phillies. The world as I knew it began and ended with Emmaus, Pennsylvania, the town where my family lived. A giant tree loomed over our front yard, where snowdrifts built canyons in winter. On weekends, after baseball games, my brothers and I sucked down cherry slushies at Dino's, the pizza place next door to the WaWa, where my father sometimes bought milk for 99 cents a gallon.

And then I read *The Little Prince*. The story of how a downed pilot encounters a bescarfed alien prince cracked my world open. Not all trees looked like the one in the front yard. There was such a thing as a baobab. There were deserts. There were princes and airplanes, and asteroids, and aliens who spoke and talked like us. Foxes who could be friends or tricksters. I was mesmerized. I read that book over and over belly down on the scratchy carpet in our front room, the hours tilting by invisibly. I have since realized that the experience of turning those pages was like taking off in an airplane. Fly often enough, you know how it works, the wings deflect air around them, creating a force pushing up and the plane has no choice but to leave the earth behind. Yet every time the ground subtracts beneath me, I hold my breath in wonder. What a thing.

Back then I didn't for a moment consider the author who wrote *The Little Prince*. The book came from my grandmother; she might as well have written it. I didn't think, *I am reading a French novella*, nor did I congratulate myself for exploring literature in translation. Everything, when I was that age, had to be translated. Something was an object or a person or an experience, then it became a word. Simultaneous to that reduction, the world beyond my front yard was expanding daily. My parents gave me a globe and I spun it like a basketball on my finger, unaware that Saint-Exupéry wrote his miraculous book after crashing his red and white Caudron C.630 Simuon in Egypt's Wadian-Natrun while trying to set a speed record with his friend André Prévot for a flight from Paris to Saigon. They had gone down without a map and carried just enough liquid—a thermos of coffee and some wine (Frenchmen!)—to survive one or two days. I learned only later they were tricked by mirages, marveled at their hallucinations, and nearly died. Their lives were saved by a passing Bedouin tribesman who resuscitated them with a native rehydration method.

When I read these details in Stacy Schiff's gorgeous biography of Saint-Exupéry a few years ago, my world split open once again. A book written about being grounded, a novel born from heartache and destruction—Nazism had chased Saint-Exupéry from France; his brother had died—brought my imagination to life several decades later in a part of America Saint-Exupéry had never seen, a town of hot rods, twirling barbershop poles, and crumbling VFW halls. This was as magical as flight. The world seen from above reveals its patterns. The way Saint-Exupéry abstracted tyranny and loss in a story about an alien had made it possible for me to understand those concepts as a child. To identify their shapes from a distance. Only I thought I was reading about friendship, and adventure.

We read differently as adults. The world around us and the people we have in it are long since named and labeled. With each passing year, our lives carry greater weight, some of it, oddly, acquirable only through loss. So most of us seek out different kinds of books. We have to—flight, as we also learn, is dangerous. Life is lived on the ground. Books are presented to us in a different way for this reason. Their covers look familiar enough to tell us what to expect, but mysterious enough to suggest we might not predict everything that will happen in their pages. Names of familiar authors attest to these pleasures on back jackets. If you live in the United States, most of the books you read will be written in English. If they are not, they will immediately place themselves in a tradition of other well-known writers from the author's part of the world. How many people began reading Gabriel García Márquez because another Colombian novelist attested to his greatness? And yet that is how most books from most parts of the world are pitched to us as adult readers.

These are just some of the barriers to being a cosmopolitan reader—which I contend is our original state. I am talking, not about what the philosopher Paul Gilroy labeled jet-set cosmopolitanism, but rather about the expansive and enlarging category that Gilroy also sets out in his books, and which the writer Aminatta Forna expanded upon in a recent gathering on the topic at Georgetown. "A cosmopolitan," she said, "is a person who has or embraces more than one way of seeing, whose perspective is not boundaried by the values of a single national culture. You can be born it, achieve it or have it thrust upon you." Think about this—the migrant is a cosmopolitan, the refugee is a cosmopolitan, the person living in two places who can imagine their plight is as well. What a beautiful idea, especially in an age when so much ugly policy and institutionalized cruelty has been rolled out in governments across the world, especially in the United States, upon an exactly opposite belief: that some people are in essence fundamentally more valuable than others.

What we read is a political matter, an ethical issue; it has always been so, but particularly now, as governments enact violence upon people who do not fit definitional purity as citizens—and as liberal democracy itself faces existential threats at its former heart, in Europe and the United States. Make no mistake, there is a culture war raging right now with the multitudinous, with hybridity, with global culture. I am not going to argue that in this time of conflict we *must* read against our own national cultures, but if we rarely do, what does that say about our values? What does that say about our imaginations? How, if we reinscribe national borders with how we talk about literature, can we ever expect to live in a free and open world as well? If we cannot first imagine it, we cannot in turn imagine its actuality.

Can we push against these forces with our own reading? I contend here that we can, and that we can do it without making literature a stern task. We must merely return to the broader experience of reading, the one so many people begin with—of reading as a gateway to surprise and delight and complexity and wonder, not as an imagined map of what we already know. This issue of *Freeman's* is an attempt to make it easier to do this. How many times have literary pages pointed to the future and given a list of writers from just one nationality? Or one genre? Increasingly, this seems a folly to me, not least because writers themselves do not work that way. Without Günter Grass, Salman Rushdie could not have imagined his way into the heart of Salaam Sinai's story of *Midnight's Children*, without which Junot Díaz could not have conjured Oscar Wao, the hero of his eponymous novel of life during the Trujillo years and then as an immigrant in America. Writers are by nature in favor of cultural and national miscegenation, because they write with the part of the mind we read with as children.

What you have here then is a celebration of the multitudinous in all its forms. Beauty has never had a passport. It arrives unbidden, uninvited, and thus in selecting the writers for this issue—the writers I believe represent the future of new writing—I set no age, genre, or translation restrictions upon who was eligible. I wanted the writers whose lives and careers are just beginning to take flight, the writers who I believe have yet to be recognized for the full scale of their greatness, and in whose pages the possible shines like a spark in the dark. They come from a vast array of backgrounds, but were in no way selected for these distinctions: the oldest is a seventy-year-old essayist who lives in Texas, the youngest a twenty-six-year-old French novelist.

A word on the selection. Typically, literary journals and magazines that compile such a list depend upon a distinguished panel of judges to read through a few dozen books to make their selection. I have sat on several such juries and each experience was a joy, and without those experiences at *Granta* magazine, I would never have been able to put together this issue of *Freeman's*. Still, I believed with a bailiwick this wide it would be far more helpful to have a very large number of casual advisers. So for the past two years I have talked to dozens upon dozens of critics, translators, writers, publishers, agents, book scouts, university professors, festival organizers, activists, and booksellers, asking them who represents the future of new writing. I have read Flemish poetry and unpublished writers from throughout sub-Saharan Africa and the Middle East, and visited countries where the language barrier is severe—such as Japan— more than once on errands of exploration. It would require many more pages than I possess here to thank all of the people involved in this quest, but chief among them has been Allison Malecha, the assistant editor of *Freeman's*, who has read virtually everything seriously considered alongside me, and who has often come to swifter, sharper conclusions than I ever could. I am so grateful to have had a copilot who packed the coffee, not the wine.

So who are these writers? Or more aptly, *what* are they? After all, a writer's true nationality is his or her style. This is the writer's face to the world. I was happy to discover that, if national and genre borders are stripped away, an enormous palette of tones, tics, obsessions, and syntactical variety surges through the world's best new writers. On the one hand, there are writers of torrential muchness and dazzling architecture, like Johan Harstad, whose recent 1,000-page novel, *Max, Mischa, and the Tet Offensive*, is excerpted here; or Ocean Vuong, who keeps a skittering momentum bursting down the page of a new poem. In her as yet unpublished 200,000-word debut novel, *America Is Not the Heart*, a section of which appears here, Elaine Castillo, with the sheer propulsive power of her voice, blasts a reader into her story of a family living under a repressive regime.

It is miraculous what a voice can do on the page. Testimony, in the best writers' hands, never has to defend its credentials as art. Édouard Louis relives the days after a horrifying violent assault when the news of that experience longed to be exploded from his lungs. Heather O'Neill pushes us fathoms deep into the life of a teenage girl whose life is unraveling around her. Pola Oloxoirac describes growing up as a beautiful young woman: the field of pressure, and the warnings constantly draped around her by mothers, aunts, and others. Mariana Enríquez's character speaks frankly and beautifully about her obsessive love of damaged hearts in a story that will make you feel the voice of Jean Genet is alive and well in the twenty-first century.

Realism is not nearly so dominant a style when you look to the world for good writing. In Mieko Kawakami's short story, a woman who recently lost her house comes up with a grim solution for how she will never have to part with it again. Sayaka Murata, who works an early morning shift every day at a convenience store to give herself time to write, describes a world in which women covet clothing made of human hair, bone, and other body parts. Sometimes the world itself refutes realism's design. In his gorgeous riff on turning seventy, David Searcy recalls how a peculiarity within the compression chamber of an aging VW bug turned the little vehicle he was driving into a rattling, unlikely supercar.

The best writers I came across in this search found a way to look at and regard the world closely from a fresh perspective. Andrés Felipe Solano moved to Korea some years ago and his journal entries of everyday activities sparkle like unsolicited satori. Diego Enrique Osorno has risked his life numerous times to cover the devastating effects of North America's transnational dependence on drugs in Mexico. In the piece selected here, he visits a town attempting to scrub itself clean of the associations of violence by holding a festival for the world's biggest shrimp cocktail. Samanta Schweblin is one of the globe's best short-story writers, and in her brief, whimsical piece a family rushing across town comes up with a novel way to signal its emergency.

Adornment, I increasingly feel, is a distraction from beauty, especially in writing. In his piece about a teacher who has survived a militia raid in Uganda, Dinaw Mengestu simply allows his subject's story to take over and speak for itself. Solmaz Sharif's poem about disquiet is poised on the knife-edge of a single moment, where despair and revelation threaten from either side. In her brief memoir of traveling in her youth, Fiona McFarlane reminds us of the way everyday life could be a revelation, or present an opportunity for self-destruction. The facts, simply stated, sometimes have an effect all their own.

There are pure storytellers here in these pages, and it's hard not to muse on the way big stories eventually must deal with justice. Sunjeev Sahota, whose novel *The Year of Runaways* might be the best published anywhere in the last five years, has contributed a short story about the way intergenerational cohabitation threatens a family marriage. In his story Xu Zechen writes of a family whose fortunes are echoed by the fate of an endlessly barking abused dog. Nadifa Mohamed conjures the life of a sailor living in Wales at the midpoint of last century, when men of his ilk prayed that a crime was not committed by someone resembling them. In Tania James's short story, a hit-and-run car accident leaves a young man dead, and a bicycle in tatters—and no one to blame. A Yi, who worked until recently as a provincial policeman, tells the hilarious story of two detectives sent to a factory in search of the thief of a missing wheel.

On occasion here, writers allow us to see them making themselves, like an artist painting his own portrait into a large fresco. In a moving personal essay, Garnette Cadogan reveals how a childhood of step-parental abuse forced him to think of himself as a character destined for abuse or revenge. Valeria Luiselli muses with shame and revelation in an essay upon the many ways she punished female writers for insufficient authenticity while going to a graduate program staffed by men. Marius Chivu, who is primarily a poet, reveals the loss that made him a poet and muses upon how gladly he would give his gift back in a second if he could have his beloved mother with him today. Claire Vaye Watkins flinches to realize she has become the kind of person her mother never would have known in her lifetime.

Even among the writers mentioned above, who are using experience as an aperture for discovery, I was surprised to discover a startling lack of self-awareness, of self-consciousness, the digital age's gaze into the mirror. There is, it feels, in the most beautifully expressed style, a deeper level to intimate contemplation, even within personal work, such as that of Athena Farrokhzad. It emerges in her poems as a slippage at the crux of contemplation, where the lack of a recognizable past creates a steeper cliff of doubt. In Ishion

Hutchinson's exquisitely baroque verse, the poet yokes together traditions to create footbridges over such yawning caverns within his past.

I went looking for my copy of *The Little Prince* not long ago, and I was dismayed to realize it had disappeared into my library, probably buried or, more likely, long gone in one move or another. My family was itinerant. I gave up on my search after I realized that if I thought hard I could imagine almost every single one of its panels, including the frontispiece and my grandmother's looping script and the year of her gift. Just as I can see the page on which my mother's hand once inscribed a copy of Dylan Thomas's poems to me for my seventeenth birthday, and I also have no problem seeing the words of love on an anthology of City Lights pocket poets given to me by an old friend.

I suspect you have books like these in your house, well-preserved or tattered copies that are so old they are no longer books but hanging door frames you once walked through. I hope you can accept this collection of new writing in the same spirit—less as a grand pronouncement and more as an invitation. With rare exceptions, I have never enjoyed or been moved by books I was told I ought to read—I was simply lucky that certain writers reached me when I needed them, whether they were from France or Wales or Colombia or Ghana, and whether they had imagined me as a reader or not. One of the great joys of sending this issue out into the world—it will be simultaneously published in Swedish, Italian, Romanian, and English—is that the writers herein make such dictates unnecessary. Their words do this in a matter of sentences—no matter how much we weigh, they can accept the load. Like them, I cannot imagine who you are, holding this, where you are. I can imagine only that we are on the same plane together and there goes the ground, away.

Seven Shorts

I'm getting old. Yet writing more. And maybe better. Or maybe only with more urgency. Which might amount to the same thing, right? To get the limitations of the system more excitingly involved. Like Lindbergh's monoplane accelerating, bouncing down the runway trying to get some air before it hits the trees—my favorite moment in the movie. The unlikeliness of everything revealed. What were we thinking? This can't possibly hold together. I've had health issues as well. So I would like to make the case for pathological revelation. What emerges as the limits are approached. When things begin to break apart.

I think of Giorgio de Chirico (I tend to think of him a lot in any case), inventor, or discoverer, of that cold surrealist surface which eventually would support the weird unlikeliness of others, too, like Dalí and Tanguy. I tend to think of him recovering from severe intestinal illness in a Florentine piazza back in 1910 or thereabouts—how, in his weakened state, in the autumn light, the ancient city square became a stage whereon could be observed, and then recorded in his "metaphysical" paintings, all laid open like an anatomy lesson, the mutual detachment of the arbitrary objects of the world. The silent, airless gulf between them as imponderable as that between the stars. You get a glimpse sometimes when things go wrong. The mechanism opens up a bit and you see through it and beyond it in a way.

All through my college years I drove a much-abused VW Beetle. Drove it pretty much into the ground—to the point where you really needed a tailwind to sustain the usual highway speed of fifty-five miles per hour. On its final voyage it carried me and three others to an air show in Fort Worth where the big attraction was the recently top-secret SR-71 spy plane guarded by a rope and an armed Marine and rumored capable of speeds beyond Mach 3. I think we might have had a tailwind going out, but coming back it was a struggle for the first few miles. And then it's like we've topped the hill or something. Cars no longer seem to pass us quite so frequently. My friend Jim Lynch is driving. He loved driving. But he was a little crazy. Now we're doing sixty-five. So I lean up between the front seats and say, Hey, what's going on? We're pushing seventy. Jim is hugging the wheel with this wild expression and a squint like he needs goggles. What the hell? He's got it floored. He's not about to back it off. He'll never get this chance again. We look around at one another. We're beginning to pass some cars. We're doing seventy-five and still accelerating. Holy crap. We're quiet now. There are these aerodynamic sounds I've never heard before. Jim's locked onto the wheel. He is committed. We're at eighty. We are passing into a new regime. At any moment we might leave the road, go into hyperdrive with fenders, mirrors ripping off, the paint igniting, flaming away in flashes as we slip beyond the envelope of atmosphere and ordinary life. When you're that age, you've no idea. A thing like this might be your destiny. Then suddenly just silence. Not transonic, but the engine cutting out. No bang or clatter. Just the whistling of the wind through those little side vents like we're plummeting from altitude. Somehow we manage to coast it off the highway into a service station. Hardly even tap the brakes. We don't need gas. It just won't go. It's done. We call someone to pick us up. I sell the car to one of the guys who can use the parts. A week or so later I'm informed it threw a rod—though how so violent an event could have been so quiet is a mystery. Maybe a day or two after that, my friend comes over to present me with the camshaft. He regards it as a marvel. As suggesting both a further mystery—how my car could have run at all with cams so worn and misshapen—and a plausible explanation for its ultimate performance. Proper cams—that lift and close the engine valves controlling intake and exhaust—have tapered ovoid profiles much like that of a hen's egg. Mine have profiles more like that of a piece of popcorn. My friend speculates that, somehow, at the end, these cams had worn into a shape that suddenly duplicated the function of what's called a "racing cam"—think of the deep, irregular gluggedy-glug of a hot rod at a stoplight, and the way it all smooths out into a roar as it accelerates away. Such engines, fitted out with racing cams, will sacrifice performance at low revs to find efficiency at speed. So, it appears we had an accidental hot rod for a moment. An ungoverned and self-generating hot rod. Had it not blown up? My God. We'd still be on our way, I guess, my friends and I, into the silent, airless gulf. Into the dark where two of us, by a different route, have gone already.

—David Searcy

Gladice Aymare has a peculiar, almost infectious lilt to her voice—a singsong cadence that softens the hard syllables of her French. She occasionally hums between sentences, her voice barely rising above a whisper, as if she were treating her words like her patients—gently, with an almost excessive kindness that makes it hard to imagine anything could ever go wrong. Among local and expat aid workers in the Central African Republic, Gladice is a veteran on multiple fronts. Trained as a midwife in Bangui, the capital of the C.A.R., Gladice followed the peripatetic path common to aid workers. There was her first Médecins Sans Frontières mission in Boguila, a small village in the northwestern corner of the country, followed by later missions in Damara and then Sibut. She was born and raised in Bangui, but her life now is built along the borders of her country, in remote villages reached either by plane or by several days' drive along the C.A.R.'s winding roads, which are so few in number that a map of every major road in the country can be memorized without much effort.

Gladice has, I imagine, traveled on every known path in the C.A.R., and that knowledge grants her more than just a privileged position. In the standard narrative of foreign aid, help, if not salvation, arrives from the outside, but on the distant back roads of a country like the C.A.R., nothing moves without someone like Gladice's direction. In 2012, when a coalition of armed groups toppled the government of François Bozizé, Gladice was working in a clinic in Damara and then later Sibut. She treated war-wounded soldiers and civilians, including forty-two rape victims, alongside her usual responsibilities in the maternity wards. When later that year Gladice returned to the hospital in Boguila, she was moved to the intensive care unit, where, she notes, she was more than just a midwife. It was a sort of homecoming for a woman who had come to know her country intimately, through its hospitals and clinics, through its sick and wounded.

She recounts this particular period with an obvious whiff of nostalgia, her gaze fixed on some indeterminate point just beyond the walls of the courtyard we're sitting in. We've just returned to the M.S.F. mission in Bambari, the second-largest city in the C.A.R., after two days of nonstop work in mobile health clinics. Despite the long hours and daylong drive to return to base, Gladice insists this is the perfect time to have our conversation. She speaks slowly and proudly about her work in the maternity ward and the responsibilities charged to her in the intensive care unit. Knowing how the story ends, she seems to linger deliberately on the bright spots. The Seleka forces that had swept into the capital and seized power at the end of 2012 had done so quickly, with little resistance from the military. When Gladice returned to the hospital four months after the coup, it was still possible to imagine that this vulnerable and profoundly underdeveloped nation would shrug off its latest political crisis. There had been coups and attempted coups before—but so far, in four decades of independence, the C.A.R. had never fallen victim to the type of violence that had afflicted nearly all of its neighbors, from Chad, Sudan, and South Sudan to the Democratic Republic of the Congo. At the hospital, there were wounded soldiers and civilians from sporadic fighting between Seleka and the former army, but it was the common daily concerns of malnutrition and malaria that demanded the most attention.

The bright spots that Gladice lingers on are centered on her former colleagues. All the staff lived next to the hospital in Boguila—a communal arrangement born out of necessity that also served as a daily exercise in bonding.

"We always ate together," Gladice says. "We lived together. We would leave at the same time to go to work. On Sunday we went to church together." Back in Boguila, she was nicknamed "Mamma Coffee."

"My friends would come to my room and they would say, 'Mamma Coffee, Mamma Coffee,'" Gladice tells me, because they knew she loved coffee, and as a lover of coffee, would make anyone who asked a cup.

Gladice never describes the bonds with her former coworkers in familial terms, although certainly there was the intimacy and proximity of family, but perhaps the term "family" is a poor substitute for the peculiar binding of work and life that comes with this type of aid work. Families separate—their members leave and go to school

5

and work and then come together at the end of the day. At the M.S.F. hospital in Boguila, like the mobile clinics in Bambari that Gladice now attends to, no one was left alone, no one had a life alone. There was only the work and the post-work gathering that followed.

As we near the difficult part of the story, Gladice lists the names and jobs of the eight staffers who lived with her. She leans over to make sure I spell each one properly.

"Before the attack we felt very secure," she says. "We had a guard day and night, a safe room. We had three blocks—I was the supervisor of our block, block 2. During the night we guarded the radio with us. And they [the guards] would call us on the radio if there was a problem."

Two days before that conversation, I followed Gladice into the back of a white Land Cruiser as it prepared to leave for a mobile clinic four hours south of Bambari. There were eight adults in our SUV—six of us squeezed onto folding benches in the rear. Underneath our seats and at our sides were the building blocks that would later be used to construct a temporary clinic on a patch of grass a few hundred feet away from the country's largest sugar factory, and the internally displaced persons' camp huddled in its shadow.

Within a few minutes of leaving the compound, we reached the edge of Bambari—a point marked by an unofficial transfer of power from the UN forces to a pair of teenage boys in military fatigues, each with an automatic rifle dangling indifferently around his neck. The young soldiers were the first official checkpoint marking the end of government-controlled territory. Almost the entire province from that point on was controlled by an ex-Seleka militia that had rejected the peace agreements that brought a measure of stability to the rest of the country.

We were casually waved through the checkpoint without the slightest hesitation, but something was obviously different on the other side of the barrier. Here, along the road to Ngakobo, the C.A.R. was still undoubtedly at war. In Bangui, the costs of that war had been evident in the camps and in the clinics and hospitals. Here in Ouaka, the proof was in the burned homes and abandoned villages that lined the narrow red-dirt road. Ten kilometers away from that initial checkpoint, we drove past what was left of Jean-Claude Pouzamandgi's village. Jean-Claude, a technician in the clinics, was responsible for dispensing medication, and when we neared his home—of which only half a wall and a pile of bricks remained—he leaned over from his side of the car, pointed out the window, and stated proudly that this was where he had lived, and, as he explained, would certainly live again.

For the next several hours, we drove through more burned villages and roadblocks—each barrier manned by soft-faced boys in military clothing a few sizes too large. With every one passed, it was hard not to feel that whatever security and authority had been present in Bangui, and to a lesser degree in Bambari, was eroding. We weren't in a dangerous area; it was, in fact, just as Gladice had described it—an insecure zone. Initially that description had sounded slightly romantic, but in retrospect, it's a phrasing generous enough to include all the threats and possible threats that make Gladice's work necessary.

On April 25, 2014, Gladice went to bed very late. She was the designated night guard and was slow to wake the next day.

"On the morning of the twenty-sixth, I came down. At one p.m., I went to the hospital for an online course on malnutrition. I went to the office for one or two hours. I was feeling tired. It was a ten-minute walk to get to the office.

"I had two hours of courses per day. When I was finished with the two hours, I returned home to wash clothes. I had just begun to wash my nurse's outfit. I had the radio next to me when I heard the guards begin to talk in their local language: Souma. It's the language of Boguila.

"When I heard them talking, I asked them to talk in Sango or in French. I then had a response—the [rebels] are starting to arrive in the hospital. And then right away, there was shooting.

"In our area—Jean-Claude and Raissa and Fiacre were sleeping. I started slamming on the doors telling them to wake up, the Seleka were here. We started looking for a place to hide.

"We quit our block to hide in block 3. There was me, Jean-Claude, and Raissa. We hid in the kitchen of block 3. It was big and there was a lot of shooting. They started around two p.m. while we were in the kitchen—the kitchen was exposed, only partially brick, so we went to go hide in the shower. It was a shower with three doors. We stayed there while they continued shooting. And because I had the radio, I turned down the volume. And we stayed like that on the floor and they continued to shoot and shoot and shoot. And it was at that moment I began to pray. 'Is it the end of my life?' I said to God. 'We're here to help the people, help us. We're here to save lives.'

"We were all in the same shower. Fiacre also began to cry. We stayed there for at least forty-five minutes of shooting. We didn't know they were killing.

"After, there was silence, we heard the cars pulling away. And then there was calm. And then I turned up the volume of the radio. We heard the voice of our project coordinator, Will. I heard him in conversation with our nurse. We heard him say there were injured at the hospital. He gave the authority to leave and go to the hospital. The first person I ran into was Raassaoul—and it was he who told us that we lost Papa Daniel. Automatically we hugged and began to cry. I went to the hospital and there were bodies everywhere.

"In addition to Papa Daniel, there was the guard supervisor, who was called Papa Jean-Paul Yainam.

"When we arrived everyone was running, crying, hugging. We went to the O.P.D. (the external consultation area)—there were eleven village chiefs killed there. That's where the meeting was.

"We did the triage—we found three survivors. And among the three was one M.S.F. guard who had a bullet in his abdomen. He had a severe hemorrhage. The doctor took him straight to surgery.

"We began to search for people to donate blood, but the guard died at the block. Then other people in the neighborhood who were attacked began to arrive at the hospital—they began to bring their survivors. We were all together—staff, expat, inpat—to stabilize those who were still alive. That Saturday everyone spent the night in the hospital.

"Will decided to evacuate the staff—on Sunday a plane came and took one part of the team. [Will] asked me if I had the courage to stay one more day while M.S.F. came to get the rest of the survivors. I stayed with my other colleagues. On Monday, two M.S.F.-France cars came from Paoua, and on Tuesday, we made a convoy with four cars. The chief of our mission, Stephano, stayed with us.

"We stopped at Bossangoa, where the team was waiting to greet us. We hugged, cried, ate together, and then continued.

"After one month, they asked if we were ready to go back to work. They offered us a choice: Grimari, Bossangoa, or Zemio—Grimari is an emergency project, which is what I chose. I didn't lose my courage to continue to work."

—Dinaw Mengestu

It is a fact universally known that in Lima, if you are a lady of beauty, you are likely to be a whore. I learned this when I was around thirteen, and my mother was obsessed with me being a lady of the night, too. She liked to check my pockets to see if I had extra money, money I couldn't account for, a domestic IRS of my little, never-been-kissed vagina. But I digress.

I've been wanting to write about the women in my family for some time, but haven't known where to start. I've always located them in a nineteenth-century rural world of dusty roads and wooden carts, like the ones carrying the thirteen-year-old prostitute Eréndira and her *abuela desalmada* in the Gabriel García Márquez story. Their Peruvian lives ooze a vague Vargas Llosa air, but the places they hailed from would have been irrespirable for his bourgeoisie. Melchora, my great-grandmother, was a native of Huánuco, a small village at the center of the Andean plain, a yellow world trapped between jungle and mountains. She couldn't read or write, though it really didn't matter; she spoke Quechua, and Quechua is a spoken language—its real life exists between mouths and ears, though it can be transcribed. Melchora loved going to the movies and yelling at the screen, especially at the villains: You are as ugly as your deeds! Melchora married an Irishman, Byrne, who beat her frequently and was drunk all the time. Eventually he left, and Melchora moved to La Victoria, a shoddy neighborhood in Lima, along with her two daughters, Olga and Ana, and a retarded little boy, Pepe.

Ana was the prettiest: by the time she was twelve a line of suitors had already formed in front of her. Men came to the house and offered their charms and gifts: platters of carne seca, furniture, ham, jewelry. Ana loved dressing up and dancing. She was wispy at the waist, she had wide Bambi eyes, and she loved getting dolled up in capri pants to dance boleros at the Lima clubs. Sometimes she wore jasmine in her hair like *La flor de la Canela*, a bolero heroine, the Madonna of the Rímac. She enjoyed the vanity of the temptress; she had fun with it.

Once a young man came to visit the family and impressed Melchora: he was well-spoken, and successful in the jewelry business. He was very short, not particularly handsome, and Olga didn't like him one bit. She assumed he was coming for her sister, but Ana wasn't staying much at home; she would disappear for days in a row, while Olga took care of little Pepe. One morning, when Olga was getting ready for school, Melchora told her she couldn't afford to return the gifts and she had to marry Jorge. Olga Byrne left the school and the house to marry my grandfather, Jorge Washington, absurdly named thus because, even though he was Peruvian and his father owned an anarchist newspaper, he was born on the Fourth of July. Ana was not planning on returning any gifts. She left school and moved out to the Rímac neighborhood, where she started seeing a man no one knew. The transition from gifts to *soles* must have happened at some point, when she had to distribute the earnings, and he became her pimp.

One night, on the way home after the bolero club, he began beating her in the street. She pushed back, took off her pumps, and tried to hit him with the heel. He went on beating her and she kept yelling but people in the Rímac were used to having their night air sprinkled with girls' screams. He pulled her by the hair down the block as she crawled and cried for help. He kicked and a part of her would move, stimulus and response, like a question and answer or a body spasm. At some point she didn't move anymore and he tied her body to a wooden cart, a *carretilla*, for everyone to see. I see him angry and euphoric, riding her dead body on the street and yelling *puta de mierda*. He did this till dawn, perhaps drunk. He was still babbling *puta* at the air, or he went into hiding; versions differ. Her body was found naked in broad daylight, rotting in the Rímac river air. Someone found the broken shoes and gave what was left of them to Melchora. She burned them.

Ana had two children who went to live with my grandmother. One of them was apparently my mother. She was careful to destroy all photographs of herself as a child, so nobody would notice the resemblance.

—Pola Oloixarac

11

In the summer of 1998, my best friend and I went to the Greek island of Kythira: birthplace of Aphrodite (sprung from her father's seed in the island's waters), birthplace of modernist disenchantment (Baudelaire, expecting a paradise of love, found instead a hanged corpse), and conveniently located between the Greek mainland and Crete. We were backpackers making our way by land and sea from Rome to Istanbul. We had spent almost all our savings just getting from Australia to Europe. We were twenty but we looked younger; we were younger. We were tender, shy, bookish girls from suburban Sydney; we lived in an ecstasy of passionate innocence rendered largely undetectable by our extreme politeness. This politeness meant we agreed to have dresses we couldn't afford sewn for us in Athens, strangely modest floral cotton shifts that made us look as if we'd just stepped off a nineteenth-century prairie. We agreed to get into the car of an aggressively solicitous man called Christos who wanted us to come with him to Marathon. These things, and others of their kind, we agreed to. And yet if E and I had been visited on that trip by golden Apollo offering a night of corybantic frenzy or an initiation into the Eleusinian mysteries, we would have turned him down. Politely.

Actually, E might not have declined Apollo. In search of beauty, she would push at the closed door of any church while I hovered behind her. I was anxious about catching the right bus, turning down the right street, having the right change for the public toilets. I was intimidated by the gorgeous bulk of the Parthenon. I was continually hustling us off public transport in the wrong places because I was so worried we'd missed the right ones. I was the one who bought our ferry tickets to Kythira and was sure, when the boat stopped at a small port on a spit of land, that this was where we should disembark—absolutely sure, although no one else got off there. The ferry terminal—the only nearby building—was closed.

Two taxis waited at the terminal; we waved them both away. Taxis were expensive. We would walk.

We had spent the day travelling and now it was late afternoon. The sea was blue and everywhere; there was much more sea than land. Land was a low greenish hill, treeless, visible across a causeway. From this distance—and the causeway was longer than it had seemed from the boat—we could make out a few buildings. We assumed that, as we grew closer, more buildings would materialise, if not by magic then because our guidebook promised them. And as we walked and evening approached and lights came on in what we assumed were windows, a town did appear to gather itself on the slope of the hill; so that when we arrived, finally, and found a village of eight or nine buildings, it seemed even smaller than it was. Most of the buildings were modest white houses along an empty beachfront; one was a small restaurant; behind them stood a complex of holiday apartments. The proprietor of the restaurant assured us that we were on Kythira, just the wrong side of it. He could call for a taxi to take us to the main town, but we couldn't afford it. We had no cash and there was nowhere to withdraw money; we could exchange traveller's checks at the ferry terminal but it wouldn't open until an hour before the next boat, on Monday afternoon. It was Friday evening.

It's not so terrible to be stranded for three days in a village on a Greek island. We accepted this at once; accepted, too, that we would live off the food we had with us (a jar of Nutella and a packet of spaghetti) and use E's emergency credit card to stay in one of the holiday apartments. These were opened especially for us. Our room was far nicer than any other we stayed in on that trip (there were, for example, no bloodstains on the mattresses). So we were in good spirits as we walked down to the beach to swim. The sun had set but the air was warm and pink and we moved through it as if through

13

soft smoke. The sea was the same temperature as the air. It seemed reasonable to imagine this as the birthplace of love.

A woman in a bathing suit emerged from one of the houses and waded out to join us. She carried her head carefully above the water; she told us this was to preserve her makeup. Her heavy mascara ran all the same, so that eventually she resembled one of the theatrical masks we'd admired in the mainland museums—the sorrowing ones meant to signify tragedy. In fact she was a cheerful woman. She had heard we were Australian. She told us that Australia was known as Big Kythira because more of the island's residents had emigrated there than to any other place, that there were considerably more islanders in Australia than there were on Kythira, and that for a time after the Second World War the island's economy was almost entirely supported by these southern emigrants. She proceeded to list the names of her expatriate friends and family. We didn't know them, but she continued to offer names and we continued to apologise for not recognizing them. There was something both friendly and melancholy about standing in the Mediterranean as this stained, smiling woman recited what might as well have been a litany of the dead.

Swimming that evening, we noticed a large cave along the coast and thought we'd like to walk to it. The next day was hot and bright and we spent it reading on our balcony, but as the afternoon cooled we set out for the cave. We followed a path through dense grasses and low shrubs. The air softened, turned pink, and as we walked I became steadily overcome by dread. The cave seemed the source of some deep, vital terror, and my fear of it was unyielding. E felt the same way. I can't remember which of us confessed first, but I remember the relief I felt when we agreed that we should go no farther. Perhaps this was, at last, Apollo's invitation, and we did after all refuse it.

Hurrying back along the path, I heard E say, "I hope we don't meet a wild dog." Almost immediately, a great dark dog sprang up

14

from the grass and ran snarling toward us. E, who seemed to have conjured it, blocked my body with hers. Just before it reached us, we heard a loud whistle; the dog, responding to this whistle, left the path.

Now we almost ran back to the village. To calm ourselves, we walked along a jetty that reached into the placid sea and sat with our feet in the water. Bright lamps illuminated the whole empty beach-front; these were the lights we had been reassured by as we walked across the causeway. The sea lapped and soothed. We talked quietly until the mood of the walk left us; then we laughed at the cave, the dog, and ourselves. As we laughed, a short, high wave rose out of the soundless sea and drenched us on the jetty. Then the water was calm again. The wave seemed so specific, so resolved, that without consultation we ran back to the hotel as if pursued.

We spent the rest of the weekend sleepless and baking in our sealed room; afraid of the island, we closed all the shutters and windows. Wrapped in wet towels and eating plain spaghetti, we waited for the Monday sun to rise. When it did, we shouldered our packs and walked to the ferry terminal to wait out the hours until our boat. Shortly before it arrived, the taxis we'd dismissed three days before came driving across the causeway.

On the ferry, E went to gaze at the food in the cash-only cafeteria. I stayed on deck, unwilling even to smell it. She returned and told me there were meatballs and a passenger playing a guitar. She slept and I stayed awake to make sure we ended up in the right place. I was hungry and tired and frightened, and because at that time I was someone who prayed, I prayed the rest of the way to Crete while E slept against her backpack. God, we were happy. We hadn't written our books yet, and no one we loved had ever died.

—Fiona McFarlane

"*Her mother finally managed to have the stroke she had been readying herself for all her life,*" Philip Roth writes in *My Life as a Man*, the novel he published in 1974, the year my parents first met. When I came across Roth's phrase, I knew it perfectly summed up my mother's life.

My mother had her first stroke when she was thirty-six, younger than I am now as I'm writing this. It was a minor stroke, a warning of what was to come, and we all knew a much greater disaster would follow, we just didn't know when. Compared with earthquakes, for strokes it's the other way around—the aftershocks are the catastrophic part. In our case, the waiting and the grace lasted for twelve years. In the meantime my father retired, I finished high school, then university, then took my master's degree and started my adult life. I sometimes think that my mother waited just the appropriate amount of time before changing my family's history.

Patience is the measure of true love, especially when illness is involved. My father and I learned this in the very first days after transferring our lives to the hospital to be with my mother, who was left in a coma by the second stroke. The official diagnosis: acute ischemic stroke within the vertebrobasilar territory.

My mother came out of the coma after several long weeks (a couple of days before New Year's Eve, which we celebrated drinking cans of beer hidden under the hospital bed) and only after two surgical procedures (the first of which was delayed several times by the lack of Rh-negative blood; the necessary bags of blood were supplied by a regional hospital and delivered by my uncle, my mother's brother, in his car, in a handheld beer refrigerator), but she opened her eyes at the cost of shutting down her memory and her speech. Furthermore—though I should probably say furtherless—she lost sight in one eye, one arm was left completely paralyzed and one leg partly paralyzed: the entire right side of her body was gone. The stroke had claimed more than half of what used to be my mother.

For nearly six months, my father and I lived with her in hospitals and rehabilitation centers, moving from one place to another as soon as the maximum hospitalization time was reached. For a whole month we were accommodated by the intensive care unit where, almost every day, someone lost the battle against his or her own body. We placed our personal belongings in a cardboard box under my mother's iron bed, and stayed at her bedside. In Romanian hospitals, when in such a critical condition, if you have no attendants, you are absolutely on your own and you wouldn't want to be at the mercy of overworked nurses. In the neurosurgery unit, relatives are attending to what's left of the lives of those attacked from within their own brain. And my mother needed us—or I had better use the passive and say that *we were needed* to supervise her coma, and then her recovery: to watch over her drips, to adjust her bandages, to feed her (with a straw shortened to a third of its length, because she was too weak to draw in through the whole thing), to clean and wash her (using tissues), to anoint her and especially to turn her over in bed, in various positions. The body of a paralyzed person is like a fruit starting to rot, once fallen on the ground: unless you move it constantly, it develops bedsores.

The hardest part, however, was that, once out of the coma, my mother no longer recognized us (at some point she called me by a strange girl's name) and had no idea what we were all doing there. But even if she had recognized us, she couldn't have spoken. And it is silence that patience finds hardest to withstand.

In those months spent in hospitals, then in rehabilitation centers—when I covered the day shift and my father the night shift—we had more than one patient to assist. With no nurses and no attendants around, out of sympathy and sudden bonding, we found ourselves in the position of attending to anyone who needed help. We fed, we washed and we turned around in their beds the paralyzed bodies of strangers, mostly old women who had been abandoned by their families. Our own closest relatives had enough of our drama and, after a while, they stopped calling. Fortunately, we ourselves benefited from the solicitude and kindness of other strangers who would bring us warm food or tacitly replace us when we fell asleep, exhausted, on a chair or leaning against a radiator. At some point a very nice woman was so impressed by my father's devotion she developed a crush on him.

Assisting in my mother's recovery was similar to raising a child. She lost almost ninety pounds in the months spent in hospitals. We bought her new clothes from the children's section. And diapers. Before changing diapers for my own child, I changed diapers for my mother. Our parts were reversed: I mirrored the gestures she had once made with me. I had to teach her to hold her head up again, to chew solid food, to use her left hand (for brushing her teeth, for example), to make her first steps dragging her limp leg along. Before helping her utter her first words and before rebuilding her memory by recounting and explaining to her the family photos (she was herself a photo that had been washed out along with the shirt in the pocket of which it had been forgotten), we had to teach her gestures and sounds by which she could let us know if she was thirsty or needed to be taken to the toilet. We built pulleys around the house (hammering nails in the door casing and attaching straps) for her to be able to move around and for her to strengthen the muscles unaffected by paralysis. We also used cords, tied to her right leg, in order to pull her foot and help her take small steps. For a while she was our personal life-size mute puppet.

My life as a man began when my mother became merely an extra on our family set. Overnight, my father and I had to play parts we weren't right for, parts we had never rehearsed. Little did we know about cooking, sewing and starching, about washing the curtains in the spring or salting vegetables in the autumn. Little did we know about caring for a home without the apprehension and the touch of a woman. Little did we know about a life without the wife and mother who had offered us everything on a plate. Little did we know about attending to her body, so different from ours. Little did we know what to do without the voice of a woman to tell us what to do.

But if you were to ask us now, neither my father nor I would say that it was really difficult, caught as we were in the turmoil of all things that needed to be done. Anyway, we never complained; we never asked for help or for compassion, and when it came, it embarrassed us. The fact that any day one of the much-awaited miracles could happen—for her to start speaking or walking on her own—gave us courage and strengthened our patience for facing the scarce and the unknown.

Today, twelve years on, we are no longer waiting for a miracle. For the first four or five years after the accident, my father clung to his hope and took my mother to rehabilitation facilities and spa resorts around the country. He even took her, without my knowledge, to monasteries in the mountains, in caves and forests, lighting dozens of candles and paying monks to say special prayers from old holy books. But now, my father and I have resigned ourselves to being utterly helpless against my mother's voiceless frustration and sadness. I can't even remember her voice anymore, the recording of which, lasting as long as a laugh and a four-second witty line, remains on a videotape from a distant cousin's wedding.

Mother, or rather what's left of her, has become the older sister I never had. I don't know what she means to my father now, but I know that his patience (or should I say his *love*) has been challenged much more than mine in these twelve years in which he has been the one to continually look after her, day after day, night after night. My father has also become an older brother, for that matter. Our family ended then, in the evening of November 22, and what we have now is something different, something spiritually superior, as I sometimes think; or just a huge injustice, as I think most of the time.

Patience describes not only the extent and the quality of my love for my mother or my relation to the ideas of fate or divinity, but also the way I confront the world and especially the cruel and sometimes useless medical system. For two years we had to take my mother every six months to be examined by an assessment board for the disabled. During a humiliating evaluation, we had to persuade the board members that my mother's limbs were truly paralyzed and that she really couldn't speak, she was not faking it. Finally, it took an intervention and a small bribe to get the permanent certificate according to which my mother fell into grade 1 disability, meaning severe locomotor disability and the due disability support pension for her and for my father, her legal attendant.

Our story has a happy end, though, and our life is only partly cloudy. We have become accustomed to living and enjoying what we have left. Fortunately, my mother is fairly autonomous now: she can get dressed and move on her own; she can feed herself without our help. She can walk, using crutches, in the garden or to the lake quite near the country house, she can thumb through family photo albums and cultural magazines (especially the ones where I'm contributing or I give interviews), she watches TV, she listens to the radio (French or Italian pop songs of the sixties are her favorites), she can put things in order in the kitchen and in the bathroom. She has amazing single-handed abilities: with only two fingers she can tie a double shoelace knot in just seventeen seconds. One day she even killed a small water snake by using her bare left hand—she happily brought it home, like a cat with a mouse!

But, most important, she has recovered her memory and her clarity of mind, even though she can't express them by ordinary language. She can't read or write either (mixed aphasia is the medical term for her condition) and her CT scan shows a huge eclipse in the left parietal lobe, where the damaged cerebral area was removed. We often joke about that together, saying that she used to talk too much anyway. The few words she can now utter, sometimes repetitively (echolalically) or in a special syntax, are, despite causing

20

her enormous frustration, an endless source of outlandishness, wit and humor. Imagine someone with a complex interior life who can express herself only in semi-haiku with a limited vocabulary.

The stroke made my mother a poet. It was not I who wrote the daily notes that were to become the long fragmentary poem that is my first book, *Vîntureasa de plastic*, but she who suggested image after image, disclosed metaphor after metaphor, dictated word after word, drumming the rhythm of each line against the hospital bed. I became her voice in another dimension. I just transcribed; I was the carbon paper between her and the rest of the world. That was the reason I kept the manuscript in my desk drawer for six years and published it only when I knew for certain that I had written for my own sake, that I had not traded on my family's tragedy just to make literature, that I hadn't flaunted my pain and my despair for the sake of literary glory. Moreover, I needed time to put up with the indecency effect triggered by displaying myself through poetry.

She gave me an artistic voice. Sometimes I think my mother sacrificed her own brain for me to make a proper entrance in literature. And sometimes I think the opposite—that my entry to literature required my mother's sacrifice. Anyway, I have no idea what kind of writer I would have become without my mother's metamorphosis and I will never be able to genuinely enjoy the gift of poetry—which I have abandoned ever since, for that matter. With every positive review, with every literary award, with every public reading, with every translation of my poems, I became more certain that I had been given poetry only to renounce it. For how could I have kept writing poetry after *that* and about *something else*? If I truly am or if I ever was a poet, then I am the poet of only one book, just as I am the son of only one mother.

In all these years, I must admit, I lost my patience with my mother several times. I was tired and I rebuked her, I yelled at her, I once lost my temper and even bullied her. I apologized in tears and felt ashamed. I feel very ashamed even now, when thinking about it. Actually—what am I saying?—sometimes it was and still is quite hard. But neither my father nor I would ever admit to that. Compassion still embarrasses us; admiration of our devotion embarrasses us even more. Because we love her the way she is, and love is not pompous, it is not inflated, it bears all things, hopes for all things, endures all things. Endures *all* things.

—Marius Chivu
Translated from the Romanian by Alexandra Coliban

My problem is I can't figure out how sorry to be for the way I've been. I'm either a little sorry, very sorry, or not at all sorry.

My problem is some nights I come in late and forget to lock the door behind me. Some nights I leave the porch light on. Some nights I have been touching my knee to another's beneath a table.

My problem is I spend a great deal of my time curating warm, inviting workspaces that I do not then use. I am always moving my desk from one room to another, always rearranging the furniture then walking into it in the night, always taking over the kitchen table.

My problem is I get an e-mail re: moment of silence but get it too late and the moment has passed and the moment was silent—I can recall it, only a half hour or so earlier—but while the moment was silent, in that I was alone, working, and silent, I did not, I don't think, use the moment to consider those we've lost, their sacrifices, nor the losses and sacrifices of their families, as instructed. At least these were not considered any more so than they ordinarily are, which is a little. My problem is I have my own moment of silence and think not of victims, their families, but of the perpetrators, and the wrong ones, the early ones, their trench coats.

My problem is not that I can't find my phone, keys, wallet, sunglasses, regular glasses, shoes, purse, book, pen, lipstick, earrings, watch, mug of cold coffee, but that I suspect these things are all hanging out somewhere without me.

My problem is I don't miss you.

My problem is I could not imagine how final death is and neither could you.

My problem is I have the job she never got to have and the education she never got to have and I'm intimidating and not as nurturing as anyone thought I'd be. My problem is I didn't convert. My problem is I'm all set.

My problem was born in Las Vegas at University Medical Center on April 28, 1957. My problem was almost fifty. My problem taught me to drive stick shift, to buy two boxes of dye, for we had the same thick hair. My problem taught me the names of all my body parts and that I decided who could and could not touch them. My problem is I never got to say goodbye, or I was always saying goodbye, goodbye, goodbye, goodbye, goodbye, goodbye, goodbye so the meaning absconded, as meaning does.

My problem is I grew up poor. My problem is I'm not as well read as he thought I'd be. My problem is I'm derivative, a copy of a copy, all faded.

My problem is I have the thing where the wires in my brain are crossed and everything that's supposed to be joyous is frightening. My problem is we married other people. My problem is I am hardly ever putting one foot in front of the other. I have a rock collection of rocks whose names I do not know and do not pretend to know.

My problem is I am only a little bothered by all of this, and want to change not at all.

—Claire Vaye Watkins

23

Today we rode in the world's most beautiful cab. A few minutes after we'd gotten in, the driver—middle-aged, and wearing glasses—passed us a notebook. Soojeong thought for a moment it was a Christian ambush, but the man explained that the book was where his clients wrote messages. While I was adding something, my wife found a second notebook, apparently much older. The first entry was from 2010. Fifteen minutes later we left the cab in Yeouido. Soojeong, who had been reading throughout the entire journey—she never does this as she suffers from car sickness—had tears in her eyes. She had read several messages, and even a short poem about the wind written by the cabdriver. It was a simple poem, pretty, not at all sentimental, she told me. But what impressed her most was that almost every one of the messages had an intimate, confessional tone. It was as if all those people had been waiting for that particular cab to unburden themselves. "I feel alone, my wife is hardly ever home, my son hates me." "I've just come out of hospital. Apparently the diagnosis is more serious than I thought, I don't know what's going to happen now." "On my way to see her for the second time. Very excited. I think she's the best girl I've met in a long time." "Our mother died today." I guess it was life in a pure state, and for that reason my eyes also misted.

I once dated a woman who used to wake up in a bad mood because she had been wasting her time having dumb dreams. We argued about this a couple of times. I told her she couldn't control what she dreamed, so there was no reason to be so enraged. No one dream is better than another. She knew this, but still went on complaining. Carl Jung said dreams aren't completely personal; in fact, they are part of a great network. During deep, early-morning sleep, for two or three hours, we become tributaries of an interminable river, a universal dream. I woke this morning with the memory of a couple of ordinary, very common dreams. One included a speech by a

Colombian politician. I lay there for quite a while, wondering why I had dreamed such a dream. It was uninspiring, and that made me feel ashamed, as if it was my duty to contribute to Jung's communal experience with more intricate examples, like the one I had last winter, which had surprised me. It involved a town made of paper, and a thrilling escape from North Korea through a tunnel excavated in the floor of a beauty parlor.

We are invited to a birthday celebration in a bar in Gangnam. The place is decorated differently from other establishments in the area: ultramodern lighting, roomy sofas, designer lamps. Ours is a bar for office workers with decor dating back to sometime in the nineties. A lot of wood and wallpaper. I order a whisky. The bow-tied waiter brings me an amber-colored tumbler, and a separate glass with a perfect specimen of ice. It is a single chunk the size of a tennis ball, cut like a diamond. I am obsessed by its geometric form, its many facets. They must have a machine just for making perfect chunks of ice. I pour in the whisky, and the ice glimmers like a star. I get bored. The birthday girl—supposedly a fashion designer—has decided to use her birthday as a sort of hijacking to promote her brand. A clothes rack begins to do the rounds, pushed by a friend who modeled for the catalogue all the guests are handed at some point in the evening. The supposed designer has left her job in a bank and wants to earn a living selling garments. A story shared by thousands of young Koreans fed up with abusive bosses, unpaid overtime, weekends spent in the office, useless meetings in which all that matters is appearances. I get bored. Fortunately there is that marvelous piece of arctic ice.

There was a flyer posted on the door. They're usually for fast-food delivery services. This one was different. I couldn't decipher it. I put it on the kitchen table rather than crumpling and binning it. In the evening, when Soojeong came back from the academy, I showed it to her. She explained that it's a kind of illegal loan scheme. With just one phone call you can immediately obtain a sum of money without a guarantor or any documentation. You just have to sign a piece of paper. It's a pretty common service. I asked her about repayments. Anyone who falls behind is beaten up, or worse. Before we went to sleep, she told me there was even an old story related to those loans: the debtors are kidnapped and taken to one of the thousands of tiny islands south of the peninsula. There, the loan sharks sell them as slave labor to the owners of anchovy boats.

—Andrés Felipe Solano
Translated from the Spanish by Christina MacSweeney

Nadifa Mohamed was born in Hargeisa in 1981 and moved to London with her family in 1986. Her first novel, *Black Mamba Boy*, was long-listed for the Orange Prize; was short-listed for the Guardian First Book Award, the John Llewellyn Rhys Prize, the Dylan Thomas Prize, and the PEN Open Book Award; and won the Betty Trask Prize. Her second novel, *The Orchard of Lost Souls*, was published in 2013 and was long-listed for the Dylan Thomas Prize and short-listed for the Hurston/Wright Legacy Award; the novel won a Somerset Maugham Award and the Prix Albert Bernard. Mohamed was selected as one of *Granta*'s Best Young British Novelists in 2013. She lives in London and is working on her third novel.

The Stoker

NADIFA MOHAMED

Red brick and leaded glass, the smell of bleach and defeat. The Employment Exchange has the atmosphere of a church; job notices flutter from the walls like paper prayers, and council workers dole out state relief with the aloofness of priests placing wafers into indigent mouths. Out-of-work miners, dockworkers, drivers, handymen, barrel boys, plumbers, and factory workers mill around, avoiding each other's eyes. The pinewood floor is dented by the tramp of work boots near the counter and littered with cigarette butts and matches.

'WELDER NEEDED'

'TEN YEARS' EXPERIENCE NECESSARY'

'UNDER 21 YRS?'

'APPRENTICESHIPS'

'CARPENTERS NEEDED'

'GRAVEDIGGING'

Mahmood shoves his hands into his sports jacket and paces from one notice to another, looking for boiler or foundry work. He has only shrapnel in his pocket, having lost the rest at poker. There is nothing worth trying for; none of the usual firms that can be relied upon to take coloured fellas are advertising. He looks again at the grave-digging notice; it's for Western Cemetery, the pay not half bad,

29

but the thought of shoveling hard, damp earth and filling it with stiff corpses makes him shake his head and mutter, 'Astaghfirullah.'

Pulling his trilby hat low over his eyebrows he takes a yellow ticket stamped 9 and waits his turn at the counter, standing beside one of the heavy coiled radiators. The heat from the cast iron blasts through his thin trousers and teases his skin, somewhere between pleasure and pain, and he rocks his body back and forth, letting the heat rise and dissipate. On the last tramper he had taken, the owners had installed new boilers and all the brass fittings had shone gold in the white light of the furnaces. He had stepped back to admire the conflagration before shoveling more coal in and turning the white light into an almost sentient, colourless gas that roved backwards and up the chimney like a jinni escaping a lamp. He had birthed that fire and nurtured it from yellow to orange to white to blue and then the colour that had no name, just pure energy. He'd wondered what it would be like to step forward the few inches that separated him from it, whether his skin would just fall from his flesh like a sheet. He had been formed by those fires, turned from a puny pantry boy into a knotted-muscled stoker who could stand at hell's gate for hours at a stretch, face roasted and grimy with coal dust.

'Number 9, come forward.'

Mahmood takes the chair in front of counter 4 and places his hat on his knee before handing over his grey identity card.

The woman in front of him wears a brown tweed suit and maroon lipstick, her hair done up with a net over the large bun. She looks at Mahmood over the rims of small wire-framed glasses. 'What can I do for you, Mr. Mattan?'

'I need national assistance, no job good for me.'

'What work can you do?' she asks, lengthening each word.

'Boiler work. Quarry.'

'Let me see if there is anything else we are yet to pin up.'

She looks through the files on her side of the partition; her manner is pleasant, better than that of some of the other clerks, who seem to resent him whether he is looking for work or drawing dole.

'There is one foundry job here but I don't think you will be suitable,' she says, leaving the rest unsaid.

He meets her gaze, swallows a bitter smile.

She stamps his card in the right places and counts out two pounds and six shillings.

'Have a pleasant day, Mr. Mattan.'

'And you, madam.'

Mahmood rises and folds the pound notes into his pocketbook before putting on his hat and leaving the melancholia of the Exchange for the thud and clamour of the racetrack.

A good day at the races in the end, just over ten pounds in winnings from an each-way bet on a colt with 11/2 odds. Mahmood had changed his bet at the last moment after catching sight of the fine black colt in the paddock, and he could have sworn the animal nodded to him as it passed by on the groom's reins. A lucky name too, Abyssinia. Names beginning with an A are always good to him and he has visited Abyssinia, another sign he should lean more on the A's; so far he has won on

Achtung
Ambitious Daisy
Apache
Artist
Angel Song
Artois
Arkansas' Pride
Atlantic Revelry

He should also hand over five pounds quickly to Doc Madison for the lodging room in Davis Street before it slips through his fingers and the fool gets on his back. The rest he will spend on the boys and Laura, treat them now that he has paid off the court fine. It had been a mistake that last time, not just theft but sacrilege on the charge sheet; he had taken things too far, and it had turned them all against him. The shoes piled up outside the zawiya on Fridays seemed fair game—you could come with one pair and leave with another with no real bother—but the zakat money was haram. Only Berlin was talking to him now. Passing the cinema, he looks up to see what pictures they have on. *The Greatest Show on Earth* still, *Babes in Baghdad*, and *Othello*. He will watch *Babes in Baghdad* tomorrow but turns his nose up at *Othello* when he realises that the turbaned figure on the poster is a white man in dark make-up and a curly wig. The A-boards outside the newsagents are still plastered with photographs from London: the flag at Buckingham Palace at half-mast, Churchill in his felt stovetop paying his respects, the newly minted queen in the backseat of a car with her eyes fixed ahead; the king's death turning into a Hollywood production when everyone knows he was a weak man, pampered from birth, unmanned by wealth and too much ease.

Mahmood stumbles over a loose cobblestone and corrects his balance self-consciously, looking left and right. His steps look strange, flat-footed, as painful corns force him to wear shoes too large for his feet. He had learnt to do the black man's walk early on in Cardiff: to walk with his shoulders high, his elbows pointed out, his feet sliding slowly over the ground, his chin buried in his collar, and his hat low over his brow, giving away nothing apart from his masculinity, a human silhouette in movement. Even now, he flinches when passing gangs of Welshmen when they've been at the boozer or on rugby days; everything might seem calm, normal, when suddenly a fist comes into his face as hard as concrete, the shock of it knocking all words out of his head. The laughter as they pass on, the attacker giddy and loud with self-congratulation, the shame hotter than a furnace. Other black sailors keep a knife or razor in a pocket but with him the risks are too high: the police know him by name, they might search for a stolen watch and find the razor or knife and then what? Two years for an offensive weapon. He has perfected not being seen, he knows people call him 'the ghost' and this satisfies him, it helps with the work and reminds him of the characters in the comic books he picks up for his eldest boy: Kid Eternity, Grim Reaper, Captain Comet.

It's late by the time Mahmood reaches Berlin's, after going home to change, ignoring Doc's calls for rent, and darting out again in a three-piece suit and dark overcoat. Berlin brings out his self-doubt; he always looks so polished, like Cary Grant. Smoothing his moustache down, Mahmood pushes the heavy black door. Calypso music fills the room and somehow makes it seem busier. There are only a few customers on this Monday night, students in black turtle-necks against the bar, a white couple dancing awkwardly beside the jukebox, their hips moving in an uncoordinated staccato. Berlin is standing fixed behind the bar, his arms stretched on either side of him, clenching the counter, his head bowed. Lost in this reverie, he takes a moment to notice Mahmood settling into the bar stool in front of him; he finally lifts his head and his distant-seeming hazel eyes settle ambivalently on him. His face is reminiscent of a shark's, a hammerhead, with his flat skull and wide, dark lips. He is hand-some but in a dangerous, bloodless way; he never loses himself or allows people to lose themselves to him. Mahmood knows that he abandoned a daughter in New York and a son in Borama; he speaks of them easily but with no guilt or regret. Mahmood likes this lack of emotionality from Berlin; it means you can tell him anything and it is like speaking to a wall: no shock, no moralizing, no pity or disgust. Berlin has low expectations and is indifferent to even the greatest tragedies; his own father was murdered before his eyes in a raid on his clan by the dervishes, and watching that dagger run across his father's throat must have turned Berlin's heart to tin.

'So the wind has blown you in again?' he asks in Somali.

'The wind has blown money into my pockets, sahib.' Mahmood drops a handful of coins onto the bar. 'Get me a pasty and a black coffee.'

'Good day at the races?'

'Not bad at all.'

'You missed some action earlier tonight. The police found a couple of Chinese sailors running opium from a lodging house on Angelina Street. Using it themselves, too, so they were walking on noodle legs to the police car, them and this little bebopper from the university. It gave the reefer boys a laugh to see the police busy with someone else.'

'The Chinamen are good at keeping their secrets. Someone must have told.'

'Like they said in the war, the walls have ears, nothing is secret for long in this old whore of a bay.'

Mahmood finishes with his pasty after a couple of bites; it's greasy and stale, but luckily his stomach has become a small, easily satisfied thing. On the ships he could eat whatever was put in front of him and go back for more; now he eats just enough to trick his mind into thinking he's had a meal.

'You think that new Somali from Gabiley is telling tales to the police? Something about him smells bad to me.'

'Who, Samatar? You got the wrong fella there. His knees start knocking if he even sees a police car. Not cut out to be an informer.'

'Grass,' Mahmood says, unconvinced, rolling the word in his mouth like a lost tooth. He hates grasses even more than coppers. You can be sitting down with a man, playing poker or warming your hands on a mug of tea, and the next thing you know everything you said is repeated back to you in the police station; no matter how much trash you were talking or how tipsy you were, it goes down against you. You deny and the police grab your neck and say they know it's so.

'I know an informer when I see one and he ain't it,' Berlin repeats. He is quieter when away from the others; he doesn't need to get up on a stepladder and perform the role of bossman, the man who made it, the man who beat it all. It's getting late and he's burning down like an old wick, wiping the counter in slow, deliberate circles, rubbing his eyes. Despite the gleaming black hair and straight back, he is in his fifties and age is starting to catch up with him; he no longer attends the rent parties and makes excuses to stay at home on weekends.

'You're still set against going back to sea?' he asks abruptly. 'Might be good for you to let it all cool down, give the Sheikh time to forget.'

'No, I want to see my boys.'

'From across the street with a pair of binoculars?'

'Better than across an ocean or two,' Mahmood replies, curling his lip.

'She don't want you bringing money in or what? You can't take these young girls so seriously. They go to the pictures and think marriage is going to be one long song and dance number. All kissy kissy lovey dovey. What, she's twenty? Twenty-one? What does she know of what a father needs to do? You don't want your sons to see you out of work and broke all the time.'

'What makes you think I'm broke?' Mahmood jumps from his stool and slams his pocketbook on the table. 'Look inside, you call that broke? I live better than those sailors with their Salvation Army coats and fingerless gloves.'

Berlin rolls his eyes and slides the pocketbook back towards Mahmood.

'You stay in Cardiff until the last trumpet call. It's not my concern. You want another coffee, big man?'

Mahmood nods and wipes his hand over his brow. His heart is racing and he can't explain why he fears that he will just end up boarding a ship soon, like a zombie, unable to keep his promise to his sons. Behaving like all the others, just floating debris.

'You're a gambler, you know that sometime you have to let fate take over.' The coffee machine hisses and steams as the last drops fall into the white cup. 'Did I tell what happened to me when I went to New York in 1919?' Berlin asks, smiling.

Mahmood shrugs.

'I went there from Barry Docks. I did good service in the merchant navy during the Great War. I thought I was some sort of hero with my chest puffed up and my medals shining. The ship spat out its cargo in New York and then went into dry docking, so I head off with my pay burning a hole in my pocket. I see all these beautiful coloured girls in furs, stockings cut low on their calves, ribbons in their slick hair and I say what! What have I been doing stuck inside boiler rooms with grimy men? I have wasted my whole life already! The girls were from the south of the country, they tell me to go to Harlem, that all the swellest, most giddy-up places are there and that it's a Negroes' paradise. I say take me there now. We ride a taxi because I want to show off and we stop at a diner to feed. The food is all their food, pig this and pig that, but I find something to chew on, and one of the girls she's a real doll, face made for kissing and she's leaning into me and laughing and I lean back and laugh too, kekeke, showing all my teeth and I've forgotten all about any ship or curfew or anything. I hadn't been near a woman in months . . . The girls are singing for me and ordering more and more and they see friends passing and call them in and I'm still leaning and laughing. We finish up and they say, there's a party! Let's go! Louis will be there and Fats and rich ofays with good scotch whisky. I pay for everyone and we take another taxi as my girl say's her feet hurt, and we go to this party and I don't see Louis or Fats but there's low light, swinging music, sharp drink. I'm getting woozy, I lose my girl in the crowd and it looks like people are dancing on top of me, like

I'm falling through the floor. I can take my booze, you know that, and I'm wondering what kind of American drink is this that makes me lose my head. I wanna find my girl and hold onto her feet and so I crawl through the crowd thinking I'll recognize her red shoes but I can't and in the end they drag me out of the party. I wake up in the street and you know what? Those girls had picked me clean. Nothing but my seaman's card in my pocketbook, drugged then cleaned me out. I drifted downtown, close to the port but too ashamed to show myself to the captain, all of these deep holes in the ground I'm trying not to fall into, where they're building this new block and that new skyscraper. I sit sorry for myself looking out over the water, holding my head, when someone push me from behind. I jump to my feet thinking it's time to fight. The man laugh and I say whatcha laughing at? My fists up already. You don't know me? Why should I know you? Hamburg oh five he says. I step back and think it can't be. He pretends to pull back an arrow and shoot me and his name hits me instead. Taiaiake.'

Mahmood feels like he is back in dugsi, watching his qu'ranic teacher pace back and forth, the stories washing over him in great waves. 'Who was he?'

Berlin's eyes glint and he pauses to throw an espresso down his throat before starting again.

'We'll have to go right back to nineteen oh five. To Hamburg, Deutschland. Me and one hundred other Somalis crossing sea and land because we were told there was good work in Europe.'

Mahmood listens as he continues, tells how he was recruited by a Somali dalaal who scouted across the Habr Awal territory and the Garhajis and Warsangeli for people willing to go with him. He was a boy with no father and when he heard so many of his clanspeople were going away there was no way his mother could hold him back. Their cattle had died, they couldn't go near their old wells because of the dervishes so the camels had only a couple of weeks in them, there was nothing his mother could give him. There they were: the decrepit, the just born, the wadaads and the weavers, the suldaan and his servants, the potters and the poets, all on a dhow to Aden. The dalaal sweet-talked them into believing the Deutsch were so impressed by what they'd heard about the brave Somalis that they demanded to see them in the flesh; all they had to do was show them their way of life and the Deutsch would pad their pockets with gold. Beneath them in the dhow were saddles, looms, spears, shields, prayer mats, baskets, prayer boards, headrests, cooking pots, dismantled aqals, all that they had. The minute they arrived in Hamburg docks there was a photographer waiting for them. His flash exploding made the babies cry.

'We met the big boss Hagenbeck,' Berlin says, 'and he took us back to his mansion and told us to make up our camp in his long green garden. I fell asleep on the grass while watching the women tie the frames together and when I woke up small pale faces were peering through the fence, giggling and whispering to each other. I took a fright at these white-haired little jinns and ran into one of the assembled aqals and stayed there while more and more Europeans arrived to stare at us.'

'Astaghfirullah,' says Mahmood laughing, 'it's still the same when you pass the railway bridge.'

'No, this was something else . . . They were not looking the way you would at a stranger whose features or clothes are foreign to you. They looked in doubt of our real existence. Their eyes like this . . .' Berlin stretches his upper and lower lids wide open, 'watching every movement we made. They looked at us as if we were creatures of their imagination, as if they might be hallucinating altogether.'

'So what about that man in New York?'

'I'm coming to him! We stayed in that garden for a few days and in the end we saw more white faces than leaves on the trees. We were ambushed but told to live normally, as if back in Africa. Africa? Where is that? I asked. I had never heard of the place. We had a hidden area to do our business but what did we find? Deutsch boys my age, and men who should have known better, climbing up trees to watch us as we do it. When Hagenbeck told us to pack up we said, 'Subhanallah' and did it gratefully, but we were not going home, no, we were going on tour. We walked to the train station with our spectators running behind us, touching our skin to see if the black came off on their hands, pulling the hair of the children, grabbing anything we dropped and stealing it. Savages. There was a special train waiting for us and on the platform there were zebras, elephants, monkeys, Asians, Africans, Red Indians, Australians gathered together as if on Judgement Day. We were part of some kind of carnival, pulled together from every corner of the earth to be exhibited in Berlin. They counted us as we boarded the train to make sure no one had got lost but inside there was complete chaos. A confusion of languages, half-naked people, and screaming children. I pushed through, looking for a seat, leaving the other Somalis behind, until I finally found a quiet carriage. Sitting around me were men with only a strip of hair running down their heads and in front of me a fella around my age with a bow and arrow in his hands. I wrapped my three metres of cotton closer around my shoulders and sat up, real tough, hardening my eyes, but the boy smiled and held his palm out to me and I took it.'

'He was the one who found you in New York?'

'That's right, Taiaiake, a Mohawk from Canada, a friend and ally. We did everything together in Berlin, we sat side by side as they measured every inch—and I mean every inch—of our bodies, took pictures of us sitting and standing up, looking this way and that, poured plaster onto our faces so they could keep casts of us. It was something else! We felt like kings. We competed against each other in the games they put on and stared as the girls walked past for the beauty contest. Lord. We didn't realize then that they saw us as little different to the elephants and zebras on parade. Later he went to

America and took to the sky, and I took to the sea. There wasn't land anywhere that we could call our own and live well.'

'So you think I should take to the sky or sea?'

'You're a man of the sea, aren't you? You shouldn't cling to this piece of flint they call a country—warm yourself up beside a nice furnace somewhere in the Indian Ocean and come back with a clean slate and money in your pocket.'

'I'm not going anywhere. The devil looks after his own.' Mahmood smiles.

'Doqon iyo malagisa lama kala reebi karo. A fool and his fate are never parted,' sighs Berlin. 'Off you go then, roohi, I need to close up.'

After turning the sign on the door, Berlin perches on a stool and lights a cigarette, his silhouette appearing and disappearing with the flashing jukebox lights. The floor is mopped, the till emptied, and the coffee machine cleaned; there's just enough time to savour a last Player before Flo begins hollering for him to come to bed. He tries to empty his mind but thoughts gallop up and down—bills that need to be paid, a court summons for street gambling, a memory of his long-dead mother's perfume suddenly as strong as the cigarette smoke, another of his daughter's downturned infant mouth. He rises and opens a drawer behind the bar, pulling out an old postcard of the Empire State Building in a blizzard, postmarked two Decembers ago. Taiaiake had written a short message in block capitals on the reverse, wishing him a good New Year and telling him that he thought he saw Lucille in a playground in Boerum Hill, and that she looked well and was climbing the monkey bars as well as any steelworker. The postcard has been in the drawer since it arrived, Berlin thinking that any day now he will reply but somehow never managing to. He struggles to keep old worlds alive; friends, lovers, even children seem to deliquesce when he turns his back, appearing in fragments in his dreams and quiet moments to claim their stake on him.

Solmaz Sharif is the recipient of an NEA fellowship, a Stegner Fellowship, and most recently a Lannan Literary Fellowship. Her first collection of poems, *Look*, was a finalist for the 2016 National Book Award. She is currently a lecturer at Stanford University.

Beauty

SOLMAZ SHARIF

Frugal musicality is how Kristeva described depression's speech

Cleaning out the sink drain

The melted cheese

The soggy muesli

My life can pass like this

Waiting for beauty

Tomorrow—I say

A life is a thing you have to start

The fridge is a thing with weak magnets, a little sweaty on the inside

A bag of shriveled lime

Arugula frozen then thawed then frozen again, still sealed

I haven't touched anyone in a year

You asked for beauty, and one morning, a small blue eggshell on the stoop, shattered open, its contents gone

Likely eaten

M asked if I've ever made a choice to live and why

I lied the way you lie to the suicidal

A few times, I said—not *Most days*

Most mornings

No, not morning

Morning I am still new

Still possible, I'm still *possibly*

Usually by 3:00

When grandmother died, she hadn't been called beautiful in at least half a century

Is never described as such

Her fallen stockings, the way she spit, thwack of the meat cleaver, the little bones she sucked clean and piled on her plate, not really looking at anyone, and certainly not me

Elaine Castillo was born in the San Francisco Bay Area. Her debut novel, *America Is Not the Heart*, will be published by Viking (United States/Canada), Atlantic (UK), and Foksal (Poland) in 2018.

America Is Not the Heart

ELAINE CASTILLO

It'll take you a long time to talk about martial law, and you'll never talk about it with anyone who lived through it with you. But for now, you don't go to the rallies, you don't join the student protests; you go silent or change the subject when someone at your table in the canteen brings it up. The fear in you predates Marcos, predates dictatorships—at least, the ones that come in the shape of a single person. No one would ever mistake you for an intellectual or an aktibista; most of the time, you don't even really understand what people are saying when they talk about the news. Reading written Tagalog has always been difficult for you, even though you've gotten more or less fluent with everyday speech. But things like old kundi-man from the thirties and forties where half the words for love are words you've never heard in your life, or the complicated dialogue in some new movie where all the characters except for the yaya come from Manila, things like newspapers—they still send you into dizzy spells. So you stay away.

But there's no staying away from this: dread's in every pore, every breath, every blink. Martial law means curfew at nine o'clock, it means streets empty except for military jeeps, it means classes that once had fifty pupils are now classes that have forty-eight, maybe forty-six. You and your other nursing student friends at the

University of Pangasinan stay together through it all, eating all your meals together in the canteen even though some girls have taken to eating alone in their dorm rooms, sometimes playing music if they have a record player, Bread's "Make It with You" crooning all the way down the dorm corridor. In the canteen, there are some girls who just start weeping into their plates, right there in front of everyone; maybe because one of their relatives has been taken, maybe just from the fear alone, stretching all of you wire-taut. Sometimes you're one of the weeping girls—but you never weep in public; you do it only in your own bed, face smashed into the pillow so the tears absorb right back into the skin, the puffiness of your face in the morning the only sign of your labors. No one knows if you'll even graduate, if there will even be a university left when this is all over, if it'll ever be over. Then, a year into martial law, you hear about your cousin Tato.

You and Tato both attend UP but you rarely see each other; the last you heard he was studying political science or law. It's your mother who tells you that one evening, when he'd come back to Mangaldan to visit his parents for the weekend, Tato disappeared. Auntie Bobette had been outside with a basket of kangkong, plucking the leaves off the long stems, planning to make monggo for dinner once Tato was back from drinking with his friends. By the time the food had long gone cold, by the time they were eating its leftovers for breakfast and then lunch, Tato still hadn't come back. A week later, Uncle David disappeared, too. That was how Auntie Bobette knew Tato hadn't just gone underground with the aktibista friends he'd made at school, that lesser maternal grief of the period. If her husband was gone, too, something else must have happened.

Your mother tells you that a few months later, men from the military came to Auntie Bobette's house in Mangaldan, parking their jeeps in the dika grass and frightening the goats into bleating. They knocked on the door, and when she opened it, they said they were there to inform her that they were willing to pay her for the death of her husband, as befitting the surviving family of a deceased military officer.

Auntie Bobette didn't ask what they meant, didn't ask why they were offering to compensate a death no one had even confirmed yet. She only said, And what about my son, Tato.

They didn't acknowledge her words, or even flinch at Tato's name, only repeating that they were willing to pay for the death of her husband. They spoke as if reciting a speech they had memorized. Bobette said, in Pangasinan, replying to an answer they hadn't given: So they're both dead.

She directed her words at the soldier who had been doing most of the talking, a Pangasinense commanding officer not that much older than Bobette. He'd probably known her husband well, drunk Diplomatico rum with him at the carinderia down the street; they'd lit each other's cigarettes, judged the beauty of each other's mistresses. Once again the officer said to Auntie Bobette, not in Pangasinan but in a mixture of Tagalog and English: We are ready to compensate you, as a military widow, for the death of your husband.

And Auntie Bobette replied, with the blazing calm of a seraph: I don't want money. If you're saying they're dead, then you give me the bodies.

When your mother told you this story, you were terrified of the next part—of what might have happened to Auntie Bobette, at the mercy of four or five soldiers. You thought maybe your mother, who had never been in the habit of calling you regularly at school and had never even visited your dorms, was about to tell you of one more death. But instead your mother told you that the frustrated officers just turned around, got back in their jeeps, and left. Nothing else. For years, Auntie Bobette waited for one more knock on the door, for it to be her husband's or her son's face she finally opened to, either gaunt and gulping at life, or bloated and ragged in death, left at her front door as a final courtesy. Or for it to be the military again, come to extinguish the last of the last flames. But it never came; it never was.

A month or so after you hear about Tato from your mother, you meet Auntie Bobette on campus, after she's done finally collecting Tato's things from his former dorm mates, who'd kept his belongings safe even when the school had already given away his room to new students. You ask how she is, sounding inane even to yourself, but you can't find the words to speak about Tato or Uncle David. Auntie Bobette seems to understand that, because she only shifts the weight of the bulging duffel bag she's carrying, full of her son's clothes, books. She refuses when you offer to carry the bag, refuses when you offer to accompany her to the bus depot. She just touches your arm and says, Asicasom so laman mo.

All of your classes at school are taught in English, and even though most of your friends at UP are Pangasinense like you, most of the time you all end up speaking to each other in some mixture of Tagalog and English, imitating the poppy Taglish of teleseryes and radio programs. So you can't remember the last time someone told you to take care of yourself in your own language.

When your mother told you the story, she never told it in a way that made it clear whether or not Tato and his father were dead. She knew, and didn't know. You didn't ask. You knew, and didn't know, too.

Shortly after Tato disappears, you'll meet the man who'll become your husband and the father of your first and only daughter, the man whose ancestral family home stands at the center of Vigan, up north in Ilocos Sur, one of the old colonial homes that used to belong to Spanish officials or Chinese merchants; his family descends from both, but mostly from the latter. He's an orthopedic surgeon, and he teaches and practices at Nazareth Hospital, the first place you work as a student nurse. People say that he's only recently come back to the Philippines after having lived in Jakarta for ten years.

It's hate at first sight. He's one of these mayaman jet-setters who've been all over the world and who speak the English of commercials and foreign movies, the English of Asian kings played by white actors. Even the silence around him is regal; you can't stand that silence. People say that he's recently divorced, that he found his first wife, the cousin of Marcos, in bed with another man. You see him sometimes on his rounds, and he has a different nurse hanging on his arm every afternoon, a different girl in the passenger seat of his dark orange Fiat every evening. He's a notorious babaero, the Don Juan of the hospital, and most of the nurses flutter when he so much as enters the room. Yet his reputation never veers toward the sordid. This, you discover, is less because of his wealth and the weight of his name, and more because of the fact that every woman who sleeps with him agrees that he's a champion at eating women out. This is what differentiates Doctor De Vera from your run-of-the-mill babaero, they say. The man loves to make women come. He doesn't just rabbit-rabbit-rabbit and then tapos na, they giggle to each other, while you jab a straw into a Coke bottle.

One day you're assigned to do your rounds with him as a supervisor. He looks you up and down and you know that if you let this happen, you'll be next.

You're not going to let it happen. You're going to get the rounds over with, even with your skin gone all strange and prickly, the tiniest hairs on your body alive, alight. In the middle of the rounds, you realize that in your haste to finish you've advanced several steps ahead of him. You turn around. He's paused in the middle of the corridor, looking at you, amused.

You walk very fast, he says. He says it in English.

You flush. Standing there smiling, you think he looks like a darker-skinned Rogelio de la Rosa, pomaded hair and all, and before you keep on thinking up stupid things like that, you turn away from him, fast. But it's too late. He's seen your face; he knows he's made you blush. Now you definitely have to avoid him.

But he doesn't chase you, the way you think he will, the way you expect men like him to. He's just—present. He's around with all the answers when you need advice about a patient's sepsis, he's opening the entrance door to the hospital for you in the morning when you're yawning and too unguarded to remember not to thank him, he's in the break room debating favorite desserts with other nurses when you've slipped in looking for a place to take a nap. What's your favorite, he's asking Evelyn, a young nurse. She replies, Brazo de Mercedes.

Brazo de Evelyn, he quips, and she titters, along with two other nurses nearby, hanging around the edges of the flirtation in the hope of getting in on it themselves.

You roll your eyes and turn around to leave. Pacita, he calls. What's your favorite dessert?

You think about ignoring him, the way you should have ignored him when he opened the door that morning, the way you should have ignored him when he made the comment about how fast you walked. You didn't even realize at the time that he must have liked it because he'd gotten the chance to stare at your wiggling ass. Only later did you think about it, in bed, hot all over with fury and something that wasn't fury.

You should ignore him, but instead, you turn around and declare, in a voice so hard it sounds like you're delivering an insult: Tupig.

One of the other nurses, Floribeth, starts laughing. Native cakes pala! she says. You can buy that on the side of the road anywhere.

Yes, you retort. Isn't that great?

You turn around to leave, proud that you haven't blushed at all, proud that you'll be getting the last word, proud to leave Don Juan and his admirers in your wake. But just before you turn your back, you see that Doctor De Vera has gone still, stricken.

Years later, when you're married, he'll tell you that tupig was the favorite dessert of both his older brother Melchior and his late mother. When they don't sell it at the small Filipino grocery store in the California town you'll live in together, you'll try to learn how to make it without ever telling him—and then, when all your attempts turn out disastrously, you'll give up, also without ever telling him. But you don't know any of that yet. So right now, you just finish turning around and leaving.

Still, no matter how much you try to avoid Doctor De Vera—in your head, you address him only as the babaero; it helps you to distance yourself—he's everywhere. And maybe it's just your imagination, but it feels like he's looking back at you, too. Even when he's meeting another date in front of the hospital—a young woman who everyone whispers is the daughter of some CEO, of some company you've never heard of—it's you that he's looking back at, as he slips into the driver's seat. It annoys you, because you see through it; it annoys you, because you're meant to see through it. He's not hiding the fact that he's looking at you, and he's not hiding the fact that he sees you looking back.

The fact that he's a babaero isn't really the problem. It's not just the celebrity, or that his first wife was Marcos's cousin, or that he's a De Vera of the De Veras of Vigan, or that he's a champion at, at, at—cunnilingus. The problem starts with the fact that he's good at what he does. If reports are to be believed, he's the best orthopedic surgeon on the island of Luzon. You've assisted him in the operating room more than once, and while he never loses the louche grace in his limbs—he and his anesthesiologist are known for singing kundiman during their procedures, so that you've become used to the sound of someone belting out Dahil Sa Iyo beneath the deafening keen of a saw juddering through a femur—there's an expression on his face, a posture in his body, which you only ever see there. In that space. Each gesture has a calm, deliberate economy, so that even the air pressure around him seems to change, like someone descending into a mine shaft. No, it's not calm; it's self-possession. Even in a cavern, he owns himself. So that's what it looks like.

The part that really gets to you, the part that gets to your quietest of parts, is the part about polio: you learn that his specialty is children with polio, that this was what he was doing in Indonesia, opening rehabilitation clinics in rural areas. It was becoming less common as you were growing up, but you still remember some kids with polio around Mangaldan and Mapandan, among the families living even farther out into the rice fields, past the bangus farms. Still, still, still—you're not going to let yourself be seduced by him, by the myths that cling to his shoulders: cosmopolitan Don Juan, pussy-eater extraordinaire, savior of children—it's all so ridiculous.

It *is* ridiculous, but not for reasons you know yet. You don't know yet about his brother, about his mother, about the beloved niece of his, also named after his mother, who joined the New People's Army in college and who he long assumed was dead; you don't know that he's going to ask to name your first child together after that niece; you don't know that you're going to say yes the minute you see the wrecked look on his face when he asks; you don't know that when your daughter is around five years old he's going to learn that this niece is still alive, that she's survived two years in a prison camp, that she needs help, money, and most of all a place to live; you don't know yet that this place will be your home in California. Most of all, you don't know yet that he'll be utterly undone by his own life, that he'll lose everything he has now, that no one who flirts with him and courts his favor in this era will remember him in twenty years, that not even the aura around his name will survive except as a source of fatigued pride, passed down to your daughter, who won't fully grasp the context or the importance of that name when she says she's proud to be a De Vera, parroting his words without knowing their meaning. You don't know yet that when he's an old man, marbled with lymphoma, one night while you're asleep next to him he's going to remove the oxygen mask keeping him alive, and that afterward, instead of burning his body and scattering the ashes over the rice fields in Ilocos Sur as per his final wishes, you'll put him in a box in Northern California, ten minutes from the veterans' hospital where you'll work sixteen-hour days, so at least you can visit his grave on your lunch break. You tell his ghost, I can't go to Ilocos Sur on my lunch break.

You don't know yet that you're going to love him, and that you won't be able to differentiate this love for him from your devouring hunger to be recognized. It's not that you're imagining that he'd whisk you away to his mansion in Dagupan City or Vigan or Manila and you'd live happily ever after. You've got a happily-ever-after in mind, and it doesn't have anything to do with being anybody's nobya. For that matter, it doesn't have anything to do with Dagupan City or Vigan or Manila at all, or anywhere else in this country. You already know that the first thing that makes you foreign to a place is to be born poor in it; you don't need to emigrate to America to feel what you already felt when you were ten, looking up at the rickety concrete roof above your head and knowing that one more bad typhoon would bring it down to crush your bones and the bones of all your siblings sleeping next to you; or selling fruit by the side of the road while people had their drivers idle their cars to buy a couple of mangoes from you, making sure never to really look at you, making sure not to touch your hand when they put the money in it. You've been foreign all your life. When you finally leave, all you're hoping for is a more bearable kind of foreignness.

But while you're still here, warming yourself in the glow of some-one like the babaero, you're just. Curious. You just want to know what it's like to be wanted by someone like that. Most of all, you want to know what it's like to get it, and not need it. Most of the time, you need things you never get; you get things no one would ever want.

But getting something you want, that you don't really need? Getting something that's just about feeding that half-sewn-up second mouth inside you, unfed and lonely, cramped somewhere between your heart and your gut? You've never had that before. You've never had it, but you want to feel worthy of it, like the woman in the hair-dye ad you've been seeing around recently. You want to feel like it's because you're worth it.

If you had a girlfriend who was telling you this story, you'd cluck your tongue, tell her to throw the guy into the trash. You'd tell her to forget his name, to practice her English and pack her bags. But it's not a girlfriend telling you this story.

Diego Enrique Osorno was born in 1980 in Monterrey, Mexico. A reporter and writer, he has witnessed some of the twenty-first century's major conflicts in Mexico and Latin America. He has been called one of the region's most important journalists by the Gabriel García Márquez Foundation for New Journalism and has received Italy's prestigious Stampa Romana. In 2014 he was awarded Mexico's National Journalism Prize, which he dedicated to the Zapatista Army of National Liberation. He is the author most recently of *Slim*, a biography of the richest man in the world, which Verso will publish in English. Like many other Mexican journalists, he has been threatened because of his work.

Christina MacSweeney was awarded the 2016 Valle Inclán Translation Prize for her translation of Valeria Luiselli's *The Story of My Teeth*. She has translated two other books by the same author, and her translations of Daniel Saldaña París's novel *Among Strange Victims* and Eduardo Rabasa's *A Zero-Sum Game* both appeared in 2016. She has also published translations, articles, and interviews on a wide variety of platforms, including *Words Without Borders, Music and Literature, Literary Hub,* and *BOMB,* and in three anthologies: *México20; Lunatics, Lovers and Poets: Twelve Stories After Cervantes and Shakespeare;* and *Crude Words: Contemporary Writing from Venezuela.* She is currently translating texts by the Mexican authors Julián Herbert and Verónica Gerber Bicecci.

Come and Eat the Largest Shrimp Cocktail in the World in the Region of the Worst Massacres in Mexico

DIEGO ENRIQUE OSORNO

TRANSLATED FROM THE SPANISH BY CHRISTINA MACSWEENEY

In the Laguna Madre, a vast area of salt water that crosses the dividing line between Mexico and the United States and comprises a dozen communities in Tamaulipas and Texas, an army of fishermen caught over seventeen thousand penaeid shrimp so the local government could organize a Festival del Mar at La Carbonera beach, and prepare a shrimp cocktail weighing 2,257 pounds. The aim was to change the negative image of San Fernando, where, in 2010, on an August afternoon, seventy-two mostly Central American migrants were massacred in the storehouse of a ranch, and where one April morning in 2011, the tortured bodies of 196 people were found buried in the shimmering green pastures. In the following weeks mass graves were discovered containing an as yet unverified number of corpses, which some local authorities estimate to be around five hundred. A macabre joke circulated on Facebook and Twitter at the time: "Come to San Fernando, we'll welcome you with open graves." During Holy Week 2014, in this place where Mexico's most awful twenty-first-century massacres have occurred, the governor of Tamaulipas state, Egidio Torre Cantú, accompanied by a dozen regional mayors, would stand around a monumental glass tumbler to celebrate a new record: the largest shrimp cocktail in the world.

Along with agriculture, fishing was one of the main economic activities in San Fernando until the war between the Zetas and the Gulf Cartel, plus the military and naval presence, brought life in the town to a standstill, and caused the cessation of mass celebrations between 2009 and 2013. And that is why the Festival del Mar became an important event for the people of the region, some of whom could not believe they would have the opportunity to see in the flesh Mariana Seoane, an actress on the Televisa channel who once posed in the nude for gentlemen's magazines and has a single entitled "I'll Be a Good Girl." Seoane would be the festival queen and, at the behest of the euphoric crowd, would sing her three hits, turning to give the crowd a view of her figure. Another important moment would be the appearance of Sonora Dinamita, among whose members were two mulattoes who, according to the mayor of San Fernando, would give the women of the town a visual experience equivalent to that offered by Seoane to the men.

But the star of Good Friday would be the penaeid shrimp, a small crustacean whose bulging black eyes contrast with its curved, cylindrical body from which sprout two pairs of antennae—one long, one short—and five pairs of legs. Its body ends in a pointed tail that, along with the head, is removed before it is eaten. With just ten or twelve of these crustaceans, water and ketchup, it is possible to prepare a small seafood cocktail, although in Tamaulipas and many other places it is usual to include avocado, garlic and lime juice; in neighboring Texas, they also add cucumber and serrano chili. When oysters and clams are added, this hangover cure is generally known as "Back to Life," a name that in present-day San Fernando is not particularly appropriate.

During the festival I had a discussion with a man who was convinced that shrimp had been created for no other reason than to be ingested in a cocktail. According to him, when placed in a glass tumbler, they have a better flavor than when deviled, cooked in chipotle sauce, or garlic, or butter; served with Philadelphia; or wrapped in bacon and cheese; or a la Veracruzana. Or even when served with that chili pepper water they make so well in Mazatlán, Sinaloa, which once held the Guinness record for the largest shrimp cocktail in the world. In northeast Mexico you can find this expensive delicacy sold dried by the highway at incredibly low prices. The roadblocks installed by the military in the region, supposedly to reduce violence, have benefited this small sector of the economy, since the shrimp vendors are able to sell their product to the lines of impatient, fearful motorists. On the journey from Reynosa to San Fernando, I came across one of these roadside vendors, and asked if his shrimp were from San Fernando, to which he replied in the affirmative; they came from the Laguna Madre. He uttered that toponym in such a solemn, respectful tone, it was as if he was referring to some species of Aridoamerican deity. The same tone was adopted by the announcers on regional radio stations every time they mentioned the lagoon. Between the Ramón Ayala corridos and Julión Álvarez ballads saturating the airwaves, there was no mention of anything but shrimp, and the great feat about to be accomplished in San Fernando. On the morning of Good Friday, just outside the center of town, caravans of pickup trucks crammed with families formed in the Loma Colorada gas station before heading off together for La Carbonera, less than thirty miles distant. The sound of Banda Sinaloense music filled the whole place, because the quick workers in the convenience store adjoining the gas station had decided to install huge speakers to liven up the morning. A mile or two farther on, three state police patrols were waiting for a group of men armed to the teeth: the latter were the governor's bodyguards and had arrived the night before by road, without their boss. The governor was coming by helicopter but needed his security team for the three-minute drive from the soccer field that formed an improvised heliport to the venue at which the feat of prowess was to take place.

The police officers agreed to pose for the photojournalist Victor Hugo Valdivia while they waited for the governor's bodyguards, whom they themselves would escort along with a naval patrol, just in case. "There's a lot of movement," said the head of the police squad with an enormous smile, pointing his machine gun toward the highway—toward a former cattle ranch that a few years before had been requisitioned by the Navy as its local headquarters. It was also in this spot that both the Zetas and the Gulf Cartel, and even some *equis*—as greenhorn delinquents are disparagingly known—set up roadblocks to keep watch over who was entering and leaving San Fernando. On Good Friday it was the police and soldiers who had mounted the series of checkpoints. For the occasion, the Army decided to roll out its most recent acquisition from the arms market: the SandCat, a very fast, highly armored truck with a diverse array of weaponry. It is the vehicle with which the regional military forces hope to confront the *monstruos*: vehicular monstrosities designed by the Zetas that have already been operating in the area for some time. The lieutenant in charge of the group was carrying a 7.62-mm MAG rifle, and didn't allow many photos to be taken of his SandCat, "because the criminals will copy it." "How can they when the vehicle's designed in the United States?" I asked with not a little naïveté. "They kidnap the people who can, and make them do it." While we were talking, the governor's security team passed, escorted by the state patrols, in turn escorted by the Navy patrols.

At the entrance to La Carbonera there was an old boat, on which a number of workmen were hanging a banner advertising the presence of Mariana Seoane. The event was scheduled to start at 10 a.m.; to hold it in the afternoon, or worse still after dark, would have been too risky, however many bodyguards, police officers and military roadblocks were in place. La Carbonera is a shrimp-fishing village with a single, unpaved main street, and this was packed with cars waiting for a parking space. Very soon a long line had formed, advancing at a snail's pace, thus allowing some of the drivers to get out of their vehicles to buy the dried shrimp sold by fishing families outside their houses. These fishermen use a trap known as a *charanga*: a net attached to a V-shaped structure, which is dropped in the marine channels through which the shrimp are expected to pass. Some fishermen work at night, when the crustaceans are most active.

When we reached the shores of the Laguna Madre, where a buzz of anticipation was already running through the crowd, a bunch of youths wearing T-shirts with the message "We are all Tamaulipas" passed by. These mass-produced tees, and plastic glasses with shrimp-inspired designs, were being handed out at the entrance. By walking along the estuary, you arrived at a pavilion, with the first rows of seats occupied by government officials dressed in shrimp-orange T-shirts, and a smattering of army bigwigs in field dress. The show had not yet started, but the emcee took the microphone from time to time and, in a guttural voice, mouthed such historic comments as: "A beautiful crystal clear tumbler that will draw the eyes of the whole world, with a shrimp cocktail weighing more than a tooooon." If his aim was to animate those present, he didn't achieve it; after his interventions, the buzz from the crowd remained unchanged, and his words evaporated into the warm morning air. Only when a couple of municipal workers removed the plastic wrapping that had protected the tumbler from accidental scratches during its journey from Mexico City did the crowd quiet a little, perhaps because everyone thought the governor was about to arrive on the scene; he did in fact turn up, approximately two hours later than initially expected. But the emcee took advantage of the silence: "Today, more than ever, we are proud of the resources provided by the waters of our Laguna Madreeeee." Around ten yards away, sitting with a quasi-scientific air behind an aged laptop, the notary who was to adjudge the record was explaining that the glass tumbler weighed 825 pounds.

Of all the shrimp-orange T-shirt wearers in the first rows, the most euphoric was Mario de la Garza, a dentist who was also the mayor of San Fernando. While waiting for the governor, he spoke with five reporters, one of them from the state press office, who asked the prearranged questions. "This is going to be highly beneficial for San Fernando," the mayor insisted several times, after admitting that lately the economy had been going from bad to worse; and all this without ever mentioning the words violence, kidnapping or war, much less narco. When I spoke to him, and confessed that despite living in Monterrey, I'd had no idea San Fernando produced shrimp, the mayor cordially replied that San Fernando's shrimp were highly valued by Mexican experts but were not widely known on the commercial market: "That's why we want the whole world to know about and eat San Fernando shrimp." The mayor was extremely enthusiastic about preparing the largest shrimp cocktail in the world; he also promised that in the coming years San Fernando would become a powerful Mexican energy producer. The municipality, he vehemently explained, was already the largest extractor of natural gas from the rich Burgos Basin that runs through Tamaulipas, Nuevo León and Coahuila.

In addition the mayor triumphantly informed me that the special guests included Thomas Mittmasht, a man with a salt-and-pepper goatee and a wide-brimmed sun hat who was leaning back, idly inspecting the gigantic tumbler before the seventeen thousand or so small crustaceans were poured into it. Mittmasht is the United States consul in Matamoros, and when faced with questions from reporters about whether his government would now advise its citizens to visit Tamaulipas, he asked them to kindly read the information on the consular website. The document found there warns US citizens that if they should need to travel through Tamaulipas, it is recommended they do so during daylight hours, and avoid "displays of wealth that might draw attention." I asked Mittmasht when he had last visited San Fernando, and he replied that he had passed through the year before on his way back from the Governor's Report in Ciudad Victoria. "I guess you're more relaxed on this occasion," I commented, with a glance at his beachwear. "Well, less formal," he answered. He had made the journey with an escort of only four armored vehicles.

The day before the San Fernando Festival del Mar, Gabriel García Márquez had died, but it was perfectly clear that the magic realism attributed to that writer was not going to disappear quickly in either Mexico or Colombia. I mention this because an official from the Tamaulipas tourist office insisted I interview two men wearing snow-white pants and guayaberas, topped by traditional Colombian vueltiao hats. They were Arnold and Plácido Verera Murillo, restaurateurs from Cartagena—owners of the Ostería del Mar Rojo—who assured me they had been drawn to San Fernando by its good shrimp, and had experienced no problems in terms of personal security. The official bulletin issued later by the Government of Tamaulipas quotes the two men as saying, "Cartagena is a wonderful city, but it cannot equal what we've seen here; it's like a dream, I never imagined I'd have the chance to come to the Gulf of Mexico and visit the Laguna Madre, the Queen of Shrimp." In addition to comparing

San Fernando to what is considered one of the world's most beautiful cities, the official bulletin noted that the two Colombians were overjoyed that "the governor and the municipal president were regenerating the beach resort, because that doesn't happen everywhere, and the authorities often just forget about a place, which isn't happening here." What the bulletin never mentioned, although some Colombian newspapers did, is that the Verera brothers were on an expenses-paid trip to Mexico to learn how to prepare the largest shrimp cocktail in the world, since Cartagena was planning to make a bid for the same title within a few years.

When I approached to interview them, the Colombians were talking to Arturo Ponce Pérez, one of the two chefs overseeing the preparation of the cocktail. Despite his worried expression, Chef Ponce said he was feeling highly motivated. Perhaps he was nervous, because he couldn't remember the last time he had made a *small* shrimp cocktail. While he preferred meat to seafood, he told me he had spent the last two weeks taking courses in preparation for the Guinness record bid, and now had everything needed for the event: just over a ton of frozen shrimp, forty gallons of ketchup and twenty-six of clamato juice; neither lime nor avocado is included in the Guinness World Records rules. While the chef was coordinating the work of his twenty assistants on one side of the main pavilion, some youths with maracas passed; it had been announced that the governor was finally about to arrive, and their task was to provide a party atmosphere to welcome him. They were joined by more youngsters with tambores, and when the official claque had assembled, the assistant cooks were given a pep talk by the second chef. The most excited of these assistants were two men carrying giant spoons to stir the tomato sauce in the cocktail tumbler. Dressed from head to toe in white, including their face masks, they were like nurses about to concoct a dish of high-quality protein, vitamins, minerals, a lot of cholesterol, and phosphorus, an aphrodisiac.

A local official came to inform me that the San Fernando shrimp was unique, and that its exquisite flavor was without compare. He then said, enthusiastically, that thanks to the shrimp and natural gas, his hometown would once again be an economic powerhouse. He spoke of the eighteen million cubic meters of natural gas shipped to Reynosa, and from there to the United States, and in a low tone, as if trying to ensure few bystanders overheard, added that two more large fields had been discovered: Trión 1 and 2. After that he began to complain that Pemex hadn't offered a peso toward the shrimp cocktail celebrations, and that the same was true of the other twenty-eight energy companies in the region, excepting Geokinetics, which had donated a sum he preferred not to specify. The Tamaulipas authorities had paid twenty thousand US dollars to Guinness just for the use of its logo in the publicity campaign. True, they had been, however, spared the travel expenses of the international team of judges, as none of the Guinness employees were willing to travel to San Fernando, given the high risk such a journey entailed. The official thought this was a shame, and said it was just an image problem, "all because of those seventy-two dead undocumenteds there on the border with Matamoros. They come dumping them on us here, and what can you do?" When I asked about the clandestine mass graves and shoot-outs of recent years, he fell silent, and then picked up his eulogy to the exquisite San Fernando shrimp where he had left off. "They really are the best in the world. I've eaten shrimp in San Francisco and Europe, and they don't even come close."

We had to break off conversation as the levels of activity increased in the pavilion. The governor's helicopter had landed. One of the bodyguards took a moment to joke with another who was helping a man in a shrimp costume to get into place. As they were passing, he said, "Hey, don't let that shrimp get too close." (In Mexico, *camarón*—shrimp—is one of the many euphemisms for the male member.) Meanwhile, the governor's head of logistics was arguing with two young organizers: "The governor is going to have his cock-tail served up there on the stage. No way is the governor going to any cooler to pick it up himself." Surprisingly, the governor decided to walk to the pavilion through the crowd, occasionally waving to those present. When he came to the row in which the two Colombians were sitting, he stopped to receive the presents they had brought from their native land, and had his photo taken with them. In the front row the mayors of Méndez, Valle Hermoso, Burgos and other regional towns were awaiting him in their orange T-shirts; also present were the colonel and captain in charge of the San Fernando military detachment. The governor, who was also wearing the requisite T-shirt, had not brought his wife; but his father, Egidio Torre López, had accompanied him, and when he took his seat in the front row, was heartily welcomed by the mayor of San Fernando, who then took the microphone to announce that very soon "we'll be in the news as an example of perseverance. They'll be talking about ordinary people who have done something extraordinary." The civic dignitary then thanked both Mother Nature and the governor for having made it possible for San Fernando to prepare the largest shrimp cocktail in the world.

Once the mayor had concluded his speech, the emcee announced they were going to show a video sent by the Guinness World Records executive committee in London. Absolute silence fell over the crowd, and on a giant screen the image of a young blond woman with a big smile and a discreetly low-cut top appeared to whistles of appreciation from the male public. In a kind of Tex-Mex Spanish, she first thanked Governor Egidio Torre (pronouncing the double "r" of Torre with great care), and while she was, with equal care, listing the names of other officials, a couple of refrigerator trucks pulled up behind the screen, and the two chefs plus their germ-free assistants dressed in white began to unload the fifty-pound packs of shrimp. When the assistant chefs had thrown in pack number twenty-two, the San Fernando cocktail weighed 1,120 pounds, and had officially beaten the previous record set by Mazatlán, Sinaloa. Jubilant cheers echoed around the venue, but this time the emcee held his tongue. The event reached its climax at the moment the tumbler weighed 2,300 pounds, and Mariana Seoane appeared, walking toward the seat allocated to her in the front row. The cries of excitement resounded throughout La Carbonera, and the emcee could contain himself no longer; in his absolutely unmistakable tone he bellowed, "Tourism doesn't come beeeetter." Seoane had only just taken her seat in the front row when she was exhorted by members of the audience to stand and show off her body. "We want to see you, Mariana," they chanted. And she stood, turned around, and said, "What a lovely audience." She then ascended to the stage to assist the governor in sampling the dish. When they got a view of the actress's shapely body from a better angle, the audience exploded into even louder outbursts of euphoria. The mayor and his wife also appeared to pose with the chefs, Seoane, and the governor beside the tumbler of shrimp. In the midst of the excited celebrations, the governor gave a speech that lasted less than two minutes, and concluded with, "This is our Tamaulipas. We work hard every day. And what do we do on our days of rest? We break world records."

After his anticlimactic intervention, the governor gave an impromptu press conference with the small number of reporters present. He made absolutely no mention of the marches in which up to a thousand people demanded peace in Tampico, nor of the petition organized by the Parents' Association suggesting classes should be suspended after the Easter vacation until there was evidence that the situation was under control, and their children's safety was guaranteed. He then walked through the crowd for a minute or two, paused for a few photos, and less than an hour after his arrival was on his way out of San Fernando. He didn't even stay for the shrimp. For her part, Seoane was besieged by fans at every step of her way to the performance stage, and then left before two in the afternoon. While she was singing, hundreds of San Fernando residents were lining up for their portion of the largest shrimp cocktail in the world. On the beach, the party was being equally enjoyed by families making giant sombreros from cardboard Tecate beer boxes and participating in impassioned games of volleyball. There were also ad hoc lifeguards, people selling mosquito spray, fathers carrying beers and tricycles, cowboys in shorts singing Norteño songs at the tops of their voices, and groups of friends in camouflage gear noisily drinking beer until four in the afternoon came around, when Sonora Dinamita finished their set, and the festivities were over. At that exact moment, I went back to the main stage. The tumbler containing the shrimp was completely empty. Over seventeen thousand small crustaceans were being digested by some four thousand human stomachs on La Carbonera beach.

That Good Friday afternoon, after spending the day on La Carbonera beach, I returned to the center of San Fernando, where dozens of houses and businesses were empty or abandoned, some of them ransacked or in ruins. The night before the municipality achieved its shrimp-cocktail feat, a youth had been kidnapped from his home by one of the warring factions still operating in the area. A week before, a taco vendor had been arrested for acting as a mafia spy. Three weeks before, the Navy had shot down the daughter of an evangelical pastor, accusing her of being an assassin. A month before, there had been an almost hour-long shoot-out in a nearby valley. Two months before, the local parish priest, who in exceptional cases acted as a hostage negotiator, had been beaten up after handing over a ransom. Three months before, a group of young people had been kidnapped by another armed commando group; they are presumed to have been forced into slave labor. Four months before, twenty people had been kidnapped in the space of a week, and then freed in exchange for sums of between five hundred thousand and a million pesos. None of these events were covered by the press. The feeling of those who spoke of them was that San Fernando hadn't yet seen the worst; in fact, the worst was a day-to-day occurrence. Some of the residents I interviewed were annoyed about the Guinness record. Just as with any other human beings, the arrival of spring brought a smile to their faces, and they were pleased that a public space like La Carbonera beach had been reclaimed—if only for a few hours—but the fear of being kidnapped or murdered prevailed. The mayor's and the governor's idea of the largest shrimp cocktail in the world as a means of removing the stench of death from the town—more a public image exercise than a daily reality—was looked upon with skepticism. For the residents it was a smoke screen, more pathetic than naive. "You can't cover up the reality of San Fernando with a shrimp cocktail, no matter how big it is," one said. Another added, "Well, when we've got a governor who hasn't even solved his own brother's murder, how are we supposed to believe he really wants to solve the security problems the rest of us suffer? This is a no-man's-land."

As the sun went down, a small Good Friday procession made its silent way through the center of town. All the parishioners were dressed in white, and it was easy to imagine that what they required from their government was not a gastronomic world record. Early the following morning, as we drove out of the San Fernando valley, with its shimmering, green pastures and beautiful grasslands stretching to the purple-tinged horizon, it took an effort of will to believe that while Tamaulipas remains a pool into which Mexican democracy is sinking, its authorities are attempting to wipe out the horror with a shrimp cocktail.

A Yi is a Chinese writer living in Beijing. He worked as a police officer before becoming editor in chief of the literary magazine *Chutzpah*. He is the author of two collections of short stories and a novel and has published fiction in *Granta* and the *Guardian*. In 2010 he was short-listed for the People's Literature Top 20 Literary Giants of the Future.

Jeremy Tiang has translated more than ten books from Chinese, including novels by Chan Ho-Kei, Zhang Yueran, and Yeng Pway Ngon, and has been awarded a PEN/Heim Translation Fund Grant and an NEA Literary Translation Fellowship. His original fiction includes *It Never Rains on National Day* (short-listed for the Singapore Literature Prize) and *State of Emergency*, both published by Epigram Books. He also writes and translates plays.

The Case That Got Away

A YI
TRANSLATED FROM THE CHINESE BY JEREMY TIANG

Thirteen years later, the case of the Aocheng Chemical Plant still nags at me like an unsolved riddle. It was broad daylight, the workers standing in the cracked concrete yard, lunch boxes in hand, voices rising and falling as they murmured how it had been fine last night, now it was gone. The Aocheng Police Department had sent Sergeant Zhao Dezhong, along with two trainees—Li and myself. We arrived to see a handcart lying there, its tire gone, looking as pathetic as an amputee robbed of his prosthetic limb.

According to the chief security officer, theft of the tire would have the same level of difficulty as a bank heist. The plant was surrounded by a wall over a meter high, topped by a wire fence to a height of two meters. There was only one gate, which was vigilantly monitored in shifts twenty-four hours a day, and there were patrols inside the factory at night. At the time of the incident, a number of employees were doing overtime in the brightly lit workshop.

They're simply mocking us, we thought.

Sergeant Zhao had been in reconnaissance during his time in the army, and he'd once court-martialed his own comrades for stealing important supplies. He quickly concluded that this was a simple case of an inside job. A precondition for burglary, he told us, was the ability to case the joint, and from the look of things an outsider would be hard-pressed to find out where everything was stored or what the layout was. Besides, statistics showed that sixty-five to eighty percent of factory thefts were carried out by the workers themselves.

Luckily for us, Sergeant Zhao said, these workers live in dorms, they haven't taken a single step out of the compound.

We worked with the security chief to come up with a plan. He would gather all the managers, who in turn would summon their team leaders, who would then get their workers together, and we would interrogate them group by group. There would be two questions: What were you doing between three and five in the morning? What proof can you provide that you were asleep or at work?

Their answers weren't important; we were interested in their physiological responses during the questioning. Sergeant Zhao detailed Li and me as human lie detectors, and we soaked up the workers' body language as they spoke. But they came in, one after another, their expressions exactly the same—flustered, they looked around the office, didn't know what to do with their hands, and were too scared to look directly at us. A few came under suspicion simply because they were young or had the wrong sort of hairstyle, but they all had the perfect alibi: ask Old Wang. When Old Wang, a down-to-earth guy, showed up, he confirmed that they'd all been working late, and hadn't so much as gone for a piss.

The fox is more cunning than us, said Sergeant Zhao. We're dealing with a cool customer.

After our investigation, the factory security chief said it was time for dinner. Sergeant Zhao insisted that he couldn't relax and eat until we were certain not a single worker would leave the premises. The chief said not to worry. He led us to a private room in the canteen where our meal was laid out, four dishes and a tureen of soup. The dishes were the size of washbasins, piled high with fish and meat and an entire chicken. Little soft-shelled turtles floated in the soup.

The chief opened a bottle of liquor and pulled a folded-up American dollar bill from inside the cap. He said to his men, Whoever finishes this gets the greenback. Sergeant Zhao said he was a lightweight, but was nonetheless persuaded to down three glasses, after which he tipsily slurred: That's enough for today, let the workers go if they want to go. Keep a tight patrol tonight, otherwise the thief might try to off-load the goods.

We returned to the factory the following afternoon. The security chief said he'd kept a close eye on the factory, but nothing had happened. Our sergeant said, That's good, that means the tire hasn't been fenced. Next, we examined every corner of the plant, with the quiet confidence of people who'd lost their keys but were certain they'd find them. We expected the tire to turn up behind some old, broken-down piece of machinery, or else tucked into the tarpaulin over some cesspool. When we passed by a storage shed, Sergeant Zhao hopped up, trying to see what was on the roof, but barely got off the ground. He asked me to try, but I couldn't do it either. I told Li to jump, and he did manage to clear the roof, but said there was nothing up there except crumbling asbestos tiles.

We even considered the possibility that the thief had hidden the tire up a tree, but among the abundant leaves and branches of the few trees in the compound, we found nothing but innocent birds building their nests. We finished the day in a despondent mood, and were still distracted when it came time for dinner. I don't remember what the chief said to us, or what we ate; I recall only that lettuce, after so much greasy food, was a godsend.

It was time for a change of strategy. Back in the station, realizing his reputation as an "elite reconnaissance soldier" had been tarnished, Sergeant Zhao tugged at his hair and raged at himself. After a long while, he said wearily: The tire isn't in the factory. We have to consider more scenarios—that it was an outside job, or an outsider in cahoots with someone on the inside.

First thing the following morning, we walked around the boundary wall instead of entering the compound. Sagebrush grew abundantly outside the factory, dew still glistening on it. The sergeant instructed us to look for signs of crushed plants. A tire might weigh twenty pounds, and if someone flung it over the fence it would surely leave a mark. We searched all morning but found nothing except some sanitary pads, black and crusty with blood, and a few dead mice, clouds of flies rising from them as we approached. Maybe sagebrush is too springy, said Sergeant Zhao. We should go have a look at the reeds.

We walked downhill, away from the wall, and split up as we entered the reed groves. We seemed to have entered a gloomy, mysterious world that stretched on forever. Soon, our shoes had disappeared into the mud. I walked and walked, until I'd worked up an appetite. I wondered if a scaly rodent might pop out of the ground and blink at me. I'd enjoyed a fair bit of wild game like that in Aocheng. I did see burrows, but they were all flooded. I muttered sternly to myself, a tire, a tire, you're looking for a tire—but I kept getting distracted. Just as it seemed that I would walk into the void, walk into night, Li's figure appeared in the last rays of light. He was having a piss.

After night had fallen, we took a shortcut back to the station. Suddenly we saw someone on the edge of a distant field waving a flashlight. When we got closer, it turned out to be the factory security chief. He said, Sorry to have caused you so much trouble. The flashlight beam wobbled down to our feet and he added, in a tone of deep regret, Your shoes, just look, they're covered in mud. Sergeant Zhao said, It's nothing, if little things like this bothered us, we'd have no business being cops.

Naturally, we went back to the chemical plant for dinner. A deputy manager came over to keep us company. After saying a few words, everyone abruptly fell silent. The manager's silence was due to a deep sense of remorse. Our silence was, likewise, due to a deep sense of remorse. Finally, both sides spoke at the same time. The deputy manager said, We're grateful, so very grateful. Sergeant Zhao said, Look, we've made no progress at all.

The security chief immediately smoothed things over: Eat, eat.

Leaving the canteen, I saw several white-haired workers in filthy overalls, banging metal spoons against porcelain jars. They seemed to be drumming out some old song, one of those our generation had never heard. As we approached, the beating quieted down; then it got louder again as we passed.

Back at the station, Sergeant Zhao didn't wash or change his shoes; he just slumped on the couch and sighed. We were going to comfort him when he jumped to his feet and said, Quick, get a flashlight, let's go up the hill and have a look. Li and I sulked; our legs were swollen from walking all day. The sergeant could see our reluctance and snapped, Fine, I'll go by myself. Of course, we had to follow him.

There was some moonlight as we switched on our flashlights and, passing through sagebrush and the reed swamp, we found ourselves on a dirt track: a road of no return. Let's imagine the thief rolled the tire along this path, said Sergeant Zhao. You two keep an eye out for tracks, I'll be damned if he carried it the whole way on his shoulder.

We saw nothing at all, and only got more tired. As we shuffled along sleepily, Sergeant Zhao suddenly shouted: Found it! We snapped to attention and squatted down, and sure enough there was a track, with a pattern down the middle like ~~. Wasn't that precisely the pattern of the tire?

Smiling like a child, Sergeant Zhao said, He must have finally taken the tire off his shoulder.

We continued in high spirits for another five or six minutes, until a mud hut loomed out of the darkness. By its window was a handcart, and next to that a tire. Elated, Sergeant Zhao went up and started kicking the door. Startled awake, the farmer turned on a light and opened up, and we went in, carrying the tire. The lamplight inside was so weak that we turned on our flashlights. Now we could see three leather patches on the tire, like ringworm scabs, which didn't fit the description of the stolen one. But anyone can disguise evidence—murderers know to change their hairstyles, for instance. Sergeant Zhao started ripping off the patches, while the farmer complained piteously, You can't do that.

But our sergeant tore them off with no hesitation. When they wouldn't lift easily, he scratched at them with his fingernail until they peeled away. He rubbed at the surface and examined it closely. It looked as if the patches had been genuine. Still uncertain, he poked at a spot with his penknife and, pressing too hard, cut into the tire, which deflated with a whoosh.

Sergeant Zhao said: This tire's too decrepit, you're obviously innocent, the tire belongs to you. Roll it to the station tomorrow, I'll get someone to fix it.

On the way back, I put an arm over Li's shoulders and leaned like a wounded man. The sergeant kept muttering to himself, So strange, how'd something that big vanish? So strange, like magic or something.

Over the next few days, we set up roadblocks, searched junkyards, dispatched people to gather intelligence, but none of these things turned up any leads. Every day, though, we had our lunch and dinner right on schedule at the factory. After a week of this, we hung back at the station, only to have the security chief turn up in person. He said they'd booked us a table at Jade Cloud Restaurant. Sergeant Zhao looked mortified, and said we'd eat when we'd earned it.

The chief said: What are you talking about, you've all made an enormous contribution.

The sergeant said: What contribution? A tire's worth fifty yuan, and we've eaten at least two thousand.

The chief said: You can't look at it that way. If you leak fifty yuan and don't plug it today, tomorrow you'll lose five thousand, fifty thousand, five hundred thousand yuan: huge quantities of state property disappearing just like that.

The sergeant said: But we can't even explain what happened to the fifty yuan.

The chief said: At the very least you've put the fear of God into the guilty party.

The sergeant said: I'm not going, you can ask them if they will.

The chief said: If you're not going, I'm not leaving.

The sergeant said: You're welcome to stay.

The security chief went and spoke to our police chief, who listened with feet planted and hands behind his back, nodding and humming like Justice Bao, and when the chief was done, he yelled, Zhao, Ai, Li, let's go.

The four of us went to Jade Cloud Restaurant, where steam was rising from two dozen dishes already on the table, and two dozen people stopped chewing sunflower seeds and stood to greet us. The security chief made the lengthy introductions, saying, This is Factory Manager Zhu, this is Factory Manager He. Our station chief waved and said, Thank you, thank you, good to know you all. Then, rather timidly, the security chief introduced the next table: This is my wife, my kids, that's Chief Officer Yang's wife, everyone's here.

The police chief stretched out a large hand, saying, How do you do, how do you do.

Later on, Sergeant Zhao used his own money to buy a second-hand tire, and sent Li and me to deliver it to the chemical plant. The security chief said, That's it, that's the one. Then he rolled it happily out into the concrete yard. At a distance I could see the bereft cart, waiting forlornly for the return of its limb.

Mariana Enríquez is a writer
and editor based in Buenos
Aires. She is the author of two
novels, two short-story collections, a biography of Silvina
Ocampo, a chronicle on cemeteries, and a novella. Her fiction has appeared in the *New
Yorker*, *Granta*, *McSweeney's*,
Electric Literature, and the
Virginia Quarterly Review. Her
English-language debut *The
Things We Lost in the Fire* has
been translated into twenty
languages.

Joel Streicker is a writer, poet,
and literary translator based in
San Francisco. He is the recip-
ient of a PEN/Heim Translation
Fund grant, and has translated
works by Samanta Schweblin,
Tomás González, and Guillermo
Fadanelli, among other Latin
American authors.

Where Are You, Sweetheart

MARIANA ENRÍQUEZ
TRANSLATED FROM THE SPANISH BY JOEL STREICKER

I have three memories of him, but one might be false. The order is arbitrary. In the first, he's sitting on a sofa, completely naked, on a towel, watching TV. He doesn't pay any attention to me: I think I'm spying on him. His penis rests in a bush of black pubic hair and the scar that runs through the hair on his chest is a dark pink.

In the second, his wife leads him into the bedroom by the hand. He's also naked. He looks at me from the corner of his eye. His hair is pretty long, even for the times—the 1970s—and I can't see his scar.

In the third he's smiling at me from close up, his face almost glued to mine. In the memory I feel myself naked and shy. But I don't know if it's real; it doesn't have the same naturalness as the others. I may have invented it, although I recognize the sensation of shyness and vulnerability that is often repeated in my dreams. I don't know if he touched me. The feeling that accompanies this memory resembles desire although, if my suspicions are correct, it should be more akin to horror. I'm not afraid of him. His face doesn't torment me, even though I try to make myself feel something like childhood trauma and its effects on my adult life. I was five when I met him. He was very sick. They had operated on his heart and the surgery had gone wrong. I found that out later, when I stopped visiting his house—really, the house of my friends, his daughters. I found it out when he died. I don't remember what his name was and I never dared to ask my parents.

A while after his death, I began to use my fingernails to score my chest, right in the middle, imitating his scar. I would do it before going to sleep, naked, and I would lift my head to see the line of irritated skin, until it faded and my neck hurt.

When it was really hot, I liked to go into the coolest room in the house. No one occupied it, because my mom used it to store books and old furniture. I adored that room: I liked to throw myself, naked, on the imitation leather couch, which was always cold, set up a little electric fan, and read all afternoon. My friends from the neighborhood and school would be at the pool, but I didn't care: in that room I had fallen head over heels in love, for the first time, when I ran across Helen Burns in a beat-up illustrated edition of *Jane Eyre*.

I hated those drawings. Because they showed Helen much older than what the book said, and because for some reason they had imagined her blond, although the book never mentioned the color of her hair. She wasn't like that, and I knew it, because during that whole summer I imagined her lying on the couch that became the bed in the orphanage, the bed where Helen, consumptive and moribund, so beautiful, was dying while I held her hand.

Helen was a minor character in the book. Jane, the protagonist, arrived at the frightful Lowood School for girls, and couldn't make any friends because the director, the villainous Brocklehurst, had shamed her in front of all her classmates. But it didn't matter to Helen: Helen became Jane's friend. She was beyond everything because she was close to death. I had a premonition that I was going to fall in love with her when Jane saw her the first time in the school yard, reading that book with such a strange name, *Rasselas*. One chapter later and Helen was dead. An epidemic of typhus had been unleashed on the school, Helen suffered a relapse of her tuberculosis, and they transferred her to a room on the first floor. Jane would visit her at night. That last night, Helen and Jane slept together. Today, when I recall that chapter (because I don't have to reread it; I know it by heart), I am aware of everything: when Jane gets into the dying girl's bed and Helen says to her, "Are you warm, darling?" Darling. Darling. It was a love scene. When Jane woke up, her friend, Helen, was dead. That chapter—every night, every single one, I would go to bed and hug my pillow, pretending it was Helen, but I didn't go to sleep like that idiot Jane, no, I watched her die, I took her hand and she, who was dying with her gray eyes staring into mine (and her breath faltering), allowed me to see something of that other place, where she was going forever.

I soon realized that my fantasy was not feasible. When I was fourteen years old, a girlfriend told me, sadly:

"You know what I heard? Do you remember Mara's brother?"

Mara was a former schoolmate who had changed schools.

"Yes."

"Well, they found he has a tumor between his heart and his lungs, and they can't operate on it and he's going to die."

A week later I was suggesting to my friend that we visit Mara. I wanted to meet her dying brother because I suspected that, well, I might fall in love with him. But when I met him . . . the boy seemed adequately sick, but I didn't like him. During that time I was confused and arrived at a conclusion that left me with a clear conscience: I didn't like real sick people, so I wasn't a pervert. Thinking like that didn't save me from obsession. For a whole year I spent the money my mom gave me on really expensive medical books, while my friends spent theirs on drugs. Nothing brought me greater happiness than those books. All those euphemisms for death. All those beautiful medical words that meant nothing, all that difficult jargon—that was pornography. By then I was pretty clear about what turned me

83

on and what didn't, and therefore I had become increasingly bored with Victorian novels, where some sick people always appeared, but you didn't know very clearly what they were dying from. I was tired of consumptives once I overcame a brutal infatuation with Hippolyte, the tubercular teenager in *The Idiot*, which lasted more than a year. I wanted pornography: sick people like Helen, Tadzio, and Hippolyte were eroticism, suggestive. And they were always secondary characters. Hippolyte was ideal: beautiful (Dostoevsky made sure to put in Prince Myshkin's mouth the words "He has a very beautiful face," which made me quiver), teenage, definitely dying and stubborn and vulnerable and evil. But he talked much and fainted little: I was tired of the descriptions of paleness and sweats and coughs. I wanted more facts, I wanted explicit sex. Books were ideal and, besides, they helped me specify fetishes. I skipped over the neurological illnesses: I didn't like convulsions or mental retardation or paralysis and, truthfully, the nervous system bored me. I couldn't care less, curiously enough, about anything oncological: cancer seemed dirty to me, overrated socially, a little vulgar (the poor lady has a *tumor*, the old women would say), and there were too many movies about heroic people with cancer (I liked heroic sick people, but not those who were an *example*). And nephrology had no charm: it was clear that people died if their kidneys stopped functioning, but I didn't care, because the word "kidney" itself seemed hideous. Not to mention gastrointestinal matters—so dirty.

It was clear what I liked, what I lingered on; and, once my specialty was discovered, I devoted myself exclusively to it: I liked people sick with pulmonary ailments (reminiscent of Helen, Hippolyte, and all the other consumptives, certainly) and cardiac diseases. This had its vulgar side, but only if they were old (or after age fifty, when frightful things like cholesterol began to appear). If they were young . . . how elegant! If they were beautiful, it was a type of ruined, but secret, beauty. All the other illnesses had their fixed terms, but this was different: one could die at any moment. Once I bought a CD in a medical bookstore (where all the clerks thought I was a student—I had prudently taken it upon myself to create that impression) that was called *Cardiac Noises*. Nothing before had brought me such happiness. I suppose that listening to the beating of those ruined hearts caused in me what listening to moans of sexual pleasure causes in normal men and women. Such variety! So many different beats, each one meaning something distinct, all of them beautiful! The other diseases couldn't be *heard*. What's more, a lot of them could be *smelled*, which disgusted me. If I went out to ride my bike with *Cardiac Noises* on my MP3 player, I had to stop because I would get too aroused. So I would listen to it at home at night, and during that time I worried because *real sex didn't interest me*. The audio tracks with beating hearts supplied everything. I could masturbate for hours with the earphones on, streaming between my legs, my arm spasming from all the rubbing and my clitoris inflamed to the size of a big grape.

I decided to get rid of the recorded heartbeats after a while. I was going to go crazy. From then on, one of the first things I did with a man was rest my head on his chest to discover whether he had some unusual beat, or a murmur, irregularity, third noise, gallop, or something else. I always asked myself when someone who was an unbeatable combination of elements would appear. Now I remember that yearning, and I smile bitterly.

I can pinpoint the moment when I lost control. After years of fruitless searching, I found an Internet site where others who had a fetish for heartbeats shared their own. They did it live, in chats, but they also had a large sound archive, downloadable, deliciously classified into normal and abnormal beats, beats during exercise, heart murmurs, stressed beats . . . I never took part in the chats. I just copied those sounds and lay down to listen to them. An accelerated but regular rhythm; suddenly a premature beat, another delayed (extrasystoles or ventricular contractions). I had thought my previous bouts of masturbation were awesome! I had had no idea, I knew nothing about the limits of horniness. I rubbed my middle finger between my right inner labia and clitoris until I touched bone, until the bone hurt, sometimes until I bled, and the orgasms came one after the other, implacable, enormous, for hours. The sheets damp, sweat pouring from between my breasts, my skin always goose pimpled, the feeling of my clitoris swollen, glorious, the contractions of my vagina and uterus. Supraventricular tachycardia, the beautiful murmur of the aortic stenosis, the unruly beats provoked by hyperventilation or Valsalva maneuvers, things that only the brave dared do. Sometimes a hidden heart, barely audible and crazed behind the ribs, a sound achieved by holding one's breath; and when oxygen finally returned, that heart would shake as if it lived inside a tomato can, bewildered, sometimes too slow, as if it were about to stop altogether.

I didn't answer the telephone. I arrived late everywhere. I would stop only when the pain in my irritated—sometimes injured—vulva took away my pleasure. In the darkness with my headphones and the hearts, that was my life, no more sex with people. What for!

Until I was able to isolate one of the hearts. Its beat never faltered. I could distinguish it perfectly even without knowing its author, whose handle was HCM1. The recordings were always very clear, and the beats always distinct, and dangerous: in auricular fibrillations, in very long tachycardia, in galloping rhythm. It was a man's heart. You could sometimes hear his breathing, and vestiges of his voice. When I discovered a file in which he was moaning because—according to the text accompanying the track—he had felt a chest pain during the session, I decided to enter the chat room to meet him.

He was evasive for a time. Too long a time for me, but I suppose it was, objectively, short. A month after the first contact, he agreed to visit me. Strange: we lived in the same city. Statistically improbable, if not impossible, because our meeting had been through an international community of fetishists. We decided to ignore it, not to think of it as a message from fate or anything like that. We threw ourselves solely into pleasure. He liked to have his heart listened to. He was very sick, and that was why he was usually shunned in chat rooms and online communities. They thought he was too extreme, to them it seemed that he was going too far, he was dismantling the idea of play and pleasure. Soon we both abandoned virtual life, and shut ourselves up in my room, with a tape recorder, a stethoscope, medicines, and substances that helped change his cardiac rhythm. We both knew what the outcome might be, and we didn't care.

His hair was as dark as that of the man I had known in my childhood, and he had the same smile. But he had three scars, not one. They had slit open his sternum: a casual observer might have seen only one scar, but I could make them all out: the first one transparent, thin, almost completely hidden by the second, which was an opaline pink that shone, as if glazed; the last one, wider, awesome, was darker than his skin. The scar that crossed his back (he had given me a detailed account of this painful procedure) was enormous, clumsy. The small, unobtrusive scars on his stomach were randomly distributed. The skin on the inside of his elbow was scored like that of an addict. There was a short scar, a dark depression on the right side of his neck. So many marks. And the labored breathing, and the enormous lips that sometimes took on a color as blue as his eyes.

You could hear his illness in those sudden inhalations when he was left breathless while speaking, in the nocturnal coughing attacks that left him pale and trembling. All the while he let me rest my head on his chest so that I could listen. A normal beat is two sounds, opening and closing. But his beats had four sounds, a gallop, a desperate effort, different, unnatural. It got worse after a cup of coffee. It was

87

scary after a little cocaine. He would often faint, and I kept listening with the stethoscope, terrified and excited, until he recovered a kind of normality and woke up. I could spend hours on his chest and afterward, excited, I would kiss and hug him almost violently, and his laughter and recklessness worried me because, sometimes, and more often as time passed and our intimacy deepened, I was certain that if I listened a second longer I was going to destroy him. To beat him, to open him up with my fingernails, more marks, a way of getting closer to him, of making him more mine. I had to contain that desire, those yearnings to satiate myself, to open him up, to play with his organs as if they were hidden trophies. To the point where I imposed on myself small punishments: not eating all day, not sleeping for seventy-two hours, walking until my legs cramped . . . small rituals, as if I were a girl who wished for her mother's death because her mother wouldn't buy her something, and then the remorse and the little sacrifices, "I'm not going to say any more bad words, God, I promise—don't let my mom die," and the bad word comes out and then the running in the night to see if her mom is still breathing in her bed while she sleeps.

But I think I wound up hating him. Maybe I hated him from the start. The way I hated the man who had made me abnormal, who had made me a sicko, with his tired penis in front of the TV, and that beautiful scar. The man who had ruined me. I hated my lover. If that wasn't the case, then some of our games would be inexplicable. I would make him breathe rapidly into a plastic bag, until I saw his forehead sweat and his arms tremble. His heart galloped over the stethoscope and he would beg, "Enough," but I asked for more, and he never said no. I had to take him to the hospital once, and when they regulated his tachycardia with cardioversion—an electric charge on his chest, as in resuscitations—I locked myself in a nearby bathroom and fell onto the toilet, howling, as my orgasm came. I bought him poppers, cocaine, tranquilizers, alcohol. Each substance caused a different effect and he acquiesced, he never complained, he barely spoke. He even paid my rent with his savings when they threatened to evict me from my apartment; I never paid him back, I no longer had a telephone, I worried only about the electricity so that the recorder would work and I could listen to my experiments again when he was too exhausted, almost unconscious.

He didn't even protest when I told him I was bored. That I wanted to see him. To rest my hand on his heart stripped of ribs, of cages, hold it in my hand, beating, until it stopped, to feel its desperate valves open and close out in the open. He only said that he was tired, too.

And that we were going to need a saw.

Sayaka Murata was born in Chiba Prefecture in 1979 and graduated from the Department of Literature at Saitama University. Her debut work, *Junyū* (*Breastfeeding*), won the Gunzō Prize for New Writers in 2003. In 2009 she won the Noma Prize for New Writers with *Gin iro no uta* (*Silver Song*); in 2013, the Yukio Mishima Prize for *Shiro-iro no machi no, sono hone no taion no* (*Of Bones, of Body Heat, of Whitening City*); in 2014, the Sense of Gender Prize and Measures to Counter the Falling Birthrate Special Prize for *Satsujin shussan* (*Breeders and Killers*); and in 2016, the Akutagawa Prize for *Konbini ningen* (*Convenience Store Woman*). Other works include *Tadaima tobira* (*A Welcoming Door*) and *Shōmetsu sekai* (*Dwindling World*).

Ginny Tapley Takemori has translated fiction by more than a dozen early modern and contemporary Japanese writers, from best sellers Ryū Murakami and Kyōtarō Nishimura to literary greats Izumi Kyōka and Okamoto Kidō. Her most recent translations are of Miyuki Miyabe's *Puppet Master* and Tomiko Inui's *The Secret of the Blue Glass*, short-listed for the Marsh Award. Previously she was an editor at Kodansha International and a foreign rights agent based in Spain.

A First-Rate Material

SAYAKA MURATA
TRANSLATED FROM THE JAPANESE
BY GINNY TAPLEY TAKEMORI

It was a holiday, and I was enjoying chatting with two girlfriends from university days over afternoon tea. Through the window, the gray office buildings of the business district sat beneath a cloudless sky. Reservations at this hotel lobby tearoom were hard to come by, and it was thronged with a female clientele. An elegant, white-haired lady with a deep purple stole across her shoulders daintily carried a piece of tart to her mouth. At the table next to us, some girls with colorful painted nails were taking photos of their cakes. One of them spilled apricot jam on her white cardigan and hastily started wiping it off with a pink handkerchief.

Yumi opened the menu and ordered a second cup of tea, then noticed the sweater I was wearing.

"Hey, Nana, that sweater . . . is it human hair?"

"Oh, can you tell?" I beamed at her, nodding. "Yes, one hundred percent."

"Fantastic! It must have been expensive."

"Yeah, a bit . . . I took out a loan. But it'll last me for life," I answered rather bashfully, lightly running my fingertips over the garment. The jet-black hair was closely knitted into rows of braids, with an intricate weave at the cuffs and neck, and glistened alluringly in the rays of light shining in through the lobby windows. Even though it was mine, it was so beautiful I gazed at it enraptured.

Aya was eyeing it enviously too. "A hundred percent human hair is just the thing for winter! Warm, durable, and luxurious. My sweater contains some too, but it's so expensive I could only afford it mixed with wool. But human hair really does feel completely different, doesn't it?"

"Thanks. It's too good to wear every day and normally I keep it safely stored away, but today I really wanted to dress up—it's the first time we've seen each other for ages, and coming to a hotel, too."

"Really? But now that you've bought it, it's such a waste not to wear it more," Yumi said.

Aya agreed. "Expensive clothes are not meant to just decorate your closet, you know. You have to put them to good use! Nana, you're engaged to be married now, aren't you? Human hair is just the thing to wear for formal occasions like meeting your future in-laws."

I toyed with my teacup. "Well, yes, but . . ." I said in a small voice, "you see, my fiancé doesn't really like clothes made from human hair."

"Whaaat?" Aya's eyes widened in bewilderment. "Why on earth not? I can't understand that!"

"I can't either, but it's not just human hair—he doesn't really like any fashion accessories or furnishings made from human materials," I said, forcing a smile.

"You're kidding!" Shocked, Yumi put the macaroon she'd been about to put in her mouth back on her plate and looked at me dubiously. "So, what about bone rings? Tooth earrings?"

"He can't stand them. We're talking about making our wedding rings platinum, too."

Aya and Yumi looked at each other.

"Really? But wedding rings made from front teeth are the best!"

"Nana, your fiancé's a banker, isn't he? He must be well off, so isn't he just being stingy?"

"No, I don't think it's that . . ." I answered vaguely and smiled. I couldn't explain it very well myself.

Aya nodded triumphantly. "Yes, there are people like that who are loaded but just don't understand fashion . . . but Naoki's always so well dressed I'd never have expected it of him. When it comes to your wedding rings, though, I'd discuss them with him a bit more. After all, they're what you'll be using to pledge your eternal love for each other," she said, raising her teacup to her mouth. On her left hand she was wearing a ring made from pure white bone. It was her wedding ring, made from a fibula for her marriage last year, and looked really good on her slender finger. I could still clearly remember how envious I'd felt when she'd happily shown it off to me, even while explaining that it was considerably cheaper than tooth.

I surreptitiously stroked my ring finger. The truth was that I did really want a ring made from either tooth or bone. I'd talked about this any number of times with Naoki, and knew better than anyone how futile it was.

"Look, go once more to the shop together. If he can just see what it looks like on his finger, he'll change his mind, you know."

I gave a little nod and looked down to avoid their eyes, and reached for the now cold scone on my plate.

I'd just said goodbye to Aya and Yumi when I felt my cell phone vibrate. I took it from my bag and saw that an email had arrived from Naoki, who'd had to go in to work even though it was a holiday.

Got away earlier than I thought. How about coming over?

Okay, I replied, and got on a subway headed for his place.

He lived in a neighborhood close to where he worked, with office blocks alongside conveniently located residential condos. Once we were married, we planned to move to a new house in the suburbs, where there was a more natural environment better suited to kids. I was looking forward to living there, but felt a little sad at the thought that I wouldn't be returning to this neighborhood where I'd spent so much time over the five years we'd been dating.

I rang the bell, and Naoki's amiable voice came through the interphone telling me to come in, so I opened the door with my key.

He must have only just arrived home since he was still in his shirt and tie with a cardigan over his shoulders, and was turning on the underfloor heating.

"I bought dinner on the way. It's cold, so I thought hot pot would be good."

"Sounds great, thanks. How were the girls?"

"They're both fine. They gave us an engagement present."

I passed him the bag containing the pair of wineglasses from Aya and Yumi, put down my purse and the bag of groceries, and took off my duffel coat. His smile instantly vanished, replaced by a scowl.

Seeing the undisguised revulsion on his face, I remembered I was still wearing the sweater.

"Didn't I tell you not to wear human hair?" he said in a low voice, avoiding my eyes, his face turned away from me so forcefully I thought his neck might snap as he plonked himself onto the couch.

"Um, well, I hadn't seen my friends for ages and I wanted to impress them. I haven't worn it at all lately, and thought it wouldn't do any harm to wear it just this once."

"You should throw it away. You promised me you wouldn't wear it. Have you gone back on your word?"

"But I haven't even paid the loan off yet. I promised I wouldn't wear it in front of you, but I never said I wouldn't ever wear it again. Why am I being told off for wearing something I bought with my own money?"

I choked up in spite of myself, and Naoki avoided looking at me as he drummed his fingers irritably on the floor.

"It gives me the creeps."

"But why? It's no different from your hair, or mine. It's more natural for us than hair from any other animal—it's a material really close to us."

"Yeah, that's exactly why it creeps me out," he spat, and picked up a packet of cigarettes and a small ashtray from the side table.

Naoki hardly ever smoked, and only ever reached for his cigarettes when he was really stressed and irritable, and needed to calm himself down. I always did my best to comfort him whenever he lit up after work, complaining about being tired, but this time it was my fault he was feeling like this, just because of what I was wearing, I thought miserably.

"You're going to Miho's shop to look at new furniture tomorrow, aren't you?" he said, puffing out smoke. "I can't go along so I'll leave it up to you, but let's just get one thing straight—if you choose even just one item made from human products, I won't marry you. Teeth, bones, and skin are all out. Otherwise I'll break off the engagement."

"Talk about a unilateral decision. What could be more normal than making people into clothes or furniture after they die? How come you've got such an aversion to it?"

"It's sacrilege! I can't believe you're so unfazed by using items hacked from dead bodies."

"Is using other animals any better? It's a precious and noble aspect of the workings of our advanced life-form—not wasting the bodies of people when they die, or at least having one's own body carrying on being used. Isn't it wonderful? There are so many parts that can be reused as furniture and it's a waste to throw them away . . . isn't that more sacrilegious?"

"No, it isn't," Naoki retorted. "What's wrong with everyone? It's crazy. Look at this!" he said, ripping out his necktie pin and throwing it to the floor. "It's made from fingernails pulled from someone's body. A *dead* body! It's grotesque. Horrifying!"

"Stop, don't break it! If you hate it so much, why do you wear it?"

"It's an engagement gift from my boss. It's revolting—even just touching it makes my skin crawl."

I held back my tears and yelled, "It's not like using human material is uncivilized. It's far more heartless to just burn it all!"

"That's enough!"

We always ended up fighting over this issue. I couldn't for the life of me understand why Naoki was so averse to wearing or using anything human.

"I'm sorry," I said. "I'll throw it away." I took the sleek black sweater off and, stifling my sobs, scrunched it up and stuffed it into the kitchen garbage can. As I stood there in my silk undershirt feeling miserable, I felt Naoki put his arms around me from behind.

"I'm sorry I got so emotional. I don't think I'll ever be able to make you understand, but somehow I just find human hair sweaters and bone cutlery and furniture terrifying."

Naoki's slim arms rubbed gently against my body. His body was enveloped in a soft cashmere cardigan. I just couldn't understand why he thought human hair was so wrong when goat hair was fine. But I noticed his hands were trembling slightly and said in a small voice, "I'm sorry, I was wrong—especially since I knew you didn't like it."

"No, I'm wrong for making you put up with me," he murmured weakly, burying his face in my shoulder. "I just can't understand why everyone is okay with something so barbaric. Cats or dogs or rabbits would never do anything like that. Normal animals don't make sweaters or lamps out of the dead bodies of their fellows. I just want to be like other animals and do what's right . . ."

I couldn't think of anything to say to that, and gently stroked the cashmere-enveloped arms that clung to me. Turning to face him, I hugged his hunched-over body to me, and rubbed his back.

He relaxed a little and sighed, his cold lips touching my neck. With his face buried in my neck, I kept on stroking his backbone for the longest time.

When I told Miho that I wouldn't consider any furnishings made from human material, her eyes widened.

"No way! You're telling me that, even with your budget you're not going to buy the shinbone chair, or the rib-cage table, or the finger bone clock, or the dried stomach lamp shade?"

"Nope."

"Nor the display cabinet of teeth strung together? The warm rug made with human hair?"

"No. I don't want Naoki to suffer. Our house should be somewhere we can both feel comfortable."

Miho closed the catalogues she'd spread out in front of me and frowned. "I wish I didn't have to say this," she said in a low voice, "but don't you think Naoki's sick? How come he's so neurotic about human materials?"

"I don't know. It's probably got something to do with having had a bad relationship with his father when he was little."

"He ought to get some counseling. It's abnormal. In any case, one day we'll all be turned into sweaters or clocks or lamps when we die. We humans are also materials—and that's wonderful!"

Miho was right, but I shook my head. "I agree with you, but . . . anyway, for now I intend to furnish our house in a way that won't cause any distress for Naoki."

Miho finally seemed to understand I wasn't going to budge, and sighed. "Okay, okay. But it's such a waste when you could get some fabulous furniture with your budget. Oh well, I guess we'll go with this dining table and chairs that don't have any human bone in them, then."

"Thanks."

"I really recommend that chandelier with scales made from human nails for your living room, but I suppose we're going to have to settle for this glass one."

"Yes, if I may."

Sighing, Miho went sticking Post-it notes in the catalogue as we decided on each item.

"I wonder why other animals don't reuse the bodies of their own dead," I said.

"Beats me. But the female praying mantis eats the male, doesn't she? It totally makes sense. I think there are some animals that know to make good use of their dead."

"Really? I guess . . ."

"Nana, aren't you being poisoned by Naoki?"

"Of course not. But I don't really understand what he means by 'barbaric.' That's what he says about using human products. But I think it's more barbaric to burn everything without reusing the materials. We use the same word to condemn each other's values. I wonder if we can really carry on like this . . ."

"Well, I really couldn't say. But Nana, you're doing your best to understand him, aren't you? If you're willing to make mutual concessions, you'll definitely be able to work it out together," she said warmly, and I gave a sigh of relief.

"Okay then, I'll draw up the invoice on these items, and place the orders. It'll take a while, so feel free to look around the store."

"Thanks."

Miho picked up the catalogues with the Post-it notes and went to the back of the store. I gazed absently around. Time flowed by at a leisurely pace here, maybe because it was afternoon, with happy-looking young couples and genteel elderly ladies all browsing around the furniture. The first floor was full of cheap plastic and glass furnishings, but the second floor had quality furniture on display. Even the armrests of the couch I was now sitting on were of white bone.

There were some bowls made from inverted craniums on a row of dining tables at the other side of the store. Hanging from the ceiling was one of the chandeliers with human nail scales that Miho had recommended. Warm light, somewhere between pink and yellow, filtered out through the nails. How happy I would be sitting down to a special dinner with Naoki beneath such a chandelier, with soup in those skull dishes on the table!

I glanced down at my own nails. They looked identical to the ones on the chandelier. After I died, how lovely it would be to have them made into such a beautiful chandelier for someone to enjoy. However much I made a show of going along with Naoki, I would never stop caring for my body, knowing it would someday be converted into furnishings. I would always feel that I too was also a material, that I would continue to be put to practical use after I died. The thought that this was a marvelous and noble process was deeply rooted within me.

I stood up and went over to a nearby bookcase. The dividers were made of bone, probably shoulder blades given their size. There were several real books placed on the shelves to model what it would look like in the home. Naoki liked books, and I thought how perfect his study would be with such a splendid bookcase in it holding his books. I picked up a small dictionary that was leaning against the divider and looked up the word "barbaric," which had been niggling at me for a while.

Ruthless, merciless, savage, heinous.

But I could only think that this applied more to Naoki's idea of burning people's bodies when they died. He was such a gentle person and I still couldn't believe he could be so harsh and cruel as to say we should discard the entire body even though so much could be reused.

But I loved him. For his sake, I was resolved to spend the rest of my life without wearing or using human material, without touching the people who, after their deaths, continued to surround us with their warmth as material and furnishings.

The following Sunday, Naoki and I went to visit his family in Yokohama.

We had already completed the formalities for our engagement and now there were all kinds of matters to discuss, like what time to hold the ceremony, whom to invite, and so forth. Naoki's little sister was going to be in charge of receiving guests on the groom's side, so we had to talk about that, too.

Naoki's father had died five years previously. Naoki's mother and sister welcomed us cheerfully.

"Come on in! Sorry to take up your time when you're so busy."

"Not at all! Lovely to see you."

Naoki's sister Mami was a graduate student some years younger than him, and had treated me affectionately ever since he and I had started dating.

"I'm so happy you're going to be my elder sister, Nana," she said delightedly as she served us homemade brownies.

Their mother poured tea to go with Mami's treats, and we chatted while enjoying them.

"Naoki, why don't you play the trumpet at the wedding? Wouldn't it be a great way to show your love for Nana?"

"No way! It's years since I played any music and I'd be far too self-conscious now. Out of the question."

Naoki looked really cute with his embarrassed smile, and I snuggled up to him happily, feeling it had been ages since I'd seen him looking so calm and relaxed.

After we'd been talking for a while, Naoki's mother stood up, saying, "I've got something for the two of you."

She went into another room and came back with a long, thin wooden box. She put it on the table and gently opened the lid. Wondering what it was, I peered inside to see what looked like some thin washi paper.

"What is it?" We both looked at her questioningly.

"It's a veil made from your father," she informed us in hushed voice, gazing at it.

She took the diaphanous fabric out of the box. It was indeed a billowy, floaty veil made from human skin.

"Five years ago, when your father got cancer, it was his dying wish to be made into a veil. It must have been just around the time you started dating Nana, Naoki. He always was too strict with you, so it was hardly surprising you rebelled against him. You never did make up after that quarrel ended in fisticuffs when he tried to force you into medical college. He used to say he'd as good as disowned you, and refused to talk about you. But then, right at the end, he said, 'The boy's a fool, but he's got taste in women,' and that he wanted to be made into a veil for the wedding ceremony."

"Ah . . ."

I sneaked a quick look at Naoki. He was staring at the veil, his face utterly expressionless.

"You didn't come to the funeral, so I never had the chance to tell you about it, but I always believed this day would come. Naoki, please forgive your father. Use this veil for your wedding."

"Nana, why don't you try it on? Isn't it magnificent?" Mami begged me, her eyes red and filled with tears.

Gingerly I reached out and touched the veil. Human skin was generally considered too flimsy and delicate for garments. It looked like rough Japanese washi paper, but it was supersoft to the touch.

"Nana, look this way."

My mother-in-law gently lifted the veil and put it over my head, fixing it with a small comb, so that my upper body was enveloped in its lightness.

The veil reached down to my lower back, covering my ears, cheeks, and shoulders in my father-in-law's soft skin. It was plain and extremely simple, but if I looked closely I could see the fine lines of the distinctive mesh of his skin, like delicate lacework. I felt as though I was swathed in an infinite number of particles of light residing in each individual cell.

"It looks amazing on you, Nana!"

My mother-in-law and Mami both looked enthralled.

Faint spots and moles left on my father-in-law's skin formed an intricate pattern, and here and there in the light the white and yellowish-brown blended to give a bluish tinge, complex hues intertwining in a way that could never be manufactured artificially. The rays of sun shining in through the window were softened by the veil as they gently filtered through and coalesced into my skin.

With my whole body swathed in the skin-tinged glow, I felt as though I was standing in the most sacred church in the world.

I looked at Naoki through the delicate, beautiful veil. Still looking down, he slowly raised his arm and lifted up the hem. I half expected him to rip it off, but he murmured in a low voice, "This scar . . . That was the one from junior high . . ."

Next to his hand, I saw a small mark in the lacy hem.

"That's right. It's from that time you hit him. It left a scar on his back, you know. I don't suppose you ever knew it, but whenever he went to a hot spring he would proudly show it off and say, 'The boy had backbone after all.'"

Naoki stared at the veil, his expression unreadable. I watched him with bated breath, thinking he might suddenly blow up like that time he threw away his tiepin. However, he just carried on staring at the veil without saying anything.

After a while, his pale face moved slowly toward me as though he was falling into my father-in-law's skin.

"Dad . . ." he muttered hoarsely, burying his face in the veil.

"Naoki!" Mami exclaimed tearfully.

"Son, you forgive him don't you?" his mother said, her voice full of emotion.

"Yes . . . of course. We'll use the veil at our wedding. Won't we, Nana?"

I wasn't sure whether I should smile or not, and just managed a weak nod. The veil trembled and softly tickled my cheeks and back with the movement. The membrane of light passing through my father-in-law's skin shimmered over my body.

In the car on the way home, I drove while Naoki slumped vacantly in the passenger seat. Despite the cold, he had the window wide open and was gazing outside.

"Hey, are we really going to use that veil?" I asked him as the box rattled on the backseat.

Naoki didn't answer, but leaned on the open window and lightly shut his eyes, snuggled in the breeze like a child who'd fallen asleep in bed.

"If you really don't want to use it," I went on patiently, choosing my words carefully, "we can always find an excuse, like the wedding planner objected to it, or it just didn't go with the dress."

Naoki still didn't respond, but just sat there as the breeze messed up his hair and clothes. Irritated, I said more forcefully, "Come on, Naoki, answer me! Which is it? Were you being honest, or lying for the sake of your family? Look, if you really do feel moved by your father's wishes then we'll use it, but if you feel using human skin is too barbaric, then we won't. I don't mind either way, so it's up to you to say how you feel about it."

"Mm . . ."

"Which is it? Come on, tell me. Are you moved, or not? Do you think it's barbaric, or not?" I demanded, raising my voice.

"I just don't know what to think anymore," he finally said. "Maybe everyone's right and making things out of people after they die really is a wonderful, moving thing to do . . ."

I frowned, and put my foot down on the accelerator, speeding up. "Look, only you can decide whether you're moved by it or not, Naoki. I'm sure I don't know."

"I can't . . . I don't . . . I really don't know what to think anymore. Until this morning I was confident about how to use words like 'barbaric' and 'moved,' but now it all feels so groundless," he muttered vacantly. He looked like a halfwit with his mouth hanging stupidly open, almost as if he were drooling.

"That word 'barbaric' has been standing in judgment over us, though, hasn't it? Where has its power gone?"

"I don't know how I could have been so confident of myself . . . but one thing I can say is that the veil really did look lovely on you. And that's because it's someone's skin. Human skin really does suit people."

Naoki shut his mouth and said no more.

The only sounds in the car were from the breeze and the veil's box rattling on the backseat.

A hundred years later, what would our bodies be used for? Would we be chair legs, or sweaters, or clock hands? Would we be used for longer after our deaths than the time we'd been alive?

Naoki was leaning back in the seat, arms hanging limply, just as if he'd become a material object. The breeze was ruffling his hair and eyelashes. Beneath his sideburns, there was a slight scar where he'd once cut himself shaving. That scar would probably still be there if he ever became a lamp shade or book cover one day, I mused.

Quietly taking one hand off the steering wheel I took his hand lying abandoned there. It was warm, and squeezed mine back. The sensation of his skin against mine was similar to how I'd felt earlier enveloped in the veil. The faint wriggle of finger bones and pulsing of veins beneath his skin were conveyed through my fingertips.

Right now the live Naoki, not yet converted into a material, was holding my hand. We were spending our very short time as living beings sharing our body heat. Feeling this life was a precious momentary illusion, I squeezed his slim fingers even tighter.

Born in the north of France in the 1990s, Édouard Louis has published two novels, *The End of Eddy* and *History of Violence*, both best sellers translated into more than twenty languages. He is also the editor of a scholarly work on the sociologist Pierre Bourdieu. He is the coauthor, with the philosopher Geoffroy de Lagasnerie, of "Manifesto for an Intellectual and Political Counteroffensive," published in English by the *Los Angeles Review of Books*.

Michael Lucey is Professor of French and Comparative Literature at the University of California, Berkeley, and the author of a number of books on modern French literature, including *Never Say I: Sexuality and the First Person in Colette, Gide, and Proust*. He is also the translator of Didier Eribon's *Returning to Reims* and Édouard Louis's *The End of Eddy*, among other works.

History of Violence

ÉDOUARD LOUIS

TRANSLATED FROM THE FRENCH BY MICHAEL LUCEY

On days when I felt calmer I would imagine myself picking out someone I didn't know in some public place, on the sidewalk or in the aisle of a supermarket, and telling them my whole story, everything that had happened. In these visions, I would walk up to this unknown person, who would shrink back, and I would just start talking, as casually and routinely as if we had known each other forever, without telling them my name, and what I would say to this person was so horrible that there was nothing they could do but stand there and listen until I was done; they'd listen and I would watch their face. I'd spend my time fantasizing about scenes in which I'd do this. I didn't tell Clara, but this fantasy of shamelessness and self-display kept me going for weeks.

The fact is that I was unable to stop talking about it. I had told what had happened to most of my friends during the week after Christmas, but not only to them; I had also told people to whom I was much less close, acquaintances, or people I had only ever spoken to once or twice, sometimes only on Facebook. I would become annoyed when people tried to respond, when they would show too much empathy or offer some kind of analysis of what had happened, as when Didier and Geoffroy speculated that Reda wasn't really his name. I wanted everyone to know but I wanted to be the only one among them who could see the truth of it, and the more times I spoke about it, the more I said, the stronger my feeling was that I was the only one who really knew, I was unique, in stark contrast to what I considered to be the laughable naïveté of everyone else. It didn't matter what the conversation was about, I would find a way to bring Reda into it, to have him appear, to bring it all back to him, as if any topic of conversation had *logically* to lead back to my memory of him.

The first week of February—barely a month after Christmas—I went out to meet an author who had written to me and proposed that we have lunch together. I didn't know him, but I said yes, and I knew why I had done that. He wanted me to write a piece for a special issue of a literary journal he was editing (a few days later, I sent him a really poorly written text, for obvious reasons), and I behaved in exactly the same way with him. This was a period in which I really wasn't in touch with the words I spoke. The author arrived at the restaurant where I was waiting for him, where I was already quivering in my seat obsessively playing with the eraser on the pencil that happened to be in my pocket; he sat down, he took off his flannel jacket, he shook my hand and was barely settling into his seat, yet already my lips were burning to speak to him about Christmas. I thought to myself: *No, you can't speak about that right now. Wait a bit. Not right away. Be polite. Wait a bit. At least pretend to talk about something else.* The reflection of the gray-blue sky outside could be seen on the walls of the buildings, something I remember not because the sky interests me, but because I wasn't listening and instead gazed out the window, distracted and uninterested, whenever I wasn't the one who was talking.

We had exchanged a few sentences and for about ten minutes I held my breath, barely able to contain myself; I could feel Reda's name on my lips. I held back, pretended to engage in the usual kind of conversation for a meeting like this, I played my role, got him to talk about his work, his books, his projects, but I didn't listen to anything he said. I replied to his questions on the same topics but I no more listened to my answers than to his; making myself stay calm was all the more difficult in that everything he said and everything he got me to say with his questions, any observations he made, felt like an indirect invitation to speak about Christmas. What I mean is that I found connections everywhere, that everything I perceived and therefore my entire view of reality was conditioned by Reda. So I spoke fearing that the words *Reda* or *Christmas* might slip out, too early, against my will.

Then I did speak. It felt to me that the time had come, and I thought *Now I've held back for long enough, now you've earned the right to speak* and I did what I'd been waiting to do since he arrived at the restaurant: I monopolized the conversation, only I spoke for the rest of our lunch, and he barely got in a few brief comments between two mouthfuls of food: "That's terrible, how horrible, oh my God, etc.," which only added to my exultation. At the end of the meal I begged him not to repeat anything I'd said; on top of all that I couldn't figure out why, and I said I was sorry for this too, this was something else I went on apologizing for, why I had told him everything, why him, someone I barely knew, how could I have behaved so inappropriately, as I knew I had, how could I have been so rude. It's along those lines that I existed, that I spoke, that I acted during the weeks that followed the assault.

This mad flood of speech had begun at the hospital. It was only an hour or two after Reda had left, and I had run to the emergency room close to where I live to get a postexposure prophylaxis against HIV. The hospital was nearly empty on Christmas morning; a homeless man was walking up and down in the waiting room. He wasn't waiting but simply wanted to be inside out of the cold. He said, "A very Merry Christmas to you" when I sat down a few feet away. That *A very Merry Christmas to you*, so odd, so improbable in these surroundings and after what had just happened, made me laugh. An uncontrollable burst of laughter took hold of me, a laugh that was loud and full and that resonated in the empty waiting room, as I remember it, a horrible laugh that bounced off the walls, as I bent forward, holding my stomach with both hands, unable to breathe, and replied between two bursts of laughing, all out of breath, "Thanks very much, thanks, and a very Merry Christmas to you too."

I waited. No one appeared. I went on sitting there. I had the feeling I was playing a role in a story that wasn't my own. I applied myself relentlessly to remembering in order to stop myself from thinking, not that nothing had happened—how could I have thought that?—but that it had happened to someone else, to a different person, and that I had watched it all from the outside; I thought to myself: *That's where your obsession comes from. That's why you are always obsessively asking yourself what the child you used to be would have thought of the adult that you've become.* I thought: *Because you've always felt like this, that your life is taking place outside yourself, in spite of yourself, that you've watched from the sidelines as it's been constructed and that it's not at all suited to you. Today's not the first time. When you were little and your parents took you to the supermarket you would watch the people go by with their shopping carts. You'd stare at them, a strange habit you'd acquired from who knows where. You'd take in their clothes, their way of walking, and you'd say to yourself: I hope I end up like that, I hope I don't end up like that. And you'd never have imagined becoming what you are today. Never. You'd never even have thought of not wanting to turn out this way.*

I craned my neck to try to see through the little windows all around the waiting room; it was a way of passing the time. Time slowed to a snail's pace. I was waiting for one of the security doors to open, I was waiting for a doctor to appear, I coughed, sniffed, I pressed the red button of a little buzzer that was on the reception desk, and a nurse arrived, twenty or thirty minutes later. That's when the torrent of words began. Its first manifestation, let's say. I had already had to restrain myself from talking to the homeless man, who was obviously drunk, once he had said *Merry Christmas*, from replying to him that what he had said to me seemed a bit ironic given that here it was December 25, and I was at the hospital, which is to say at a moment when I should have been somewhere else, just like him, I had to restrain myself from beginning to tell him everything that had led up to my being there, in the emergency room. But this time I didn't hold back, and so I told everything to the nurse, who only wanted to know which department to send me to—although thinking about it, he probably wasn't a nurse, but maybe an attendant, or a receptionist, or a switchboard operator. I didn't hold back my tears. I didn't even try to hold them back, since I was convinced that if I didn't cry he wouldn't believe me. My tears weren't fake; the pain was real. But I knew that I had to play the role well if I wanted anyone to believe me.

Obviously, all this anxiety only went on getting worse in the days that followed. Later, in a different hospital, despite my determination to move the doctor so that he would understand and believe me, my voice remained stuck in a metallic monotone, I spoke coldly and with distance, my eyes stayed dry. I had cried too much already, I had no tears left to offer. *If you don't cry he won't believe you*, I thought to myself, *you need to cry*. But my eyes seemed now to belong to a stranger. I made a huge effort. I tried to force the tears to come, concentrating on images of Reda, his face, the gun, so that the tears would flow, but there was nothing to be done, the tears wouldn't come, my efforts were all to no avail, no tears welled up at the corners of my eyes, my eyes stayed resolutely dry, I was still as calm as I had been when I first arrived and the doctor nodded his head behind his glasses, which were slipping down his nose.

I turned to other scenes from my life for help. I brought back to mind other painful memories, the saddest and most painful I had, in order to produce some tears. I thought back to hearing the news of Dimitri's death.

Didier had phoned me in the middle of the night to tell me Dimitri had died, on a night when I was out walking, alone in the dark night when the telephone first buzzed and vibrated in my pocket. It was Didier sending me a text asking: "Can I call you?"; and I feared the worst since normally he didn't ask if he could call before calling, I was afraid something serious might have happened to Geoffroy, I was imagining an accident of some kind. I forbade myself to think of his body lying on a stretcher, but the image still appeared, and I wrote back: "Of course," already trembling, my fingers unsteady on the screen.

My cell phone rang for a second time, and I hesitated, and then Didier announced, in a voice that was both controlled and shaking, shaking precisely with a calmness that was too overdone, too artificial, that Dimitri, who had been traveling for an important meeting far from Paris, and to whom I had spoken a few hours earlier on the phone, was dead.

I was doing my best to provoke a bout of crying so I could convince the doctor of what I was saying, but it was too far in the past, it didn't affect me any longer. I was compelling myself to cry and he, on his side of things, was holding on to his skepticism, and I felt that these two opposing forces meeting in the same moment could allow us to establish or rather to reestablish the truth of the matter, that the truth was to be found in this meeting, and that it would be born out of this tension. I did everything I could to cry but I didn't succeed.

So there I was standing in front of the nurse in the first hospital, and on that night I was crying with no problem at all. He was trying to reassure me: "Someone will come take care of you, there's not much I can do personally," and it was all I could do not to scream: "I don't think you understand." In the end a nurse arrived. When she came up to me and asked me why I was here, I spoke, and went on speaking and speaking.

Tania James is the author of the novels *Atlas of Unknowns* and *The Tusk That Did the Damage*, and the short-story collection *Aerogrammes*. She lives in Washington, D.C.

The Liberator

TANIA JAMES

Saeed steps out of the barbershop to find that a stranger has locked her bike to his. The other bike is a Trek, slant-framed and sky blue, with a pink Planned Parenthood sticker over the *k*. Its U-lock has them both yoked to the rack.

He weighs the lock in his hands. His brother could break this thing. Haider, who calls himself the Liberator, who stole him this janky Rawhide instead of a Giant like Saeed wanted. But the Liberator has to finish his shift at Best Buy.

Saeed texts him anyway. *Stuck in Shaw. Someone locked her bike to mine.*

The reply comes immediately. *Sucks for u.*

Take off early. Bring cutters.

The Liberator doesn't deign to reply.

Saeed picks at the Planned Parenthood sticker. She's probably at the juice shop across the street, buying a smoothie that tastes like gritty salad in a glass. When she comes out, he'll be magnanimous. He'll say he lives out in Takoma Park with his brother, which is closer to true than false. Maybe they'll swap numbers.

Over the next ten minutes, the playground grows wild with middle schoolers. They climb and curl around every bar, screaming under a bright fall sun. A heavyset boy, bold enough to wear a Cookie Monster

115

sweatshirt, wanders over to Saeed. The boy is low-lidded, a little numb about the mouth. "Mister," he says, "do you have a dollar?"

"What for?"

"Ice cream." The kid points to the ice cream truck across the street.

Saeed gives him his grimiest dollar bill. Kid mumbles a thank you and takes his time over the crosswalk, paying no mind to the cars speeding from either direction.

Saeed's phone hums—a text from his mother.

Where r U? Jignesh is here.

He curses softly. He'd forgotten all about the tutor his mother had hired, some malnourished H-1B with mathematical timing.

Got a problem with my bike.

Three blinking dots indicate her typing something elaborate.

U Liar come now. Hinges has to go.

He can't help smirking whenever his mother is bested by autocorrect.

The metro is only a block away but no harm in waiting a few more minutes in case the bike girl is a seven. Hinges can wait.

Saeed takes a photo of the bikes, swipes a filter over the image, and posts it to Instagram with the caption: *Siamese bikes.* Instantly, regret overtakes him. How would anyone know the bikes are locked together? You can't tell from the photo. This is why he's got thirty-seven followers. This is the bike girl's fault, kind of. Why is he waiting around, snapping stupid pictures with stupid captions on account of a feminist seven who can't work a lock? Fuck this shit. And his shitty bike. Which he'll have to come back and get tomorrow. He locks it properly and sets off for the metro.

The Cookie Monster kid stops him on the sidewalk. "Hey, mister, can I have another dollar? My cousin wants an ice cream too."

"Where's yours?"

"I ate it."

"Which kind?"

A pause. "I like all kinds."

"Do I look like a chump to you?"

The kid cocks his head, as if arbitrating an answer that Saeed, all of a sudden, wants to know.

"I'll take fifty cent," the kid says.

Saeed heads for the crosswalk.

In the condo next to the playground, Lori Piotrowski takes the elevator back down. A half hour before, she was pedaling up Seventh, off to meet her special friend, boyfriend being too symbolic a term, when she realized she had no wallet. Hastily she locked up her sky-blue Trek and spent about twenty minutes scouring her apartment.

Now, wallet in hand, she steps aside so a man and his little boy can enter the elevator. The boy is wearing a sweater-vest with a pug stitched on the front. "Hi," she says to the boy, who is staring at her.

The boy says nothing.

"I like your sweater," she says.

The boy looks up at his father and says, "I don't want to talk to her."

The father places his hands on the boy's shoulders. "You don't have to," he says.

This is what she gets for talking to strangers: skepticism and disdain. It's the same on the wards. Nearly every patient she meets is appalled by her ignorance, her youth, her surname. Even the nice ones are unsettled by the thought of leaving their health to a first-year resident. Rightly so. On Lori's last rotation, she was supposed to give a vaginal exam to a grossly obese woman who whooped when Lori's fingers went questing into her anus.

Still wincing at the memory, Lori comes out of her building and halts.

There's a guy messing with the lock on her bike. Right out in the open! Nervy as city squirrels, these thieves, darting into and out of condo garages. That's how her last bike got stolen. She waits for him to produce a pair of cutters; that's when she'll pounce. Instead he consults his phone, something professorial in the way he's stroking his chin. After a while he walks away, stopping to chat with a little kid he seems to know.

By the time she gets to her bike, the little kid is walking her way. Her lock looks somehow wrong, and then—oh. *Oh.* She searches the sidewalk for the bike guy, who is stepping into the crosswalk.

"Miss," says the kid, "do you have a dollar?"

"Sorry, one sec—hey!" She calls after the bike guy. "Hey, wait!"

He turns his head and a car slams into his legs, tossing him through the air before the street pounds him flat. The car—a Camaro—brakes sharply, then swerves around the body and speeds on, tires twisting around the next corner. She runs to the body: facedown, limbs spread. "Hi," she says to his ear, "hi, do you hear me? What's your name?" The bike guy rolls onto his side. Bits of gravel stubble his cheek. He's so young. He watches her as she bends close to his mouth and feels his breath wisping against her cheek.

She finds the pulse in his wrist, bucking against the press of her fingertips. She checks his head for blood or signs of injury. "Let's get him off the street," someone says, and before she can protest, the bike guy is being shouldered to the curb.

There she sits with him and waits for the ambulance. On the opposite side of the street, schoolchildren cluster and gawk until an older woman herds them away. The bike guy stares through them, looking like a child waiting for someone to slip his socked foot into a sneaker. Lori tries to keep him talking. What's his full name? (Saeed Hassan Seyal.) Where does he go to school? (Takoma High.) What's his address? (2310 Ritchie Avenue.) Who is he taking to prom?

He blinks at her, his expression bored and disoriented. "I'm seeing like two of everything."

"Are you dizzy? Do you feel sick?"

"I don't think I can ride my bike."

"I'll take care of your bike. I'll get it to your house."

He names his bike—the Rawhide—and hands her his key. When she asks for his cell number, he can't remember the last four digits. He has her write her name and number on the back of his hand. The blue ink of her pen spreads like cracks in porcelain.

The paramedics arrive, siren lights sparkling. A cop is scratching her description of the Camaro into a small notebook while she strains to keep an eye on Saeed Seyal. A paramedic presses a palm into his abdomen, and he sits there holding up his shirt, so tame to the touch of strangers it's as though his body isn't his.

She doesn't get to speak to Saeed before they lay him on a gurney and load him into the ambulance. The kid in the Cookie Monster sweatshirt runs up and passes a sneaker through the closing doors.

By the time she gets Saeed Seyal's bike upstairs, Travis has texted her ten times, in quick and angry succession. He has been waiting in the lobby of the movie theater for thirty minutes. They could've gone to their neighborhood theater, but as her attending, Travis insists on going where none of their colleagues will see and report them.

Come over, she texts. *Something happened.*

It takes him an hour to reach her apartment. In all that time, she has swiped the hair from her sink and placed herself on the futon, her thoughts disappearing into the bottomless black of the TV screen.

"What's going on?" Travis says, stepping into her apartment, bringing with him a whiff of fruity shampoo. He looks around the room. "Whose bike is that?"

She describes how she witnessed a guy getting hit by a car, leaving out the part about her U-lock. "Wait," Travis says, "how'd you get him to the curb? Did you move him?"

"Not me, someone else."

"But didn't you tell them about immobilizing the neck?"

"Stop it," she says. "It feels like you're pimping me."

"I'm not pimping you."

"I hate that that's what it's called."

She wants to describe the sound the body made when it landed, the fat thump like meat tossed on a scale. She can't. Not with Travis rubbing circles on her back like a masseur-in-training.

"It's good you were there," he says, followed by a careful pause. "But with a trauma, you're always worried about cervical fracture, so you really shouldn't move the patient. You really should immobilize the neck."

The next day, during a break at work, she calls Saeed to arrange a time to deliver the bike. His voice mail is full. She Googles him to look for an e-mail address, and lands on his Facebook page. He looks hopeful and handsome, eyebrows gently raised as if surprised by someone to the left of the camera. The latest post begins *Our most beloved son and brother*, and a cold heat fills her face. *Janaza will be held tomorrow . . . led by his elder brother Haider . . . buried in the Muslim portion . . . To Allah We Belong and To Him We Return.*

She is late to rounds. Travis is pimping the group without mercy, going from person to person with a single question that no one knows the answer to.

"Hematoma," she says, before he gets to her.

Travis looks at her, surprised. She usually remains quiet during rounds. "What kind?" he says.

"Does it matter? His hemoglobin is dropping, he was on Coumadin."

"Retroperitoneal hematoma."

"That's basically what I said."

Travis raises his eyebrows. "So by your logic, all hematomas are *basically* retroperitoneal hematomas?" A snicker from one of his minions. "Is that what you're saying, Dr. Piotrowski?"

That night, over the phone, she dumps Travis.

"Is this because of the hematoma thing?" he asks.

"No, it's because you wash your hair with Herbal Essences."

"Lori." He sighs. "You were late, and you were being weird and aggressive. How did you expect me to respond? Is it something else? Is this about that car accident?"

She cuts him off to say her mother is calling.

Next, she doubles down on her to-do list. She orders several cacti online and signs up for a composting service. She donates a goat to an impoverished woman through Heifer International and is sidelined by the YouTubing of baby goats. She calls her sister and leaves a message. She rents an SUV for the following Saturday with the goal of folding down the seats, loading in the bike, and driving it to the Seyals' house.

Saturday arrives. She never claims the car.

She finds Saeed Seyal on Instagram. She lingers over the last picture he took, of their bikes locked together. His caption: *Siamese bikes.*

Beneath this, someone wrote *Rawhide had a way with words. the Bard of Takoma Park RIP*
Saeed wish we hung out more. U seemed like a really cool guy. fuck that driver IMO he shld burn in hell.
Saeed Im praying for u and ur family.

The comments go on and on, hundreds of them, sealed with black hearts and cryptic emojis.

Again, Lori rents an SUV, and again, she cancels. The Rawhide continues to lean against her wall, acquiring the permanence of furniture.

One day, walking down her block, she's stopped by a voice calling, "Miss! Hey, Miss!"

On the other side of the street is the little kid in the Cookie Monster sweatshirt. He's sitting on the wall that borders the playground, bouncing his heels off the bricks. "What happened to the guy?"

She starts toward him, and stops, as if they're divided by a rickety rope bridge instead of a crosswalk. For weeks, she has avoided the crosswalk, preferring to cross at the stoplight at the end of her block. But the boy, watching, still as an elk, reminds her that she is a grown woman and so she joins him on the other side, by which time her mind has been drained of euphemisms. "He," she says to his sneakers, "died. He died."

The sneakers go still. "He didn't look like he was dying."

"Sometimes it happens that way. You can't always see the bleeding when it's somewhere deep."

The boy scans the street, his expression inscrutable.

"Was he your friend?" she asks.

"He gave me a dollar for ice cream."

"Sounds like a nice guy."

"Not that nice. He was mad. I think 'cause you locked your bike to his."

She nods, her throat wadding up. She feels undone before this kid, all kids, their awful honesty.

The boy looks at her. "You were gonna bring him his bike."

"I haven't, yet."

"Why?"

"I don't want to see his mother. I don't want to tell her what I did."

"You're keeping it?"

"No," she says sharply. "I mean, no. That would be stealing."

"So you have it. But you're not keeping it."

"Right."

The boy nods slowly.

"Can I have it?" he says.

It's nine at night when she rolls the Rawhide up Ritchie Avenue. The metro was nearly empty, the elevator seething with the scent of pee. Pumpkins leer from porches, reminding her of one of Saeed's last Instagrams. He had snapped a photo from inside a jack-o'-lantern so that a clear blue sky filled its grin and eyes.

At last she reaches the mailbox of Saeed Seyal. A red banister leads up to a porch with no decoration or furniture, the windows hollowed of light. She rolls the bike into the yard and props it against the banister. She slides her letter between the spokes. Three hours she spent on the first draft, which was only a paragraph long yet whose tactility and permanence made her labor over every detail, every word, the margins, the lettering, the look of the thing, as if the recipient might press the piece of paper behind glass.

She wrote: *I locked your brother's bike to mine by accident.*

She wrote: *I saw him walk away, but before I could reach him, he got hit by that car. I waited with him until the ambulance came.*

Beneath her name, she included her number.

There is a noise somewhere in the house, maybe the clap of a cabinet door. She crouches—her whole body waits. When no one comes to the door, she leaves the bike and hurries away, noiseless as a thief.

The next morning, she ventures into the living room, which looks larger without the bike against the wall. She goes to her marker-board and wipes a finger across the word *RAWHIDE*.

After breakfast, she bikes to the farmers' market and buys some apples and a squash the size of an infant. She splurges on sunchokes and baby ginger, neither of which she knows how to use, but there is time left in the day to learn. Her geriatrics rotation begins on Monday. For now, the hours lie ahead, open and all hers.

Walking to her bike, she gets a call. The name at the top of the screen says *Saeed Seyal*.

She stares at the name. She lets her backpack drop, possibly bruising the apples. She could screen it. Among her friends, she is famous for screening. But then she thinks of the way she sneaked

123

off in the night, crouching out of some primitive instinct, and the shame of it makes her press *Accept.*

"Hey," says a voice that sounds just like Saeed's, deep and kind of sinusy. "Is this Lori?"

"Yes, this is me, hi—"

"It's Saeed."

She hears the distant bleat of a truck backing up, the pop of tennis balls off strings. She plugs her free ear with a finger.

"Saeed Seyal," he says casually. "You know, from the car accident. You dropped off my bike last night."

"Saeed." She catches her reflection, stretched and gliding over the door of a passing car. "I thought. There was an obituary."

"Yeah, I was in this coma thing, and just when they were about to pull the plug, I woke up."

She steadies the phone with both hands. It's his voice, it's the voice she remembers. "Oh my God. Oh Jesus." She sinks onto a nearby bench, her face in her hand, bowed by so many emotions she can't even weep. "Saeed? Are you serious? Is it you?"

"No," he says. "It's not."

"Not what?"

"I'm his brother. I'm the one who found his bike this morning."

Her hand falls to her lap. "Why did you say you were him?"

"I sound like him, don't I."

"What is the matter with you?"

"You thought he was back from the dead, right?"

"What the fuck," she says softly, "is the matter with you?"

"Well, now you know how I felt this morning. Now you know how it feels."

Haider presses *END* and takes a last gulp of Natty Light. He slings the can into the wastebasket; it clanks off the others. Wedged between is her letter.

That morning, he'd gone to get the mail. He turned away from the mailbox to find the Rawhide resting against the banister, unlocked like it was any other day. He smiled for a few seconds like a dumbass. Then his hand went to the mailbox and it took all his will to stay standing.

He hid the Rawhide under the porch. His mother didn't need to see it, to add to her collection of Saeed's leavings. Last week Haider saw her thumbing the shreds of his brother's beard from the sink into her palm, every last thorn.

He understands. It's the same way he keeps thumbing through his texts, the ones between him and Saeed. *Can u come? Bring cutters.* Now his screen is cracked from when he smashed it against a wall.

While his mother takes a shower, Haider bikes the Rawhide thirty minutes away, to a shopping plaza where shit gets lifted all the time. The wind has whipped him of his buzz. He props the Rawhide against a parking sign and gives the handlebar a squeeze, his eyes stinging. When a woman in high boots glances his way, he removes his hand and walks to the bus stop.

He'd given Saeed the Rawhide as a gift, though Saeed had been a thankless little poon about it, wanting to know why Haider couldn't nab him a Giant. In part, Haider was trying to protect him against thieves. "Only two ways to keep a pro like me from taking your bike," he told his brother. "One: ride a shitty bike. Or two: leave your bike unlocked. Because then you're telling the thief, *I'm not far away. I've got my eye on my ride. I'm coming right back.*"

Daniel Galera is a Brazilian writer and translator. He was born in São Paulo but lives in Porto Alegre, where he has spent most of his life. He has published five novels in Brazil to great acclaim, including *Blood-Drenched Beard*, which was awarded the 2013 São Paulo Prize for Literature. In 2013 Galera was named a *Granta* Best Young Brazilian Novelist. He has translated the work of Zadie Smith, John Cheever, and David Mitchell into Portuguese.

Eric M. B. Becker is a literary translator, a journalist, and the editor of *Words Without Borders*. In 2014, he earned a PEN/ Heim grant, and in 2016, he was awarded a Fulbright to translate Brazilian literature. His work has appeared in the *New York Times*, *Guernica*, and elsewhere. With Mirna Queiroz dos Santos, he edited the PEN American anthology *Women Writing Brazil*.

Twenty After Midnight

DANIEL GALERA
TRANSLATED FROM THE PORTUGUESE BY ERIC M. B. BECKER

The sudden urge to bring about the destruction of the world had to do with the smell of human shit on the sidewalks, with the fumes rising from the city Dumpsters, with the bus drivers' strike, and with the general sense of helplessness brought on by the heat wave that bore down on Porto Alegre late that January, but, if there was a before and after, a marker between the life it appeared I was going to lead and the life I led, this marker was the news that Andrei had been killed in an armed robbery the night before, near the Hospital de Clínicas, a few blocks from the area near Rua Ramiro Barcelos where I was walking. I came to a halt so rapidly when I processed the news that had passed through my Twitter timeline that my right foot—damp with sweat—slipped inside my sandal and my ankle turned, causing me to tumble down onto the hot sidewalk, my left arm ridiculously stretched toward the sky to protect my cell phone.

Near the spot where I fell, a homeless woman rummaged through a Dumpster, bent over the edge like an ostrich with its head in the sand, black legs and bare feet emerging from her pink dress with its pleated skirt. As she heard me groan, she slid back out of the opening, closed the lid to the container, and began walking in my direction. I was already leaning over one of my knees, adjusting my sandal strap, when she asked if I was all right and offered help, and only then did I realize she was a male transvestite, exhibiting fine curly hairs along her sculptured thighs and arms. I responded that I was fine, thanks for asking, I only needed to sit down a while. She observed me with great interest as I made myself comfortable on the front steps of the nearest building, giving the impression that she'd like to draw closer to help me but maintaining a prudent distance. A thick layer of oiliness covered her beautiful face, recalling icing, and her smile full of straight white teeth was much more unlikely than the way the clothes she wore fell most naturally over her body. I assured her I was all right and she didn't insist, walked off in the direction of Avenida Osvaldo Aranha, crossing her legs ever so slightly as she walked, like a young girl in a biquíni headed to the pool at the house of some friends of her boyfriend.

I tested moving around on my ankle to make sure I hadn't ruptured a tendon. I was scared to look again at my cell phone screen, since upon doing so I would confirm that, not long before, Andrei had taken a bullet at the hands of some thug somewhere around here and was dead, at the age of thirty-six, I calculated, recalling that he was three years older than me. The step I'd sat on was covered in burned matches. The thought that the matches could have been lit by Andrei's assassin, a crackhead inclined to kill to ensure the next rock, gave me a horrible shiver down my spine, followed by nausea. Drops of sweat emerged from behind my ears and ran down my neck. I asked myself whatever had happened to the city in my absence, a ridiculous question, since until just a few minutes earlier nothing seemed to have happened to the city, it was the same city it always had been. It was probably then, during those moments of perplexity that came one after the other, that the notion burrowed into me that the days we were living were a passage toward a slow and irreversible catastrophe, or that whatever force, law of nature, or entity breathed life into our hopes—and by "our" I meant my expectations, those of my friends, those of my generation—was beginning to die out.

It was my first visit to Porto Alegre in nearly two years. I had arrived a week before, carrying with me recollections of an airy and colorful city suspended in the amber tones of certain spring days adorned with blue skies and the flowers of purple ipê trees in the Parque da Redenção, recollections that were undoubtedly real but which pointed back toward a past that was unclear and irreconcilable with the present. Throughout that week, the city covered in a carpet of filth, baking beneath the radiation of the worst summer in decades, had brought to mind a cirrhosis patient abandoned to his death beneath the sun. Vehicles and people stayed off the streets on that thirty-first of January, amid summer vacation and the approach of Carnaval; and the bus strike, which had resulted in a total freeze in service for the fifth day straight, was the final surge in the wave of lethargy that engulfed everything. Workers from the outskirts of the city cried into news cameras because they had no way to get to work and their pay was being docked by their bosses. Jitneys, school buses authorized by the mayor's office for emergency use, and rickety clandestine buses flew down the empty bus lanes, crammed full of people on the verge of overheating. The taxi drivers honked and wreaked anarchy to their hearts' content, wild with the overdose of passengers, and some charged overnight fares in broad daylight simply because they could.

The taxi driver who, days earlier, had taken me directly from the airport to the hospital where my father had been admitted told me that the strike had been deemed illegal by the Labor Court, but that the striking workers didn't give a damn and it didn't look as if the stoppage would end anytime soon. Buses that dared to leave the garages were pelted with rocks by union members. Bus workers fought with one another and against their bosses, the latter accused of causing the impasse to pressure the government into raising bus fares, something the government wouldn't do, not in the wake of the protests of June 2013 that, spurred on by violent police repression, had managed to undo the rise in fares throughout the entire country. While all this was going on, plants were scorched beneath the sun, the heat index in the early morning recalled a rain forest, and in the afternoons the thermometers in the city center surpassed forty-five degrees Celsius. The water gushed out hot from the faucets. Not luke-warm. Hot. Nearly scalding. Water and electricity were out in various parts of the city, sometimes for hours or even days on end. Those living on the outskirts of the city had it the worst, of course, and were beginning to block roads and highways in protest against such negligence. The homeless spent early mornings huddled together in the shade, resting on cardboard beds, sleeping an improbable, pleading sleep, their eyes half open. My desire was to nestle up there on the front steps of the building and sleep that very same sleep.

I looked again at my cell phone screen, which still displayed the story of Andrei Dukelsky's murder on the website of the newspaper *Zero Hora*. I scrolled through it, wetting the entire glass screen of my iPhone with the sweat of my finger. According to Andrei's girl-friend, some Francine Pedroso, he had gone out for a run sometime around nine-thirty at night and had taken only the house key and his smartphone, which had been stolen by those who killed him. There were no witnesses, despite the fact that the site where the crime took place was an area with a fair amount of traffic, even at night. "One of the most promising new talents in contemporary Brazilian literature," was the honor the text conferred upon him. "Duke, as he was called by friends." There was a hashtag, #GoodbyeDuke, offering an instant record of the expressions of shock and sadness on the part of his readers and friends on social media. I didn't have the courage to click through.

We were no longer that close, Andrei and I. I'd last seen him a few years earlier, in São Paulo, at the last of his book signings, or at least the last one I'd heard about. He had stopped updating Twitter and, as I confirmed soon thereafter, committed Facebook suicide as well. Our closest interaction had been fifteen years earlier, during college, when we wrote together in our e-mail fanzine, Orangutan, and had a few conversations we would later recall as exchanges of great intellectual depth. He made me read Camus, João Gilberto Noll, *Moby Dick*. I tried imagining where the other contributors of the e-zine were at that moment, especially Emiliano, who I missed the most living in São Paulo. I remembered when I saw Andrei for the first time in the courtyard of the journalism school, smoking as though he'd been doing it since he was in diapers, stout and severe as a judo fighter, with a receding hairline that foretold a precocious baldness. He wore nice blue and white shirts and would go to the bars in a suit, total extravagance for a young college student at the end of the nineties. His fingernails were always long and dirty and he had a bit of a smell to him. Duke never stopped being a mystery to us. Among his friends, but above all among those of us from Orangutan, there was a sort of unspoken competition to see who would become the first to figure him out, to gain his confidence, to become his confidant. But Duke never opened up to anyone. And reading his short stories and novels did nothing to unriddle the enigma. From what I'd read, I had the impression there were things he hid even from his writing. As though he awaited some distant future in which he would find himself ready to write about them.

The funeral in the Jewish cemetery on Rua Oscar Pereira, the news story went on, would be closed to the public. No wake, in accordance with Jewish tradition. As I sat there on the front steps of some residential tower, yearning to be overcome with the numbing sleep of the homeless, I thought of Andrei's body lying on the sidewalk some five hundred meters from where I found myself, how his dried blood across the flagstones must have left stains that now mixed with dog piss and traces of the muck leaked from trash bags, and then I caught myself thinking, against my will, that in actuality he had been spared, that perhaps he was lucky after all, since he had escaped something terrible that was approaching, something we'd all have to learn to get used to.

I remembered then that I was carrying the nicotine patches for my father in my purse. I tried to concentrate, I turned off the cell phone screen, stood up, and continued walking toward Avenida Ipiranga. A column of black smoke rose from the concrete embankments at the edge of the Dilúvio and, as I crossed the bridge over the water, I saw two boys dressed in rags bent over a crackling fire, likely melting copper wires to sell to the scrap yard. The Dilúvio riverbed had been reduced to a creek snaking between sandy banks exposed to the sun, but in the few spots that were deeper it was possible to see schools of fish swimming in the gray, pulpy sewage. On the other side of the avenue, where the neighborhood of Santana stretched on, located on a tiny block on Rua Gomes Jardim lined with tiny houses, their verandas almost hidden behind gardens in need of some attention, near a glassworks and an old butcher shop that had always scared me as a young girl, was the house belonging to my parents, for whom the world—as a matter of health and longevity—was closer to coming to an end than it was for me.

And the world had nearly come to an end for real for my father. At the age of sixty-six, he'd had a heart attack and was at home recuperating from bypass surgery. When I was awoken before sunrise by the ringtone of my cell phone in my apartment in São Paulo, eight days earlier, the operation, which would last four hours, had already begun. On the other end of the line, my mother sounded more angry than scared. Details of the episode came only later from my father, after the ICU, when his memory was refreshed. After eating a dinner of a salami and cheese panini, delivered by motorcycle from his favorite luncheonette, and after watching TV while drinking two glasses of Campari with tonic water and smoking with his habitual voraciousness, he'd lain down to sleep. He woke up in the middle of the night with heartburn and a slight pain in his chest, walked around the living room a bit, and, noting that the pain wasn't going away, decided to pay a visit to the emergency room. He saw no reason to disturb my mother's shallow sleep, and so he grabbed the car and drove alone to the Hospital Mãe de Deus, suffering a heart attack without realizing it, smoking Marlboro Lights with one arm hanging out the window and the other hand on the wheel of his Honda Fit Automatic, probably listening to something like Simply Red on Rádio Continental, certain that he was suffering from gas or some other relatively harmless thing. As soon as he mentioned the pain in his chest to the doctor in triage, they took his blood pressure and hurried him to the cardiologist. A short time later he was on the operating table.

I arrived at the hospital with suitcase and backpack in hand and caught him at the end of the first full day following the procedure, hugging a pillow as he coughed up mucus before my mother's eyes. He was disoriented and constantly asked whether it was day or night. When the sheet was pulled back for some exam or procedure, I found his naked body unbelievably white, and I thought that couldn't possibly be my father's color, he was darker than that. They had drained too much fluid from him, he had a shortage of blood, something wasn't right. I tried not to look too closely, imagining he felt shame at being exposed before me in that situation, and for my part I felt repulsion at seeing him so debilitated. Lying on the hospital bed at the mercy of probes and needles, his sternum sewed up with steel wire that would remain there in his skeleton even after all his other body tissue turned to dust, he was the emblem not only of his own death but also of mine. These morbid thoughts began to retreat to the background the moment he was transferred to his room. He regained his good humor and joked that his useless body was at my disposal for experiments, that the time had arrived to donate it to science.

I told him I didn't need anything aside from *Arabidopsis* seeds and sugarcane for my research but that I had a friend at the University of São Paulo who studied the effects of cigarettes and processed meats on the bodies of stubborn old men and would perhaps have an interest in his carcass. My father was visited by a few colleagues from the college preparatory courses and high schools where he taught literature and Portuguese, and also by a trio of students who held him in high esteem. I supported him on his walks down the hallway, during which he complained about Mother's recent obsessions, the economic interventionism of the federal government, the permissive pedagogy of our time, and spoiled students who thought they had a right to everything, all the time looking at me from the corner of his eye to measure my reaction to the things he was saying. After five days of hospitalization, he was able to return home, where his spirits took a nosedive. Sometimes he cried out of the blue and looked at us perplexedly, saying that he didn't know why he was crying as the tears streamed down his cheeks. He insisted on taking a shower standing up, he cleaned his own wounds and dedicated himself to the breathing exercises prescribed by his physiotherapist. He still had years to live, I thought, who knew if he wouldn't come back from it all even stronger, strong enough to see the world waste slowly away toward its own end.

The morning I learned about Andrei's death, I had gone out to buy nicotine patches at my father's request. He wanted a specific brand that wasn't so easy to find and, as the buses were off the streets, I had to walk to a pharmacy in Bom Fim. I returned home looking like a malaria patient. I saw that my father was sleeping, left the bag with the patches on the dinner table, and walked into the kitchen. I filled a glass with ice cubes and iced black tea, right beneath the stream coming from the air conditioner. The old, worn-out sofa had its own distinct smell that overwhelmed the roses and lilies my mother kept in a vase on the center table. I called that smell the smell of dust mites. Ever since I was a young girl, when I learned about dust mites from a magazine article about respiratory illnesses, I associated the smell of the sofa with an army of these tiny creatures, which I imagined had infiltrated the rough fabric of the sofa cushions by the millions. The magazine article was illustrated with a close-up from an electron microscope in which the dust mites looked like green olives with legs poised above balls of gray spaghetti. I must have been nine or ten when I saw the image, and at the time the threat of dust mites had reached the status of a household phobia in homes across Brazil. My parents, following the example of everyone else, had installed air filters that looked like tin robots in all the bedrooms. I would listen to the mechanical hum of the filters and imagine the dust mites being chewed up in a massacre committed by minuscule gears. What had happened to those filters? Nobody paid the least attention to dust mites anymore. "Four pairs of paws and a pair of palpi," I said under my breath, remembering a fragment from one of the biology books I read and reread as a child. Those were the traits of arachnids, the class that included dust mites, spiders, and scorpions. I liked pronouncing that phrase, its alliteration and almost comic sonority reminiscent of the lines from some children's song. Sometimes I found myself singing "four pairs of paws and a pair of palpi" in my head as I dried the dishes, took a pee, or sat before the computer screen trying to work on the incomplete draft of an article.

I spent some time repeating those words like a mantra, sipping my iced tea, feeling the sweat dry on my cold skin. Andrei was dead. The anxiety I'd just experienced on the street wouldn't go away—on the contrary, I felt it was permeating me irreversibly, as though I were soil absorbing poisonous water. I looked at the glass in my hand, I imagined it transforming into hundreds of shards scattered about, and I thought there was something perverted and undesirable in that glass that remained intact, it was as though it were conscious of being a glass, something it definitely had no right to be. I squeezed the glass tightly, wanting and not wanting to break it, in an impulse similar to the cruel desire people sometimes feel to squeeze a puppy.

Living with my parents at thirty-three, even under the circumstance of the medical problem that had nearly killed my father, brought the predictable sensation of an emotional step backward. I loved the things in that house, sure, but this didn't stop them from generating a certain discomfort in me. I cast my eyes from the framed photos of Tatuíra, our deceased mutt with her tiger-stripe fur, to the violets in little vases in the kitchen to the collection of cookbooks with their faded spines, and I visualized the showerhead spitting out air when we took a shower, my father's enormous library full of literature, the reference books my mother left piled on the floor of the little shed behind the house where she worked on her illustrations, the guest room that still preserved idiotic vestiges of the time it was the bedroom of an only daughter, a poster on the wall of Johnny Depp and Winona Ryder in *Edward Scissorhands*.

The familiarity of the house intensified my fear of having left unguarded a strategic border far away from there, of having opened a flank for them to take my life away from me. The rent for my apartment in São Paulo was past due, more than half the lightbulbs needed changing, and my research about circadian rhythms in sugarcane plants was stuck in the wreckage of a petty quarrel that had resulted in my failing the qualifying exams for my doctorate. The next exam was scheduled for the beginning of April, and I had taken care to schedule it on a date that would force Professor Cesar, my nemesis, to send a substitute to assume his place on the examining board. This practically guaranteed that I would pass, but I trembled with rage and anxiety each time I remembered the humiliation that maggot had put me through. I was convinced I'd been the victim of faculty misconduct, but going that route would have been counterproductive. Cesar could have quashed me if he wanted.

My fingers grasped the glass with such force they'd turned yellow. I asked myself what would happen if I simply left everything behind. If I didn't return. Disappeared into the woods, ran away to Uruguay and stayed there listening to the distant echoes of civilization's death throes. My weakness and my loss would follow me to the grave. Version One: I would experience freedom of a kind that I had never imagined existed. Version Two: The question was whether, beyond the narrow lens of our vanity, our ambitions in life truly became gratuitous, futile, and forgettable, as I sometimes, in secret, suspected.

I relaxed the pressure in my fingers, swallowed the last ice cube, and set the glass down on the table. I needed to do something to escape the vortex of anxiety. Then I remembered my favorite way to pass the time in that house. The habit, which I developed as a child, of riffling through my mother's visual reference guides, among them the illustrated zoology, botany, and anatomy volumes that had so fascinated me since I was a young girl. I walked out the back door of the kitchen. The heat outside, even during the few seconds necessary to cross the backyard to reach the shed, bore down on me with such cruelty that I asked myself whether those conditions weren't hostile to human life. Man's fragility was pathetic. Millions of years of evolution had led to creatures incredibly unadapted to the planet's environment, as displayed by our suffering from lack of sustenance or the smallest changes in temperature, a humiliating vulnerability to all sorts of atmospheric conditions, to exposure to physical matter and other organisms, not to mention the still further humiliating vulnerability of our minds to any old nonsense, to anxiety, to hope. We were unfit for nature. It wasn't surprising then that we wished to destroy it.

Fortunately, my mother was working in her studio with the air conditioning at full blast, listening as she always did to Rádio Itapema, which at that moment was playing a Nei Lisboa ballad that took me back, who knows why, to afternoons when I would go drinking with my classmates in the open-air bars on Rua Doutor Flores, in the historic city center, after class during the college entrance exam course. My mother's desk was wide and uncluttered, without any drawers, just a wooden top over tubular metal legs. The iMac, the scanner, and the digital drawing tablet seemed like technologies from outer space in comparison with the FM radio, whose antenna extended into the air. The devices shared space with several pencil holders full of pens, and sheets of paper covered with sketches. It had already been years since she began doing her drawings on the computer, but I could clearly remember the pre-digital era, when her desk was replete with enormous sheets of heavyweight paper with their creamy texture, cases full of colored pencils, rulers, utility knives, watercolors, and paintbrushes. Still a squirt, I would get sheets of tracing paper from her to copy illustrations from books using Chinese 0.5-mm ink pens. I was dead scared of breaking the tip of one of those pens. My mother's specialty was technical illustration and what she called realist drawings. The delicate movements of her wrist gave birth to hearts and throats for medical textbooks, bowls of cereal encircled by ripe strawberries for boxes of granola, Amazonian birds for collector postcards tucked inside milk chocolate wrappers, tractors and harvesters for farm equipment catalogues. All she needed were reference photos. Once, seeing one of her illustrations on a bag of bread during breakfast, I asked why they didn't simply use photographs instead of drawings so realistic they looked like copies.

"I don't copy photographs," she responded. "I don't draw things. Photos do that. I draw ideas of things. Imagine a perfect apple. I draw everything you imagine an apple to be—not the real apples you find in our fruit bowl."

In the majority of cases, her illustrations were near-identical reproductions of the photos, it was difficult to discover details that differed, as in a game of spot the differences, but there was no question that the images did differ in some deeper way. Her drawings were

closer to Renaissance paintings than to photographs, imbued with
an idyllic magnetism that the communications agencies, publishers,
and companies that wanted her services certainly understood much
better than I did. From an artistic point of view, the illustrations
were of no value. In some cases, however, when the client briefing
permitted greater liberty or allowed for a more uncommon direction
than was usually the case, she was capable of creating images that
were strangely poetic, less prisoner to labels and catalogues, and
closer to hyperrealist painting, in which the presence of the technique employed and the nearly undetectable anomalies bestowed on
expressivity what could easily pass for a documentary photograph.
Among my favorite illustrations was a piece she herself was proud
of to the point of having it framed and hanging it on her studio wall.
It was an illustration of a brand of sunscreen for a magazine ad. A
family at the edge of the sea, enjoying themselves—father, dog, young
girl, a mother applying sunscreen to the young girl, who was playing
near a sand castle. My mother used several different photographs
to create this illustration, casual photographs taken with her own
camera during the summer in a town called Shangri-La in southern
Brazil, where we had a house on the beach that was later sold to
pay off certain debts. The ocean in the background had neither blue
water nor perfect waves capped with white foam. It was the ocean
along the coast of Rio Grande do Sul, brown as chocolate milk with
the rough and chaotic surface of floodwaters. Across the mother's
belly was the scar from a C-section. It wasn't hidden or anything like
that. The woman in the reference photo had a scar and my mother
decided to leave it. To her surprise, the image was approved and
printed. It had come out tiny on the magazine page and you could
barely note the transgression, but there it was. To me, the enlarged
version hanging on the wall communicated a feeling of truth behind
appearances, of the briny stench intoxicating the sunny day and the
inconvenient wind that was always gusting along the coast.

139

I walked quietly into the studio so as not to disturb my mother, but she turned her head at the very same instant.

"Did you find the patches?"

I told her that I had, that my father was still sleeping in the bedroom, and I noticed, as I drew closer, that she closed a window of her Internet browser where Facebook had been open, leaving within view the workspace of her drawing software, where she was working on an illustration of some inscrutable contraption. I asked her what it was. "A new type of fruit peeler. It's a fad right now." I wasn't sure what to say and she added that she would finish working soon and heat up some lunch. Not wanting to interrupt her further, I walked over to the stacks of books scattered around the floor and among various bookshelves. A sudden recollection lifted my spirits.

"Mom, remember how I left my *Encyclopedia of Cryptozoology* here?"

She took a while to answer as she finished typing something, most certainly part of the Facebook chat I had interrupted.

"It must be in the middle of the other books you left here. I think they're all on the white shelf."

The shelf was a small Formica slab in the corner, nearly buried under the larger shelves and the piles of books and file folders. From a distance I caught sight of the yellow spine of the large hardcover book, too heavy to take to São Paulo when I moved there for my doctorate. I sat on the floor with the book between my legs and began turning to pages at random. "The Great Sea Serpent of the *HMS Nestor*." In September 1866, in the Strait of Malacca, the crew of the steamship *Nestor* caught sight of a creature swimming in wavelike movements next to the ship. It reminded them of a frog or a giant lizard and had a tail more than fifty meters long. Its entire body had black and yellow stripes. "Lake Sentani, Indonesia." At some point during the Second World War, as he and his troops set up camp in what would become Papua Province in Indonesia, anthropologist George Agogino threw a grenade into Lake Sentani in hopes of catching fish for a meal. A shark three meters long appeared dead, floating on the surface. There was nothing strange about the creature, except for its presence in freshwater, which was abnormal. One hypothesis was that the shark was in fact a sawfish of the species *Pristis microdon* whose sawlike nose had been destroyed by the explosion. "Diablito." Between September 2000 and February 2001, residents of Pitrufquén, nearly four hundred kilometers west of Buenos Aires, sighted on several occasions a tiny humanoid creature that was given the nickname Diablito, Little Devil. The first reports of sightings came from children and weren't taken seriously, but it wasn't long before adults, too, began to hear the creature's wailing—"a cry like that of a baby"—and to find their chickens and dogs mutilated. One farmer who said she'd seen Diablito described him as "a tiny little man with the wrinkled, hairy face of a pig." Investigators noted several similarities between this case and various sightings of the chupacabra throughout Latin America since 1995. "(Blue) Tigers." In September 1910, Methodist missionary Harry Caldwell, an unrelenting tiger hunter, came face-to-face with something extraordinary in Fujian Province, in southeast China. Caldwell described the specimen this way: "The beast's fur was wondrously beautiful. Its base was a dark grayish-blue color, almost a navy blue in the belly region. Its stripes stood out and, as far as I could see, were similar to those of a regular tiger." Bernard Heuvelmans, who created the term "cryptozoology" in the 1950s, also compiled reports of blue tigers in the same region of China in 1986.

Jumping from entry to entry, I made the time pass and assuaged my anxiety, which began to give way to a sort of enchantment that was difficult to attain past childhood. I revisited giant owls, modern sightings of pterodactyls and other dinosaurs, legendary hominids like Bigfoot and the Abominable Snowman, and an endless series of sea serpents and other aquatic monsters. The majority of entries didn't document terribly spectacular cases. The cryptozoology catalogue was composed in large part of unconfirmed species that featured only tiny variations in relation to known species, or of well-known species sighted in unexpected regions or habitats. It may not have been a science, but it had a scientific side to it. The *Encyclopedia of Cryptozoology* had no entries regarding supernatural events, UFOs, or anything of that kind. There was no space for werewolves, ghosts, zombies, or aliens. Those who witnessed the encyclopedia's thousands of creatures believed they'd seen, not creatures from some other planet, but rather animals of flesh and blood, children of nature in the same way as pigeons, horses, and humans are—undiscovered animals, in strange shapes, at times fantastically bizarre, but still animals. The illustrations were numerous and, in nearly all cases, exceptionally crude. They were sketches done in a hurry by stupefied ship captains and naturalists, or composites drawn from reported sightings that suggested skepticism and derision, and were often based on indigenous tales shrouded in myth or on the testimony of individuals who inspired little confidence, such as inveterate believers in superstition and creationists going out into the field to obtain evidence of the divine origins of our planet and all its creatures. The encyclopedia did not endorse such sources and irrational interpretations; it merely recorded them with a critical distance, suggesting that, who knows, one day the truth behind such reports might be revealed. But it was exactly these rudimentary records and the lack of validation that had sparked my imagination when, at the age of ten or eleven, I grabbed the encyclopedia for the first time from a pile of my mother's biology books. Those pages had revealed to me a capacity for invention that surpassed in every way religious and mythical explanations of the origin of the world, a capacity for invention that operated within Newton's laws of motion and the process of evolution, in full agreement with the geologic, biochemical, and ecological sciences.

After all, the existence of a giant anaconda thirty meters long, like that reported by Father Victor Heinz during a boat trip along the Amazon River on May 22, 1922, was unlikely and had never been confirmed, but it wasn't impossible, and confirmation would hardly affect accepted scientific theories, even if it were then necessary to ask where the metabolism of fatty acids sufficient to support, in terms of calories, an animal of that size would come from. The first video images of a giant squid in its natural habitat had only recently been captured by Japanese scientists, in July 2012, bringing a whole lineage of legendary marine animals from the Kraken to the Leviathan of the Old Testament onto the unhallowed ground of digital documentation. Reports of dinosaurs surviving to the present day were certainly false, but in 1938, Western scientists discovered that the coelacanth, a fish presumably extinct for seventy million years, still swam in the waters off South Africa and was known to the region's indigenous population. And, if the infinite varieties of sea serpents present in folklore and in modern tales the world over did not exist, they were at the very least a testament to the fascination and horror awakened in the human soul by the deep sea and its still mysterious inhabitants. The fact was that, thanks to that book, throughout my childhood I saw no reason to waste time with gods or ghosts, since I could instead imagine mega-sharks, Chinese monkeys trained to prepare ink for scribes, enormous eagles that snatched human babies from their mothers' breasts, and bloody confrontations between sea serpents and sperm whales, like the one detailed in 1875 by the crew of the *Pauline* in Brazilian waters, near the Cape São Roque, a story that eclipsed even the wildest passages of *Moby Dick*—if not in its philosophical weight, at least in its power of suggestion of just what astonishing creatures the natural world might hold. What I read humbled and captivated me. The animal kingdom's stranger members were more fascinating than the occult, than literature, than television shows.

For a couple of years after I discovered the book, when people asked me what I wanted to be when I grew up, I responded in complete seriousness and with great conviction that I intended to become a cryptozoologist, which to me in my naïveté was a perfectly normal, if hardly popular, profession. As if that weren't enough, I also had a concrete goal: to find the white pampas deer, whose entry in the *Encyclopedia of Cryptozoology* described two sightings, one in 1940, another in 1946, of a pampas deer with a coat of fur that was almost entirely white. One of the eyewitnesses was a farmer in the region of Camaquã, in Rio Grande do Sul, who described the animal as "a full-grown pampas deer white as a cloud, with brown spots on its back and head, with antlers black as coal," and who tried to subdue the beast with a bullet from his shotgun but missed the mark. The other white deer had been seen on the border with Uruguay by the staff and patients of a sanatorium by the name of Three Acacias. The creature may merely have been a mutation of *Ozotoceros bezoarticus*, the pampas deer, perhaps of the *celer*—or southern—subspecies, which could be found in the Argentine pampas and was practically extinct. The eyewitness reports could have been false, and some pampas deer were whiter than others. But there could also have been a rare and isolated species, seldom seen and never before captured. That's what I believed at eleven years of age, and a life dedicated to confirming the existence of the white pampas deer seemed like a good life to have ahead of me.

Much later, I realized that people had held back their laughter or reacted as though they were speaking to a young child when I explained the objective of cryptozoological studies, and one Christmas night an uncle of mine told me that soon deer would be extinct throughout Rio Grande do Sul because those who lived in the countryside, believing that these animals transmitted foot-and-mouth disease to their cattle, shot them on sight, rendering them impressive trophies for the walls of their homes. In the end the reactions of adults began to make me feel ashamed and I never again spoke of those things. I spent my middle school and high school years saying I would be an architect. It sounded more like a serious profession. When I graduated from high school, I decided to take the entrance exam for journalism school, in pursuit of one of those professions fetishized among teenagers who were more or less well-read in the late 1990s, the last time there existed something that resembled a job market for that profession. One year later, however, I had already changed my major to biology. The *Encyclopedia of Cryptozoology* was at the root of my latent desire to become a scientist. It was that book that made me see the world as a place of real mysteries that were worth discovering and investigating. The whole enigmatic aura surrounding fauna that were yet to be discovered—which gave me the feeling that each animal illustrated in the encyclopedia was something out of a fairy tale or the bestiary of some extinct people— dwindled over the years, though. The time came when it was more common for the distinctions between new species to be uncovered by means of molecular biology performed in a laboratory than through underwater expeditions to ocean trenches, the exploration of caves, or information gathered in remote villages. Then came the cryptozoology of DNA sequencing, which existed in abstract calculations performed by computers, a realm that was untouchable but paradoxically gave life to our conviction that we knew the world then more than we ever had, and that we were separated from the unknown merely by the time needed by a processor to remedy the situation. Part of me didn't accept all of that. The era in which the unknown was "more real" than the known remained, in my memory, still a recent one. In my lost youth, I recalled as I sat there on the floor of my mother's studio, I didn't know what to do with all that desire to shed light on the most obscure corners of the planet and the universe. The whole thing was stimulating and at the same time hopeless, because I wasn't sure where to begin. I would read each issue of *Superinteressante* magazine (my parents had bought me a subscription) filled with the desire to be like all those scientists who studied superconductivity and dug up dinosaurs, but I still didn't know how to get there, I simply wasn't sure what to do with my life, and that was good, it was stimulating. The years passed and, after a certain point, not being sure what to do with my life began to be a bad thing, and there was something much worse, which was the desire to no longer do anything at all.

I closed the book that was open over my crossed legs. A feeling of anxiety washed over me like a cramp. I tried to keep it at bay but soon I was sniffling. I heard my mother get up from her chair, I listened to her sandals scratching the tile floor as she crouched down, I felt her hand on my shoulder. I wanted to explain to her what was upsetting me, but, even if I had found the words, I wouldn't have had the courage. I imagined myself saying: "The only thing left in this world is destruction, Mom, and the worst thing we can do is interfere," but I wasn't even sure I really believed that, I knew only that the idea had begun to take hold of me. I spoke instead of my father's heart attack, how it was only beginning to sink in. He'd barely escaped death. I wasn't ready for him to die. I also told her about my situation at the university, that I even ran the risk of losing my scholarship after failing my qualifying exams on account of a vile, spiteful professor. My mother already knew all about the whole tragedy, we'd talked it over several times via Skype, one of those times being when I was drunk on vodka mixed with limoncello and spoke in all seriousness about sabotaging the freezers that held Cesar's research supplies, and showing him that he'd fucked with the wrong student. But she listened to it all over again and waited for me to finish before saying anything.

"Your dad is getting better. The worst is over. And we already spoke about your doctorate, didn't we, dear?" my mother said with the tone of voice she used in attempts to project her own

imperturbability onto others. "Your adviser and your peers understood perfectly the real reason you failed. Didn't they? You'll find
a way to fix this. Your research is too valuable for them to let
something worse happen."

She ran her hand through my hair, lifted her eyebrows, and smiled
from cheek to cheek. Our conversation might well have ended there,
she was right, I would pass on the second attempt, no one had ever
heard of candidates failing their qualifying exams twice at the Institute of Chemistry. Cesar's substitute was a professor who didn't have
anything against me.

"Mom, do you remember Andrei? My friend, the writer."

"Yes, of course. The Duke?"

"He died yesterday. He was killed in a robbery on Rua Ramiro
Barcelos."

She began to open her mouth and then her face became all
twisted.

"My god, Aurora, how awful . . ."

"They shot him in the face so they could take his cell phone."

"When was this?"

"Last night. Near the Hospital de Clínicas. He died around there,
I think."

"What a tragedy. Every now and then they'd publish something
about him in the newspaper. He was quite the success."

"He was."

"Did they find whoever killed him?"

"I'm not sure, I don't think so."

"Are you going to the funeral? Did you two still speak?"

"I hadn't spoken to him in a long time. Ever since I moved to São
Paulo I haven't really kept in touch with people here."

My mother stood up and walked out into the backyard. I went
after her and found her staring at the grill. A few meetings and parties with the Orangutan group had been hosted there, barbecues

147

that stretched on into the night and had, on occasion, turned a bit psychotic and semipornographic.

"I just remembered the bottle of alcohol," my mother said. One time, Andrei, completely wasted, had tried lighting the grill with a liter of alcohol, producing an impromptu flamethrower that lasted a few seconds and singed some of my mother's vases full of flowers as well as the hair on the arm of another boy, who ended up in the emergency room. "There was that friend you all had who was always taking off his clothes."

"Antero. I'd forgotten about that, he did that all the time."

"To your father and me, you all seemed like children still. It was difficult to swallow certain things, but later we got used to it."

Thinking about the way we were back then, I also thought we were just a bunch of kids. But we had thought we were adults. More adult than the adults. I could remember in vivid detail the way, on the threshold of twenty, I thought of my parents as children. And now we were all more or less the same thing.

"Let's go see how your father's feeling," my mother said all of a sudden.

Together we walked into the house to find him awake on the living room sofa, in his pajamas, remote control in hand, watching the videos of Buster Keaton that he so adored and had collected since the time of VHS tapes. I had given him that collection of DVDs as a birthday present.

"The doctor said you're not supposed to laugh," my mother warned.

"I've already seen this movie five hundred times, I don't laugh anymore," he replied.

I sat down at his side, laid my head on his shoulder, and concentrated on the TV screen for a few minutes. That was the movie in which Keaton plays a young man who has only a day to get married in order to inherit seven million dollars. After he has been turned

148

down by various women, his friends publish an ad in the newspaper for a girl to marry a millionaire groom, and soon Keaton is being chased down an enormous avenue by hundreds of women in wedding dresses. The chase turns absurd, with a mix of cranes, wild acrobatics on cliffs, and a rock avalanche that overtakes the hero and his brides as they scurry down a mountain. What I never managed to tell my father was how Buster Keaton's unchanging expression directed my imagination toward the muscles of his quick, athletic body, and the indefatigable posture of his characters—always fighting, in their awkward way, against forces that so comically outweighed them— awoke in me an empathy so intense it was easy to confuse it with sexual desire. As a teenager, I would watch the tapes when I was at home alone, the way boys watch porn films.

There was one scene, however, that disturbed me in a different way. It happened in the closing moments of a film called *College*. After an entire Olympics of frustrated attempts to participate with a modicum of dignity in campus sporting life, a young college student played by Keaton finally wins over the girl and they marry. They leave the church together and then there's a series of three shots that pass as fast as lighting. The three images, one after another, can't last more than five seconds. First we see Keaton and his wife at home with their young children, doing chores around the house. Then we see the two of them much older, sitting side by side in rocking chairs. Then, two graves. And then a title card that reads "The End." I found that ending absolutely terrifying. It seemed to contain an urgent message: you will bend over backward and swallow your pride to achieve what you want, and you'll get it, but from that point on life won't be worth more than three short cuts. The film was over, effectively, *before* those three shots. When the couple left the church, it was already over. That was the secret tragedy of the film, its hidden subtext, a gesture toward the absurdity that is life. Of course this only increased my desire for Buster Keaton. I had masturbated one or two times dreaming of that melancholy mask and that chest puffed up with naive heroism.

Sitting next to my convalescing father on the sofa, I observed, with some relief, that my erotic relationship with those films was behind me. What caught my attention at that moment was the film's unbelievably daring action, a suicidal madness filmed almost entirely without the aid of special effects. My father did not, in fact, laugh at the scenes, just as he'd assured my mother. He stared at the screen with a calm sort of concentration, a frown on his face, sharing in that sweet sorrow. His body had a sharp smell laced with cinnamon, a scent I breathed in with a sense of transgression. My little old man who'd nearly died. I felt so close to him.

Keaton's energy, his range, and his unruffled expression were not within our reach, but the pacing of the action that absorbed us was real, the way it gathered speed was real, not only real but realistic; it had been a long time since it had spilled out from the realm of cinema and into our lives, and our end would be composed of three quick cuts that would be difficult to recognize as a chapter of our story.

My cell phone vibrated in my pocket. The call came from someone who wasn't in my contacts.

"Aurora?"

"This is she. Who's calling?"

"Francine. We've never met."

But I could remember having read her name in the newspaper article.

"It's about Andrei," she said.

Ishion Hutchinson was born in Port Antonio, Jamaica. He is the author of the poetry collections *Far District* (Peepal Tree Press, 2010) and *House of Lords and Commons* (Farrar, Straus and Giroux, 2016). He teaches in the graduate writing program at Cornell University.

Sympathy of a Clear Day

ISHION HUTCHINSON

By melon carts and feral cats skinning off adobe
walls, we thread the white heat of day on the square,
to the café minarets level at our eyes, vapor coils
of virgin snow peaks through them, ready to spring.

Travel is sympathy. Not so, you point at what's below:
birds and monkeys shuck to perform by their cages;
snakes rise in fragrant droppings on carpets children
squat with whisks while tourist dollars and coins fill baskets.

Souks edge the lubric traffic. Commerce, from the good
cool of this café, prowls and gnaws the city to the bone.
Mighty caravans appear still with oaths and murmurs
from across the equator, no longer with tents, for cheap

hotels proliferate as madly as the war raged for oil.
From this height we are in a spell of fabrics, lavender
and saffron, those loggias of black soften in the haze
glow basalt and move in fluid swaths against shadows.

Bless Churchill's cruel, romantic eyes, in one regard,
for painting the sky's fragile lilac and radio wafer,
no longer audible, over the bazaar's broken watercolours.
His self-centred ego now turns unseen, incessant drones.

"To celebrate," you tell me with mock triumph, "a holiday
is to become free for the unaccustomed day: the clear day."
The clear day I repeat, then shudder remembering another
phrase, the God-land compressed within itself, and remind you.

Any reprieve but none from the unredeemable world.
Weighted voices. Clouds cover the propane tank on the terrace;
we come down to go to the desert, that final archive where
dragnet of stars blanch at sunset over travellers in slow progress.

Sunjeev Sahota was born in
1981 and lives in Yorkshire with
his wife and children. His first
novel, *Ours Are the Streets*, was
published in 2011. His second,
The Year of the Runaways, was
short-listed for the 2015 Man
Booker Prize. He is a *Granta*
Best Young British Novelist.

Good Girls

SUNJEEV SAHOTA

'Maybe you need to speak to her?' Balbir said, sliding across to her side of the bed now she'd warmed his spot for him.

'I'll decide what I need to do,' Gurdev said. 'But I'm not forcing her into a nursing home. We'll just have to look after her here.'

'You mean pehnji and I will have to look after her,' Kulwant said, in the bedroom next door. 'Fine! Fine! You look after both the shops and we'll look after your mother.'

'I'll help, darling,' Jagroop said. He'd been so much more conciliatory since she'd discovered the results of their tests. 'But we're the Directors. We can't do that *and* be on the shop floor.'

'Home help, then,' Balbir suggested. 'You can get twenty-four-hour nursing care. One thousand pounds a week.'

'One thousand bhanchod what?'

'We can't leave her home alone all day anymore.' Kulwant removed Jagroop's hand from her thigh. 'Every day I wonder what I'm going to come home to this time.'

'It was only a bit of flooding.'

'But how much did the new carpet cost? Wouldn't a nursing home be cheaper? In the long term?'

'Maybe,' Gurdev said, extracting the comb from his topknot. 'Off the light. On fours . . . please.'

The attempts to oust their mother-in-law from the house had been going on for three months, since the day Kulwant had stormed out of her shop, across Burngreave, and into Balbir's store in tears. 'They lied!' she said, and slapped the creased yellow paper so hard on the counter that the chewing-gum stand lost a couple of sticks. Balbir handed her customer his change over Kulwant's shoulder, then took up the note. It was headed with a stamp belonging to the late friend of the family Dr. Ramasingha, and it stated that without doubt non-conception was due to Jagroop's poor sperm motility and, furthermore, in all likelihood, his wife was 'all there'.

'I was cleaning out Mum's old trunk and I found . . .'

'Don't cry, sister.'

'For thirty years they've let me think it was my fault. All that gossiping behind my back. All those pitiful looks. Just wait till I get my hands on him.'

But this was news to Jagroop, too. It seemed the only person who'd known the truth was Mum and everyone else had been told (by Mum) that the results had only confirmed what they'd always suspected. That contracting mother pox in adulthood had done for Kulwant. That they'd been tricked into marrying Jagroop to a dead end.

'What names she called me. Half-a-woman. False flower.'

'A desert on legs,' Jagroop mused, forgetting himself.

'She called me what?'

'But, darling'—this was the first ever 'darling' of their marriage—'this doesn't change anything. I don't love you any less.'

'What you mean *you* don't—? And take your hands off me! It's your mother I'm going to strangle.'

She didn't confront Mum in the end. Far better, she decided, to remove her from the house, forever. She'd been guilt-tripped into doing every last thing for her—not only her ironing, washing and cooking, but cutting her corns, rubbing Johnson's baby lotion into her armpit every Sunday, for God's sake—and now enough was enough.

'But she's our mum,' Balbir said.

'Do you want to see Jassi ever again? Do you think you will while she's living here? Once she's gone you can talk to Gurdev properly. Like a husband and wife. Without her poisoning your business all the time.'

That night, with Kulwant's words high in her mind, Balbir stole away to her bedroom and logged into Facebook under her pseudonym. She had only one friend: her daughter, Jaswinder. There was no little red subscript number beside the camera icon, so Balbir carefully—as if each click risked a detonation—navigated to some recent photographs, freezing on her favourite, of a grumpy-looking toddler in a 'Frozen' Elsa dress. As Balbir stared at the image, the ball of pain in her stomach grew, swelled, until it seemed to be showing through the folds of her fifty-four-year-old body, choking up her throat. Typing with only her index finger, she sent Jaswinder a message: *hello beti . . . how is zubys cough . . . hope she lots better now. Xxxxx*

All morning Balbir put off making the phone call and setting into motion Kulwant's latest idea. Instead, she checked the takings against the till roll; refilled the cash machine (squatting like a fishwife in her salwar kameez to drag the screeching thing away from the wall); tallied the scratchcards' revenue to the display on the lottery terminal; set aside the PayPoint income; flattened the towers of cardboard boxes and carried them to the recycling bin (avoiding eye contact with the lipsticked ten-year-olds who seemed never to attend school); recast the beer shelves in anticipation of the afternoon alkies (a very different breed from the 6 a.m. ones); bagged up the newspaper returns and sealed them in the rusted iron chest on the forecourt; mopped the floor, wiped the counter and scrubbed the shutters, her greying head by now prickly with sweat. Then, with nothing more to do, she flexed her fingers, sounding arthritic cracks, and dialled from the shop payphone, muffling the receiver with the end of her chunni and holding one hand to her throat, as if that would fix her voice at the lower register.

'Maji? Tusi theek hai? It's Harmohan, from the gurdwara . . .'

As soon as she was off the phone she switched to her mobile and called Kulwant. 'I did it.'

'Good girl. I'll set off now.'

'Are you sure? Be careful.'

'Don't worry,' Kulwant said. 'I've done it before,' she added, which confused Balbir, but before she could say anything Kulwant hung up and perhaps two hours later Gurdev hurtled down from his office above the shop shouting that the Merc had blown up.

'Deal! Deal you pucking idiot!'

'Mum? Mum? We need to talk,' Gurdev said, sitting beside her on the busted square seat cushions of the sofa.

'About what?' She didn't take her eyes off the TV.

'About the car,' Jagroop said.

'I told you. It wasn't me.'

The brothers exchanged looks and Gurdev's forehead constricted as if to say *Leave it to me*.

'But it was you, Mum. They saw you.'

'Who pucking saw me?'

'The neighbours. They saw you carrying the petrol can.'

'I keep telling you. Harmohan from the gurdwara rang to say they needed some petrol for their mower. What is a good Sikh to do?—Arré, I told you to deal—what you to do now, hain?'

'But there is no Harmohan at the gurdwara. And no one from the gurdwara rang. We checked.'

'Are you thinking about Harmohan your neighbour?' Jagroop suggested, placidly, sweetly. 'From the old Attercliffe house?'

Mum, a small, tremendously wrinkled woman with silver hair scraped back into a ratty little tail, turned her glittering black eyes to her younger son. 'No, bhanchod. Because he died. In 1973. And not once did his wife cry.'

'They say the long-term memory starts to compensate,' Kulwant said, ostensibly to Balbir who was standing in the doorway with her, but loud enough for their husbands' ears.

Mum slapped the side of Jagroop's turban. 'I am not going into a home. Over my charred remains will those people come here again. And I did not burn your Mercedes. I was in this room watching those loose women when this desert-island dish you married came running down from the bathroom saying the car was on fire.'

'It's lucky she was here,' Jagroop said, in a tone of protectiveness that made Kulwant soften towards him a little. 'The garage, the whole house could have gone up.'

'It wasn't me.'

'And the flooding?' Gurdev said. 'You were the only one in the house.' (Balbir felt her cheeks start to glow.) 'And phoning round wishing people a happy birthday when it wasn't?'

'I swear that's what my Guru Gobind calendar said.'

'Thirty-five thousand pounds that car cost me.'

'I am not going into any dirty cunting home. So puck choo.'

"The bastards put me in a home!' Mum exclaimed, charging across the peach shagpile of her room in Sheffield Rosewall Accommodation as furiously as her four-year-old hip would allow. One month on and she still sounded shocked.

'How was Mum?' Gurdev asked that night.

'Better,' Balbir said, nodding insistently. 'She didn't throw any chairs at us. And in her own way she said she misses you.'

He pursed his lips across to one side of his face. 'Well, of course I want to see her. But the shops are busy.'

'Of course.' She shuffled a little closer to him, so close he put down his copy of *Des Pardes* and looked right at her. She smiled, hesitantly. 'I was wondering. It's Zubaidah's birthday in a few weeks.' She waited. She looked for some change in his face, for some concession, or even just an acknowledgement that their granddaughter, who had his bow-shaped mouth, his thick brows, was about to turn four.

But he said nothing, not a tremble in his overdyed, stiff facial hair.

'Maybe I could meet her? Just for a few hours. One, even. Maybe?'

'You know how we feel. They're dead to us.'

'Jaswinder's all alone. And Zubaidah's your *granddaughter*. I'm only asking for a short visit. Mum will never find out.'

On the fourth night he agreed to a meeting in a park somewhere in Leicester, where their daughter lived and far away from any aunties who might spy them.

'He even said he'd drive me,' Balbir said, skimming the pages of a toy catalogue with her free hand while on the shop phone to Kulwant. 'What do you think of a tractor? Like in India. One she can ride.'

'Why's he driving you? He might do something to her. Take the train, sister.'

'He wants to. I bet his heart melts when he sees Zuby.'

'He really doesn't—down there, by the eggs, try opening your eyes—he really doesn't seem like the melting type,' Kulwant said and Balbir felt a tiny flutter of worry in the bowl of her stomach.

Less than a week before the trip to Leicester, news came of a fire at the nursing home. The following day Mum returned to the house.

'I'm so sorry,' she said to the pastoral care officer as Gurdev loaded her luggage into the van. 'I really didn't know they were flammable. But I have a history of it, you know. Ask him about his car.'

'The scheming little mad witch!' Kulwant said, snatching the baby lotion from the bathroom cabinet because Mum was now waiting in the lounge, hands raised, armpits exposed. But Balbir was scarcely listening, too befuddled by what this return might mean for her first sight of her daughter and granddaughter in nearly three years.

'It means it's not happening,' Gurdev said in bed.

'Maybe I can go on my own. In the train. I won't stay long.'

'Did you not hear me?'

She lay there watching the still blades of the gold ceiling fan, edges crimped in moonlight, and once Gurdev was snoring she stepped to her wardrobe and held the tractor in its Fisher-Price bag and wept on and off until the alarm bleated and she had to make his tea and get to the shop.

Prank calls, rearranging the furniture, even leaving the gas on for so long their Somali neighbour alerted the fire service: it didn't matter what new tactics Kulwant deployed. The sons refused to return their mother to the home.

'She didn't like it there,' Jagroop said.

'So that means she can blow us all up in our sleep? She'll kill us.'

'She'll kill us,' Kulwant (washing) repeated to Balbir (drying) the following night.

It seemed as if Kulwant had started to believe that Mum really was going senile. 'Maybe we need to stop,' Balbir said, exhausted by the whole thing.

'You mean I have to carry on living with the woman who's made my entire married life hell? Don't you want to see Jassi ever again?'

The door swung open and Gurdev moved to wash his hands at the sink. 'The table needs clearing.'

'Fucking bastard,' Kulwant said.

'Ki keya?'

'Making custard,' Balbir said. 'Would you like?'

'I've worked out how we're going to take care of Mum,' he said, casting the towel onto the worktop. *The hook. Please can't you use the hook?* 'You're both going to do it.'

'Oh, wonderful,' Kulwant said.

'But the shops?' Balbir asked. 'Who'll work the shops? You two?'

'Mein tera baap da naukar ni. So speak some sense once in a while. I've hired a few faujis. One pound fifty every fucking hour so I hope it's worth it. And that you appreciate what all I'm doing for you.'

'What faujis, ji? I don't understand. Where did you find them?'

'What questions! They're from the pind. They were at the gurdwara looking for work. Is that enough? They're coming tomorrow.' He shut the door with a parting: 'Bring the custard upstairs.'

They were all young, the four faujis, none yet thirty, and in pairs they were each allotted a shop to look after.

'Two men to do what one woman has been doing for thirty years,' Kulwant said. 'And how has it happened that I've gone from trying to never see that woman again to spending every hour of my life with her.'

'Jo Rab ne likha,' Balbir said gnomically, tying the belt of her trench coat and checking the pockets for her bus ticket. 'Whatever God has written.'

Gurdev's van wasn't in its spot, and inside the shop only one of the faujis was present. 'Where's your uncle?' she asked, indicating the gold-framed picture of Gurdev above the fag stand.

'Ji, he's gone with chotu to get some samaan. Beers and cigarettes.'

One of his dodgy Eastern European deliveries no doubt, given how late it was. She slid the Closed sign into its plastic hatch. Beside that: 'Only two children at a time please. We're a tidy premises. Debit cards accepted here.' The young man—Manjit, though his fake passport gave some other name—moved out from the counter and began rolling down the blinds on the chiller cabinets and fridges. Balbir dallied until he was in the furthest corner of the store and then balanced the till and removed the money. Which was silly, she knew, because he had all the access he could want during the day. The cash machine was emptied, the lottery terminal reset, the cardboard recycled, the place swept and mopped—and still Gurdev wasn't back.

'You go. I can wait on my own,' she said, lifting the counter flap but not moving through it.

'Uncle told me to wait. To help unload.'

The lights had all been dimmed and the Coke fridge against which he crouched gave off a steady buzz. The veil of gloom allowed her to look at him properly, directly, in a manner that would have been considered immodest in daylight. He was older than she'd first thought: thirty, thirty-five, even. A slim neck gave way to sloping shoulders. There was a covering of dust in his hair, like fine ash. He must've been cleaning out the rear store earlier on. The gloom, generously, also admitted a few words.

'You're from Jandiala?' she asked.

'Ji.'

'Which patti?'

'Saanki. Do you know it?'

'I've heard of it. I only spent a few weeks in Jandiala after my marriage. We're from one of the other ones. Badi patti.'

'I know. My family looks after your land there.'

'Oh . . . good. Thank you,' though she had no idea they still had land there.

'You have good land. It's one of the best plots. Especially now. The new laws. And you should taste the saag you grow. Not that we ever have,' he added hastily, eyes worried.

She moved onto more familiar ground: 'Are you shaadi-shudda?'

'My sisters first. That's why I'm here.'

'Of course. Daughters' weddings are expensive,' she said, suppressing a still-painful image of Jaswinder in a red hijab. 'God willing it will happen.'

'God makes nothing happen,' he said with vehemence, as the van's headlights swerved across the shop window and onto his face.

When she knew that Gurdev would be out collecting another Romanian delivery she cooked saag, throwing in extra mustard seeds—the way people from India like it—and spooned great dollops of it into a plastic Haribo sweet tub. To eat with it, she made four makki-di-rotis.

'Ask him about the land,' Kulwant said, coming into the kitchen to find Mum's corn cream.

'Why?'

'Why not?'

Manjit ate the saag and roti there and then, squatting on a milk crate and using a case of Carlsberg for a table.

'Have you not had saag while you've been here?' she asked.

'Not like this.'

She'd forgotten how Indians ate: he confidently trapped the food in the roti, as if the bread were an extension of his fingers, and then swept it into his mouth as smooth as anything. How clumsy the Indians born of this country seemed ('British-Asians,' did they call themselves?), chasing the sabzi around the bowl and then tentatively, shakily, lifting it towards their lips so that by the time the roti reached their mouths most of the sabzi had spilled anyway. She'd even seen some who used a spoon to load their roti!

'Is something funny?' Manjit asked, paused in his chewing.

'No, no. Carry on. Please. I was just thinking of something. It's not you.'

He used words and phrases she'd not heard for decades, words that no one seemed to have any use for in England. *Lehaaj. Sareeka-pye-chaara. Bahtt.* Why did no one in this country say 'bahtt'? So much more precise than 'doorr'. When she asked if he had enough saag: *Badu*, he'd said. Such a simple, nothing word, yet it took her back forty years, to her mother buying gourds in the bazaar while she and her two sisters marvelled at the green hawks overhead. *More, pehnji?* the vendor asked. *Badu, badu*, her mother had said. *It's already more than I know what to do with.*

'So who looks after the saag in Jandiala now?'

'Ji?'

'Our land. Who looks after it now you're here?'

'Oh. Aand-gwaand.' Another one she'd not heard in years. 'But people we trust. There's nothing for you to worry about.'

'I just want to make sure it's in good hands. Since you said it's worth a lot of money now.'

'Yes. Since the new laws. You get four times the value. And yours is in prime position. Commercial developers would pay a fortune for it.'

'That's so strange. It's hard to believe.'

He explained that it had started as a sweetening policy to get the agri-vote on Modi's side. Because there'd been a lot of feeling, you see, especially in Punjab, that the BJP was anti-farmer. But the policy coincided with a huge surge in Punjab's urban economy and developers were now desperate for land to build on, especially land bordering a road that leads to the city.

'Like yours,' he finished.

As he washed the Haribo tub and handed it back to her, she said, 'Don't mention the saag to your uncle. He might think I'm spoiling his staff,' she added, laughing a little to disguise her awkwardness.

'Ji.'

'Or our conversation. About the land.'

He looked at her for perhaps a moment too long. He must be thinking, What other secrets did this woman keep from her husband? She felt herself start to blush.

'The Right to Fair Compensation and Transparency in Land Acquisition, Rehabilitation and Resettlement Act, 2013,' Kulwant said, reading the words on the monitor over Balbir's shoulder. Then, taking over the mouse: 'For direct purchase of land . . . including farmers . . . rural areas . . . compensation fixed at four times the land value. That's interesting.'

'Have you got what you want now?' Balbir asked, eager to switch to her Facebook page and see if any new photos had been uploaded.

'Hm. Maybe,' Kulwant said, and for the next three nights she teased information out of her husband. On the fourth, she waited until Jagroop advanced his hand onto her thigh. He seemed shocked that it wasn't shoved away again and braved going a little further down.

'Please, na,' she said. 'You're pretending only. You don't find me attractive anymore.'

She turned round, showing him her back which he was quick to press up against, his hand on the end of her nightie, his topknot swinging into the rim of her vision. 'You're still beautiful, darling. So very beautiful. I tell you every night.'

'And I keep telling you. All these years in that shop have turned me into a hag. How many more will I have to endure?'

'You're so hotty-hotty, darling.'

Kulwant grimaced—he wasn't listening—and stayed his hand before it reached her knickers. 'Just tell me, na. Will we ever have enough money to sell up? I want only to spend some more time with you . . . jaan.'

'Oh we will, we will,' he said, trying his hand again, frustrated by her again.

'You keep saying that, but when? We don't have anything apart from the shop. No properties, no huge savings. No'—she risked it—'no land.'

'But we do have land,' he said, so voluntarily, so openly that she wished she'd just asked him in the first place and not gone through this nightly charade.

'Oh, back in Jandiala? But it's not worth anything. It won't get us far, I mean.' She slid her thighs apart and his hand dived in and she felt his beard against her neck.

'It's worth a lot now, you know. There's been a change in the law.'

'Really? How much?'

'About fifteen crore.'

She gawped in the dark.

'Bhaji wants to sell it'—his hand rubbed her bum—'and once we have our share we can sell the shop and spend as much time together as we want . . . Do you like me doing that, baby?'

'Yes, yes, very much. But surely we won't get it all. What would we do with all that money?'

'We will get it all, darling.' He chuckled against her ear. 'Every last penny for you and me.'

Her knickers were off—how had that happened?—but she supposed she'd now have to go through with it. His reward, she told herself.

Manjit returned from the tiny toilet-cum-kitchen and held up the washed Haribo tub like a game-show assistant, to show that this time he'd left no smears of sabzi on the bottom.

'Well done,' Balbir said, stowing the tub in her shoulder bag, stowing it right deep down. Hiding it, really. She noticed his long mouth tighten to a frown.

'You don't have to keep giving me food. If it's going to make trouble for you.'

Samasi'a. Not since she was a betrothed girl about to leave India had she heard that word. She wasn't even confident that, prior to his using it just now, she'd have been able to recall what the proper word for 'to experience trouble' was. How much of herself she'd lost, to time, to this country. And for what gain?

'It's no *trouble* for me. But if you don't like my cooking you only have to say.'

'It's the best meal I have all week.'

'Good. Let's leave it at that.' And then: 'Your uncle's thinking of selling the land.'

His forehead—smooth, unblemished (could a forehead be described as perfect?)—narrowed, as if asking why she was telling him this.

'I thought you should know. As you looked after it,' which sounded like the most ridiculous thing she'd ever uttered in her life.

'Well, he'll get a lot for it.'

'Fifteen crore,' she admitted. Was there anything she wouldn't disclose?

'And all tax free. It's pays to lie, doesn't it?'

'I don't think you should call my husband a liar.'

'They all do it. Not a penny do they pay in tax.' He shook his head, as if in wonder at what some people can get away with. 'The rich know all the schemes.'

'That's enough,' she said. 'If you can't say anything good about him then let's just wait for him in silence.'

While they waited she remembered she hadn't topped up the cash machine. Squatting, knees flared so the apron of her kameez hung between her legs, she wrapped her arms around the machine's wide grey base and pulled. It seemed heavier today, or maybe she was only getting older. Manjit crouched opposite and said he'd do it.

'I can manage,' she said, clearly not managing.

He circled his arms around the thing, and they were like two people attempting to shift a tree. This close he even carried a faint smell of India, some old dark smell that made her want to weep and inhale all that was around his neck. They forced the machine away from the wall so Balbir could get to the safe hidden in its hollow stand and add the new cash. What a lie those 'We don't have access to the machine' and 'No cash kept overnight' stickers were! As they crouched and pushed it back against the wall Manjit's hand—accidentally?—touched hers, rested on top of her fingers, over the middle one that was singly ringed. Balbir, gently, as if nothing had happened, took her hand back and told herself that the tingling shooting up her arm was only the hum of the Coke fridge. Because she was nearly twenty years older than him for God's sake. Old enough to be his amma. Old enough to know better.

'That's one heavy machine,' he said.

'Hm? Oh yes. Heavy. Very heavy.'

He smiled, as if perplexed. It must have been an accident. Definitely an accident. Why else would he look so confused? Why else would he be walking round to her? With his words and his smell. Oh his smell. His smell and his lips and please God help me but yes his kiss.

'You're looking worried, ji,' Kulwant said to Jagroop, sliding her just-shaven legs under the duvet, placing one calf across his knee. Any higher and her back gave a twinge.

'Hm?' he said. 'Oh no. No. Come here.'

'You sure? It's been three nights you've been like this. Not talking. Thinking. You never think. I can tell something's the matter. I am your wife.'

'Uff, woman, I said it's nothing.'

Huffing, she wriggled to her side of the bed.

She heard him sigh. 'We've had a letter.'

She rose onto her elbows. 'What letter?'

He brought a photocopy up with him the next night, a formal-looking communication on strong white paper. Running along the

171

top, about two inches wide, the lion-and-scrolls imprimatur of the Government of India Tax Commission, Investigative Office.

Dear S. Gurdev S. Aulak and S. Jagroop S. Aulak (sons/o S. Bachittar S. Aulak)

A complaint (ref. no. 877D3G#1) has been registered with regards to plots 7A, 7B and 7E on the New Cantt Road in the town of Jandiala of district Jalandhar in relation to the selling of these three plots. We believe the documents for these plots are with you and that you are therefore the rightful owners of these plots. However, these plots have not been registered with the Government of India Tax Commission (Punjab State Division) which is legally required for you to do so before any sale, trade or exchange can be made. The penalty for completing a sale without informing the GITC (PSD) is potentially custodial. To register your land please visit our website at indiataxoffice. gov.org.in/rurallandregistration (we recommend you have your bank details with you).

The letter continued for another paragraph, giving the contact details and auto-signature of a Major Jarnail Singh, followed by some words on the role and remit of the GITC, which Kulwant had cribbed from its website. She was particularly pleased by her use of the word 'custodial'. Her first draft had simply and crudely declared 'The penalty is jail' until she went over it all again with a dictionary and a thesaurus at her side and the letter templates she'd snagged from the Internet.

When she showed the letter to Balbir, Balbir read it and immediately handed it back, as if it were a cursed object. 'I can't believe you wrote that. I can't believe you sent it.'

'I told you I would.'

'They'll kill us.'

'Isn't this a form of death? They've robbed us both of kids. We've worked like dogs for them.'

'It's not that bad,' Balbir said. 'There are worse ways to have lived.'

'Lived. Exactly. We should still be living.'

Balbir pulled her knees to her chest, revealing orange-stockinged feet ('No heating after nine,' Mum insisted, in her electric blanket).

'I know you're scared. Think of Jassi. Of Zuby.'

'We won't get away with it. We can't.'

Sitting on the bed, Kulwant put her hand on Balbir's knee. 'We can try. Let's give them a run for their money at least.' Then: 'How are you? Better?'

Balbir shrank back against the headboard, as if distancing herself from the lies she'd been telling, because it had been two whole weeks since she'd been to the shop, feigning illness—'Womens' problems,' she'd said to Gurdev, who'd made an odd grunting noise and probed no further.

Kulwant despatched three more letters over the next month, each growing in impatience and the last mentioning a 'seizing of land rights if registration not completed in a timely fashion.'

'Harami bhanchod bastards!' Jagroop said, hitting the letter with the back of his hand.

'All this shor-tamasha. Why don't you just register it?'

'Why don't you once in a while try talking some sense? Do you know how much tax we'll have to pay if we do that? Sixty percent. Sixty bhanchod percent.'

'Hm. Well. That is a lot.'

'Isn't it?' he said, sneeringly. 'There'll be no you-and-me-time if we get lumbered with that. You can stay in that shop the rest of your life.'

'What do other people do?'

'How am I supposed to know. Bhaji's looking into it.'

She reached over his belly for the iPhone beside his blood pressure pills.

'What are you doing?'

'We can do our own research, can't we? It is our money as well.'

He wrested the phone back but his face conceded that she had a point and he brought up his home page, a search engine. 'What shall I type?'

'Oh, how should I know? You know I'm no good with these things.'

'Land tax in India?'

'Hm,' she said, shrugging. 'Something like that. Like "avoiding rural land tax in Punjab for foreigners" or something. Maybe.'

With a down-scroll of the screen here, and a well-placed question there, she led him to the sites advising on the least shady way to evade rural land taxes. She knew their content pretty much by rote and the main advice on them all was practically identical: 'Hide your assets . . . Spread your wealth . . . Spouse, adult children are good . . . Don't lump it all together under one name . . . Sell after six months . . .'

'What's all that mean, ji?' Kulwant asked.

He bookmarked the page and killed the screen. 'Doesn't matter.'

The afternoon the accountant arrived, Balbir spilled the tea because her hands were trembling so much. She fetched a cloth and wiped the puddle away, avoiding all eye contact with Gurdev and the suited Hindu at his side—Gujurati even, going by his name—a sixty-something with trimmed white hair. She returned to the kitchen, her face hot with fear.

'Calm down,' Kulwant whispered.

'What calm down. We're going to be found out. Oh God, where will we go?' She put her hip to the sink and covered her face with her hands.

But the accountant left after a couple of hours, taking with him a blue bag of Balbir's samosas, and nothing more happened until one evening, ten days later, when Gurdev and Jagroop called them both into the lounge. On the mahogany coffee table was a set of bound papers, the front page folded back so the title couldn't be read.

'Sign these,' Gurdev said, holding out a pen.

'Oh? What are they?' Kulwant asked.

'Since when do you backchat?'

'Just sign it,' Jagroop said.

'But why can't I ask what it is?' Kulwant pressed.

Jagroop clutched her upper arm and pushed her forward. 'Sign. I'll explain later.'

So she did, Gurdev turning the pages—'Here, here . . . here . . . and here'—and then Balbir, wiping her damp, dishwashing hands on the end of her chunni, did too.

They had six months to sell the land that was now in their names. There'd be a twenty percent penalty, Kulwant explained, because of some unavoidable early selling charge, but they couldn't risk waiting longer. No doubt Gurdev and Jagroop were planning to sell up as soon as the half year was over and before the tax people would notice. There was, however, the problem of how to sell land in the bureaucratic maze that was India.

'That is a problem,' Kulwant said.

'A samasi'a,' Balbir replied, absently, and Kulwant looked across, by degrees, as if absorbing this strange past-life word.

Balbir had not been alone with Manjit since the kiss: there'd been the fake illness, then for a week she had timed her arrival at the shop to coincide with Gurdev's return from any deliveries. It had never occurred to her, she realised as she passed the van's empty parking space and entered the store, that he might tell anyone of her shame. She'd just seemed to know that he wouldn't. And this realisation—his discretion, her wantonness—only made her feel worse. What kind of gutter woman must he think her to be? He was refilling the cigarette

lines—Lambert & Butler, Rothmans—getting ready for the next day
when he looked back and saw her standing there. He moved out from
the counter, throwing the cellophane into the potato-sack bin, and
she waited for him to pass before starting to till up. She kept her eyes
on the money, counting, recounting, distracted. He was deep in the
middle aisle, mopping the linoleum. She bagged up the notes; sorted
the cash machine, the PayPoint and lottery terminals; then adjusted
her chunni over her shoulder and approached.

'I need your help,' she said.

Later, Kulwant locked the door to Balbir's room. 'But what if he tells?'

'What other option do we have? And he won't tell.'

'You don't know that.'

'There's five lakhs in it for him.'

'Still, pehnji. Are you sure he's trustworthy?'

'Yes.'

Perhaps she'd been too adamant, too immediate in her defence,
because Kulwant sat beside her and asked with quiet suspicion, 'How
can you be so certain?'

Balbir said nothing, only looked at the wall, and Kulwant put a
hand to the small of Balbir's back as if to relay a promise that she'd
ask nothing more.

For a quick sale they stuck a price of twelve crore on the land—an
alarming one million pounds even after everything was deducted—
and asked Manjit to ensure that not a word was mentioned in any
newspaper or on any website, nowhere anyone from the pind might
see it and call Gurdev and Jagroop. Instead, Manjit contacted a close
friend who knew someone who, in turn, knew someone who'd had
dealings with a man at the Punjab Development Authority. Everyone
in this chain insisted on his own one-lakh cut of the sale, but it meant
that within a month Manjit was on the phone to buyers at three of

the biggest commercial developers in the district, all of whom were panting to make the purchase.

'How long will it take?' Balbir asked.

'I don't know.' He placed a USB stick on the ice-cream fridge between them. 'There are some papers on here you need to print out and sign. Your sister-in-law, too.'

'More forms,' she said, zipping the stick into the inside pocket of her handbag. 'Thank you.'

'Where will you go?' he asked suddenly.

She was surprised. He'd never asked questions. 'We haven't decided. I want to see my daughter and granddaughter. In Leicester.'

'You might need to go further.'

'Yes, well, like I said, we haven't decided.' Then: 'You must think I'm a very besharam, loose woman.'

'The opposite. I think you're very brave.'

The door buzzed and Gurdev came in and maybe he witnessed something difficult and intimate in the way she had to force her eyes away from Manjit's face, because he said not a word on the drive home and the next morning Kulwant spent half an hour applying concealer to the bruise around Balbir's mouth.

A completion date was agreed upon—still some five weeks before the six-month deadline—and on the night before the funds were to be transferred Balbir arrived at the shop to close up as usual.

'You won't be able to keep it quiet for much longer,' Manjit said. 'As soon as the money's handed over someone will talk.'

She nodded. 'We've made plans.'

She walked down the aisles, lingering, staring at the large white squares that made up the ceiling. How many years? How many hours? She'd given her life to this little shop. Her life. Would anyone notice she'd gone? That the little Indian woman from the shop—what *was* her name?—was no longer there?

'Will your cut be deducted before the money's moved?' she asked, circling back to him.

'Ji. I thought that would be easier.'

She nodded again, looked round the shop one final time, and back to his face. She tidied some grey hairs away from her cheek and rose up onto her toes and kissed him very deliberately, very fully, and very slowly on the mouth.

'What's with the suitcase?' Jagroop asked as Kulwant wheeled the gleaming box to the van. 'We're only going for the day.'

'Supplies. Food. Mum's medications.'

It had taken several weeks of planning, this trip to Hull, once they'd got the completion date. They'd considered absconding in the night, then in the day, or saying they were only going to the gurdwara, even concocting an elaborate plot involving a choking fit and a late-night dash to hospital. But there was always the question of how to get their belongings, noiselessly, inconspicuously, past their shrewd-eyed mother-in-law.

'Let's not, then,' Kulwant said. 'Let's do it in plain daylight.'

Hints were dropped, there were throwaway mentions over roti of how wonderful a trip to the beach would be, that the sea air would do Mum no end of good. They spoke of a family day out, a day trip, and showed their husbands how cheaply it could all be done. None of it was taken seriously. Only when Balbir chanced upon news of a trade fair in a city called Hull ('Cheapest prices guaranteed.' 'Make contacts from all over Europe!') did Gurdev start to take grudging notice and finally agree to the idea of time away from the shops. Balbir moved the completion date back by one week so it fell on the same day as the fair, and from then until the morning they left she lay awake at night listening to her heart thump thump thump.

They took the van up the M18, the M62, Gurdev, Jagroop and Mum in the front while Balbir and Kulwant sat swaying on the rear wheel arches, Kulwant holding on to their suitcase. It seemed like every minute Kulwant would check their bank balance on her phone and glance over to Balbir and shake her head.

'Did you register us for the fair?' Jagroop asked over the noise of Sunrise Radio.

'Ji!' Kulwant replied. 'It starts at one. Maybe let's go to the beach first?'

'Who cares about the beach?'

'For Mum! The sea air!'

They found a car park across from the water and the van doors were opened to let the women out. Balbir reached back in for the suitcase.

'We're not carrying that bhanchod thing around,' Gurdev said.

'But—we might need it. I'll wheel it.'

Gurdev slammed the doors shut. 'If you need it, you can come back for it. Here–' and he passed the keys for her to put in her handbag. As the five of them headed for the lift Kulwant, pushing Mum in her wheelchair, kept looking back, memorising the van's location.

It was a blustery day, the sky a grey dome, and their coats remained fully buttoned up, right to their chins.

'Who's pucking idea was this?' Mum said as they lifted the front wheels of her chair onto the promenade.

'It's good for you, Mum,' Jagroop said. 'It's a different kind of air here. Cleaner.'

They made it to the pier, then up it, Gurdev striding ahead, as if on his way to fight the sea, and still the phone showed no increase in their bank balance.

'What now?' Gurdev said, turning round at the candy-striped railing. 'There's the sea. We've seen it.'

'Something to eat, maybe?' Balbir suggested, chin-jutting towards the tables in what looked to be some sort of indoor viewing point. 'We could eat the paratha we brought.'

Kulwant made sure to lead them in, choosing a spot folded into a corner, away from the windows. 'Less noisy for Mum.'

Paratha were unfoiled and handed round, with achaar and butter. A flask of tea. As Balbir served everyone a second cup she noticed Kulwant looking at her phone with lips starting to part, as if in awe, and it took all the strength Balbir had to steady her hand and keep pouring the tea.

'I need the toilet,' Kulwant said, rising slowly from the table. 'Pehnji?'

'Why you both—?'

'Women's,' Kulwant said and Jagroop bent back to his food. 'Pehnji?' she said again and this time Balbir stood and picked up her handbag. She remained standing for a while, watching the three of them eat, watching Gurdev, her husband, fixing this image in her mind. Kulwant touched her sleeve and Balbir nodded and followed her through the room.

'Where are they?' Gurdev asked. Twenty minutes had passed.

'Women's problems,' Jagroop said, as if to elucidate.

Ten more minutes and Gurdev got up onto his big flat feet and located the toilets. He waited until the door opened and a middle-aged blonde woman came out, bent under a huge backpack.

'Is my wife in there?'

'I don't know. What she look like?'

'Indian.'

'Then no.'

He tried Balbir's phone, Kulwant's—voicemails both. 'Where the hell are they?' he said, back at the table. 'The fair starts in forty-five minutes.'

'Lost your wives?' Mum said. 'What kind of men are you?'

'Hang on,' Jagroop said, going to his phone. He had an app, in a cloud, he added, confusingly, and Kulwant's phone was synced up.

'Give me a minute. They're probably shopping.' He used his fingers to zoom in. 'The harbour? The port?' He looked to his brother. 'Maybe their phone was stolen? Do you think they've been kidnapped? Shall we call the police?'

Then Gurdev's phone rang. It was the sarpanch—the leader—of Jandiala calling to congratulate him on the amazing sale of his land.

They made it to the port, wheeling their mother, but the ferry had already detached from the harbour and a volume of scummy greenish water was widening between them.

'Is that them?' Jagroop said, pointing to the rear of the deck.

'BALBIR!' Gurdev called.

'Clever little bitches,' Mum said in what sounded almost like admiration.

On board, Balbir and Kulwant huddled together against the railing, the wind flapping their chunnis across their faces. Tears stung. Behind them, in her 'Frozen' Elsa dress, Zubaidah spun the wheels of her red tractor and Jaswinder watched, chin and mouth tucked into the upturned collar of her coat.

'They've seen us,' Balbir said, shivering.

'It's too late. It doesn't matter.' Then: 'Where's your bag?'

Balbir opened it and Kulwant removed the van keys and over-armed them into the water. Gurdev and Jagroop were shouting, gesticulating, their words swirling in the wind.

'What are they saying?' Balbir asked.

'I don't know but'—Kulwant held Balbir's hand—'ready?'

And together: 'PUCK CHOO!'

Athena Farrokhzad was born in 1983 and lives in Stockholm. She is a poet, literary critic, translator, playwright, and teacher of creative writing. Her first volume of poetry, *Vitsvit*, was published in 2013 by Albert Bonniers Förlag (translated by Jennifer Hayashida and published as *White Blight* by Argos Books). In 2016, her second volume of poetry, *Trado*, which was written together with the Romanian poet Svetlana Cârstean and from which these poems are excerpted, was published.

Jennifer Hayashida is a writer, translator, and visual artist. Her most recent projects include translation from the Swedish of Athena Farrokhzad's *White Blight* (Argos Books, 2015) and Karl Larsson's *Form/Force* (Black Square Editions, 2015), named one of the ten best books of 2015 by *Partisan*. She is director of the Asian American Studies Program at Hunter College, CUNY, and serves on the board of the Asian American Writers' Workshop.

(15)

ATHENA FARROKHZAD
TRANSLATED FROM THE SWEDISH BY JENNIFER HAYASHIDA

Svetlana said: If you want to write about loss someone you love must leave so you understand the meaning of the word.

Svetlana said: When someone leaves she has already ceased being the one you love.

Svetlana said: The one you love will stay with you, regardless of the havoc you wreak.

(16)

ATHENA FARROKHZAD
TRANSLATED FROM THE SWEDISH BY JENNIFER HAYASHIDA

I said: The more important it is to me that what you say is true, the
more I doubt it. Once I was as certain as a returning bird of passage.
I never wavered in my goal, never confused a rest stop with a des-
tination, never turned around for a forgotten bundle, did not allow
myself visions when, parched, I hovered above the desert. I was the
master of a vast horizon, a clear, cloudless longing. Now I understand
how dangerous it is to not prepare for the loss.

(33)

ATHENA FARROKHZAD
TRANSLATED FROM THE SWEDISH BY JENNIFER HAYASHIDA

I said: Where I come from we die for foreign enemies and domestic traitors during days history does not bother making note of.

Svetlana said: Where I come from our inherited talent for dying has made us survivors.

I said: Where I come from a hostage drama is played out between us and history, where no ransom can alter the outcome.

Svetlana said: Where I come from we reach our expiration date before we get to the refrigerator case.

I said: Where I come from our tongues are greased and our elbows sharp, or if it is the other way around, or if the wind which blows away history's injuries has passed, without us noticing any difference.

Svetlana said: Where you come from you struggle for what became our ruin with a fire only those whose struggles have not yet fallen into ruin can struggle.

Samanta Schweblin was born in Buenos Aires in 1978. Her collection of short stories *Pájaros en la boca* won the Premio Literario Casa de las Américas. In 2010 she was named a *Granta* Best Young Spanish-Language Novelist. In 2012 she was awarded the Premio Juan Rulfo for her story *Un hombre sin suerte*, and in 2014 she won the Premio Konex-Diploma for her career as a short-story writer.

Megan McDowell has translated books by many Latin American and Spanish authors, and stories she translated have appeared in the *New Yorker*, the *Paris Review*, *Tin House*, *Harper's*, *Vice*, and the *Virginia Quarterly Review*. She lives in Santiago, Chile.

An Unlucky Man

SAMANTA SCHWEBLIN
TRANSLATED FROM THE SPANISH BY MEGAN MCDOWELL

The day I turned eight, my sister—who absolutely always had to be the center of attention—swallowed an entire cup of bleach. Abi was three. First she smiled, maybe a little disgusted at the nasty taste; then her face crumpled in a frightened grimace of pain. When Mom saw the empty cup hanging from Abi's hand, she turned as white as my sister.

"Abi-my-god," was all Mom said. "Abi-my-god," and it took her a few seconds longer to spring into action.

She shook Abi by the shoulders, but my sister didn't respond. She yelled, but Abi still didn't react. She ran to the phone and called Dad, and when she came running back Abi was still standing there, the cup just dangling from her hand. Mom grabbed the cup and threw it into the sink. She opened the fridge, took out the milk, and poured a glass. She stood looking at the glass, then looked at Abi, then at the glass, and finally she dropped the glass into the sink as well. Dad worked very close by and got home quickly, but Mom still had time to do the whole show with the glass of milk again before he pulled up in the car and started honking the horn and yelling.

Mom ran out of the house in a flash, with Abi clutched to her chest. The front door, the gate, and the car doors were all flung open.

There was more horn honking and Mom, who was already sitting in the car, started to cry. Dad had to shout my name twice before I understood that I was the one who was supposed to close up.

We drove the first ten blocks in less time than it took me to close the car door and fasten my seat belt. But when we got to the main avenue, the traffic was practically stopped. Dad honked the horn and shouted out the window, "We have to get to the hospital! We have to get to the hospital!" The cars around us maneuvered and miraculously let us pass, but a couple of cars up we had to start the whole operation all over again. Dad braked in the traffic, stopped honking the horn, and pounded his head against the steering wheel. I had never seen him do such a thing. There was a moment of silence, and then he sat up and looked at me in the rearview mirror. He turned around and said to me:

"Take off your underpants."

I was wearing my school uniform. All my underwear was white, but I wasn't exactly thinking about that just then, and I couldn't understand Dad's request. I pressed my hands into the seat to support myself better. I looked at Mom, who shouted:

"Take off your damned underpants!"

I took them off. Dad grabbed them out of my hands. He rolled down the window, went back to honking the horn, and started waving my underpants out the window. He raised them high while he yelled and kept honking, and it seemed that everyone on the avenue turned around to look at them. My underpants were small, but they were also very white. An ambulance a block behind us turned on its siren, caught up with us quickly, and started clearing a path. Dad kept on waving the underpants until we reached the hospital.

They left the car by the ambulances and jumped out. Without waiting, Mom ran into the hospital with Abi. I wasn't sure whether I should get out or not: I didn't have any underpants on and I wanted to find out where Dad had left them, but he was already out of the car and slamming the door, his hands empty.

"Come on, come on," said Dad.

He opened my door and helped me out. He gave my shoulder a few pats as we walked into the emergency room. Mom emerged from a doorway at the back and signaled to us. I was relieved to see she was talking again, giving explanations to the nurses.

"Stay here," said Dad, and he pointed to some orange chairs on the other side of the main waiting area.

I sat. Dad went into the consulting room with Mom and I waited for a while. I don't know how long, but it felt like a long time. I pressed my knees together tightly and thought about everything that had happened so quickly, and about the possibility that any of the kids from school had seen the spectacle with my underpants. When I sat up straight, my jumper stretched and my bare bottom touched part of the plastic seat. Sometimes the nurse went in or out of the consulting room and I could hear my parents arguing. At one point I craned my neck and caught a glimpse of Abi moving restlessly on one of the cots, and I knew that, at least for today, she wasn't going to die. And I still had to wait.

Then a man came and sat down next to me. I don't know where he came from; I hadn't noticed him before.

"How's it going?" he asked.

I thought about saying "Very well," which is what Mom always said if someone asked her that, even if she'd just told me and my sister that we were driving her insane.

"OK," I said.

"Are you waiting for someone?"

I thought about it. I wasn't really waiting for anyone; at least, it wasn't what I *wanted* to be doing right then. So I shook my head, and he said:

"Why are you sitting in the waiting room, then?"

I understood it was a great contradiction. He opened a small bag he had on his lap and rummaged a bit, unhurried. Then he took a pink slip of paper from his wallet.

"Here it is. I knew I had it somewhere."

The paper was printed with the number 92.

"It's good for an ice cream. My treat," he said.

I told him no. You shouldn't accept things from strangers.

"But it's free, I won it."

"No." I looked straight ahead and we sat in silence.

"Suit yourself," he said, without getting angry.

He took a magazine from his bag and started to fill in a crossword puzzle. The door to the consulting room opened again and I heard Dad say, "I will not condone such nonsense." That's Dad's clincher for ending almost any argument, but the man didn't seem to hear it.

"It's my birthday," I said.

It's my birthday, I repeated to myself. *What should I do?*

The man held the pen to mark a box on the puzzle and looked at me in surprise. I nodded without looking at him, aware that I had his attention again.

"But . . ." he said, and he closed the magazine. "Sometimes I just don't understand women. If it's your birthday, why are you in a hospital waiting room?"

He was an observant man. I straightened up again in my seat and I saw that, even then, I barely came up to his shoulders. He smiled and I smoothed my hair. And then I said:

"I'm not wearing any underpants."

I don't know why I said it. It's just that it *was* my birthday and I *wasn't* wearing underpants, and I couldn't stop thinking about those two circumstances. He was still looking at me. Maybe he was startled or offended, and I understood that, though it wasn't my intention, there was something vulgar about what I had just said.

190

"But it's your birthday," he said.

I nodded.

"It's not fair. A person can't just go around without underpants when it's her birthday."

"I know," I said emphatically, because now I understood just how Abi's whole display was a personal affront to me.

He sat for a moment without saying anything. Then he looked toward the big windows that looked out onto the parking lot.

"I know where to get you some underpants," he said.

"Where?"

"Problem solved." He stowed his things and stood up.

I hesitated. Precisely because I wasn't wearing underpants, but also because I didn't know if he was telling the truth. He looked toward the front desk and waved one hand at the attendants.

"We'll be right back," he said, and he pointed to me. "It's her birthday." And then I thought, *Oh please Jesus, don't let him say anything about my underpants*, but he didn't: he opened the door and winked at me, and then I knew I could trust him.

We went out to the parking lot. Standing up, I barely cleared his waist. Dad's car was still next to the ambulances, and a policeman was circling it, annoyed. I kept looking over at the policeman, and he watched us walk away. The air wrapped around my legs and rose, making a tent out of my uniform. I had to hold it down while I walked, keeping my legs awkwardly close together.

He turned around to see if I was following him, and he saw me fighting with my skirt.

"We'd better keep close to the wall."

"I want to know where we're going."

"Don't get persnickety with me now, darling."

We crossed the avenue and went into a shopping center. It was an uninviting place, and I was pretty sure Mom didn't go there. We walked to the back toward a gigantic clothing store. Before we went in he said to me, "Don't get lost," and gave me his hand, which was cold and very soft. He waved to the cashiers with the same gesture he'd made toward the desk attendants when we left the hospital, but no one responded. We walked through the aisles. In addition to dresses, pants, and shirts, there were work clothes: hard hats, yellow overalls like those the trash collectors wore, smocks for cleaning ladies, plastic boots, and even some tools. I wondered if he bought his clothes there and if he would use any of those things in his job, and then I also wondered what his name was.

"Here we are," he said.

We were surrounded by tables of underwear for men and women. Right in front of me was a large bin full of giant underpants, bigger than any I'd seen before, and they were only three pesos each. With one of those pairs of underpants, they could have made three for someone my size.

"Not those," he said. "Here." And he led me a little farther to a section with smaller sizes. "Look at all the underpants they have . . . Which will you choose, my lady?"

I looked around a little. Almost all of them were white or pink. I pointed to a white pair, one of the few that didn't have a bow on them.

"These," I said. "But I can't pay for them."

He came a little closer and said into my ear:

"That doesn't matter."

"Are you the owner?"

"No. It's your birthday."

I smiled.

"But we have to find better ones. We need to be sure."

"OK, darling," I ventured.

"Don't say 'darling,'" he said. "I'll get persnickety." And he imitated me holding down my skirt in the parking lot.

192

He made me laugh. When he finished clowning around he held out two closed fists in front of me, and he stayed just like that until I understood; I touched the right one. He opened it: empty.

"You can still choose the other one."

I touched his other hand. It took me a moment to realize it was a pair of underpants because I had never seen black ones before. And they were for girls because they had white hearts on them, so small they looked like dots, and Hello Kitty's face was on the front, right where there was usually that bow Mom and I don't like at all.

"You'll have to try them on," he said.

I held the underpants to my chest. He gave me his hand again and we went toward the changing rooms, which looked empty. We peered in. He said he didn't know if he could go with me because they were for women only. He said I would have to go alone. It was logical because, unless it's someone you know very well, it's not good for people to see you in your underpants. But I was afraid of going into the dressing room alone. Or something worse: coming out and finding him gone.

"What's your name?" I asked.

"I can't tell you that."

"Why not?

He knelt down. Then he was almost my height, or maybe I was a couple of inches taller.

"Because I'm cursed."

"Cursed? What's cursed?"

"A woman who hates me said that the next time I say my name, I'm going to die."

I thought it might be another joke, but he said it very seriously.

"You could write it down for me."

"Write it down?"

"If you wrote it you wouldn't say it, you'd be writing it. And if I know your name I can call for you and I won't be so scared to go into the dressing room alone."

"But we can't be sure. What if this woman thinks writing my name is the same as saying it? What if what she really meant was letting someone else know, putting my name out into the world in any way?"

"But how would she know?"

"People don't trust me, and I'm the unluckiest man in the world."

"I don't believe you. There's no way she'd find out."

"I know what I'm talking about."

Together, we looked at the underpants in my hands. It occurred to me that my parents might be finished by now.

"But it's my birthday," I said.

And maybe I did it on purpose. At the time I felt I did: my eyes filled up with tears. Then he hugged me. It was a very fast movement; he crossed his arms behind my back and squeezed me so tight my face pressed into his chest. Then he let me go, took out his magazine and pen, and wrote something on the right margin of the cover. Then he tore it off and folded it three times before handing it to me.

"Don't read it," he said, and he stood up and pushed me gently toward the dressing room.

I passed four empty cubicles and kept going. Before gathering my courage and entering the fifth, I put the paper into the pocket of my jumper and turned to look at him, and we smiled at each other.

I tried on the underpants. They were perfect. I lifted up my jumper so I could see just how good they looked. They were so, so very perfect. They fit incredibly well, and because they were black, Dad would never ask me for them so he could wave them out the window behind the ambulance. And even if he did, I wouldn't be so embarrassed if my classmates saw. "Just look at the underpants *that* girl has," they'd all think. "Now those are some perfect underpants."

I realized I couldn't take them off now. And I realized something else: they didn't have a security tag. They had a little mark where the tag would usually go, but there was no alarm. I stood a moment longer looking at myself in the mirror, and then I couldn't stand it any longer and I took out the little paper, opened it, and read it.

I came out of the dressing room and he wasn't where I had left him, but he was a little farther down, beside the bathing suits. He looked at me, and when he saw I wasn't carrying the underpants he winked, and I was the one who took his hand. This time he held onto me tighter; we walked together toward the exit.

I trusted that he knew what he was doing. That a cursed man who had the world's worst luck knew how to do these things. We passed the line of registers at the main entrance. One of the security guards looked at us and adjusted his belt. He would surely think the nameless man was my dad, and I felt proud.

We passed the sensors at the exit and went into the mall, and we kept walking in silence all the way back to the avenue. That was when I saw Abi, alone, standing in the middle of the hospital parking lot. And I saw Mom, on our side of the street, looking around frantically. Dad was also coming from the parking lot and was headed toward us. He was following fast behind the policeman who'd been looking at his car before, and who was now pointing at us. Everything happened very quickly. Dad saw us, yelled my name, and a few seconds later that policeman and two others who came out of nowhere were already on top of us. The unlucky man let go of me, but I held my hand suspended toward him for a few seconds. They surrounded him and pushed him roughly. They asked him what he was doing, they asked him his name, but he didn't answer. Mom hugged me and examined me head to toe. She had my white underpants dangling from her right hand. Then, patting me all over, she noticed I was wearing a different pair. She lifted my jumper in a single movement: it was such a rude and vulgar act, right there in front of everyone, that I jerked away and had to take a few steps backward to keep from falling down. The unlucky man looked at me and I looked at him. When Mom saw the black underpants she screamed, "Son of a bitch, son of a bitch," and Dad lunged at him and tried to punch him. The cops moved to separate them.

I fished for the paper in my jumper pocket, put it in my mouth, and as I swallowed it I repeated his name in silence, several times, so I would never forget it.

Xu Zechen is the author of the novels *Midnight's Door, Night Train,* and *Running Through Beijing.* He was selected by *People's Literature* as one of the best Chinese writers under forty-one. The recipient of numerous awards and honors, he lives in Beijing.

Eric Abrahamsen is the recipient of translation grants from PEN, to translate Xu Zechen's *Running Through Beijing,* and from the National Endowment for the Arts. He has written for the *New York Times,* among other publications. He also hosts the website *Paper Republic,* which features Chinese literature in translation.

The Dog's Been Barking All Day

XU ZECHEN
TRANSLATED FROM THE CHINESE BY ERIC ABRAHAMSEN

Patching up the heavens was something only Chuan would think of trying. He stood on our roof—hammer in his left hand, nail in his right—banging at the sky. A cloud came over: "I nailed it." A plane flew past: "I nailed that, too." Zhang Dachuan and his wife Li Xiaohong said, "Look how clever our son is: he knows a needle and thread would never do it. You need a hammer and nail to patch up the heavens." They stood in the courtyard, looking upward. Under a rare blue Beijing sky, their eight-year-old son Chuan held his hammer and his nail high, looking for all the world like a heroic giant. From their point of view I towered just as tall: I was on the roof next to him, hovering over Chuan to keep him safe.

Chuan was wrong in the head. His parents were fruit sellers, and they spent all day every day in the cab of a motorized three-wheeled flatbed, selling piles of apples in apple season, oranges in orange season, watermelons in watermelon season. On occasion they had bananas, mandarin oranges, pineapples, or pears. Cherries were most expensive. Li Xiaohong couldn't understand why city people were crazy for the tiny, overpriced things—they insisted on calling them by their English name, *che-li-zi*. Chuan was happy to follow me around. When I wasn't out pasting advertisements, Zhang Dachuan and Li Xiaohong would lead him into our yard, bringing apples and oranges with them: "Chuan, you play with big brother Muyu." They'd bring his lunch in a box, of course, and I'd warm it up for him at noon. If my roommates Xingjian and Miluo were around, there'd be extra apples and oranges. Then their three-wheeler would start its rattling roar, and they'd call to Chuan, who stood cocked-headed and drooling, with his hammer and his nail in a sack:

"Be good! Say bye-bye to mommy and daddy."

This isn't about Chuan, or Zhang Dachuan or Li Xiaohong, much less is it about that motorized three-wheeler that went trundling from dawn to dusk through the streets and alleys of Beijing, piled with fruit. This is about a dog, the one that Zhang Dachuan and Li Xiaohong kept to guard their courtyard. They rented the courtyard and two-room building next to ours. They lived in one room, and kept their fruit in the other. The dog was tied outside the fruit room to keep thieves and children away. We hated that dog. Every morning, as the three-wheeler started rattling, it started barking. As the three-wheeler pulled away, it was still barking. As the three-wheeler spent the day trundling through Beijing's alleys, it never stopped barking.

"Someday that fucking dog is going to get it," my roommates said.

The dog woke early, which meant no rest for us. All three of us made a living pasting advertisements around the city, which meant we were more or less nocturnal, and were usually crawling into bed around dawn, right as the little shit started up. Even if we weren't out at night we might take a nap at noon, and that thing could have you awake and sweating at the ankles with a single yap. Someday that fucker was going to get it.

We hadn't gone out that day. After lunch I took Chuan up to the roof to fix the sky. Xingjian was poring over *Prince Gong's Interpretation of Dreams*—he'd had a dream that a white hog with peach flowers on its face was knocking on the door, and when he opened it he'd woken up. Miluo was inserting line breaks into a paragraph he'd written the night before—he thought he might have the potential for poetry. They wanted to have an afternoon nap, but it was impossible: the dog kept barking. And barking, and barking. And barking. Who knew how its wires had gotten crossed. From the roof I could hear the two of them cussing and bitching. The earth-shattering rattle of the three-wheeler became audible, approaching from a distance, and Chuan raised that same damn hammer and the same damn nail and said:

"My dad! My mom! Look, my mom and dad!"

His parents were back.

Xingjian and Miluo came out of the room and called up to me, "Tell them to take their rug rat back!"

"I'm playing with him," I said. "No skin off your nose."

"Hell with that," Xingjian said. "That dog is driving me nuts!"

"Not only do we have to listen to the dog," added Miluo, "we have to help them raise their retard. It's not right! Send him home."

The three-wheeler stopped outside the courtyard, and Chuan's parents got out, all smiles. They'd sold a whole load of oranges that morning, and were planning on restocking and doing it again.

"Are you having fun playing, son?" asked Zhang Dachuan.

Li Xiaohong added, "Remember to call Muyu 'brother.'"

I had to lie and say I was going to my uncle's place to pick up a fresh batch of advertisements. Chen Xingduo was keeping up with the times, I said; had they ever heard of a fake-ID peddler with business cards? Soon we'd be handing those out instead of advertisements. Anyway, I'd have to return Chuan to them.

They seemed a little unhappy, but made sure to keep their smiles on. The kid *was* theirs, after all. The dog was still barking. I passed Chuan down to Li Xiaohong, who pursed her lips and asked for the lunch box, too. "Did you do something to annoy them?" she asked Chuan under her breath. Chuan twisted his head and body around to look at me, stuck out his tongue, and grinned.

"Big brother likes me."

His eyes never seemed to be focused on the same spot. It drove me nuts, I always felt he was looking at someone else when he was talking to me. But he was right: I did like him. He always said what he was thinking, or what he wanted to do—he hadn't learned hypocrisy. His dad could have taken a lesson from him. Zhang Dachuan was always going on about how much they loved their son, how they couldn't bring themselves to have another—government policy allowed for a second child if the first was disabled. "But if we had another," said Zhang Dachuan, all smiles, "little Chuan wouldn't be happy." He took Chuan from Li Xiaohong, holding him by the armpits, and heaved him into the three-wheeler's cab. Chuan's head smacked audibly against the cab's back divider. Zhang Dachuan's face twitched, and he hissed under his breath:

"No crying!"

The three-wheeler passed through the gate of the courtyard, piled with oranges, apples, and bananas, and rattled away. Chuan was next to his father, and Li Xiaohong was in the back, on top of a heap of apples. The dog barked with greater abandon.

The two of them were from the countryside but they'd traveled all over, and their accents had followed them. You couldn't tell, exactly, what kind of Chinese it was. Zhang Dachuan was always adding the Beijing *arrr* sound to the end of all his words: *They wurrr lining up for the apprrrs and orangerrrs*. It infuriated Xingjian: "Where the fuck does he get orrrf, with his '*wurrrs*' and his '*apprrrs*'?"

He transferred his irritation about Zhang Dachuan's accent to their family dog.

"It's *still* fucking barking!" he said. "I'm going to kill the little mutt! It would be one thing if it were a German shepherd, but it's not even a Pekingese, it's just a filthy mutt. I'm going to kill the little shit!"

No sooner said than he and Miluo were out the door, both of them in a rage. It wasn't just the fact that their nap was interrupted.

I suspected that Prince Gong's interpretations were turning out bogus, and Miluo's line-breaking career wasn't panning out. But they couldn't simply kill the animal, it would be obvious who'd done it, so they decided just to mess with it for a while. Miluo was holding a bowl of leftover pork-rib stew, the broth half congealed in the cold.

"You stay up on the roof," Xingjian directed me. "Tell us the second you hear them coming back."

I grabbed an old copy of *The Arabian Nights* I'd found in a book stall, and crawled back up on the roof.

There's no better place to read than on a roof. The buildings in the western suburbs were low to the ground; life there held low to the ground, too. From my elevated seat I felt I could see the whole world clearly. Even a book makes more sense, read up there, than it would in a classroom. I sat down near the edge bordering the alleyway. The dog barked even more wildly as the two of them climbed over the wall. Miluo fished a bone from his bowl of broth and tossed it to the dog, which snuffled at it and immediately stopped barking.

Truly, there was nothing remarkable about the dog, it was just a mutt. It was black and white, but so filthy from rolling in the dirt and its own muck that there wasn't much difference between the black and the white. It made its home outdoors, in a crude doghouse, and was so accustomed to being cold that it curled up into a ball anytime it sat down. I doubted whether it had ever eaten its fill: its curved ribs seemed about to poke through its hide. The dog's name was "dog." That's how Zhang Dachuan and Li Xiaohong called it: "Come here, dog! Quit barking, dog! Fuck off and die, dog!" Now it lay with the bone between its front paws, almost too excited to gnaw it. Xingjian and Miluo dragged two folding stools from the corner of the yard and sat down to watch the dog trembling as it chewed. Xingjian looked back at me and snapped his fingers. The afternoon sunlight was weakening, and the dog's shadow inched out into a blob.

"We're giving him a taste," Miluo said to me.

The Arabian Nights was a good book. Up on the roof, it was an even better book. It brought me instantly out of my low-to-the-ground life. I flipped through it randomly, reading bits here and there.

The dog still hadn't managed to crunch up and swallow the bone; in its frustration it was wheezing like an asthmatic. But it wouldn't give up, and kept biting the bone, then spitting it out, then biting it again. Xingjian stuck his finger in the congealed broth then brought it to his nose, his eyes closing in pleasure as he smelled it. The dog had to have understood his expression: it suddenly went quiet, then came over and lay docilely at his feet. Xingjian raised his chin, and made a sign at Miluo, who came over and gave the dog a kick. The dog had no idea what was happening. It leaped up, gave a single bark, then went quiet and lay back down. Miluo gave it another kick, and it leaped up again, looking back at him, its bark becoming a drawn-out growl that trailed off strangely. It hesitated for a few seconds, then lay down again. Miluo looked at Xingjian, who grinned and nodded, and a third kick landed on the dog's belly. This time it really did get angry; it jumped up and spun around several times, as Xingjian and Miluo instinctively scooted their stools back. They were in no danger, though: the dog was already at the limit of its chain. It barked, but they no longer found the barking annoying. They looked back at me and grinned.

"Want to come down?" asked Miluo.

"What are you going to do?"

"Don't worry, we're just playing with the little fucker," Miluo answered, landing another kick on the dog's haunches.

The dog was really going nuts, yanking at its chain so that it clanked and jangled. Xingjian hurriedly scooped out another blob of congealed broth and flicked it on the ground, and the dog went after it. It licked the whole patch of ground. It must have been delicious. Afterward it slowly lay down again, smacking its mouth, put its head on its front paws, and continued barking. There was a note of pleading and of sorrow in its barks. Xingjian passed the bowl to Miluo and moved his stool over next to the dog, then began petting it as if it was his own dog, working through its fur from its head, over its back, to its tail. The dog closed its eyes. From where I was sitting, it looked as though Xingjian had been planning to give it a punch in the head, but the moment he'd made a fist he relaxed his hand again—perhaps he'd seen the dog's furiously wagging tail. He continued rubbing it, starting at the head and moving again over its emaciated back to its bony haunches, then he moved to its tail, smoothing the fur from base to tip. He stood up.

"Take a look if they're coming back, will you?" he said to me.

I stood up, my faint shadow stretching broad and long over the roof, all the way to the other side. On days like today the sun was as weak as a sick man, whose strength was exhausted by a few sneezes. In the distance were single-story buildings; in the greater distance were more single-story buildings, and a few trees with bare branches like pencil sketches on the horizon, and the occasional taller building. The sun seemed ready at any moment to drop on those buildings and those trees. I looked up the alleyway and saw nothing, not even a pedestrian, as if the western suburbs of Beijing had suddenly emptied. I waved a hand at them.

"Quit reading that stupid book," said Xingjian. "It won't bring you any fairy tales, not in this life or the next. I've got something to show you."

He gestured to Miluo, and took the bowl back. It was Miluo's job to do. He dipped his hand in the bowl and came up with a handful of congealed broth, then smeared it on the dog's tail. The dog caught the scent and began barking excitedly.

"Still fucking barking!" Xingjian gave it a kick.

The dog stifled its barks, and began twisting around in search of the scent. The broth did smell good—I even caught a whiff of it from the rooftop. A plane passed overhead; one of Chuan's patches. If you hadn't seen Chuan's perpetually unfocused eyes, his strangely cocked head, and his endless string of drool, you wouldn't think anything was wrong with him at all. He had more imagination in him than most normal people, more than *The Arabian Nights*—who would have thought of patching the sky? Who could have understood that needle and thread wouldn't do it, that you needed a hammer and nail?

The dog was spinning in circles after its own tail. The chain slowly wrapped around its legs; it didn't know to step over it. It managed a few times to lick the tip of its tail, which made it all the more frantic to get another taste.

Everyone's seen a dog chase its tail, but we'd never witnessed such a clumsy, frenzied, disorderly pursuit. We started laughing. It was grunting and yelping as it attempted to lick its own tail, and barking when it couldn't reach it. Eventually it discovered that if it twisted its body violently it could just reach the tip, and soon had licked it clean.

Xingjian and Miluo held a discussion. Clearly, putting more broth on the dog's tail was tantamount to simply feeding it directly, and where was the fun in that? Soon they'd reached a consensus: they'd add more broth bit by bit, higher and higher up the tail. How high could he reach?

This made things difficult for the dog: it needed to bend itself practically in half, and by the end it simply couldn't manage. The chain wasn't making things any easier, tripping and tangling it, until it finally fell in a heap and became so frustrated it bit the chain and began shaking it back and forth. Xingjian and Miluo only stood to one side and laughed. I had to admit, it was a rare bit of fun. I stood on the roof and shouted:

"Take the chain off!"

They liked that idea. Xingjian flicked a little broth on the ground, and while the dog was busy with it, Miluo undid its collar.

A new round of tail-chasing ensued. The removal of the collar and chain didn't actually give the dog much more freedom of movement, but it was certainly an encouragement, and it strove all the harder to bite its tail. I didn't know what sounds a person in complete despair might make, but as the dog failed to lick the root of its own tail it made a sound of boiling rage that for a moment sounded almost human. The sound caused a chill to run through me, as though it were ice water and not the chill breeze of dusk that was passing over me. The game seemed to have gone far enough.

The breeze brought the sound of a diesel engine. I cocked one ear, but it seemed to have disappeared. Yet there it was again. It was time to remind Xingjian and Miluo that enough was enough. They were watching the dog twisting itself up like a potato bug, themselves doubled over with laughter. The dog gave a last desperate yelp, folded itself up, and sank its teeth into its own tail. In pain and shock, it levitated straight into the air, body still locked in a circle, and seemed to hang there for a couple of seconds before it smacked down with a seemingly audible crack of bone on ground. It let go of its tail, yelping all the more piteously, and made straight for the gate of the yard.

It was an old-style courtyard, with an iron gate that opened in two halves. Zhang Dachuan had chained them together. The gate was large enough to admit the three-wheeler directly into the yard. The gap between the locked halves was wide, but not wide enough to let a dog squeeze in and out as it pleased, no matter how skinny. That day, however, it was maddened enough to try, but succeeded only in ramming one half of the gate. It made a turn and tried again, ramming the other half of the gate. It made one more turn, circling into the far corner of the yard to get a running start, and this time went for the stump of a long-dead toon tree next to the courtyard wall. It leaped onto the stump, then successfully scrabbled up and over the wall, landing on the road outside with the solid smack of bone and flesh on concrete.

"Get out!" I yelled. "They're back!"

The sound of the diesel engine had already moved into the alleyway. It was Zhang Dachuan's three-wheeler, no mistake. Still shocked by the dog's escape, Xingjian and Miluo stood openmouthed for a moment before vaulting over the wall themselves.

The dog struggled up and took off running with an unsteady gait. It staggered like a drunk, but going fast. The three-wheeler had just turned into the alleyway and was approaching at a jaunty speed—the fruit had sold well, the back was empty. The dog headed straight for it, as if welcoming long-lost relatives, and Zhang Dachuan was obviously taken by surprise—he didn't swerve until the last minute. As he did he hit the brakes hard, and the three-wheeler flipped. The cries of dog, man, and woman rose from the alley.

By the time I'd gotten down from the roof and run over, the front wheel of the three-wheeler had already stopped spinning. The dog was splayed on the ground to one side, still barking. Li Xiaohong knelt in front of the three-wheeler, weeping as she tried to get into the cab from the side. The door yawned open to the darkening sky; on the other side, Chuan had ended up—God knows how—jammed in the door, his upper body inside the cab, his lower body outside it, wedged between the cab and the ground. The weight of the unloaded three-wheeler bore down on the half of him that was caught outside, and dark blood was winding out across the pavement.

Li Xiaohong cried for Chuan, her voice already hoarse. He made no response. Not the slightest sound. Zhang Dachuan had gotten one shoulder under the cab of the three-wheeler and was trying to heave it back upright. I set my shoulder next to his. The dog was still barking, but somehow still sounded nothing like a dog.

Night was falling. Two figures approached, as unsteady as the dog: Xingjian and Miluo. They joined us in righting the three wheeler. I heard Zhang Dachuan's flustered, urgent voice.

"Stop your crying, Li Xiaohong, all right? Now we can have another! One that's right in the head, and right in the body. And you won't have to feel sorry for him. And you don't have to worry we won't be able to raise him. Just stop your crying, won't you!"

A couple of weeks later, rummaging through a book stall, I found a book that mentioned one of the uses of a dog's tail: to help it keep balance. "In running fast or accelerating, a dog's tail will stretch out straight behind it; in turning corners it will swing back and forth; in decelerating it rotates in a circle, similar to a parachute deployed behind a swiftly decelerating aircraft." So far as I could remember, as Zhang Dachuan's dog ran, its tail had drooped like a broken feather duster.

By the time I was rummaging in the book stall, the dog was dead. It had kept bashing itself against the door, until it eventually killed itself. Zhang Dachuan and Li Xiaohong left Beijing, and went back to their hometown. None of us knew where their hometown was.

Garnette Cadogan is an essayist. He is currently a Martin Luther King Jr. Visiting Scholar at the Department of Urban Studies and Planning at MIT, a Visiting Fellow at the Institute for Advanced Studies in Culture at the University of Virginia, and a Visiting Scholar at the Institute for Public Knowledge at New York University. He is editor-at-large of *Nonstop Metropolis: A New York City Atlas* (coedited by Rebecca Solnit and Joshua Jelly-Schapiro) and is at work on a book on walking.

With Nothing to Hide

GARNETTE CADOGAN

Back then, hammered upon by fists, I took cover under fantasy. I clung to my imagination in order to survive. A brutal stepfather and bystander mother made life miserable-to-unbearable, and so my wish was to be someone else. As far as I was aware, no one my age was dealing with the outpouring of fire and brimstone I longed to escape, so I had no choice but to take flight in my head. Often, when I got a reprieve from the pendulum crash of my stepfather's stumpy knuckles, I would daydream a normal life. More often, I'd dream about being Bruce Lee. *Bruce Lee* the character, he of *Fists of Fury* and *Enter the Dragon* fame: lithe, super fit, ready to enact punishment on his enemies with breakneck speed and assured style. I wanted to be a character—the character—that could readily defend himself and inflict pain on the man who entered his home like a wrecking ball, ready to leave it in ruins. Little, puny, bruised me found comfort in the reverie of revenge: scene after scene of me side kicking my stepfather's face, slamming him to the ground with my extraordinary Kung Fu technique and merciless force.

But I was nurtured by a grandmother who thought revenge was the worst sort of failure—you were giving too much time to someone who had already taken away too much. Perhaps that explains why my other childhood hero was Charlie Brown. Here was a kid who, week after week when I met him in the *Peanuts* comic strip, with its funny gang of exuberant kids and their animal companions (plus, an additional delight for me, nary an adult in sight), was teased and mocked and bullied but somehow, insecure and anxious though he could sometimes be, he pressed on. Call him "blockhead"; pull the football away from him, time and time and time again; humiliate him—this kindhearted lovable loser would not contort from who he was to hotly confront the world. He would persevere, maybe even kick that ball someday. (Years later I read a remark made by an opponent of eighteenth-century preacher and theologian Jonathan Edwards that reminded me of how my young eyes viewed Charlie Brown: his "happiness was out of the reach of his enemies." Melancholy might grab the kid, but it didn't have full hold on him—I looked at lil' Charlie Brown and saw joy, found joy.) In him was a courage harder to grasp, near-impossible for me to imitate.

But fearful, flimsy me didn't have the strength to mount a physical fight. Nor did I have the resilience and generosity to be untroubled by the blows that regularly rained down on me. So, much as I dreamt about becoming *Bruce Lee* or Charlie Brown, I couldn't copy either. Who I did become, though, was another fictional character— the Jamaican trickster figure Anansi. This character, a spider who made his way from Ghanaian folktales—in Akan, the word *ananse* means spider—to Jamaican lore, was the star character in many of the folktales I heard as a child in Jamaica, where he was usually a symbol of resistance and survival, taking on his oppressors with slick talking and sleight of hand. The stories describe a world where Anansi encounters more dangerous animals—characters with aptronyms like Tiger and Snake—and cheats his way out of defeat and death. An Anansi story is a concealed proverb: a wallop of wisdom lies in wait at the end. But that's not what I took away from those tales—what attracted me was that one could outmaneuver one's oppressors through trickery. Not only could I get out from under someone's rough grasp: I could also have the last laugh. I relished Anansi's nimble deceit, and envied how he used his sly mind to gift-wrap his opponents' stupidity and cruelty and hand it back to them. By the time his predators recognized they were being fed their own bitterness, Anansi was gone, out of harm's way with a grin. I yearned to evade like Anansi, and soon enough he became my patron saint. I decided that the burden of imagination, then, was learning how to manipulate: there was safety, after all, in being slippery. Anansi was a mental *Bruce Lee*, so to speak, and I began to behave like his overeager disciple.

So it became a cat and mouse game. I'd make a sly move, my mother and stepfather would try to trap me, I'd lie to escape and avoid harm. (My grandmother, the only safe adult, would usually be on the lookout, ready to provide sanctuary.) My home became, in my mind, a torture chamber, and I wanted to be away from it as much as possible. My rationale was that I could get home from school around 3 p.m., like any normal ten-year-old kid, and get humiliated and pummeled for a few hours until bedtime. Or I could get in past bedtime, on the wrong side of midnight, and be greeted by my grand-mother who would wait up to sneak me in, hear the truth of where I'd been, share laughter, and help me figure out a story that would sound believable to my mother in the morning.

Eventually, my mother started to stay up, suspecting that I wasn't always showing up a few minutes after she turned in. Sometimes, in the wee, quiet hours as I scaled the front gate or scurried up the grill that led to the second-floor balcony by my room, I'd hear a shout: "Yes, Mr. Bloodcloth Tarzan!" Anansi had met his opposition, and would have to talk his way out of a less severe beating than the one the truth would attract. But my mother refused to settle with the fictions I weaved. She would match my trickster with her detective. Days later, like a psychic who had suddenly regained lost powers, she would confidently declare me a liar, unspool my concealed activities, and pile on punishment or beatings—or worse, send me to my step-father, who was like an executioner who was only sated once he fulfilled his sadistic role. I couldn't figure out how she knew what I did—I was half-convinced she went to an Obeah practitioner—until my grandmother, who decided to play counter-detective to her daughter's detective, figured out that my mother would put questions to me about my whereabouts and wanderings after I fell asleep. When semiconscious I had a habit of answering anything asked, only to be unaware of the conversations when I awoke. Now tipped to her device, I began to pretend to sleep for the first hour or so after I turned in; when poked and questioned, I repeated the deceit I told with eyes wide open. Sherlock Holmes was no match for Anansi.

My lies were armor. They protected me by keeping me a step ahead of my mother and stepfather after my peregrinations got me home late. They protected me from bullies at home and from bullies outside. But they didn't protect me from the bully within: soon enough, what began as self-defense was now a way of life. Anansi was no longer a persona. I stopped playing a trickster and became one. The truth had painful consequences and being a trickster, I reasoned, was a life-and-death matter. But the delight in outmaneuvering others brought with it a corrosive element: I was all too ready to deceive.

In my first year of high school I received a bad report card; I had been treating school like a social hangout, and homework and study as suggestions to be ignored, and had the grades to show for it. My stepfather beat me bloody. I was unable to sit for weeks, had wounds that needed dressing, had scars that took forever to fade. As a result, I decided he'd never see a bad report card again. So I did what made best sense to a young slacker—intercepted and hid my report cards. With the help of my grandmother (who stashed them), he and my mom stopped receiving my report cards (and, not paying attention to my schoolwork, they never seemed to miss them). I had gotten report cards that showed such low academic performance and high disciplinary run-ins that I needed a parent to come speak to my teachers at my school's regular parent-teacher meeting. I paid the neighborhood drunk to come in as my dad. He put on a bravura performance. Weeks later, a teacher bumped into my mother while she was shopping. She expressed sympathy over my mother's home situation. My mother explained she wasn't married to a drunk. The teacher assured her that she needn't feel ashamed; she, too, was married to a drunk. My mother repeated that her husband wasn't a drunk. The teacher, an embodiment of sensitivity and insensitivity, asked: Why, then, did he come drunk to school to discuss your son's report card?

I worried about my lies catching up with me, not recognizing that they already had. In a home where the truth would often lead to pain, I practiced lying—until I didn't need to practice anymore. I was a liar. I too much enjoyed having the last laugh, too much worried about disapproval, too much cared what others thought. Worse, I loved an audience. (To love the crowd is to love untruth, warned Søren Kierkegaard, a lesson I ignored to my peril.) I lost the thing worth protecting—my very self. The ingenious child became the duplicitous adult. And he couldn't imagine himself out of this state, dominated by an internal bully. But, thankfully, he made friends who would not put up with the fictions, friends who insisted and reassured him that he could disappoint them with no dire circumstances to follow. Disapproval, they constantly reminded me, was nothing to shirk from—especially not when it meant I would dodge the truth.

I decided to throw off the trickster because I made friends who demanded honesty from me, and they modeled it beautifully. Around the same time, embarking on my twenties, I developed a love for reading—I finally learned to sit still—and my imagination wandered to new worlds, rushed to new models. My grandmother, who always knew the true stories, who was never made to interact with the trickster in me, and friends who were like family, made me despise and combat the trickster I'd become. And the books I was reading taught me new ways of being. ("Reading makes immigrants of us all," writes Hazel Rochman, speaking of readers' imaginations. "It takes us away from home, but, most importantly, it finds homes for us everywhere." In books I found new homes that gifted me the solitude I craved; reminded me, too, that I was not left alone.) I had grown past *Bruce Lee*, Charlie Brown, and Anansi. I was now being reshaped by new models, real and imagined.

Later, when I took to the page to start writing about my life, the old fantasies reappeared—well, not exactly. They came back not as fantasies so much as they came back as potential muses. As I wrote, I found myself wanting to take revenge on people who had hurt or oppressed me. *Bruce Lee* was vying to be my muse. (Some days my friend Philip will remark, after reading some intemperate remark of mine that should never have left my brain, "I saw that *Bruce Lee* wrote on Facebook today.") But I also recognized myself wanting to write in a spirit my grandmother would have approved of—to write as one with a capacious, generous heart who doesn't try to get even but who meets the world on open-minded terms. Charlie Brown beckoned to be my muse. And so, draft after draft, essay after essay, *Bruce Lee* and Charlie Brown duke it out. And perhaps, for the only time in the history of the world, Charlie Brown, that lovable loser, kicks *Bruce Lee's* ass.

Valeria Luiselli was born in Mexico City and grew up in South Africa. She is the author of *Sidewalks*, a collection of personal essays; the essay "Tell Me How It Ends"; and the novels *Faces in the Crowd* and *The Story of My Teeth*. The latter novel, which was written in installments for workers in a juice factory, won the Los Angeles Times Book Prize for fiction and was a finalist for a National Book Critics Circle Award. She lives in Harlem.

I Is Another

VALERIA LUISELLI

A few weeks after I moved to New York, almost a decade ago, I had a medical emergency and ended up in the waiting room of St. Luke's Hospital in the middle of the night. While I waited my turn with all the other lost souls, I was given a questionnaire to fill in. The first questions were straightforward and easy to answer: "Cancer in your family?" "Any allergies?" In the final section, though, one question took me by surprise. I don't remember the exact phrasing, but it was a question about race. The only other time I'd been asked anything remotely similar—but it was not even about race—was during my first day in fourth grade, at an all-girls school in South Africa, where my family and I had just moved. The girl sitting behind me in the classroom had tapped me on the shoulder and asked: "Are you Greek or Lebanese?" I'd answered "Greek," displaying no hesitation but crossing my fingers under my desk. To my relief, in response, she smiled wide. I wiped my sweaty palms on my pleated blue skirt and smiled back. From that day on I was allowed into a group of girls who I later learned were Lebanese and Greek, so I could have chosen either option. In any case, I was able to pass as Greek for long enough that when I finally confessed one day that I was in fact Mexican, the alliances I'd formed had already become friendships, and so withstood my dark secret.

My body sinking into the waiting-room chair at St. Luke's Hospital and my palms sweating in a familiar way, I hesitated in front of the question for a while, traveling up and down the ladder of choices with the tip of my pencil: White, Black, Hispanic, Asian, Native American, Other. Then, possibly driven by my high fever, I decided to exteriorize my discomfort. I walked over to the receptionist and, in a voice that came out more meager and modest than what I'd aimed for, I asked:

"Sir, which box do I check here, sir?"

He scanned me from the depths of his ennui, saying nothing. Slightly emboldened by what I interpreted as now my right to feel offended by his indifference, I raised my voice a bit and explained:

"Hispanic is not a race, sir! Right?"

He raised his eyebrows, still said nothing, and went back to his task. So I walked back to my seat, defiantly put my feet up on the chair next to mine, and checked "Other." Next to my answer, I wrote, in small but clear handwriting: "And fuck you." Then, thoroughly satisfied with myself, I walked over to him again and placed the questionnaire down on his desk.

I was twenty-four, so the self-righteous little scene I was acting out before the eyes of an overworked, underpaid and of course unimpressed receptionist was not entirely in keeping with my age. I suppose I still had more stances than ideas, though I wouldn't have known the difference at the time. I was full of causes, and was convinced that my individual resistance to any manifestations of the status quo embodied a kind of heroism and an advancement of global justice. I had just graduated from the Universidad Nacional Autónoma de México with a thesis in political philosophy. It was an ambitious but not very well-written critique of John Rawls's *Theory of Justice* from the point of view of "illegal" immigration. As Borges used to say about someone he despised, it was more complicated than complex.

The main argument in the thesis, more or less, was that the kind of contractualism underlying Rawls's theory encompassed a solely *domestic* conception of justice and did not address the most pressing contemporary problems of *global* justice. The critique I attempted, if I remember accurately, drew on ideas developed by several cosmopolitanist philosophers, Martha Nussbaum, Thomas Nagel, and, especially, one of Rawls's star pupils, who later distanced himself from Rawls and formulated critiques of some aspects of his theories. I interviewed this political philosophy professor in his Manhattanville apartment in the summer of 2007, exactly one year before I moved to New York. He offered me a glass of apple juice when I walked into his apartment, and then showed me into his living room. I noticed his wiry, bright red hair, and observed, my jaw probably dropping a bit, how he kneaded his head as he talked, as if he was squeezing truth out of his scalp. I fell in love with him, completely and ephemerally, the way philosophy students fall in love with anything or anyone eccentric; the way rocks might fall in love with passing birds. I asked him winding, circular, ungrammatical questions about the philosophical soundness of contractualism vis-à-vis contemporary immigration patterns. I think I had just learned the phrase "philosophical soundness" and probably overused it.

One year later, I was living in a student housing apartment in Manhattanville. I never saw the political philosophy professor again (though I later read he had been involved in a sexual harassment scandal). I had become one of the philosophy dropouts I had once scorned, abandoning a serious professional path in political philosophy to pursue a PhD in comparative literature (the second-most useless specialization, after non-comparative literature). My monthly rent was as high as my graduate student stipend was low, so I had to hunt down any paid gig that did not violate the rules of my F1 student visa.

Sometime later I got an e-mail from an editor. He offered decent payment for a weekly column in a terrible magazine. When I dialed the number he gave in the e-mail, he specified that the column had to be about dating in New York "as a woman of color." Never having encountered the term, I consulted several friends about the exact meaning of "of color." Thanks to one of my closest friends—by far my most intelligent friend, a brilliant writer and scholar specializing in the black diaspora, and also a professional satirist—I learned that this magazine editor was in fact quite right in assigning that precise term to me. In the politics of exclusion and inclusion in America—and the language that goes with it—I was, by all means, a woman of color. However, despite this, and despite my very real need for the extra cash, I decided to turn down the offer. I essayed many possible opening lines for my e-mail. Some were intended to sound prophetic but read like cryptic Chinese fortune cookies: "Generational dating paradigms will soon shift." Others tried way too hard to sound sarcastic: "I am a woman of greenish color." I finally settled for a one-line lie, because I remembered my mother always said that if you're going to lie you must keep it short: "I'm married."

I think, for the few months that followed, I still tried to make sure my ego—which was swiftly thinning into bare self-esteem—received a daily, though more and more homeopathic, dose of a delusion of otherness. I told myself that I would never reduce my identity to the incorrect racial categories of medical questionnaires; that I would never allow preconceived notions of what I was in the eyes of others to define who I was. (Had someone back then given me "intersectionality" as a conceptual weapon, I would have misused it with pathological debauchery).

Having to sit through endless lit theory classes did not help temper my growing confusion and resentment. What I had first considered as a kind of taxonomic violence circumscribed within only certain institutional practices—airport customs, hospital questionnaires and fashion magazines—extended, I now discovered, to other spaces. The readings we were assigned in our seminars, it seemed to me, all neatly packed entire literary traditions, such as the Latin American one, into boxes labeled with concepts like "third world" and "marginal." The writers I had read all my life up until then, and had always conceived as the almost mythical titans of a rich and robust canon—Rulfo, García Márquez, Lispector—were suddenly thrown together in the pile of marginality. I felt that comparative literature, at least in American universities, was nothing but a constant effort to reduce other literatures to categories of readability that I found humiliating.

If my first months of graduate school were confusing, the ones that followed were enraging. I was on the defensive, and my professors, brilliant people with good intentions, were unknowingly feeding the little paranoid monster inside me. (Now, almost ten years later, as a university professor myself, I often wonder what kind of misunderstandings I may be fueling.) I started getting everything all wrong. I read Gayatri Spivak, who was then the director of my program, and thought that her seminal essay "Can the Subaltern Speak?" was a demonstration of hypocrisy. How did her interventions in the field give voice to young Caribbean women who swept and mopped the corridors of our university every night, or to the lives of the Yemeni men in the nearby delis, or the destinies of the Mexican deliverymen who pedaled through the city no matter the weather? I thought that categories such as "margin" and "subaltern" were, in the mouths of all those privileged and prestigious academics and writers, an enormous hoax and a cynical act of appropriation. How was their work at all relevant to the people to whom they purportedly gave a voice? Weren't they stealing or simply using other people's voices and identities to their advantage? In my indignation, I spared no one and nuanced nothing. One day, for example, I was asked to write a critique of Toni Morrison. I read her novels and essays, falling in love with some, resisting others. But I ended up writing an imbecilic rant.

My views about the United States were still monolithic, lacking nuance, and full of contrived animosity. I read all American writers, like Morrison, through eyes foreign and angry, conceiving of them solely as privileged Anglo-Saxon writers, the intellectual elite of the world's leading cultural, economic and military power. (I had no idea of what it takes, precisely in America, for a woman of color to even be published.) The way I saw it, American writers did not have to go through the trial of either cultural or linguistic translation—the trial, that is, in which "the accused" first has to demonstrate that he or she is readable, in the exact terms of readability that are expected, and only then will be given the chance to speak in English; but even so, will never be given equal treatment with respect to his or her Anglo-American counterparts. I was not so wrong about the politics of translation, but how wrong I was about Morrison, and about Spivak, and about so many other things. I had no idea that even the smartest and most original thinkers living in this country—like Spivak and Morrison, two figures that I now can understand with more clarity and therefore highly respect—must comply with the categories under which they are expected to subsume their creative and intellectual production because they are women of color (much like translated authors, by the way).

I still had not seen the much more sinister side of America and the power dynamics of its society, though it had always been right there in front of my face. I did not know there was simply no choice in the matter, that nobody is free to choose the very rigid categories that make up social identities here. You are a woman of color, you are an immigrant, you are an alien, you are a minority. No questions asked. (But who even came up with these terms? I suspect it was not a person who later wore them.) And, if you don't speak from your assigned minority niche, no one even cares to listen. Despite all this, having the apparatus of a minority discourse is better than not having it, because before it existed there were fewer ways, fewer words to name and denounce the daily atrocities that took place under everyone's eyes.

The one question that still drives me crazy today, and still makes me irreparably angry at myself, is why as a young woman I directed all my rage and confusion toward female giants like Morrison and Spivak, and not toward my many mediocre—at least by comparison—male professors and mentors. Why did I grin and sigh at every one of the many philosophy professors who passed through my life, while raising a defensive wall against the women whom I listened to and read? Young women beware! Even more dangerous than philosophy professors who turn out to be sexual predators is the silent, surreptitious, autoimmune emotional disorder that drives young women to spare everyone except the female figures whom they could look up to, and aspire to one day resemble.

In *A Season in Hell*, Rimbaud wrote the oft-quoted line: "I is another." When you're very young and moving around from place to place, trying to find a life for yourself, and have perhaps just moved to a new city or a new country, and hospital rooms still seem more like literary metaphors than concrete places, and philosophy professors still seem sexy instead of scary, it's fairly easy to navigate through life carrying the Rimbaudian flag: "I is another." That is, it is tempting to hold on to the belief that you can be anything and anyone, and will not allow others to incarcerate you in a single category of identity. Cultural assimilation, especially in a country like the United States, requires compliance with a single form of being "other." Being assigned a fixed, ready-made identity and forced to accept it is perplexing and frustrating. For me, at least, it was a slow, painful process. But there really is no way out of the American identities labyrinth, so it is best to learn to find your way around all the dead ends inside it. Slowly, during the process of assimilation, I moved beyond my initial frustration and anger—or did I just learn to live with them?—and chose to fully embrace the identity I was handed, understanding it as a potentially emancipating political instrument instead of a muzzle. Not that I'm proud of all the implications of assimilation: now, at the doctor's office, I sit up straight in waiting-room chairs, like the well-behaved schoolgirl I never was; offer a wide, docile smile to the receptionists; and check "Hispanic."

Mieko Kawakami has published numerous books including novels, short stories, essays, and prose poems. Her second novella, *Breasts and Eggs* (2008), won the Akutagawa Prize and was translated into Norwegian, Spanish, French, Chinese, Korean, and other languages. In 2016, *Granta* selected her for its Best of Young Japanese Novelists volume, which included her story "Marie's Proof of Love."

Hitomi Yoshio is an Associate Professor of Japanese literature at Waseda University. Her translations of Mieko Kawakami's works have appeared in *Granta, Words Without Borders, Denver Quarterly, Pleiades, Electric Literature,* and *Monkey Business: New Writing from Japan.*

The Flower Garden

MIEKO KAWAKAMI
TRANSLATED FROM THE JAPANESE BY HITOMI YOSHIO

It happened at three o'clock in the afternoon on a sunny spring day, three months ago exactly.

There she was, standing on the terra-cotta tiles of the entryway to my house, next to my collection of colorful Repetto ballerina flats and my husband's polished shoes. I had carefully chosen those tiles considering the balance of colors and the overall nuanced effect.

Just then, I heard a voice.

The woman's lips remained still as she stared into my face. I heard the voice again. I listened, but couldn't decipher the words. I knew, intuitively, that they were directed toward me. I held my breath and focused on the voice. It was solid, a distinct alto. What was it saying? I couldn't tell. All I knew was that it was speaking to me. I stood there, staring silently at the woman who had appeared before me.

She was petite and demure looking, not the type of beauty that immediately attracted attention. But her long eyelashes, especially when she averted her gaze, left an impression that they were meant to attract the opposite sex. I felt strangely irritated by her plump lips and perfectly straight teeth. Her parents must have paid a fortune to fix them when she was young. Everything about her seemed calculated, from the way she moved her eyes to the way she held her head, from her perfect posture to the tone of her voice. You could see the marks of effort that you often see in women who are neither beautiful nor unattractive. These women surround themselves with cheerful colors and objects of the finest quality, pretending to enjoy them. They perfect the charade for so long that they convince themselves, and those around them, that their cheerfulness is the natural result of their inner confidence. That was the kind of woman that appeared before me. She was accompanied by the real estate agent whose voice I could barely stand to hear, who, for several months now, had brought strangers to my house, day in and day out, to leave their ugly footprints in every corner. In short, the woman was a potential buyer.

"This is it. I had a vague sense of what I wanted, but I didn't know exactly. Oh, this front porch! It's perfect."

Bowing her head slightly, the woman looked into my eyes with a smile. The real estate agent was nodding vigorously next to her. "I'm glad the house pleases you. It's quite different from what you had requested, but I see you rather like these *charming* types of homes. Well, this really expands our choices." With a smile flashing across his face, he introduced me as the owner's wife. I bowed in return and, offering each a pair of slippers, walked toward the living room.

I never volunteered any information unless they asked me a specific question. You can learn all you need to know about a house by walking around. If I were eager to sell, I would have said all kinds of things—for instance, how the house was designed by the British architectural firm that undertook the famous restaurant and garden in Gaienmae, or how we used the finest stucco for the walls and ceilings, even inside the closets. I could have told them how the light filled the rooms according to the season, how serene the neighborhood was, or how the dishwasher was top of the line, made by the German manufacturer Miele. But I said nothing. I didn't have the slightest desire to tell a random stranger how I had groomed and loved the house, or how much time and care I had devoted to perfecting it. The fact was that I was being driven away from my own home.

"Just look at the door, the color of the walls, these bay windows . . . everything is perfect. And with such a spacious dining room, you could put a sizable table there. It's always been my dream to have a solid wood dining table." Peering into the dining room and the kitchen, the woman sighed and exclaimed in an exaggerated fashion. *Of course everything is perfect. What could you possibly know about it?* I scoffed inwardly, trailing a few steps behind her.

Who was this woman anyway? Her bag and shoes were not expensive looking—it was hard to gauge how old she was. Plus, it was rare for a woman to come to a viewing alone. Since it was a Saturday, her husband should have come with her if she were married, and if not, she would have been accompanied by a parent or some other relative. (I gained all sorts of useless knowledge like this in the past few months.) Yes, it was indeed unusual that a woman would come to a viewing alone. She didn't seem like the type that would buy a house all on her own, and was definitely too young to buy one worth well over a hundred million yen, even with a mortgage. Who knows, perhaps her husband was buying the house for her, and he happened to be busy. That's how it was for me after all. Or could it be a gift from her parents? Yes, that must be it. But if so, wouldn't they want to come see the house for themselves?

Under normal circumstances, the seller has the right to choose the buyer, and to even inquire about his or her background to the extent that the information is not confidential. All parties are more or less equal between the seller, the buyer, and the agent who works on commission. But this was not so in our case. We had no right to ask questions or to make decisions. They would have laughed in our faces if we had insisted. When my husband's company filed for bankruptcy, we had no choice but to let go of our house, which was still under mortgage. "Voluntary liquidation," they had called it. Neither my husband nor I—who had designed the house and grew to love it over the years—was to decide on the value and its future occupant. No, it was to be handled by a random stranger who had never seen or set foot in the house.

Everything happened so quickly. It was worse than a situation defined by the common expression "downward spiral"—I may have felt some kind of pain or fear then. Instead, with no end in sight, I felt like a tiny grain floating amid a giant blank space where I could see and touch nothing. Everyone was laughing at me behind my back, though people never voiced their scorn—those who called or came to see me, neighbors who greeted us on the street, anonymous passersby, friends I hadn't seen in years were all laughing because the ostentatious house had caused our downfall.

Quiet by nature, my husband rarely spoke to me about his work. The accounting was processed internally by his employees, and I had no interest in that sort of thing to begin with. I knew he was involved in asset management and stocks, but those were handled at work and had nothing to do with me or my house. My role was simply to manage the household with the money left over after the monthly mortgage and insurance payments had been made. One day would pass, followed by another, and before long a whole year had passed without significance.

I couldn't recall a single occasion when I felt we were financially lacking, even when my husband was an ordinary salaryman before he started his own business. He was never concerned with how I spent our money, since we had neither children nor extravagant taste to speak of. From his demeanor, I always assumed that business was going well, and had no cause for worry. When we built our present house six years ago after getting rid of the house his father had left behind (how I had detested that traditional Japanese house with its gloomy gray tiled roof), the paperwork was taken care of by my husband and his company. All I had to do was sit down over tea with the architect my husband had chosen, discuss the layout of the house that I had drawn up, and confront the challenge of turning my vision into a reality.

So, like a child under parental care, I was completely oblivious as to what was happening to my husband's company and to my own home. Perhaps my husband had wanted it that way. I was kept in the dark until the very end, until the day he announced out of the blue that we would have to sell the house. I was aware that our nation was facing a financial crisis, and had even expressed concern when the topic came up among the neighborhood wives, but I never dreamed that the recession could affect us personally.

My life until then was made up of a series of numerical repetitions. The familiar numbers that appeared in the bank statement every month. The bill from my favorite antique furniture shop. House fixtures and furnishings would arrive carefully packaged. New fabric of the season. The bill from the farm in Kyushu prefecture that delivered fresh vegetables and meat. These appeared simply as numbers on the credit card bill, and I never imagined that they would come to an end. Those things happened to other people, living in other parts of the world. It was like politics—we understand that political issues are real and important, but still imagine that they exist in another realm separate from our everyday lives. I couldn't imagine that words like "bankruptcy" and "foreclosure" would have any relevance to my own life. It never occurred to me that the two realms might come together.

"You have such girlish taste."

"Pardon me?" I said, startled, with a smile frozen on my face.

"Oh it's just that everything feels so *delicate*," the woman said. "And so *deliberate* too, from the wallpaper to the windows to the overall look of the house. We women never grow out of it, do we? I'm the same—I've always loved this kind of aesthetic. Take what you're wearing—it's so girlish in the most tasteful way. Straight out of a childhood dream."

"Thank you," I uttered, and said no more.

The woman proceeded to praise every item in the room in an exaggerated manner. "How lovely the wallpaper is. Oh, the colors, the patterns. The height of the sink is just right. The tiles give such a foreign feel. Everything is just *lovely*." Couldn't this woman keep her mouth shut for a second? Why must she babble on and on? She must believe that people like to be flattered—perhaps she was in that line of work. There are those who believe that as long as you flatter, people will like you and help you get on in the world. Or, was there disdain behind all her flattery? Perhaps it was both. In any event, the woman's exaggerated behavior annoyed me, leaving discomfort as if something was stuck between my teeth.

"Could I take a look at the bathroom?"

"Of course."

She opened the cabinet where the toilet papers were stored, checking the width and the door. She made sure the water ran properly. Buyers always inspect every corner of the house—the layout of the closets, the shelving unit in the powder room, the inside of the dishwasher, the position of the showerhead, the depth of the bathtub, the grout of the tiles—everywhere from the storage room to behind the shelves. The only things they refrain from opening are the wardrobe drawers. The woman went around the house nodding approvingly and making mental notes, while the real estate agent followed closely behind her. After inspecting the kitchen, she opened the back door and asked about the garbage collection schedule. I answered.

"Do you get a nice breeze? It must come in from here and go out over there. Could I see the second floor? Do you mind?"

In silence, we ascended the small spiral staircase made of solid natural wood, designed to perfection. I always took special care to polish the handrail, but as I placed my hand on it, I noticed that it was already growing dull. My heart ached. The woman walked briskly down the hallway. "May I see the bedroom?"

"Please."

"What's that over there?"

"A walk-in closet. You can also enter from the other side."

"What's on the other side?"

"A room I use as an atelier."

"An atelier? Oh, is that a sewing machine I see?"

"Yes, I use it to sew clothes."

"My goodness," the woman exclaimed in a high-pitched voice. "Are you a designer? Or do you make patterns?"

"No, it's just a hobby of mine." I noticed that my voice was faint.

"What a fairy-tale room," the woman burbled on. "I love the way the triangular roof frames the walls against the high ceilings. So charming. The wallpaper echoes the living room, yes? And look at all this lace. You make clothes, you said? What a refined hobby."

The woman seemed to smirk at me. As she turned and walked back toward the bedroom, I noticed that her footsteps and mannerisms had changed. Now, it was as if she were showing a visitor around her own house, proud of every little detail. "Oh, that tiny door over there?" She scurried back into the bedroom.

"It leads to a kind of dressing room," I answered.

"Oh, so this is the 'boudoir' in the layout. What a lovely dresser. This room has such a *foreign* feeling."

I watched as the woman walked across the carpet in my little room and stood next to the window with its delicate, ornamental shutters. The room would fill with gentle light in the morning and cool air in the evening. The woman was about to have it all. *She's standing where I should be.* When she reached for the curtain, I almost cried out, "Keep your hands off!" But I didn't. Then, looking through the window, the woman let out a short gasp. "Oh, the garden! Those flowers!"

I remained silent. Out of everything I was proud of in the house, what was most precious to me, what I had most invested my time and energy in, was the flower garden. The ground was covered in different varieties of thyme, so that from afar, it gave the impression of green waves. And floating among the waves were anemones, forget-me-nots, violets, ranunculus, and tulips, all of which had just begun to deepen their color. In the shaded parts of the garden, there bloomed spring starflowers, ajuga, and impatiens. Flowers also filled the front porch, which was custom designed. How carefully I had chosen the front gate! The fence with the angel relief would soon be covered with climbing roses. Every year, when the weather got warm, the Lady Banks' roses bloomed in clusters. Next to them were the Dorothy Perkins, and on the other side were the Japanese roses. And let's not forget the Iceberg roses. The Uncle Walters drew attention with their stubborn faces, the only red you saw in the garden. Their petals felt smooth and rich, like velvet. How many hours had I spent choosing the perfect pot for each type of flower, considering the overall balance? I searched for weeks for a shade of brick for the flower bed that would match the outer walls. I buried the bricks—just the right tint between beige and pink—one by one, creating a gentle curve along which I carefully interwove the conifers and dead nettles. It was an utterly unique garden that I had created with immeasurable care. The mailbox, the curve of the exterior walls, the lamppost, the signature Juneberry tree—I labored to find perfection in every detail. In Tokyo, where houses resemble large gray tombstones straight out of a generic architectural catalogue, I had created a fanciful haven overflowing with blooming flowers that dazzled the mind and momentarily transported one to the Cotswolds. I had created the house that I had dreamed of since childhood.

"I love it. I really do. Should I go ahead and buy it?"

Having inspected the house, the woman sighed deeply and contentedly. Then, with the words, "May I?" she made herself comfortable on the living room sofa. "Isn't it cozy?" she said to the real estate agent in an eager tone.

"We're so pleased the house is to your liking," he answered with a look of satisfaction, as if he had just given her a gift. *We*, he had said.

The woman glanced at the decorative shelf near her and noticed the photograph of my husband and me smiling happily. It was taken on our wedding anniversary last year at our favorite steak restaurant. Last year . . . we were smiling then. I felt a sting in my throat and leaned against the wall. All I could do was press my fingers against my temples and wait for the lump in my throat to go away. "Should I go ahead and buy it?" she had said. I repeated the words in my head. *Should I go ahead and buy it?* I almost laughed out loud. I wanted to burst out laughing to her face. But instead, I leaned against the wall in silence.

"I love it. A charming little house with a garden—I bet life would be pretty cozy here. And so many flowers—it's like living in a fantasy manga world of Yumiko Ōshima."

The woman kept rattling on to herself with a contented look on her face. I kept my eyes firmly closed and my arms crossed over my chest. *Should I go ahead and buy it?* How dare she? How could that be possible? And who was this Ōshima? You might be filthy rich, but you were a stranger to this house until today. You found it by chance through a real estate agent. You know nothing about what it takes to maintain a place like this—all the work that goes into getting the roses to bloom every year, to keep the garden lush and green. You couldn't care less about the Kohler enameled cast-iron sink, William Morris textiles, Laura Ashley fabrics, or James Jackson's Jacpol antique wax polish. You think the house looks like a *fairy tale*? You were irrelevant to my house, my life, my past until now . . . how could you possibly *buy* all of this? What does that even mean? To make it all yours? I don't understand. Who are you anyway?

The woman thanked me and the real estate agent informed me that I would be contacted at a later date. They drove away.

I went back into the house and glanced at the clock. It had just turned five. At this time of day in spring, the flowers are engulfed in the mysterious aura of the evening mist, making you feel as if you've wandered into a Monet painting. How I loved gazing at the garden from the left-hand window of the living room. I would imagine myself from the outside, looking out through the small window of the house with its triangle roof, surrounded by modest yet well-groomed flowers amid the deep green. I never tired of gazing out as the garden faded in twilight, as the green leaves, the white petals, and the house melted into the darkness that fell soundlessly, the gentle fragrance of the evening accumulating.

And just like that, the house became hers.

The cutting board is all dried up. The edges of the cardboard boxes are frayed and black. The mattress is as hard as the bottom of a shoe. I imagined an empty toilet paper roll as I lay listlessly looking out at the electric wires hanging limp outside the window. *I am like an empty toilet paper roll*, I thought to myself as I looked around the cheaply furnished weekly apartment that was managed by someone my husband knew.

We had been able to take most of our dishes and clothing. Yet, for the past several days, I had been wearing a tattered old summer sweater that was covered in lint. It was almost three weeks since we moved into this apartment.

We left all of our furniture behind. We had no say in the matter. The realtor and the woman had agreed on the buying price, but apparently it was not sufficient according to whoever managed our debt. They ended up raising the price quite a bit, which resulted in renegotiations that delayed the closing date. We were allowed to continue living in the house until the deal was closed, so for a while, I imagined that we could live there indefinitely as if nothing had happened. But of course, that came to an end.

The woman settled on a price that was thirteen million yen above the initial asking price, but with the condition that she would have the right to buy all of our furniture for a price to be negotiated. This was convenient for both parties involved, so a price was agreed upon. The house was sold, as it was—only the inhabitants changed.

The same doors, the same tables, the same walls, the same garden, the same ornamental shelves, the same chairs. In my house, the woman became me. When I heard of the arrangement, I became so upset that I reproached my husband for the first time in twenty years. He responded with a look of fatigue. "We had to sell the furniture anyway to pay back the debt. If we hired a middleman, we would have had to bring money to the table." He was not trying to explain, or to convince or console me—he was simply stating the fact.

"Couldn't we have put everything in storage until we sorted things out and found a proper place?" I asked with tears in my eyes.

My husband answered in a low voice, "It was hard enough to take the clothes, the dishes, and all the little things with us. Plus, when we stepped out of the house, the furniture was no longer ours." Still unconvinced, I continued to question him for over an hour after we turned off the lights. "It's not going to be easy from now on—you know that, right?" was all he would say. Though he had stopped responding, I felt strangely excited and was unable to calm down. I buried my head under the thin summer futon in the stifling heat and cried until morning.

I can no longer recall the events that took place after the contract was signed—how we were driven out of our house and ended up here. What did we say to the neighbors? Did we slip away in haste or make up some elaborate lie? When did we pack our belongings? What did we eat? What time did we wake up and go to bed? Everything was a blur.

My husband was now driving a secondhand domestic car. I seem to recall him saying that it belonged to an acquaintance of his. Where was he during those hectic few days—or was it weeks? How did it all end? Was it really over? Come to think of it, it must have been my husband who took care of everything, but I had no recollection of discussing anything or even exchanging words with him. How did we get through it all? Surely, I was there, awake, and moving my body. Yet my memory was vague, as if something were pouring out of me despite my efforts to contain it. It was the same when I tried to remember my childhood. How did I spend those last days? How did I end up here?

Then I remembered something the woman had said. "Don't worry, I won't be keeping the bed." We were standing at the entryway before the house was handed over to her. We happened to run into each other just for a moment.

The woman said those words to me after a polite greeting. The real estate agent had assured us that he would keep our misfortune confidential, but I knew then that he had lied. The expression on the woman's face, the way she looked at me—she knew everything and was enraptured by her own benevolence and sympathy. She knew it all—that I had lost everything and had no choice but to lead a miserable life with my old, bankrupt husband. She was laughing at us both, who had never questioned our values and life choices until now. She was filled with a sense of superiority over the fact that she, who could be our daughter in age, was doing us a favor by taking on the girlish fantasy house that nobody else would want to buy.

With a wide-brimmed hat covering my face, grasping the straps of my purse, I set out to visit the house, which was now an hour away, and required three trains. This was already the fourth time I was going there. Fortunately, there was no one on the street in the middle of the day. It was so hot that sweat seemed to pour out when you just tried to keep your eyes open.

The house shone in the summer light. The neighborhood was dead silent, as if all the people had been annihilated, leaving the houses empty. On this summer afternoon, I sat on a bench in a small park down the street from the house. Under the bare branches of the wisteria no longer in bloom, I sat staring intently at the house. Hearing the rustle of branches in the wind, I watched a Juneberry tree—one I had planted—gently sway by the entrance gate. The color of the walls behind the tree was exquisite—a color that I loved, a color I had helped paint. The triangular roof. The tiny square windows. An abundance of green. Flowers blooming. Everything was as I had left it.

When I became thirsty, I would walk to a convenience store twenty minutes away and buy something to drink. Back on the bench, I saw no one save a few cars and an old woman with a bent back walking down the street very slowly.

The woman had bought the house on her own. I found out only two weeks ago, when the topic came up with my husband. I was lying on the futon when he told me, and propped myself up upon hearing the news. How long had it been since I looked into my husband's eyes? His face had a dark hue, having aged ten or twenty years.

"On her own? You mean, she lives there all by herself?" I asked in surprise.

"It seems that way," he answered.

"What does she do?"

"Apparently, she's a lyricist."

"A lyricist? You mean, someone who writes song lyrics?"

"Yes, that's what I heard."

241

"Is she famous?" My heart was beating fast.

"I don't know the details, but it seems that way." My husband replied in an uninterested manner with his head turned toward the TV screen.

"Do lyricists make so much money?" I continued in disbelief.

"It depends, I guess. You know that popular band, the Phantom Thief, is it? You've heard of them. I hear she writes for that band."

"So she must be very rich. And at her young age . . ."

"Only thirty-one apparently. Well, I suppose age has nothing to do with talent or royalties for that matter."

Our conversation ended there.

As I awoke from my reverie, the air was reverberating with the sound of the cicadas. Clenching a plastic bottle, I imagined the woman sitting at my desk inside the atelier. You could see a small forest off in the distance through the right-hand window, and at this time of year, the pale green of the trees would stretch vertically, coolly swaying in the wind. When evening came, I used to listen to the church bells. I would stop what I was doing and go downstairs to prepare dinner while listening to Mozart on low volume, played by the beautiful pianist Irina Mejoueva.

I had no idea what kind of life a lyricist led. I never saw the woman once during the past two weeks. I noticed what looked like a red Alfa Romeo, rounded and toylike, where my husband's white Mercedes-Benz used to be. The only person I saw from the bench approaching the house was the mailman driving up in a scooter to deliver the mail. On all three previous occasions, not a single person had come in or out.

Did the woman spend all of her time inside? The house was far from the train station and the supermarket, so she would have to drive to go anywhere. There was no bicycle on the porch. Well, it was so hot these days, perhaps the woman ran all her errands in the morning and spent the rest of the day inside the house. Or perhaps her days and nights were reversed. Come to think of it, it wouldn't be surprising if a writer slept during the day and worked at night.

But the woman was a lyricist, not a writer. There was a big difference. A lyricist simply plugged words into songs, which were much shorter than books. It couldn't possibly be a meaningful occupation. Writing lyrics was simple—unlike writing the songs themselves. You just repeated the same words over and over, and all those popular songs had the same lyrics anyway. They had nothing to do with a song's success. All she had to do was string together cliché words like "dream" or "love" or "hope" to delight those teenage girls whose heads were stuffed with cotton candy. Who paid attention to lyrics anyway? If you exchanged one set for another, no one would notice, not even the singers themselves. You might miss them if they were gone altogether, but they held no value in themselves. The woman had surely manipulated her way into the industry. What a cheap, silly business. It wasn't because she was accomplished or talented that she managed to buy my house. The only talent she had was to suck up to the producers or some powerful man in the industry. She was nothing but a selfish single woman concerned only with herself. I saw right through her the first time we met. And it was through her manipulative ways that she succeeded in acquiring my house.

When I looked down, I saw fresh dirt on the ground where I had apparently dug my heels in. I took a sip from the water bottle. Glancing at my watch, I saw that it was just turning four o'clock. The sun was still high in the sky with no sign of relief. I was surprised that only two hours had passed. I felt I had been sitting on the bench for many hours, if not days, looking at the house for a long, long time. My handkerchief was soaked from the sweat trickling down my forehead and neck. Even in the shade, it was insufferable—but where else could I go? I thought of the flimsy futon in the weekly rental.

243

I thought of the low ceilings, the cheap magnets on the cabinets, that atrocious vinyl that covered the floor, the dirty windowsill, the stained bathtub, the wrinkled tablecloth. Everything lacked imagination. I thought of the empty toilet paper roll. That was no place for me. It had nothing to do with me whatsoever.

I could see the Iceberg roses blooming so profusely that they covered the ground. They seemed so gallant, blooming just as they had last year, even though I was no longer there to take care of them. *It's okay, everything will be all right*, they seemed to be saying to me. I felt my chest tighten. I wondered how the dayflowers and the jasmines were doing. That corner of the garden lacked steady sunlight, so you had to be particularly careful how you watered them. Were they still blooming? Did that woman take care of them? I was worried, since I saw no sign of her watering the garden during my three visits. She probably did so only when she felt like it, if at all— that's the kind of person she was. I could tell just by looking. She had no idea you needed to give them plenty of water every morning and evening.

My roses. My darling little flowers. It's not easy to live with flowers. When you think about it, it's far more work than keeping pets. My lovely flower garden. *Are you in pain? Are you lonely? If you could speak, if you could walk, I know you would be by my side. You would have followed me. Who would want to stay with that woman? You had no choice.* What could I do? Oh, my house. My flower garden. What could I do?

It was then that I saw the front door open, without warning. I had been staring at the house with handkerchief in hand, and the house, silent until then, seemed to rouse itself. Involuntarily, I lowered my head as if to hide. The woman emerged in a navy dress and was carrying a red purse. She locked the door, made sure that it was locked, and started walking. I could feel my heart beating so loudly that my ears hurt. I couldn't move. Without noticing me, the woman came out of the gate and walked down the street toward the train station. When she was out of sight, I stood up with some hesitation and walked briskly to the edge of the park and watched, obscured by a tree, from behind the low fence. She was just about to turn the corner and disappear from sight.

I returned to my bench and took a breath, staying still for a while. I wiped the back of my neck with a handkerchief, then pressed it against my eyes. I exhaled deeply and looked straight at the house. *It's time.* My heart started to pound, so strongly that when I put my hand to my chest, I could feel it moving.

It's time. Yes, but time for what? I didn't know. All I knew was that the woman was no longer in the house. The woman was no longer in *my* house. That much I understood, but what was I to do? What *could* I do? No . . . what did I *want* to do? What I wanted was to get my house back. But what did that mean, to get it back? To live there again? How would I do that? I had no idea. But if someone asked me what I wanted, I would wish for things to go back to the way they were. The way they used to be when that house belonged to me.

Just look at it—the garden I cultivated, the flowers I cherished, the house I designed. It wasn't about money or property. That house was *mine*, period. Putting aside rigid ideas like ownership and legal rights, what I saw before me was simply . . . mine. It stood there, just as it used to. Think about it this way. If your child were taken from you, never to return again, the child would still be yours no matter what. Whatever changed on the surface, the core remained the same. The truth would withstand any change in circumstance. It didn't matter what people thought—even if no one understood, that house was *mine*. I could say so proudly. Look. There it was, *my house*.

I emerged from the park, slowly crossed the street, and stood in front of the house. I walked up to the gate and turned the doorknob. The ground looked dry, as I had expected. The varieties of thyme, which normally grew abundantly this time of year, looked deflated. They felt limp to the touch, and the green waves were now shallow and murky. There was not enough water. I walked along the side of the house to the back. The bellflowers hung their little heads as if their energy was sucked out of them, and the larkspurs were all huddled together barely withstanding the heat. The only plants that managed to hang on were the wild strawberries and the ivies.

Finding the hose abandoned in the corner, I connected it to the water spigot, turned the faucet, and let the water flow. It flowed and flowed. The ground instantaneously turned dark and began to emit that earthy smell. I closed my eyes and inhaled deeply. It was a smell I knew so well—the smell of summer, of vegetation, of flowers. I breathed in the humid air through my nostrils and into my lungs, savoring the smell and the flow. I took it all in, filling myself up, then releasing it slowly. With the hose in hand, I walked up and down the garden, giving water to everything in sight.

The earth drank greedily. When I had watered enough, I picked the wilted flowers and the discolored grass and leaves inside the flowerpots, and placed them all in the compost by the shed. I took a bag of fertilizer and buried the pieces one by one in the soil. With slight hesitation, I returned to the shed and filled a large watering pot with diluted Hyponex plant food, and sprinkled it over the flowers and the leaves and the grass.

When all that was done, the garden seemed to come back to life.

I sat on the small terrace, and gazed contentedly at my flower garden that glistened in the summer light. Relishing the smell and the colors to my heart's content, I put away the hose, washed my hands, and sat on the terrace once more to enjoy the garden. The terrace was perfectly calculated to take in the undulating green landscape. Caressing the soft wood with my fingertips, I released a sigh from the bottom of my heart. The water drops on the leaves and flowers shimmered in the sunlight, which seemed gentler now.

I could have sat there forever. *But the church bells will be ringing soon.* I took off my sandals to go to the kitchen, reaching for the knob behind me. I stood up unhurriedly and turned around toward the sliding glass door. I saw the woman's face.

The woman was looking at me through the glass. Our faces were so close that our noses would have touched if it hadn't been for the glass door separating us.

It was as if we were looking in a mirror. How long had we stood looking at each other like that? I didn't know what she was thinking or whether she was breathing. All I was aware of was the absolute silence as the woman stood immobile before me. She never took her eyes off mine. Then, the glass door slid open and we were now facing each other directly. Her eyes and nose and mouth were at the same level as mine. I had never looked at another person's face so closely and extensively. I no longer knew what I was looking at. When I shifted my gaze to her mouth, I could see that the edges were slanted slightly upward, as if she were smiling.

"Come in."

She said this in a low voice, her gaze still fixed on mine. Her voice was much deeper than I remembered, but it sounded like a voice I knew. Then it occurred to me. It was the voice that sounded in my head when I saw the woman for the first time. Yes, that was it. Breathing through my nose quietly, I walked into the living room as if drawn by some mysterious force.

"How is everything? Living here, I mean . . ." I blurted out awkwardly, standing by the ornamental shelf and toying with my fingernails. The woman had a curious smile on her lips as she looked at me, and didn't answer my question.

"What do you want?" she said.

Oh, I was in the area and happened to pass by. I rang the doorbell but there was no answer, so I went around to the back to see

*if you were there, and noticed that the garden looked a little dry.
So I thought, why not go ahead and water it?* I was about to say all
this, but the woman continued before I could utter a word.

"You've been hanging around the house since last week. It's
creepy. What do you want?"

I glanced down, at a loss for words. The woman's toes were painted
dark pink, but her little toe had barely any nail.

"How can you stand being out in this heat for hours?"

"There's a wisteria . . ." My voice sounded strangely raspy. I
coughed. I was going to say, "It provides a bit of shade," but the
woman cut me off by sighing loudly through her nostrils.

"Look, I can imagine how you must be feeling," she said.

I continued to stare at her little toe with no nail.

"You're having trouble accepting reality. It's normal. This used
to be your house, but your husband went bankrupt and you were
kicked out. Your house becomes your identity as a housewife, doesn't
it? I could tell at a glance that this house meant everything to you.
You still can't accept it, can you? You can't accept what happened?"

I nodded, as if to agree with everything she said.

"You can't let go of your former life, so you come back to the
house. And you don't even know why."

I nodded again, as if to agree with everything she said.

"But did it never cross your mind that when you're kept by someone, this sort of thing could happen at any time?"

"Kept by someone?" I repeated.

"Exactly," she said. "You may not like the sound of it, but that's
how it is, isn't it? You don't have a job. When your husband told me
so during the closing, I wondered what the difference was between
a housewife and a domestic animal. If something happens to the
owner, the pet shares his fate. That's what's happening now, isn't it?
I suppose a dog or a child can't help being kept, but you're a woman
in your prime . . . well, you may be past your prime now, but you

were at some point. What would you say if someone asked you, What have you done with your life?"

I couldn't answer right away as the word "kept" was still ringing in my ears. *What have I done with my life?* After a while, I came up with an answer. "I managed the house."

"You managed the house . . . yes, there's something in that," she nodded. "Listen, I understand how you must feel, but that doesn't make it okay to barge into a house that belongs to someone else. That's called trespassing. It's a crime."

She threw a piercing glance at me. Tension built behind my ears, and I nodded several times in silence.

"What about the keys?" The woman demanded, as if the thought suddenly occurred to her.

"The keys?"

"Yes, the keys. You must still have keys to the house. Did you make copies before handing over the set?"

"Oh no, I didn't," I answered. The woman peered at me suspiciously, then sat down on the sofa and leaned against the cushions.

"You love the house, don't you?" She said in a tone that was half mockery and half pity, her arms folded across her chest. I wasn't sure if my feelings toward the house could be summarized in the single word "love," but nodded nonetheless.

"Yes, well . . . I do have a strong attachment to the house. I designed and furnished it myself, so I feel deep inside that it belongs to me somehow . . . and as you said, I've lived here for a long time so it's hard to let go of that feeling. Perhaps . . . I think you might understand better if you thought of the house as a child . . . the tie between a mother and child is inseparable, right? That's how I feel about my house, like a mother and child . . ."

I felt something warm surge in my chest as I voiced the words that I had repeated over and over in my mind while sitting on the park bench, or lying under the covers of the coarse futon in the dark of the night when I felt so alone despite my husband who lay next to me. It was all I could do to keep the tears from spilling out.

"But even when you lived here, the house wasn't yours, really. It belonged to your husband." The woman looked confused. "Or was it purchased under your name?"

"No, not technically . . ." I answered in a weak voice. "It was my husband who bought the house, but we're proper husband and wife . . . and I was the one who made the decisions, down to every detail. So in that sense . . . for me, it's my own house. Of course, it's my husband's house too, but fundamentally, finances aside, I feel that it's mine."

"*Finances aside*?" The woman looked surprised. "*Proper husband and wife*? Everything you have, someone bought for you. The house, the furniture, the dishes, the silverware, the bed, all the knickknacks that struck your fancy . . . the flower beds, the gate, every piece of clothing you own . . . your husband bought them all for you, didn't he? How could you say so confidently, without a hint of hesitation, that those things are *yours*? Is there a switch that goes off when you're married that makes it okay to think in that way?" The woman continued, as if she truly didn't understand. "You said before, *managed the house*. Is it because of this that you gained a sense of entitlement? You never thought of getting a job?"

I shook my head. I had never seriously given a thought to working since I got married, nor had I ever discussed it with my husband. I felt uneasy and my head was foggy. It was all I could do to keep up with what the woman was saying.

"I'm not saying this to upset you," she continued. "Believe me. It's just that I'm intrigued. How could you put yourself in such a precarious situation? That's the part I don't understand. How can you trust someone so naively? How can you put your whole life into someone else's hands? Weren't you scared? Or anxious?"

I couldn't keep up with her deluge of questions, nor could I figure out how to convey my thoughts in words. All I knew, however vaguely, was that she was wrong. I wasn't sure which part exactly, but I knew it instinctively and abstractly. That's not what it meant to be husband and wife. I couldn't express it well, but that's not what marriage was either. All this woman was concerned about was money. She was missing what was truly important. I felt this in my gut, but how could I make her understand?

"Anyway, all of this is beside the point," the woman said, seeing that I wasn't going to explain myself. "I don't really care what you think or how you choose to live your life. People do whatever they want—it has nothing to do with me."

I kept silent, staring at her toes.

"It's just that I feel strange sometimes, living here, surrounded by all the furniture you left behind . . . or rather, that I bought from you. It's that strange feeling that bothers me. I've stayed in hotels for extended periods, but it's not the same. Plus, this is one hundred percent my house—I'm not a guest or a tenant—I have nowhere else to live but here. But something strange is going on. It's not that I feel guilty or pity or think you deserved what you got—in fact, I don't think of you at all. Emotions don't interest me. It's just that . . . there's something strange about the house itself. Maybe because I'm still new to the place, but I've grown used to living here. Surprisingly so. The furniture, the doors—I feel I've known them for years. It's almost uncanny how *natural* everything feels. When I moved in and slept in the bedroom for the first time, I woke up feeling as if I'd spent countless nights here before. As if my body already knew the house and everything was connected to my memory. It was really uncanny."

I didn't know how to respond. I continued to stare at the woman's toes in silence.

"I'm not talking about ghosts or anything like that," the woman laughed. "I'm even less interested in that kind of thing than in feelings."

"It's just that . . ." the woman held her breath and looked at me. "There's this scent. It's overwhelming. Do you know what I'm talking about?"

"A scent?" I asked.

"That's right. It's not that it smells bad. It's a peculiar sort of scent that's neither bad nor good. It's the scent itself that bothers me. When I catch a whiff, I . . ." The woman fell silent.

"Do you mean . . . the scent gives you a headache?"

"No, that's not it," the woman answered after a slight pause. "It just bothers me. The scent creeps in every day from out of nowhere, at random hours. Every single day. When I catch a whiff I become . . . confused. About what, I don't know, but it makes me feel shaken at my core somehow. I escape into the bedroom, into the closet even, but the scent comes after me. I light an aroma candle, take a shower, cook, all to no avail. I was so desperate once that I asked an acquaintance to come over and check it out, but she couldn't smell anything. I was at my wit's end—then one day, I noticed you sitting over there in the park, looking over here. Do you have any idea where the scent is coming from? I'm not talking about flowers or plants."

"No, I don't," I answered.

"Then . . . perhaps you're the cause of it after all," the woman snapped coldly. "It doesn't make sense logically, but I can't think of any other reason. It's crazy that you can sit in this heat and stare at someone else's house for such a long time. It's not normal. Maybe the scent has something to do with it. I must be sensing some sort of physical danger, and my body is responding to it through the sense of smell. I'm not into superstition, but there's no other way to explain it. Plus, you've committed a crime by trespassing. The thought of you continuing to hang around the house gives me the creeps. I get a headache just thinking about it. All of that must be connected to the smell. My head is starting to throb as we speak."

I was still looking at the ground.

"So what are you going to do about it?" the woman said after a pause, sounding exasperated.

I no longer knew what to think. Why was this woman asking me what I planned to do? I knew nothing of the scent she was talking about, nor was I interested in it. So what if there was a mysterious scent? What was surprising about not feeling well? Wasn't it simply that my house had not welcomed her? To state it more plainly, wasn't it a clear sign that she had no right to live in my house?

I raised my head and looked around the living room. Nothing had changed. It was as if time had stopped inside my house. Everything was as it had been, from the sofa to the cushions to the curtains to the light that stretched across the floor this time of day in the season.

Did I not just come down from the second floor? Had I not been sewing a moment ago in my atelier? Was this not my house? The inhabitants may have changed, but things remained the same. Now that I had returned, everything could go back to the way it used to be. Like the garden just a moment ago. The house felt alive once more—I felt alive. These past several months had all been a mistake . . . and just like waking from a bad dream, I could come back.

"What's over is over." The woman's voice interrupted my thoughts. "No matter how much you long for it, the house is no longer yours. It's all over. You need to move on."

"Move on?"

"That's right. I'm being greatly inconvenienced here. You're wasting my time as we speak. What you did was criminal. I could report you to the police, but I don't want to waste any more time."

I nodded in silence.

"You need to think about how you can refrain from coming here. Are you listening? You're hung up. You're still attached to the house psychologically."

"Yes . . ."

"That's right," the woman continued. "In TV shows or in novels, people like to burn and destroy things to get revenge—but you don't do that in real life. You've lost your house, and now it belongs to me. That's a fact. Period. If you killed me now, the house still wouldn't be yours. The only thing left to do, then, is for you to change. So the important question is, How can you make this change? How can you get over the attachment you have to the house?"

I nodded weakly at the woman's words.

"Listen, this is something you should be thinking about yourself. I just want to resolve this as quickly as possible. What does it take for you to move on? If this was a romantic affair, well . . . you could have closure by having sex or a huge blowout—something that aims for a final sense of unity before going separate ways. Once you've given it your all, you can move on, or so I hear. How about doing something like that?"

"Like what?" I asked. "Do what exactly?"

"That was just an analogy. I'm just thinking of ways for you to get over the whole thing. Let's see . . . what's your favorite thing about this house?"

"Everything," I answered. As I listened to the woman, my mind became foggy and my head was beginning to throb. What was she talking about? Although I felt my head tighten, the pain felt abstract and my body seemed to become more and more remote with every minute. I could no longer tell what was real and what was not.

"You can't say *everything*. Try to be more specific."

"The flower garden," I whispered after a while.

"The flower garden." The woman became thoughtful and fell silent. Then, she looked straight at me.

"The flower garden . . . That might work."

"Hmmm," I said vaguely.

"It could be a kind of therapy. More practical, even. Why don't you become the flower garden itself? Who knows if it will work, but then, one thing may lead to another . . . you might come out feeling better. It may be worth trying—becoming one with what's most important to you, something you normally can't attain unity with. Why don't we try it while the sun is out? Who knows, it may even be connected to that scent I've been talking about. Plus . . . this is the last time I'm offering you help. Next time, I'm handing you over to the police."

"But how?" I was puzzled.

"You become part of the flower garden," the woman snapped in a cold voice, "by burying yourself. Next to all of your precious flowers. To reach a catharsis, they say you either have to burn it or bury it. And we can't exactly burn you, can we? So instead, you can connect with what's most precious to you from a different perspective, a different approach. You might have an epiphany. Or, who knows, you might lose interest in the house altogether. It's worth trying in any case. I'm sure no other fifty-year-old housewife has done such a thing before."

With a chuckle, the woman glided across the living room and opened the sliding glass door to the garden. She turned around and motioned for me to follow. I walked toward her, dragging my feet, which were nearly asleep from standing for so long.

The woman stepped into the flower garden and put on the gardening shoes. She walked over to the shed where the gardening tools were kept, and brought over a large shovel and spade. I stared at the spade as she placed it in my hand. The memory of buying the tools came back to me. How I couldn't decide on the design of the handle. The first time I used them to dig up soil. How the ground was so tough because of all the roots. The sound of the soil being pierced through. Dirt crumbling. Digging up potatoes. Wait, wasn't I a child then? The gardening gloves. My husband. He was busy with work and rarely around, but sometimes I would turn and see him watching me with a pleased expression as I poked around in the ground. *The flowers are beautiful*, he would say. *Thanks to you, our garden is always in good shape*. Yes, that was here. The two of us. When I let my guard down, when I let my thoughts wander, all kinds of memories came flooding back. They enveloped me completely. Where were they taking me? The spade was rusty. They came rushing back. What did any of that have to do with the shovel and spade?

The woman stepped on the bed of thyme. Pointing to the ground with the shovel in her right hand, she drew an outline just above the ground. "Is this big enough? We can't dig too deep, so we'll have to bury you horizontally. A rectangular shape, like a coffin." I began digging into the bed of thyme as the woman directed. Because of the water I had just given it, the soil gave in to the spade easily and soon I could see the dark, moist part. In silence, I dug the edges of the rectangle, then began digging deeper. I dug and dug, in silence. The bed of thyme was shallow and came out without resistance, its white roots exposed and severed from the soil. All around me were piles of black soil mixed with green and white. After half an hour or so, there was a dark hole big enough for a person to lie in.

"Go ahead and lie down," the woman said.

I sat down on the dark, moist soil and stretched my legs, placing my arms to my side. I breathed in the gentle smell of the soil. *Stay still*, the woman said, *I'm going to bury you now*. It was that voice again. I felt a cool sensation on the back of my hands, my arms, my neck. The voice began to cover me with the soil mixed with thyme. At first it felt light, then I began to feel the weight on my chest and thighs. After a while, I felt a new sort of weight fall upon me with a thump. It seemed that she had added compost she found in the shed. The voice continued to cover me with soil as I lay in the middle of the garden.

The summer evening sky extended as far as my eyes could see. When I opened them wide, the sky became wider with them. The sky became so wide that, curious to see how far it would stretch, I opened my eyes as wide as I could, and opened my mouth along with them. The tinted cirrocumulus clouds appeared faint and ephemeral in the distance, and I could see a small airplane floating among the clouds. The voice continued to cover me with soil. My limbs became heavier and heavier as the hands pressed down the dirt meticulously. The seeds, the bulbs, the roots. I could see myself tending to the flowers wearing my gardening gloves. *May you bloom beautifully. May you take root.* Each time I dug the spade into the earth, fresh dirt would fall upon my body. *What have I done?* One scoop at a time, I became heavier and heavier. Then, I became lighter and lighter. My limbs were no longer free and I could hardly breathe, but somehow, somewhere, I could feel myself growing upward toward the sky. *What have I done?* The voice, now silent, covered me with dirt. I could hear it breathing. Whose voice was it? I couldn't see the face, but it seemed to be struggling. Whose voice was it? It covered me with dirt. I covered myself with dirt. Each time I breathed, each time the voice pressed down with its hands, I became heavier and heavier. One scoop at a time, I became lighter. Managing to shift my neck slightly to the side, I saw the leaves of petunia flowers. A water drop swayed and reflected the light. A newborn ladybug was about to spread its wings. I had a feeling that I had seen this moment long, long ago, but could no longer remember when. But I will tell him. When my husband comes home, I will tell him about the ladybug, about this tiny delicate creature ready to spread its wings and take off. Beyond the windows of my house, I hear the usual church bells ringing. I will leave my room, descend the stairs, and tell all kinds of stories. About these flowers that breathed gently, existing quietly in peace. About myself. About all that I can see from here. I will tell you everything.

Ocean Vuong was born on a rice farm outside Saigon in 1988. When he was age two, after a year in a refugee camp, he and his family arrived in the United States. He was the first in his immediate family to learn how to read proficiently, at the age of eleven. With Ben Lerner as his mentor at Brooklyn College, he wrote the poems that would become his first collection, *Night Sky with Exit Wounds*. A Ruth Lilly and Dorothy Sargent Rosenberg Poetry fellow and winner of a Pushcart Prize, he has received honors and awards from Poets House and the Academy of American Poets. In 2016 he received a Whiting Award. Ocean Vuong lives in New York.

Partly True Poem
Reflected in a Mirror

OCEAN VUONG

i want to find a gun / and change myself / he said / in the dream
only a week before his mother called / no hello only / her breath a
windmill crashing slowly into my head / this face already changed
since heavy rain left november too bloody / to read in a boy finds
a bridge and becomes / everywhere and i decide against / tuesday
/ vandross on the stereo muted tv / the room pink / with images of
a bloody dictator / my face the shade of strawberry icing / as i sit
through one war / another hold / the page closer to the glass dammit
/ imagine yourself in / real life / there should be tears / there should
be / a reason but all i have / is the voice: seventeen *children are
gunned down in afghanistan today* / and i think: shouldn't it be
gunned up? / doesn't the bullet / in a child / become an angel-seed
/ the beginning / of "heaven" / *how dare you* / i mutter to myself
/ and the face / is only a little "prettier" than yesterday / which is
enough / so i step into the n train doors opening / the line break i
finished / schuyler's book / his grip still warm on my shoulder / words
all blurry / the last time / someone borrowed him was may 13 1981
/ which makes me sadder / than mondays in the library / reading
all the heroes who killed themselves / trying to save / my life / but
the pills were like / "the teeth of an angel" i said / into the mirror /

said i'd make it / to 34th st. but now i'm not sure / what i smoked
is working / i take long hits / cause i don't have healthcare / a line
here / and there keeps my hands from shaking / barely made it to
brooklyn college / without palms wet again / clutching the seats i'm
sick / and sorry / for the scar on your face even / at night the day
brighter / as a memory / the young poet with a mustache / sitting
in the dusty classroom says / *don't worry you have an edge / your
friend died plus / you're asian* and i want / to take his hand and lie
down in the room / lit only with broken glass / a coffee table axed
to pieces / the statue of a plastic buddha / decapitated / and there
no more prayers / at the prow of you / instead / i said *have you ever
been fucked in the ass?* . . . *no / no i don't mean figuratively* / you
see / all this trouble / just to make some sense / just to make a ghost
appear / on paper / so you can see me in this mirror and maybe it's
8pm there / after all / this face already gone / maybe this is just to
say / that i found the gun / and changed / the world instead / and
now it's just you and me / dear reader / meeting each other for / the
first time in a room dark / as the insides of / our skulls / and look
i'm sorry i'm reflecting / the two gashes in your face / i would stitch
them up / but you'll never see again

Heather O'Neill is the author of three novels: *Lullabies for Little Criminals,* which was short-listed for the Orange Prize for Fiction; *The Girl Who Was Saturday Night*; and *The Lonely Hearts Hotel.* She is also the author of a collection of short stories, *Daydreams of Angels*; and a book of poems, *two eyes are you sleeping.* Born and raised in Montreal, O'Neill lives there today with her daughter.

A Song for Robin

HEATHER O'NEILL

They've asked me to sing a song at Robin's funeral. I'm going to do it, of course. Even though I haven't seen him in a while. I know exactly what song I'm going to sing too. Let me tell you how I chose it.

My dad's family business was robbing gas stations. That was what his family had taught him how to do. And he did it really well until I was born. His parole officer got him a job because he wouldn't have known how to find one otherwise. His parole officer's name was Martin. He said he thanked God every day that Martin had turned him from a bum into a man. He started working as a janitor at the train station when I was two and he's done it ever since.

He said it was his job that made him happy. Like he would make jokes at the dinner table and we would laugh and laugh and laugh. We were always choking on our spoonfuls of Kraft Dinner. He stood up at the table once and did a Pavarotti impersonation with like made-up Italian words. "Oororosolomeoo. . . ." We thought it was so funny.

He would tell us all the dumb things that happened at his work. All the stupid-assed things people said. He would put on a sign that said the floors were wet because he had just mopped them. But people didn't care and they still walked across them really quickly and then they would slip and all the papers would fly out of their briefcases. I know that doesn't sound funny. But when my dad would tell the story, we would like die laughing. He would imitate their facial expressions right at that moment when their body was in the air and their asses hadn't broken yet.

I don't know if my sister and brother have any particular talents. But I liked songs.

Even when I was really little, when my mom used to turn on the radio in the kitchen, I'd always go really quiet, I wouldn't make a peep. The music was like a magic spell on me. They all liked when I sang commercials. My mom said I sang the orange juice commercial better than the woman who was on the orange juice commercial. I loved that. I was so proud of myself.

When I got older, I would be able to remember all the words to whole songs and not just advertisements. I used to sing a Dolly Parton song. My dad would invite his friends over. He would get me to sing "9 to 5" for them. They loved that. I didn't have any idea what it meant.

My family didn't know what in the world I was supposed to do with the ability to sing orange juice songs. They didn't know how in the world a person was supposed to get anywhere in the world. It wasn't their fault. They were just ignorant. Their parents hadn't passed on any knowledge when it came to getting by. And so they had nothing to pass on to me.

At school I was average, average, average. I wasn't left behind any years or anything like that. But I didn't get my tests back covered in stickers or praise the way some kids did either. And I never got any badges in gym class. I was surprised when the teachers remembered my name.

I didn't mind going to school, only I found it boring. I probably would have gotten more out of it if I had applied myself. I just looked out the window and killed time. I spent the whole morning looking forward to lunch.

Then this one morning I saw the sign for the talent show auditions on the wall near math class. I really thought, I'm going to miss out on something if I don't do this.

I didn't tell anyone in my home what I was doing. Sometimes I think my family had an inferiority complex. When we were in the living room, we would feel like we were kings of the world. But outside they were all about keeping your head down and not drawing attention to yourself.

I'm not sure they knew what they were afraid of. But I think they were afraid of being judged. And there I was literally asking to be judged. In the auditorium there was the drama teacher and the music teacher. And three of those kids who get involved in everything, the ones trying to pass themselves off as teachers, would be there to judge me too.

I was wearing a pair of plastic red jelly shoes and a yellow terry-cloth dress with bows on the shoulders. And my hair was way up in a blonde ponytail!

All the other kids who were performing musical numbers had full bands. They were doing rock and roll songs. There were kids that were all dressed in the same outfits doing hip-hop numbers. I knew looking at their elaborate productions that I was probably doomed.

When it was my turn, I stood there in the center of the stage. I didn't get into character or anything. I said that I would sing the Life Savers commercial. My whole family said there was nothing better than when I sang that jingle, so I decided to believe them. I didn't have a score for the piano guy because I wanted to sing it a cappella. The kids in the auditorium and backstage were laughing the whole way through the thirty seconds of my song. They thought I was as dumb as dumb can be. I didn't disagree.

As I was leaving, a kid in my class I never spoke to named Robin came running up to me and tugged at my ponytail to get my attention. He said I had the most beautiful voice he'd ever heard.

I looked him up and down to see if he was making fun of me. He was skinny and had bangs in his eyes. He was wearing a jean vest that was covered in so many studs that I thought it made him look like a lizard.

"Seriously," he said. "That was totally wicked."

"Nobody said anything," I answered.

"That's because they were spellbound! They didn't know what to make of your voice. It's unique. It's sweet. It's like God gave you some cough drops when you were born. You're better than most stuff on the radio."

"Then how come they said sorry, you can't be in the talent show?"

"Because they are afraid of greatness."

"You're crazy."

"You got any more commercials you can sing me?"

I sang him the oatmeal ad that had been on heavy rotation on television. Then he said he wanted to be my manager. He was seventeen years old. I had no idea what he meant by that. But I let him walk me home the next few weeks. At first he was always talking about how good I was at singing. Which I liked. Of course you're going to listen to anybody complimenting you. It's so addictive. Listening to just one compliment is like eating just one chip. Impossible but after a couple of days of talking about me, I got bored, and we started talking about other music.

And that was so interesting. Because I'd had all these complicated thoughts about rock and roll songs that I was totally in love with. I didn't know there was anybody else who was thinking these thoughts. And if there were, it wasn't someone my age and on my block.

We were both really into the Eurythmics. Annie Lennox's voice is so deep. It's like she's speaking from far away, from another dimension. Like she's just the low notes on the piano. And her words are so smooth. They are like cream. Like all those little plastic cups of cream you get at Wendy's for your coffee.

And Tina Turner. She has this crackly voice like she's singing over a loudspeaker. Like her words are written on paper but the paper is burning. All these women who get beat up by their husbands are so tough afterwards.

I had an aunt just like Tina Turner. After she left my uncle, she wouldn't let anybody look at her the wrong way. And she wore a fur coat everywhere and she was like a queen! She was the Queen of Overdale Avenue.

Robin really liked Fleetwood Mac. There was something about Stevie Nicks that bothered me though. She was like one of those girls who are always about to have a nervous breakdown. Or stand outside on the street begging their boyfriends to take them back. Also, I always thought that if a guy had a chance of dating either me or Stevie Nicks, he would choose Stevie Nicks.

Michael Jackson! I could spend my whole life talking about him. He's so talented. If I was going to be stranded on a desert island, and I could only take one album, it would be Michael Jackson's *Thriller*. That album is like my autobiography. Michael Jackson is in every memory I have. Like at all the birthday parties that I went to at McDonald's, he was playing at them.

We talked about "Time After Time." I never even took Cyndi Lauper seriously because of the way she dressed. Like those middle-aged ladies who try and dress kooky to make up for the fact that they are so ugly. I hate those crazy white cat ladies. There were like one too many of them on Overdale. My dad says it's what happens to a woman if she doesn't get laid enough. But she was wonderful. It was like I'd been punched in the gut when I heard her singing that song. That's how shocked I was. But in a good way.

After we'd walked home together for a couple of weeks, Robin asked if I wanted to come over to his apartment. His mother was a skinny crazy junkie. She was always putting him in foster care and ignoring him whenever she had a new boyfriend around. He didn't tell me about this. It was just one of the stories that the whole neighborhood knew about. All the parents would shake their heads at how he was raised. One time, years ago, when Robin would have been about seven, my dad said he saw him sitting on the stoop outside his building all by himself at midnight.

When I walked in Robin said his mother hadn't been home in a couple of weeks. You could tell because the place was a dump. There was an Indian carpet on the floor that had been stepped on so many times that you could hardly see the pattern anymore. There was light blue wallpaper with white flowers on it that had been ripped in a spot. There were teacups on the coffee table. Some were filled with different-colored tea, shades of red and burgundy and brown. Some had cigarette butts in them. One was filled with sales receipts.

He showed me his box of cassettes. We lay on the floor next to his boom box and listened to them. He stuck in one by a singer named Tracy Chapman.

I had never heard Tracy Chapman before. She was brand-new. What a surprise! It was as if I had gone to a bank to take ten dollars out of the ATM machine and my bank statement came back saying I had three million dollars in my chequing account. That's what the song was like when it went to my heart like it was an ATM machine.

I was surprised that it didn't kill me. You would think all that emotion would make my heart explode. Sort of like when you plugged in too many appliances, and the fuse couldn't take it anymore, so it just blew.

Maybe that was what had happened to the dinosaurs, someone dragged out a boom box to the middle of a field during Jurassic time and stuck in a Tracy Chapman cassette. And their big-ass hearts couldn't take it and exploded like water balloons.

Afterward, we went to the kitchen to see if there was something in the fridge to eat. Robin opened a beer and the suds poured down my hand and onto my toes and it was like I was standing on the beach at the edge of the waves. He said that it gave him a hard-on how beautiful my body was. Because although I probably didn't mention it, I was quite developed for my age. And then we took off all our clothes and we fucked each other senseless. Although I wouldn't have described it like that at the time.

My bra was lying on the floor like a clamshell.

After that first time we were together, I kept crying and crying. I didn't know whether I was happy or sad or what. I think he wanted to cry too. I remember him standing at the side of the bed. He was all naked. Except he had a gold chain around his neck with a cross on it. I found out later he got it when he was a baby and he never took it off.

I felt a little bit different when I got home after sex. It was a little bit like I was pretending to be myself. I had to trick everybody into believing that I was Theresa.

And it broke my heart that they believed it. Their little girl had been killed, but they didn't know it. They didn't have any idea. And the person who was responsible for murdering her was right there sitting beside them! And she was wearing Theresa's velour jumper and her favourite socks, the ones with the strawberries on them.

I was sitting on the chesterfield and I started to cry. And they were all like, What the hell are you crying about? We're watching Newhart. Nothing sad can happen!

You lose your virginity, then you have to keep it a secret. I couldn't do that! I mean I wasn't going to tell them that I had busted my cherry, but I did want to tell them that I had a boyfriend.

So I invited Robin over for dinner. I thought it was the thing to do. It seemed polite after we had slept together. Before we had been kids together, but now we had had sex, and so we were adults. Right?

I got dressed up in my Sunday clothes when he was coming over. The whole family got dressed up because it was the first time that I was bringing a boy home.

My mother took out the fancy plates. When we weren't having guests over we would use the dishes with roosters on them. The roosters were always strutting their stuff. Roosters on every plate and on the side of the soup bowl. Now they were just plain white.

We brought out all the plastic doilies. And set them on the white tablecloth. Setting a table like that makes everybody have to pitch in. We had to bring out every chair from the house and put it somewhere around the table.

I was worried that Robin wasn't going to fit in. The vice principal of the school gave him a hard time about a lot of the outfits he came to school wearing. She would yell out to him that his sweater looked like Swiss cheese. He had these silver Michael Jackson gloves that he used to wear. He had black army boots held together with pink duct tape. Every time he got onto a public bus everybody turned to look at him. He liked that. He had these big sunglasses with white frames, sort of like the ones Jackie Onassis wore.

He rang the doorbell. When I opened the door, he was wearing a button-up shirt and corduroys. He had a bouquet of flowers that he handed to my mother. I don't know where he got them. Maybe he broke into the botanical gardens, I never asked. He had a box of chocolates too. Honestly, when he showed up with all that stuff, I thought that we were married.

He was so polite to everybody. He had really nice manners. My mother asked him all sorts of really boring questions. But he looked at her like she was asking him important philosophical things. She kept asking him about his apartment like was it cold in the winter and did his mother put plastic up on the windows. Did he have any idea how much she paid for the heating bill? Did they ever have mice?

My mom had made her stuffed green peppers. That was her specialty. But I thought they were disgusting. They looked like ordinary green peppers, but when you lifted the lid off the pepper, there was tomato and hamburger beef mush inside. I hated the taste of it myself. But it was an engineering feat, so we got to be impressed. It was like those commercials about who put the caramel in the Caramilk bar. Except in this case I suppose the question was, Who put the meat loaf in the green pepper bell.

My dad started telling us a story about being in line at the grocery store. He was buying ten bags of Cheez Doodles because they were on sale. But the cashier said he could only buy three at a time. That killed us. I thought my appendix was going to burst from laughing so hard. It was the way he told the stories too. He was funnier than Richard Pryor. My mother begged him to stop before she used up all the oxygen in the room.

Then Robin started talking about the way I sang. My family didn't really understand the purpose of music. I mean they certainly didn't see it as an art form or anything like that. It was something that was played inside delis while people were picking out their favorite chewing gum. Or at the beginning of a television show so that you would know you were right at the beginning of it and hadn't missed a thing. And to make commercial slogans stick in your head.

The only cultural thing we did was when we went to see *E.T.* That was like the biggest deal. We never went to see movies because there were so many of us that it cost too much money. But my dad said that it was historically important for us to go. He said people would be talking about that alien for years. So it was necessary for us to know what they were talking about.

Robin started saying that the universe was very careful when it handed out talents. It was exceedingly careful when it considered who it was going to give beautiful singing voices to.

"It gives voices to people who need to tell a tale," Robin said. "Theresa was given her gift because she's supposed to give a voice to the people on the street. When she sings, she isn't only telling her own story, she's singing about everybody's dreams and sorrows whether I liked it or not."

"Get out of here," I said.

He said that with every gift there came responsibility. He said that people had no right to keep a gift to themselves. They were obliged to share it. You were stealing from others by not sharing it.

I liked the way my family was listening to him. They all quieted down to hear what he had to say. I always wonder how come there can't be more of these nights. You know.

Robin still wanted to be my manager. He was going to get me a record deal. He was going to get a 6-track player from the pawn-shop and record me singing. But he said we had to pay our dues on the road too.

He had a keyboard that he really didn't know how to play. But he could program songs in and pretend to play them. So what was wrong with that? And he sang backup vocals for me. I always liked to hear him chime in, just when I thought I was all alone in a song.

He got us our first gig, playing at the Portuguese Community Center. There were these old-timers there wearing uniforms. It was some sort of veterans' night. They had little paper plates to put hors d'oeuvres on. They would take their dentures off and put them in their pockets and eat the tiny cakes. One was wearing a wristwatch and it began to go off in the middle of my solo. He took out some pills from inside his jacket and then swallowed them.

Then we had a show at a retirement home on Thanksgiving. They all got up and started their strange dancing. They looked like how your dolls look when you get them to dance together. We played at a kid's birthday party. We played at a convention. We played at a retirement

272

party. We did a lot of weddings. Once we played the opening of a grocery store. It was like the fortieth anniversary of this grocery store. They had us go play in the back by the frozen goods section for a couple of hours. When we were done, along with our paycheque, they gave us a complimentary chicken all wrapped in gold foil.

Robin would wear a suit. He was always able to put together some sort of odd flamboyant outfit he picked up at the thrift shop.

I was going to need a trademark outfit. Because that was the outfit that I was going to be photographed in about a thousand times. And it would be on all my record albums. Like Édith Piaf with her little black dress. It would be the dress that people pictured me in when they were at home listening to my records with their eyes closed.

My mom said I could take her old wedding dress. She started going at it with a pair of scissors. She started pulling it in different directions with pins and needles. She had a measuring tape and she started holding it up to different parts of me. I had never been fitted for anything. It actually made me think of Cinderella. When it was done, it was really pretty. It had all these beige ribbons in the back.

You're supposed to dry-clean wedding dresses, but there's no way that I could have afforded something like that. I just washed it by hand in a bucket in the bathtub and then hung it from a clothes hanger from the showerhead. Or if it was a sunny day, I hung it out on the clothesline on the balcony.

I must have worn that dress forty times that summer. Sometimes we even played two gigs in one day.

Oh and, of course, we'd pin as many flowers as we could to my hair. Robin was always excited about how flowers looked in my blonde hair.

We went outside the city to perform at weddings being held in the country. When Robin and I were onstage, we were so harmonious. Maybe because we always just got along really well and had a lot in common. I think that comes across when you perform. No matter where we were, someone always requested Stevie Wonder's "I Just Called to Say I Love You." And that is one of the most important love songs of all time. It's all about being with someone and it being so comfortable and perfect and spiritual. And that's what we were putting across onstage, two people in a Stevie Wonder paradise.

On the bus ride home, you'd see the city in the distance, looking like a Lite-Brite set. Robin had bigger dreams for us. He liked to talk about them on the ride home sitting with his cheap keyboard on his lap. He had a plan where we would play on a cruise ship. But after a little while I knew that our band would never get that far.

Partly because he was getting stoned all the time. I saved up my money and bought all kinds of things, like a black coat with round white buttons that my dad said reminded him of a domino piece. Robin spent all of his on drugs. When I tried to say something about it, he said it was because he was an artist. It makes sense to be stoned if you are in a rock and roll band and playing at places like CGBG's. But if you're like at a ten-year-old's birthday, I don't think that it makes sense. Once Robin was sitting on a pink plastic chair with his legs crossed holding a paper cup with iced tea in his hand with his eyes closed for fifteen minutes. He had confetti in his hair the next day. He didn't even bother to comb it out.

Also he didn't make love to me anymore because of the drugs. And he stopped wanting to talk about music. He just wanted to borrow my share of the money we made all the time, which I didn't like. Once I refused to give him five dollars and he called me a bitch right in front of everybody on the street.

"I made you who you are. I got you all these gigs. Why are you being such an ungrateful bitch now?"

"I don't like the way you're starting to talk to me," I said. "You used to like to talk about music."

I paid attention to all those after-school specials. They made an impression on me. The drug-addict life seemed about as appealing to me as getting cancer. I saw junkies out on the street corners all the time. I did not want to stand on a corner my whole life begging people for crumbs, you know. And having to move out of the way when they wanted me to move out of the way. And scurrying across the street all the time, almost always like two seconds away from getting run over by a car.

Robin was ambitious about what he expected from the world. But I didn't really need anything like that. I just wanted to be happy. All I desired was a sweet little nest to come home to in the evenings— with all my people in it.

My dad was so proud of his job. He would do push-ups next to the bed in the morning. We always argued about whose turn it was to sit on his back while he did push-ups when we were little. That's the good life. Get yourself a job that no one else wants, my dad used to say, and no one will try and steal it from you.

So I got a job at Dunkin' Donuts. I got myself one of those little brown dresses with orange lapels. I got to put pink icing on the donuts every morning. I found that I really liked it. The best part was that I got to bring home donuts for everyone at the end of the day. That's a perk. The only drawback is the pay stays basically the same until you are like ninety years old.

My parents always made a big sloppy deal out of one another. I think they thought that it was important to kiss in front of us kids. Once my dad said that for dessert he wanted a kiss from my mom's big sweet lips. She went over and sat on his lap and kissed him. We always screamed and giggled when they did that. I wondered as a kid how come my mother didn't crush him with her big ass. But I think she was weightless when she sat on him. She was like a beautiful deflating air balloon.

My mother used to say that we weren't rich in money, but we were rich in all sorts of other things. Like love, I guess she meant.

I broke up with Robin. I started dating Peter, who worked at the donut store with me.

I heard from Robin two years later. He called me from prison. He had one phone call to make. I didn't know why he was calling me. I didn't know what I could do for him. But I was yelling at everybody in the apartment to shush. When someone calls you from prison, it is holy and you have to treat it with respect.

He wanted me to sing a Whitney Houston song. He wanted "How Will I Know." And everybody in my family got quiet and gathered in the hallway. They were all listening too. He liked that song because I think he never really believed that anyone really liked him. He was feeling lonely and wanted to know that even though you felt all alone and like everything was wrong, you might be all wrong about that feeling.

All those nights out playing in our rinky-dink band were really fun, but I never took it seriously. I don't like those big, big ideas. They are kind of like drugs. I don't have it in me to be somebody like Whitney Houston. She would fight with Bobby Brown all night long—I could never be in a relationship like that. I just wouldn't care at all. She cared so much about Bobby Brown that she let him drive her crazy. She just was so afraid of nobody loving her that she would let a dude treat her any way he wanted.

It's really not my business to figure out who killed Robin. The best thing I can do at the moment is just sing the Whitney Houston song at his funeral. I don't know if that'll do Robin any good. I think I need to sing it to me as much as to him. I think I'll be singing a love song to some sort of dream that was too big for us to have.

Johan Harstad is a Norwegian novelist, short-story writer, playwright, and graphic designer. His novels include *Buzz Aldrin, What Happened to You in All the Confusion?*—a *Kirkus Reviews* best book of the year, which has been published in thirteen countries—and *Max, Mischa, and the Tet Offensive.* He is also the author of *172 Hours on the Moon,* which won the 2008 Norwegian Brage Prize in the young adult/children's literature category; four plays; a collection of short stories; and a prose collection. He lives in Oslo, Norway.

Tara Chace has translated more than twenty-five novels from Norwegian, Swedish, and Danish. Her recent translations include Jo Nesbø's Doctor Proctor's Fart Powder series (Aladdin, 2010–2017); Johanne Hildebrandt's *Unbroken Line of the Moon* (Amazon Crossing, 2016); and Sven Nordqvist's Adventures of Pettson and Findus series (NorthSouth, 2014–2017). She translated Johan Harstad's YA sci-fi thriller *172 Hours on the Moon* (Little, Brown Books for Young Readers, 2012). An avid reader and language learner, Chace earned her PhD in Scandinavian Languages and Literature from the University of Washington in 2003. She lives in Seattle with her family and their black lab, Zephyr.

Max, Mischa,
and the Tet Offensive

JOHAN HARSTAD
TRANSLATED FROM THE NORWEGIAN BY TARA CHACE

Marin in the morning. I sit on a bench, surrounded by tourists with iPhones and SLR cameras with limitless memory cards and the ability to snap pictures at the same firing rate as a Minigun. Like me, they're looking down at the Golden Gate Bridge. They're happy to be here. We're all happy to be here. We all have our reasons. Our smiles are a language with a million dialects. It's quarter to eight in the morning and the night's chill is still in the air. It hasn't eased even though the day has long since begun. The city at the other end of the bridge, San Francisco. Alcatraz and Berkeley farther away. I haven't been here before. It's a beautiful city, not like Los Angeles. In San Francisco, I would have really fit in. We got here yesterday. Slept here last night, in the car. I slept well, undisturbed for almost eight hours, until a German rapped on the windshield and woke me up to ask if it cost anything to park here. Then it was time to get up. Stand up and sit down again, that's how it is. No reason to go if there's no place you need to be. I sit on one of the two benches here; I've been claiming it for more than an hour, smoking cigarettes and drinking water. Sure, only one of these two activities is socially acceptable around here. Somewhere over there in the city is the theater. I can't remember off the top of my head what it's called, but what does it matter? The address is stored in GPS, as is that of the Fairmont, where currently I'm technically checked in. In name if not in spirit as they say. The ensemble has been looking forward to coming here; San Francisco is known for its theater audiences and I wish the cast easier days now, they deserve an audience who'll welcome them with open arms even if most of what's slung from the stage is enough to make a person fling himself off the bridge down there. If so, he wouldn't be the first. Or the last. A troubling number of people kill themselves from that reddish-brown bridge every year, enough that the authorities are considering installing a net to catch all those unhappy and desperate people before they're lost to us for good. Maybe we should have had that for the theater as well. I'm ashamed to have put on *Better Worlds Through Weyland-Yutani*. What was I thinking? I suppose it was rage that made me do it; I think I wanted to air the rage onstage in hopes that it would abate. It doesn't. The audience members obediently accept the text, which tells them that they're all irrelevant and no one cares about them after all. Terrible to watch. How they applaud their own demise because they don't think they deserve anything different. I spot a guy jogging across the Golden Gate coming toward Marin County, and for an instant I'm worried he'll be one of the ones who suddenly give up, climb over the railing and vanish, one of the ones who don't even hesitate. But he just keeps running, leaning into the headwind down there, a man in his early or late forties, not easy to say for sure from this distance. A half hour later, he comes huffing and puffing up the winding hills and passes me, winded and flushed, with an empty water bottle and sweat pouring from his cap, on which is written the word *AWESOME* in big, yellow letters on a light blue background. He looks like a man who regrets everything.

Sooner or later he, too, will get there. This, I know: at one time, I was one of the ones running.

We meet in the gym at the school outside Stavanger every Monday, Wednesday, and Friday in our dark blue tracksuits with *Forus and Gausel Athletic Club* printed on the back, always on time, well, at least Stig and I always arrive at the same time; we slide our bikes into their spots on the bike rack and shiver in the cool afternoon air. Then Andri comes, a few minutes later. "Sorry," he says, "my mom kind of took her time with dinner." She always does. Cooking isn't her forte.

We've been told we have a lot of potential, that we can go far, we have athletic potential, and our coaches, mostly local parents who have varying degrees of a clue about sports, complain incessantly about all the kids who suddenly stop coming when they hit fourteen, fifteen. But we're going to stick with it, we're sure of it. I've started to believe it, because neither of my parents has said a word about moving anywhere at all and it's 1989, more than a year has gone by, it's early October and I'm twelve years old. I think we're going to stay. So no way am I going to disappoint Sean, the physiotherapist from Ireland who always overestimates the shape we're in and sends us out on impossibly long runs with built-in hill interval training inspired by Spetsnaz forces, or Ola, the bald, good-natured meditation guru who can never figure out the floodlights and lets us run hurdles and throw the javelin in the dark on the soccer field and who, when we come inside where it's warm for the last half hour, puts together these bizarre, multidimensional obstacle courses in the gym which are just as hard to comprehend as to complete.

Yeah, we're going to stick with it, even after we turn fifteen. Of course we will.

We run and it feels like we're going to die. And it's cold out. That's how I remember all the training back then, as something that took

281

place in the fall, or late in winter, while it was dark in Norway, and there were reflections on the asphalt from the cold rain that had fallen. We must have trained in the spring, too, and in the summer, but anyway that's how I remember it, and our breath always showed and we had to keep moving to stay warm and the streetlights disappeared behind us as we ran farther and farther each time, always to places we'd never been before, with no idea when we'd get back to school again. It's Stig, Andri, and me, together with Sean's eldest son and another seventeen-year-old from my sister Ulrikke's class who digs Springsteen, both of them to our horror. The two older kids always take the lead and know where we're supposed to go, probably hoping that we three youngsters panting along after them will fall behind and eventually throw in the towel, turn around, and go home again crestfallen. But we never give up. We really sink our teeth into it as we pass the twenty-kilometers-of-nonstop-running mark and are sure we'll never make it back alive. We stick it out for the first fifteen minutes, the first half hour, always the hardest, the toughest, with a stitch in our sides and breathing that's impossible to control, we converse in dependent clauses to shift our focus or just to prove that we still have enough breath left to do this; we run throughout all of Forus, and all the places have their own names, too, I remember all the street names: We run up Ulsbergbakken and Heddeveien, through the woods, and along Godesetdalen; eventually our voices go completely quiet, they're replaced by the sounds of our running shoes against wet asphalt and our regular breathing, in and out, in and out, in step, our breathing synchronized, we're like full-speed human metronomes, organic machines that just go and go and go, and soon it gets darker around us, the distance between the streetlights and the houses increases, we're out in the countryside now, past the farms and the fields on Jåttåveien. Something strange happens in our heads as we stop thinking about how tiring what we're doing is, as body and brain part ways, each leaving the other to do its own thing. This is what Ola has described so many times to his meditation students, *letting your head fly.* So, that's exactly what I do. I let it fly and we run down toward the highway and Hinna, and I leave myself and am raised, higher and higher, I can no longer hear our sounds, and the landscape opens up, I see us from above as we run through the last evidence that the industrial neighborhood we live in was ever an agricultural area, far from the city, far from the world. I rise higher and stare down at the housing developments and streets and schools and stores and factories that surround the dark green fields where the last of the horses stand still and graze, oblivious to what's happening, and in the middle of all this I can just barely make out five people running, faster than they were in the beginning, their legs jut out again and again from their lower bodies and pull them forward, it's an amazing sight, and then I lose us in the cloud layer for a second. I don't find us again until we're past Jåttåvågen where the Condeep bases for oil and gas production platforms are built before being sent out into the North Sea. We're on our way back now, and I think we're glowing, at least I know I am, but I'm not tired, none of us are; we're indefatigable, we're on the cusp of something big, we're going to start middle school soon, our lives will begin as soon as next year and it's impossible to know what will happen after that, reality will open wide and we'll be in the thick of it. We fight our way up the final stretch, the interminable Gauselbakken, still alive, still with energy left. I can see my own face as I reach the top, see the school and know we're there, I can see myself and I know what I'm thinking, because I'm thinking about my parents, I'm thinking that it's Friday and soon, after a final half hour indoors where we'll get to play our way through an intense round of floorball before we break for the evening, I'll say goodbye to my friends and hop onto my bike, ride home, and my mom will take a loaf of garlic bread out of the oven and set it in front of me, along with a glass of soda, I'll eat a little and then I'll go shower, and while I'm drying off and putting on clean clothes, I'll hear the theme song at the beginning of *Norge Rundt*, the show everyone watches on Friday nights, and smell the scent of wood burning in the fireplace and hear my dad say something to my mom and hear her laugh shortly before she comes and knocks on my door and says the pizza's ready, and then we'll sit there together in the living room, on the brown sofa across from the fancy sofa that we never dare sit on unless we have guests which we almost never do, and Ulrikke is out with her friends so I have them to myself, my parents, who I believe love each other. My dad asks if practice was hard and I tell him what route we took and how the landscape changed and he asks if I saw those three enormous concrete legs down in the bay for the newest Condeep which will be done soon and I nod, move more of the homemade pizza onto my plate and refill my soda and that's how these evenings usually proceed, until they drift into something more unclear that begins to dissolve. I think it's because I'm tired, it's been a long week, I ran so far and now I'm going to bed, so I go back into the bathroom again, brush my teeth as thoroughly as I can and hang my clothes over the side of the tub before returning to my room, get under my covers and wait for someone to come kiss me good night, because I still like that, I'm not too old for that, and my mom comes in only minutes later, she walks so quietly, that's the way her feet are tuned, differently from my father's who stomps through the world in a way that gives the impression he's wearing snowshoes trudging through heavy snow and needs to make sure his footing is secure. With my mother, it's like she's always afraid the ice will give way and that the icy-blue water will well up at her. Although they express it differently, what my parents share is that neither fully trusts the ground beneath them.

"Are you tired?" she asks, sitting down on the edge of my bed.

"Think so."

"You can sleep in tomorrow, you know, since it's Saturday."

"Yeah," I respond. "Tomorrow's Saturday."

This is the same Saturday that my parents—while Ulrikke sits on the armrest of a chair with her arms folded demonstratively because she has places to be and doesn't have time for impromptu family meetings like this, and I sit expectantly on a dining table chair beside her—tell us we're going to move to the United States that summer, as soon as school gets out.

It is fall. It is fall 1989 and then the new decade. The winter and spring of 1990. These are the final weeks of life in elementary school and the graduation party at Anne's house after the last regular day of school in the middle of June, a party that starts at exactly 6:00 p.m. and ends at 10:00 p.m. At the latest. We dance to Percy Sledge and eat rolls and buns and someone has hung a disco ball from the ceiling to nudge the atmosphere slightly in a nightclub direction. A lot of the people present have actually been out dancing several times and seen how things are done. Not Stig or Andri or me. But to some extent we're all in the same boat, each of us from this class that has been together for six years spends the evening in a celebration that conceals our sadness and nervousness about the group we've belonged to no longer existing, we've bidden a respectful farewell to our homeroom teacher and promised to come visit (probably only two of the girls will actually do it, and only one time, slightly embarrassed as they realize that this is one of those things people say but don't do because now they're busy with new classes), when fall comes we'll all be enrolled in other classes, some of us will end up at other schools farther away. We will have longer commutes to school, new teachers, new classmates to compete with or be teased by. We've existed together for almost as long as we can remember, we've had our assigned seats and we know everything about each other. Who sat across from whom, behind whom, two rows behind and to the right: none of that will carry forward. But at the same

285

time, we can hardly wait, summer will feel incredibly long before we reach the other side of it, where the future awaits and middle school begins. Luckily there's no coming back here. From here on out you just get older and things get steadily harder. It's a matter of seizing the opportunities that arise. The world is going to smell different now. Like victory.

But I won't be here then. No one knows, because I haven't told a soul that we're moving in a couple of weeks. Leaving Norway for good. I should have, and I had every intention of doing it, at least telling Stig and Andri. But I just haven't, I've been pretending nothing is up, even when we talk about what classes we hope we'll be in that fall and the welcome letter from the middle school that I lie and say I received, too. I've put it off and put it off so long that I've started thinking it might be best to just disappear one day.

The first two weeks of that summer. They never end. They crawl along through the scorching June days. Hiding behind the curtains in my room, I slowly pack my things and my life thus far. I have the two boxes my parents gave me that I can bring to the United States and many boxes I'm supposed to fill with everything else I "want" to give away, donate to the Salvation Army or wherever it ends up. Actually, it's strange that no one has asked us what's going on, because there's no doubt some of the neighbors must have noticed all the activity at our place, the heavy velour curtains in the living room being taken down and the trucks being filled one by one with our furniture and driven away the closer we get to our departure date. Maybe people think we're remodeling or redecorating or something. Most of our furniture is from the sixties anyway and I suppose people do fix things up in the summertime.

And then suddenly the day arrives. I should be home already, but I don't want to go. I'm sitting on top of Ulsberget with Stig and Andri, the gravel sports field is behind us and if we want we can just barely see the eleven-year-olds who just started training track and field, running back and forth across the short side of the field while the coach, probably the father of one of them, yells at them to run faster, better, cleaner, with more control—but we're facing away from them so we just hear them, as if from far away, the yelling and their feet running back and forth across the gravel and in front of us, below us, is Forus, with its factories and gas stations and the Scania plant, rows of trucks parked for the night, and I should have been home already, but I'm here. I don't want to go, I want to keep sitting here, because it's a hopelessly nice night and we're sitting together on top of Ulsberget with Forus below us and it's starting to cool off even though the sun hasn't set yet, it won't do that for another hour, and maybe how nice it is doesn't have anything to do with the whole thing, maybe it's not the kind of night where it matters what the weather's like. Maybe it could have been raining and I'd have been just as happy, I don't know, I just know that it's an almost uncomfortably nice evening and I don't want to go home, but I have to, because everything that's not packed and ready, labeled with my name, and placed in the specified locations before my dad goes to bed for the last time in our house will be left behind.

Tomorrow at 6 a.m. it will be too late.

We're leaving then. For good. Before the neighbors are awake. A taxi will pick us up at 5:50 a.m. and after that all traces of us will be removed, as if we'd never been there to begin with. A moving van will park where our Mazda has parked all these years, and men none of us know will unlock our house with the key my father gave them, carry box after box with our names on them out into the van and make sure that they're sent to our new address. Soon new people and new voices will fill our rooms, they'll bring their own furniture, their own curtains and habits, their lawn mowers and clothes to dry on the clothesline and a totally different car

287

in the garage. And the neighborhood around the house, the streets and roads, the factories and the North Sea oil offices, the traffic and the woods, the railroad and the rocky outcroppings, the shore and the fjord, none of it will be mine anymore, other people will take it over, I will have only the memory of once belonging here, to this exact place, where the summers are humid and unreliable at best and the winters never completely cold, with sideways rain and forecast storms with incessant sleet and sporadically icy streets from November to April.

And I'll lose my two best friends. That's why I haven't said anything to Stig or Andri.

It's after ten. It's starting to get colder, I zip up my jacket, pull my knees in closer even though the sun is still in our eyes. It's one of the first days in July. There's usually bad weather when everyone's on vacation, but a lot of things are wrong with this summer. Just hours before we walked down the hill to the fjord, down to the wharf behind the Sønnichsen metal tube and fittings plant where Andri usually goes fishing (even though there's no way what he catches there can be all that healthy to eat); we strolled over to Gausel Beach and went swimming in water that was probably slightly too cold, but Stig believes it's important to swim in the summer, it's good luck, and I know he just made that up on the spot, but I stagger along after them across the rocky intertidal zone with goose bumps all the way up to my face and I step on a starfish before it's deep enough to switch to swimming and make my way out into the fjord, swim hard enough to warm up, and think that if nothing else at least I can swim better than all of them. I swim the seven hundred meters around the little islet of Gauselholmen, where three boys and three girls in their mid-teens sit barbecuing and smoking, they've set up a silver-colored tent and will surely spend the night out there, it looks nice, I envy them, and one of them, a guy with shoulder-length hair in a wool sweater and bell-bottoms with a freshly rolled cigarette hanging from his lips, stands up as I swim past them, smiles and cheers me on, and for a second I almost think he looks like me, but then he turns and says something to the others, they laugh, I can't tell what at, and I swim back toward the shoreline below the big houses where Stig and Andri are sitting by the edge of the water, throwing rocks at the crabs to break their shells and waiting for me to come ashore. We sit there and dry off without saying much and afterward we retrace our steps back up the same hills, just walking, we roam around in Forus, down Storaberget Terrasse to Heddeveien, down Kviestølen and Bamsefaret, Ulsbergbakken, Petroleumsveien, and Løwenstrasse and back again, I don't remember what we talk about, I just remember that it feels like a procession, all of it, like the end of something that was meant to last much longer and along the way, by the grocery store in Kviebakken, we run into several of our former classmates who will be in class with Stig and Andri in the fall; I enter the store instead, walk back and forth between the shelves to kill time while they chat outside, and I don't go back out until I see that they're alone again. Afterward we each buy a bottle of Coke and a big baguette that we eat plain, sitting with our backs against the warm, red bricks on the store's facade. Then we keep going, as if we're busy, and we are, too, we cross our own tracks and enter the woods behind the big residential area, up on Ulsberget, the highest point we can find, that's where we sit down, that's where we've already been sitting for way too long before I finally say it:

"I'm moving away tomorrow."

There's a long silence before Stig says, quietly, "I knew something was up. Have you known for a long time?"

"A while."

They nod slowly.

"I guess we're not all going to end up at the same school in the fall after all," Andri says. "The trio and all that."

"Looks like you guys are going to be just fine," I respond.

"Well yeah, but . . . I mean, the three of us were supposed to . . ." He doesn't finish the sentence. Instead he says, "Where are you moving, anyway?"

"To America. Long Island."

All three of us are shocked as it sinks in, just how far away that is.

"Is that . . . in California?" Andri asks.

"No, I think it's near New York City."

"California would definitely be cool, Hollywood. Maybe you could go there sometime?"

"Maybe."

And then we talk about California for a bit and what we think it's like there, since there's no point talking about Long Island which we don't know the first thing about, and Andri says that in California people sometimes get killed right in their cars if they're driving too slow in traffic on the freeways, *shot right through the windshield*, he says, Andri read about it and it's probably true. But at the same time, we tell each other that the U.S. also has movie stars and money and the best bands and enormous helping sizes no matter what you order, and we all totally agree that America is cool, nothing wrong with the U.S., we can all picture ourselves living there, moving there and living exactly how we want. *Someday*. But not right now, not tomorrow. It's just too darned soon.

"This is for us," Andri says and looks out at Forus.

"Huh?"

"I said that this one time to some lady who came to our house and rang the doorbell, I think it was sometime last year, she only spoke English and was looking for Ullandhaug, I guess she was trying to get to the university or something like that, and then she asked: *Is this Ullandhaug?* so I told her it was Forus. But I guess it came out wrong, I think she misunderstood me, because she seemed offended and turned around and left."

"This is for us," I repeat.

"And in a lot of ways that's true," Andri says.

"This place sucks," Stig says. "Look around, would you? I don't get it. How the hell can people even stand to live here?"

"But it's *our* sucky place," I answer.

"The Nazis were the ones who made Forus livable, did you guys know that?"

We did not know that.

"It's totally true," Stig says. "Nobody talks about that out loud, but it's the truth. The Nazis saved Forus from sinking."

"I don't buy it," Andri says.

"Oh yeah, it's true. Even Satan has one good turn in him," Stig says. "They came up the coast in 1940, crawling inland over the sandy beaches along Jæren and they moved north from there into the countryside. Until they got here, to Forus. I think they picked the place sight unseen. They must have. If they'd only taken the trouble to check the eta . . . etamolo . . . molotology—"

"E-ty-molo-gy?"

"—behind the name of the place first, they would have realized that Forus means *swampy terrain*. And that spells trouble, right? But they came, the Third Reich waded into the swamps and decided to locate the headquarters for their fighter plane forces right in the place with the region's most hopeless wind and weather conditions. They built concrete runways and a five-kilometer-long taxiway, shatter-proof hangars, they floundered around in the mud wreaking havoc, then they finally built solid, efficient channels and drained the swamp water out into Gandsfjord and Hafrsfjord and shored up the soil in Forus forever. And then they flew away, which must have been the only time the runways were ever used."

It's easy to picture. That first and final sortie. If you blinked you would surely miss the Messerschmitts departing Forus in a bright steely swastika formation in the sky.

"Later," Stig continues, "thirty years later, after the oil started gushing and the high housing prices crept outward from downtown Stavanger and became insurmountable for most people, a few took their Sunday walks out to what had once been pure farmland to see if maybe Forus might be a place where they could put down their roots."

Easy to picture that, too: My parents, Stig and Andri's and everyone else's, how they all drove out here, independently, and studied the real estate prospectuses and the lots with skepticism or enthusiasm, discussed among themselves and spit into their fists, stuck the shovel into the dirt and called the bank to set up a meeting about a mortgage loan. We put down our roots here, tentatively and hesitantly at first, eventually with increasing conviction. And those of us who stayed, among the factories and the industrial buildings that rose around us on all sides, we bore our belonging to Forus like a badge, proof that people can survive in any kind of conditions. We were citizens. We were in the house. In the burbs. With dry feet in the swamp.

"Well, just tell them you don't want to move," Stig says. "Say you refuse to go."

"Don't you think I've tried?" I respond.

We're quiet again, it's not so easy to think of anything else to say about it.

"But we can come visit you, right?" Andri says, trying to find something positive. "Maybe we could come for summer vacation next year. We could stay until school starts again."

"Of course," I say.

But that'll never happen.

All three of us know that, we just don't say it out loud.

Instead I tell them about the reorg at SAS and how my father got a tip that American Airlines in New York was looking for pilots, and I tell them that American Airlines has those really big planes that my dad has always dreamed of flying, the jumbo jets, Boeing 747s, and that that's why we're moving, so he can fly longer, bigger planes, earn more money, have more predictable work hours, and maybe we'll move back again after a few years, that could happen, I say, but mostly because I want it to be true, and I talk and talk about the differences between the Boeing 737 and the DC-9 and the 747 and the other types of planes I know about, all to keep silence away, and we agree to at least write letters, of course we can do that, I promise to send them my address as soon as I can, and we make plans to see each other the following summer, as if that were realistic, and by then it must be getting close to 11 p.m., we finally get up and come down from the rocky knoll, through the woods, and we say goodbye to each other on the gravel path between the soccer field and the houses, they each shake my hand as if I'm leaving for some official mission. I turn my back to them and walk home, hear them parting ways a little behind me, each walking off in his own direction after having agreed to meet up the next day, maybe go down to the beach if the weather is nice, you never really know how long the nice weather will last after all, it's usually always raining in this cruddy town, and it's not cold anymore, the heat is coming back, it's humid now, my sneakers stick to the asphalt on my way home and I swear the thunder and lightning started that night, a terrible storm over the entire Stavanger region, which probably lasted until well into August and gave way to an unseasonably early winter.

Ross Raisin is the author of three novels: *A Natural*, *Waterline*, and *God's Own Country*. In 2013 he was named one of *Granta*'s Best of Young British Novelists, and he has been the recipient of several other awards, including the *Sunday Times* Young Writer of the Year Award and the Betty Trask Award. He has been short-listed for various others, including the IMPAC Dublin Literary Award and the *Guardian* First Book Award. He has recently written a book on creative writing, *Read This If You Want to Be a Great Writer*, to be published in 2018. He has written short stories for *Granta, Prospect, the Sunday Times, Esquire*, BBC Radio 3, among others, and has contributed to anthologies such as *Best British Short Stories*. Raisin teaches creative writing at Goldsmiths University and as part of the UEA/Guardian Masterclasses programme, and is a writer in residence for the charity First Story.

Bearded

ROSS RAISIN

The changing room is loud, chaotic. A swimming lesson of young boys charged in just before you and the tiled space resounds with the noise of shouting and lockers and wet slapping feet. You give a little smile to the teacher as you come past him, and he acknowledges you with a shake of his head before going to deal with one large boy who is moving away from the others, padding off towards the other end of the room.

You collect your belongings from the locker. The swim has done you good. The anxiety that you felt on waking this morning has eased, lost to the water, the hurtle of oxygen. Seventy lengths. After all those summer swims in the churning outdoor pool, and the reluctant switch back to the leisure centre now that the weather has turned, it was easier than you had anticipated. The extra lengths have left you invigorated, clear. Two more, you told yourself at each of those last turns beneath the lifeguard's twitching feet—enjoying, every time you breached the surface, the flat blue glare of the sun through the far glass wall. You open the door of an unlocked cubicle, to find a boy inside. He is sitting dripping in his trunks, looking at his phone. You begin automatically to apologise, but stop yourself. 'You must lock the door, please,' you say.

He looks at you for a moment, bewildered, then goes back to his phone.

As you continue to search for an unoccupied cubicle, the thought of this morning's meeting rises again. You look for a clock on the walls—and see, up ahead, a young Asian man in front of the mirrors, using two hairdryers at the same time to dry a beard that hangs almost to his nipples. The spectacle of it halts you. You sense the opportunity of a photograph. It will not be possible, however, without offending him.

You get changed swiftly, anticipating the use of one of those hairdryers that you have missed all summer, before the cycle to the magazine's workspace, preparing yourself for what they will have to say about your portfolio. You have left enough time not to rush, to get a coffee from the little artisanal wagon on the pavement outside their building, which you will drink in the smoking shelter going over your pitch until you are ready to go inside, past the bicycles hanging on the walls of the entrance, the expensive disordered furniture, into the hub. If they approve of the Ebro photographs for their autumn issue—the first of several *River Roadtrips* they want to do through Europe—there is a good chance that they will commission you for the whole series.

The Asian man is still there, drying his great beard, when you step half-dressed out of the cubicle. You walk round him to the final hairdryer. It is astonishing, this beard. Deep chestnut. Luxurious. It has the celebrity pomp of a small pedigree animal. The man is using one steady shaft of air from underneath, to lift it, while with the other hairdryer he twists and flicks with surprising dexterity. You will enjoy telling Charlotte about this beard.

The final dryer does not work. You try it a couple of times, then stand aside to wait for the Asian man to finish. You try to relax with the thought of cycling to Old Street, your coffee, how important it is that you do not hurry any of that.

Somebody from Stephen's team will be preparing the sofa space now. Your photographs will be splayed across the glass table, beneath their indoor tree. Stephen will want to know what ideas you have for other rivers. As the anxious thought of it comes again you train your eyes on the beard and you experience the strong, comforting impression of resting your head against it, stroking it.

You look abruptly away—at yourself in the mirror, and see how much more toned your chest is than the other man's; how much better your hair will look dried with the blower and not a towel. The man has a towel wrapped around his waist and beneath it a pair of trousers, shoes, but his head hair and chest are completely dry. It occurs to you that he has not been for a swim. He is here only to attend to his beard.

He has not used overshoe protection. A yellow leaf protrudes from the damp cake of mud under his left foot. A thin brown dribble is leaking across the floor. You check your watch, and know that you should leave, but you remain where you are. You are wearing over-shoe protection. You look down with deliberation at the ruched blue bonnets covering your feet and see suddenly the paired heads of your grandmothers, and you understand precisely their opinion of this Asian man, who has not used the pool, taking all of the functioning hairdryers to blow-dry his beard.

From inside one of the cubicles there comes the sound of a man's voice: '*Amazing. See. Amazing. Told you she would, didn't I? Look, mate, I'm just leaving the pool.*' It has been five minutes that you have been standing. And he was already here, installed, when you came in from the pool. The beard, clearly dry now, has grown. The reds and browns of its thick foliage catch the light as it quivers in the wind. He does not appear even to have noticed you. Again you look at your watch. If you do not leave right now you will be late. You are about to step forward and speak to him, but some strange force holds you back. All at once the schoolchildren are thundering towards the exit. The teacher at the rear by the lockers, shepherding them through. 'Okay boys, nice and orderly, wait in a line outside.' They stream past the Asian man, and though they all glance up at him there is not the hint of a smirk, a giggle. Only one boy, near the back of the group, is staring. He cannot stop himself, until he is beyond the man and you catch his eye, giving the boy a little complicit smile. He turns his head away, ignoring you.

In the still aftermath of the boys, only the buzzing of the hairdryers in the air, you step forward.

'Excuse me.'

He does not hear you above the motors of his hairdryers.

'Excuse me.'

He looks at you over his flapping beard.

'You will be finished, yes? Soon you will be finished?'

He continues to look at you, not stopping the hairdryers, before turning back to the mirror, and you understand that he does not speak English.

'Ridiculous,' you say loudly, walking by him, your anger quickened by the knowledge that he does not comprehend.

You go back inside the cubicle to finish getting dressed. Water has bled across from the neighbouring stall and the whole floor is wet. In the irate fluster of pulling your remaining clothes out of your bag, the noise of the dryers invading the cramped space, your shirt drops to the floor. 'Fuck,' you shout, picking it up. It is a fine, white material, and instantly it is sodden. It will need drying. You place it damply beside you and put your head back against the partition panel, trying to regain your composure.

High up on the opposite panel is a yellowed slice of masking tape on which somebody has written, years ago: *not cleaned since October 2014*. You begin, roughly, to towel your hair. A child's crying, on the other side of the wall in the women's changing room, cuts through the hairdryers. It did not come easily to you, learning

English. Those first months, in the Palmer's Green bedsit: the constant struggle of textbooks, expensive CDs, tenses. You think about how far you have come since that time. In the beginning, before you met Charlotte, you made yourself go to places—a running group, a five-a-side morning—where you would meet English people, never allowing yourself to fall back on the Greek clubs and cafes that were only minutes down the road. You dream, now, in English. Is that not proof enough that you belong here? The noise of the hairdryers fills your brain. There is a shout on the other side of the wall, a woman: *'Molly! Stop that!'* You pick up the wet pudding of your shirt and tighten your fist around it. Water drips to the floor. Outside the cubicle the Asian is still pampering his beard, oblivious to you, to anyone else. He has never once, even now, had to face the prospect of going back. He will remain, installed in the same streets and cafes and barber shops as the rest of his people, surrounded by themselves, dreaming about a place that they have never left, in Pakistan, Bangladesh, wherever.

You should have texted Stephen by now to tell him that you are going to be late. You wring out the shirt, sling it over your shoulder, and gather the rest of your things, thinking about how impossible it would have seemed to you once that people like Stephen, his team, consider you a colleague. There is nothing for you back home now. You do not call it that anymore. Home. You rarely think about that place, where your parents lived and died, the water still lapping against the blackened walls of the harbour. Cats moving in the shadows of old boats, slipping between buckets to scavenge the piled wet guts of fish. Your father's hand against your back, the smell of him against you, imploring you to stay. Charlotte would never live there, anyway. It is a conversation that you have had, once, jokingly, at a dinner party with her friends.

The drone of the hairdryers is inside you. It is obvious that the Asian knows you are here, hiding inside your cubicle. He is mocking you, laughing at you. You move to the door, ready to confront him. To wrestle one of the hairdryers from him, if he will not give it up. What can he do? You are stronger than him. If he seeks a member of staff—he has not used the pool; he does not even speak their language. Your bright blue feet transport you over the slick tiles, out of the cubicle. He has gone. An English man stands there, drying his hair. A slug trail of shining floor leads towards a squeegee propped by the exit. In the reflection of the mirror the Englishman regards you standing behind him; the other hairdryer, in the space next to him, cocked in its holster, silent.

Contributor Notes

Eric Abrahamsen is the recipient of translation grants from PEN, to translate Xu Zechen's *Running Through Beijing*, and from the National Endowment for the Arts. He has written for the *New York Times*, among other publications. He also hosts the website *Paper Republic*, which features Chinese literature in translation.

Eric M. B. Becker is a literary translator, a journalist, and the editor of *Words Without Borders*. In 2014, he earned a PEN/Heim grant, and in 2016, he was awarded a Fulbright to translate Brazilian literature. His work has appeared in the *New York Times*, *Guernica*, and elsewhere. With Mirna Queiroz dos Santos, he edited the PEN American anthology *Women Writing Brazil*.

Garnette Cadogan is an essayist. He is currently a Martin Luther King Jr. Visiting Scholar at the Department of Urban Studies and Planning at MIT, a Visiting Fellow at the Institute for Advanced Studies in Culture at the University of Virginia, and a Visiting Scholar at the Institute for Public Knowledge at New York University. He is editor-at-large of *Nonstop Metropolis: A New York City Atlas* (coedited by Rebecca Solnit and Joshua Jelly-Schapiro) and is at work on a book on walking.

Elaine Castillo was born in the San Francisco Bay Area. Her debut novel, *America Is Not the Heart*, will be published by Viking (United States/Canada), Atlantic (UK), and Foksal (Poland) in 2018.

Tara Chace has translated more than twenty-five novels from Norwegian, Swedish, and Danish. Her recent translations include Jo Nesbø's Doctor Proctor's Fart Powder series (Aladdin, 2010–2017); Johanne Hildebrandt's *Unbroken Line of the Moon* (Amazon Crossing, 2016); and Sven Nordqvist's Adventures of Pettson and Findus series (NorthSouth, 2014–2017). She translated Johan Harstad's YA sci-fi thriller *172 Hours on the Moon* (Little, Brown Books for Young Readers, 2012). An avid reader and language learner, Chace earned her PhD in Scandinavian Languages and Literature from the University of Washington in 2003. She lives in Seattle with her family and their black lab, Zephyr.

Marius Chivu's first published book was a poetry collection, *Vîntureasa de plastic* (*The Plastic Windess*), which won several awards and was translated into French. He is also the author of the short story collection *Sfîrşit de sezon* (*End of Season*) as well as two travel journals *Trei săptămâni în Himalaya* (*Three Weeks in the Himalayas*) and *Trei săptămâni în Anzi* (*Three Weeks in the Andes*). He has edited various anthologies, including *Best of proza scurtă a anilor 2000* (*Best of Short Stories of the 2000s*) and *111 cele mai frumoase poezii de dragoste din literatura română* (*The Most Beautiful 111 Romanian Love Poems*, with Radu Vancu). He is a literary critic at *Dilema Veche* and has his own radio show, *All You Can Read*, on Radio Seven. He lives in Bucharest, Romania.

Alexandra Coliban has translated into Romanian a wide array of works by British and American authors including Kurt Vonnegut, Philip Roth, Sylvia Plath, Will Self, Nick Cave, and Jeffrey Eugenides.

Mariana Enríquez is a writer and editor based in Buenos Aires. She is the author of two novels, two short-story collections, a biography of Silvina Ocampo, a chronicle on cemeteries, and a novella.

Her fiction has appeared in the *New Yorker*, *Granta*, *McSweeney's*, *Electric Literature*, and the *Virginia Quarterly Review*. Her English-language debut *The Things We Lost in the Fire* has been translated into twenty languages.

Athena Farrokhzad was born in 1983 and lives in Stockholm. She is a poet, literary critic, translator, playwright, and teacher of creative writing. Her first volume of poetry, *Vitsvit*, was published in 2013 by Albert Bonniers Förlag (translated by Jennifer Hayashida and published as *White Blight* by Argos Books). In 2016, her second volume of poetry, *Trado*, which was written together with the Romanian poet Svetlana Cârstean and from which these poems are excerpted, was published.

Daniel Galera is a Brazilian writer and translator. He was born in São Paulo but lives in Porto Alegre, where he has spent most of his life. He has published five novels in Brazil to great acclaim, including *Blood-Drenched Beard*, which was awarded the 2013 São Paulo Prize for Literature. In 2013 Galera was named a *Granta* Best Young Brazilian Novelist. He has translated the work of Zadie Smith, John Cheever, and David Mitchell into Portuguese.

Johan Harstad is a Norwegian novelist, short-story writer, playwright, and graphic designer. His novels include *Buzz Aldrin, What Happened to You in All the Confusion?*—a *Kirkus Reviews* best book of the year, which has been published in thirteen countries—and *Max, Mischa, and the Tet Offensive*. He is also the author of *172 Hours on the Moon*, which won the 2008 Norwegian Brage Prize in the young adult/children's literature category; four plays; a collection of short stories; and a prose collection. He lives in Oslo, Norway.

Jennifer Hayashida is a writer, translator, and visual artist. Her most recent projects include translation from the Swedish of Athena Farrokhzad's *White Blight* (Argos Books, 2015) and Karl Larsson's *Form/Force* (Black Square Editions, 2015), named one of the ten best books of 2015 by *Partisan*. She is director of the Asian American Studies Program at Hunter College, CUNY, and serves on the board of the Asian American Writers' Workshop.

Ishion Hutchinson was born in Port Antonio, Jamaica. He is the author of the poetry collections *Far District* (Peepal Tree Press, 2010) and *House of Lords and Commons* (Farrar, Straus and Giroux, 2016). He teaches in the graduate writing program at Cornell University.

Tania James is the author of the novels *Atlas of Unknowns* and *The Tusk That Did the Damage*, and the short-story collection *Aerogrammes*. She lives in Washington, D.C.

Mieko Kawakami has published numerous books including novels, short stories, essays, and prose poems. Her second novella, *Breasts and Eggs* (2008), won the Akutagawa Prize and was translated into Norwegian, Spanish, French, Chinese, Korean, and other languages. In 2016, *Granta* selected her for its Best of Young Japanese Novelists volume, which included her story "Marie's Proof of Love."

Born in the north of France in the 1990s, **Édouard Louis** has published two novels, *The End of Eddy* and *History of Violence*, both best sellers translated into more than twenty languages. He is also the editor of a scholarly work on the sociologist Pierre Bourdieu. He is the coauthor, with the philosopher Geoffroy de Lagasnerie, of "Manifesto for an Intellectual and Political Counteroffensive," published in English by the *Los Angeles Review of Books*.

Michael Lucey is Professor of French and Comparative Literature at the University of California, Berkeley, and the author of a number of books on modern French literature, including *Never Say I: Sexuality and the First Person in Colette, Gide, and Proust*. He is also the translator of Didier Eribon's *Returning to Reims* and Édouard Louis's *The End of Eddy*, among other works.

Valeria Luiselli was born in Mexico City and grew up in South Africa. She is the author of *Sidewalks*, a collection of personal essays; the essay "Tell Me How It Ends"; and the novels *Faces in the Crowd* and *The Story of My Teeth*. The latter novel, which was written in installments for workers in a juice factory, won the Los Angeles Times Book Prize for fiction and was a finalist for a National Book Critics Circle Award. She lives in Harlem.

Christina MacSweeney was awarded the 2016 Valle Inclán Translation Prize for her translation of Valeria Luiselli's *The Story of My Teeth*. She has translated two other books by the same author, and her translations of Daniel Saldaña París's novel *Among Strange Victims* and Eduardo Rabasa's *A Zero-Sum Game* both appeared in 2016. She has also published translations, articles, and interviews on a wide variety of platforms, including *Words Without Borders, Music and Literature, Literary Hub,* and *BOMB,* and in three anthologies: *México20; Lunatics, Lovers and Poets: Twelve Stories After Cervantes and Shakespeare;* and *Crude Words: Contemporary Writing from Venezuela.* She is currently working translating texts by the Mexican authors Julián Herbert and Verónica Gerber Bicecci.

Allison Malecha is an associate editor at Grove Atlantic and the assistant editor on Freeman's. She lives in Brooklyn.

Megan McDowell has translated books by many Latin American and Spanish authors, and stories she translated have appeared in the *New Yorker*, the *Paris Review*, *Tin House*, *Harper's*, *Vice*, and the *Virginia Quarterly Review*. She lives in Santiago, Chile.

Fiona McFarlane was born in Sydney, Australia. She holds degrees in English from Sydney University and Cambridge University, and was a Michener fellow at the University of Texas at Austin. Her first novel, *The Night Guest*, was a finalist for the Guardian First Book Award and the Los Angeles Times Book Prize. She is also the author of a short-story collection, *The High Places*. She lives in Sydney.

Dinaw Mengestu is the award-winning author of *The Beautiful Things That Heaven Bears*, *How to Read the Air*, and *All Our Names*. He is a graduate of Georgetown University and of Columbia University's M.F.A. program in fiction and the recipient of a 5 Under 35 award from the National Book Foundation and a 20 Under 40 award from the *New Yorker*. His journalism and fiction have appeared in such publications as *Harper's Magazine*, *Granta*, *Rolling Stone*, the *New Yorker*, and the *Wall Street Journal*. He is the recipient of a 2012 MacArthur Foundation grant and currently lives in New York City.

Nadifa Mohamed was born in Hargeisa in 1981 and moved to London with her family in 1986. Her first novel, *Black Mamba Boy*, was long-listed for the Orange Prize; was short-listed for the Guardian First Book Award, the John Llewellyn Rhys Prize, the Dylan Thomas Prize, and the PEN Open Book Award; and won the Betty Trask Prize. Her second novel, *The Orchard of Lost Souls*, was published in 2013 and was long-listed for the Dylan Thomas Prize and shortlisted for the Hurston/Wright Legacy Award; the novel won a Somerset Maugham Award and the Prix Albert Bernard. Mohamed was selected as one of *Granta*'s Best Young British Novelists in 2013. She lives in London and is working on her third novel.

Sayaka Murata was born in Chiba Prefecture in 1979 and graduated from the Department of Literature at Saitama University. Her debut work, *Junyū* (*Breastfeeding*), won the Gunzō Prize for New Writers in 2003. In 2009 she won the Noma Prize for New Writers with *Gin iro no uta* (*Silver Song*); in 2013, the Yukio Mishima Prize for *Shiro-iro no machi no, sono hone no taion no* (*Of Bones, of Body Heat, of Whitening City*); in 2014, the Sense of Gender Prize and Measures to Counter the Falling Birthrate Special Prize for *Satsujin shussan* (*Breeders and Killers*); and in 2016, the Akutagawa Prize for *Konbini ningen* (*Convenience Store Woman*). Other works include *Tadaima tobira* (*A Welcoming Door*) and *Shōmetsu sekai* (*Dwindling World*).

Pola Oloixarac is a fiction writer and essayist. Her novels, *Savage Theories* and *Dark Constellations*, have been translated into seven languages. Her writing has appeared in *n+1*, the *White Review*, the *New York Times*, and *Granta*, which named her one of its Best Young Spanish Language Novelists. She wrote the libretto for the opera *Hercules in Mato Grosso*, which debuted at Buenos Aires's Teatro Colón and had its North American premiere at New York City's Dixon Place. She lives in San Francisco.

Heather O'Neill is the author of three novels: *Lullabies for Little Criminals*, which was short-listed for the Orange Prize for Fiction; *The Girl Who Was Saturday Night*; and *The Lonely Hearts Hotel*. She is also the author of a collection of short stories, *Daydreams of Angels*; and a book of poems, *two eyes are you sleeping*. Born and raised in Montreal, O'Neill lives there today with her daughter.

Diego Enrique Osorno was born in 1980 in Monterrey, Mexico. A reporter and writer, he has witnessed some of the twenty-first century's major conflicts in Mexico and Latin America. He has been called one of the region's most important journalists by the Gabriel García Márquez Foundation for New Journalism and has received Italy's prestigious Stampa Romana. In 2014 he was awarded Mexico's National Journalism Prize, which he dedicated to the Zapatista Army of National Liberation. He is the author most recently of *Slim*, a biography of the richest man in the world, which Verso will publish in English. Like many other Mexican journalists, he has been threatened because of his work.

Ross Raisin is the author of three novels: *A Natural*, *Waterline*, and *God's Own Country*. In 2013 he was named one of *Granta*'s Best of Young British Novelists, and he has been the recipient of several other awards, including the *Sunday Times* Young Writer of the Year Award and the Betty Trask Award. He has been short-listed for various others, including the IMPAC Dublin Literary Award and the *Guardian* First Book Award. He has recently written a book on creative writing, *Read This If You Want to Be a Great Writer*, to be published in 2018. He has written short stories for *Granta*, *Prospect*, the *Sunday Times*, *Esquire*, BBC Radio 3, among others, and has contributed to anthologies such as *Best British Short Stories*. Raisin teaches creative writing at Goldsmiths University and as part of the UEA/Guardian Masterclasses programme, and is a writer in residence for the charity First Story.

Sunjeev Sahota was born in 1981 and lives in Yorkshire with his wife and children. His first novel, *Ours Are the Streets*, was published in 2011. His second, *The Year of the Runaways*, was short-listed for the 2015 Man Booker Prize. He is a *Granta* Best Young British Novelist.

Samanta Schweblin was born in Buenos Aires in 1978. Her collection of short stories *Pájaros en la boca* won the Premio Literario Casa de las Américas. In 2010 she was named a *Granta* Best Young Spanish-Language Novelist. In 2012 she was awarded the Premio Juan Rulfo for her story *Un hombre sin suerte*, and in 2014 she won the Premio Konex-Diploma for her career as a short-story writer.

David Searcy is the author of the novels *Ordinary Horror* and *Last Things*, and the essay collection *Shame and Wonder*. The recipient of a grant from the National Endowment for the Arts, he lives in Dallas, Texas.

Solmaz Sharif is the recipient of an NEA fellowship, a Stegner Fellowship, and most recently a Lannan Literary Fellowship. Her first collection of poems, *Look*, was a finalist for the 2016 National Book Award. She is currently a lecturer at Stanford University.

Andrés Felipe Solano is the author of the novels *Sálvame, Joe Louis (Save Me, Joe Louis)* and *Los hermanos Cuervo (The Cuervo Brothers)*. His work has appeared in the *New York Time Magazine*, *Words Without Borders*, and *Anew*. In 2010 he was named one of *Granta's* Best of Young Spanish-Language Novelists. He currently lives in Seoul, South Korea.

Joel Streicker is a writer, poet, and literary translator based in San Francisco. He is the recipient of a PEN/Heim Translation Fund grant, and has translated works by Samanta Schweblin, Tomás González, and Guillermo Fadanelli, among other Latin American authors.

Ginny Tapley Takemori has translated fiction by more than a dozen early modern and contemporary Japanese writers, from best sellers Ryū Murakami and Kyōtarō Nishimura to literary greats Izumi

Kyōka and Okamoto Kidō. Her most recent translations are of Miyuki Miyabe's *Puppet Master* and Tomiko Inui's *The Secret of the Blue Glass*, short-listed for the Marsh Award. Previously she was an editor at Kodansha International and a foreign rights agent based in Spain.

Jeremy Tiang has translated more than ten books from Chinese, including novels by Chan Ho-Kei, Zhang Yueran, and Yeng Pway Ngon, and has been awarded a PEN/Heim Translation Fund Grant and an NEA Literary Translation Fellowship. His original fiction includes *It Never Rains on National Day* (short-listed for the Singapore Literature Prize) and *State of Emergency*, both published by Epigram Books. He also writes and translates plays.

Ocean Vuong was born on a rice farm outside Saigon in 1988. When he was age two, after a year in a refugee camp, he and his family arrived in the United States. He was the first in his immediate family to learn how to read proficiently, at the age of eleven. With Ben Lerner as his mentor at Brooklyn College, he wrote the poems that would become his first collection, *Night Sky with Exit Wounds*. A Ruth Lilly and Dorothy Sargent Rosenberg Poetry fellow and winner of a Pushcart Prize, he has received honors and awards from Poets House and the Academy of American Poets. In 2016 he received a Whiting Award. Ocean Vuong lives in New York.

Claire Vaye Watkins is the author of *Gold Fame Citrus* and *Battleborn*, which won the Story Prize, the Dylan Thomas Prize, the New York Public Library Young Lions Fiction Award, the Rosenthal Family Foundation Award from the American Academy of Arts and Letters, and a Silver Pen Award from the Nevada Writers Hall of Fame. A Guggenheim Fellow, Claire is on the faculty of the Helen Zell Writers' Program at the University of Michigan. She is also the codirector,